S O U L
SURVIVORS

BOOK 1

RIVER KAI

SOUL SURVIVORS

BOOK 1

RIVER KAI

Edited by Kayla Vokolek
Cover and Illustrations by River Kai

ISBN (Ebook): 979-8-9900293-6-1
ISBN (Paperback): 979-8-9900293-7-8
ISBN (Hardback): 979-8-9900293-8-5

Library of Congress Control Number: 2024917560

Our books may be purchased in bulk for promotional, educational, or business use. Please contact your local bookseller,
or send a request to River Kai Art at riverkaiart.com/wholesale
or PO Box 1414, Wilsonville, OR 97070.

First edition, October 2024

10 9 8 7 6 5 4 3 2 1

END THE CYCLE BOOKS

PSYCHOLOGICAL THRILLER IMPRINT
OF RIVER KAI ART

To all those experiencing violence in silence,
whether it's re-lived or happening now
in what feels to be an unstoppable cycle.

You matter,
you are loved,
and you belong here.

Your voice deserves to be heard.

CONTENT ADVISORY

I believe survivors.

Survivors' stories are often overlooked, and to add to survivors' trauma, perpetrators are often glorified or used as a tool to perpetuate ableism against those with mental health conditions. The terrible irony is that many survivors are disabled, possibly even by their perpetrator's abuse. Far too often, survivors are also the only ones to face the ramifications of the trauma their perpetrators forced upon them.

I've written *Soul Survivors* to showcase survivor perspectives, highlighting their emotions, challenges, and lived experiences in managing the consequences of trauma. Topics arise that may be difficult for some to read.

Please take care of yourself with the following in mind: *Soul Survivors* contains topics of war, military, cults, abuse, PTSD, pregnancy, miscarriage, and chronic illness. While sexual abuse is never "shown," survivors' resulting feelings and trauma's physical consequences are discussed.

If you or someone you know is struggling through the impacts of trauma, there are those of us out there ready to witness your truths. Please seek the care you deserve, as you matter immensely to me and your loved ones. Unsure where to start your search for support? Feel free to visit the Resources page at the back of this book for a list of mental health resources.

One final note: oppression harms everyone. I stand with survivors, and I refuse to look the other way.

And since it can't be said enough times, and I imagine you may need to hear it from someone again…

I believe you.

With All My Love,
RIVER KAI

CHAPTER 1

Niko

By the time I'm aware of her, my five-year-old sister has already decorated my entire left arm with a permanent marker. I notice the lopsided cat face on my bicep, but I still can't move. I can only look into her enormous black eyes. Surprised by the sudden eye contact, Hana bolts down the hall, screeching and laughing.

"Nikolai?! What did you do to your baby sister?!"

Mom's anxious glare awaits me at the hallway's end, her fiery hair spilling out of a frazzled bun. She looks like she's carrying a mini, brunette copy of herself on her hip. Tilting her head, Mom urges me to speak, but the words won't come out. Either way, she'd never believe "I just looked at her" as anything but a cheap excuse from her scary son.

Hana throws her tiny arms around Mom's neck. "Mommy! Don't be mad!"

"I'll kick your brother's butt if he hurts you, baby."

"R-really?"

"Yes. Really." Mom kisses Hana's forehead, placing her onto the floor.

Hana dives for my legs, burying her face into my hip. "But he didn't do anything! He didn't even say hi."

Mom shifts from I-want-to-beat-you-up-for-hurting-my-baby to genuine concern. "What do you mean?"

I sigh, knowing what's coming.

"You know what I mean, Mommy." Hana picks the asphalt from my combat-stained pants. "He was day-sleeping again."

"*Hana*," I groan, throwing my head back to beg the ceiling for mercy. "Why me?"

Her tiny brows furrow into a serious scrunch. Such a mature face on a little kid brings a sad smile to my face.

"Did I do something bad?" She whispers.

I smooth back her hair before it escapes from its lopsided ponytail. "No, little sprout. Don't worry about it."

"Hana, why don't you go tell Izzy to come get dinner?"

At the sight of Mom's serious expression, Hana runs off without another word.

But I grit my teeth. "Izzy?"

Rolling her eyes, Mom sends a clear message; she's unwilling to waste her breath to argue with me over Lilith's name yet again.

When we agreed to foster my older sister, Lilith re-named herself. My parents, however, went along with the Department's suggestion of calling her "Isabel" because "Lilith is a demonic name." We, the legal killers of America, "don't want to offend the Christians" by calling a refugee by her name. But Jay, Emmalee, and I refuse to call Lilith a name she doesn't identify with, a contentious point between my parents and us.

Mom crosses her arms. "What do you need to snap out of it? Your older sister already broke the whole punching wall last night because she was really pissed, so that's out. Your dad will install a new one tomorrow. Do you need me to fight you, instead?"

I stare at the floor, unsure what I do need, but I'm sure it's not *that*. Honestly, I'm still processing that I must need something, according to my mom and baby sister. I can't feel yet.

"Niko? Do you need me to call your dad to come home and get a read on you?"

This grabs my attention. Dad's sixth sense would know too much. "No, not Dad. I'm fine. I'll just… sit in my room for a minute."

She watches me unhook empty holster after holster until finally, my bulletproof vest clatters to the scuffed-up laminate.

"Are you sure? You're not going to suddenly, like, flip out and kill one of us, are you?" She chuckles, and I'm glad my back is to her. Mom's humor doesn't amuse me, but this is how the Department of Tactical Defense members "bond."

"No." I whip around, deadpan to her smile. "I won't."

"Good. Pull yourself together and come eat, kid." She gives me a shoulder slap, closing the door behind her.

I stare at the doorknob, my bedroom's last sign of movement. Eventually, my head blurs into nothingness, and the thoughts start again. I guess Mom and Hana were right; I'm not doing too well. It's not the worst, but I do hiccup for air as soon as I'm alone. On the outside, I look like an angry, empty shell, maybe breathing a little weirdly if you look up close. I'm dying to scream, break something, hurt myself, throw up, or maybe even cry, but I can't. All I can do is sit.

No time has passed in my mind when Mom screams my name. She snags my attention on the first try with a rare hint of panic.

In this atmosphere, my body knows how to exist.

I march into the living room and find Mom's empty expression—a glimpse into what I must look like these days. "Mom? What's wrong?"

"Isabel is gone," she whispers.

My heart clenches. "Gone" can mean multiple things here.

Storming into Lilith's room, I find a handwritten note on her bed.

> I wasn't joking.
> Don't come looking for me.

I prepare to do exactly that, darting back to my room. Lilith isn't dead. That's all the information I need.

Mom fumes in the doorway. "You won't find her, Nikolai."

I tense my arms, definitely feeling something now. "You won't even try?"

"There's no point if she's anything like you," she says. I

swallow hard, and she softens her voice. "That was definitely Isabel who wrote the note."

I'm seething. "Her name is *not* Isabel."

"Okay, *Lilith*," Mom snaps back. "*Lilith* warned me she was going to leave last night. That we never were family, anyway, and she's sick of this place. This is what she wants. Or needs, maybe. I don't know."

Mom's crying now, but I'm pissed.

"I don't give a fuck what she thinks she needs. She's my sister! I'm not going to just let her go! Where the hell is she gonna go? We've got eyes everywhere! And she's fifteen! W-well no, sixteen today, but—"

"You're only fifteen yourself, kid. Lower your voice right now."

It's too late; Hana is already bawling. But I'm reaching my limits. Beyond my limits, I won't kill someone like my mom assumes; that's the last thing I ever want to do.

Which is why I understand Lilith. I hate being treated like a cumbersome life hazard after they raised me to be one.

But it's not safe for Lilith out there, no matter her combat expertise. Leaving identifies her as a traitor. Our private paramilitary sector will use endless data pools to track her and make an example of her. I have to find her before anyone else does, no matter what it takes. Step one is to abandon everything I've been told and disrespect authority.

"No," I say. A hot spike of anxiety grips my heart.

Mom clenches her jaw. "Excuse me?"

My stomach rolls, but I think of Lilith. I have to try. "I said, no. I'm not going to shut up and obey orders anymore."

"Hana, go to your room."

My mother's threatening tone summons a shiver so deep that my chest tightens, stifling my lungs. Hana slips closer to panic, her eyes darting between us. My heart aches for her. She's not like us, and we always manage to scare her.

Hana's eyes land on me for reassurance, so I kiss the top of her head. "It'll be okay, Sprout. Go to your room, my love."

We watch in silence as Hana pitters down the hall, escaping into her room and slamming the door to muffle her sobs. It guts me.

Mom pounces at my throat, pinning me to the wall. "Come on, fight. Get your aggression out."

"No." My choked throat squeezes out my words in a tight rasp.

She presses harder, trapping the blood in my head. They've trained us to withstand choking for a long time, but there's still a limit where anyone struggles on instinct. Mom knows this, daring me to attack her and let my emotions out "before I do anything worse."

I said no, I want to say, but it's been a full minute. I've almost run out of air.

My own mother is ignoring my "no," too.

Reflexively shoving her off me, my oxygen-deprived brain forgets to account for our weight difference, but my facial expressions have been drilled out of me so effectively that she doesn't anticipate it. My brute force slams her across the hallway, her head bouncing against the drywall with a hollow thud. I dive for her in a guilty panic, desperate to cradle her head and rub it until she feels better like I'd do for Hana. But she slaps my hands away, whipping me around and arresting me against the floor.

"You're growing too soft," she hisses. "You expect to go out there like this and survive?"

"I don't care if I survive," I mumble.

She digs her elbow into my back, where the diaphragm meets the spine, and my strength reels. "You better start fucking caring. I'm not answering the door when they bring me the news your sorry ass gave up and died for no reason. And you think you can deploy like this on Monday? They'll eat you alive if you don't pull it together, fast."

I struggle beneath her in silence, wishing I didn't have to fight back. I've already done enough of that today.

It looks like Mom read my mind. Her voice softens. "Where were you earlier? Why didn't you come home right away?"

I grunt. "I did."

"Three fucking hours late! What are you doing lately at night?!"

At this point, I begin to sob. This shocks my mom into lightening up.

I don't know what's wrong with me, either. I never cry. Now I can't stop.

"Niko?! Answer me right now, baby. What are they having you do?"

"Nothing."

She leans over my ear, cradling my jaw in slender, chilly fingers. "Don't lie to your mother."

Catching her off guard, I roll into the small opening she left and escape her grasp. I spring to my feet—feet that stagger around beneath me for a second, giving my weakness away. It feels like I've been hit by a truck, and not because of Mom's gentle sparring; my secret triples my weight. The secret I'll keep forever.

"I'm never going to tell you." My voice sounds fake, expressing my emotions with a harsh rasp.

Mom throws desperate arms in the air. "What the hell is wrong with my kids tonight? I expected it from Lilith, but since when do you not respect authority? They'll kill you if you pull this shit anywhere else, Nikolai."

I shrug.

She scoffs. "My teenagers have lost their fucking minds."

"Yeah, we have. Thanks to this wonderful fucking place you're raising us in!"

She stares into my eyes, frozen in her response. I can't decipher what she's thinking. She must've lost track of her words like she lost track of her adopted child.

Finally, she says, "You need to properly defend yourself and get your shit together. I wasn't a perfect mother, but I raised you to survive the life we have to work with. You're right. Lilith has lost it. She won't survive, like any other traitor." Analyzing my bulging eyes, she continues in a whisper. "What happened to you, really? Tell me. I don't care if it's confidential. I don't even have to tell your father." My aching heart bleeds into my expression, threatening to give me away. But then she says, "Did you kill someone today? Is that it?"

Panting through rageful tears, I grip my shirt in an attempt to hold myself together. "No, I didn't."

Her shoulders drop. "Okay, then what is it?"

"I don't want to fucking *kill* people! That's what!"

She thinks for a moment, standing taller as she seethes. "Then why did you sign up for it?"

"Because I thought you wanted me to!"

"I don't believe that. Part of you wants this life. And now this is the life we have to live, Nikolai. You promised me last year that you wanted to go further in your training, no matter what. There's no take-backs when you kill someone, and unfortunately, that's what they'll ask of you from now on. You have to face this. Whether you think it's right or not, they chose *you* to protect this country. It's too late to live a different life. You already have killed people."

My nails dig past my shirt and into my skin as I gasp for air. An image invades my mind—my first target's empty eyes—and I'm light-headed. I was ordered to do it, but maybe I should've killed myself instead, sparing us both from the Department's grasp. They told me he was a terrorist that could kill hundreds and I cling to that like a prayer, but I think Lilith was right. I think *we* might be the terrorists.

I can't stay in this house another minute, so I say the first words that come to my head. "Yeah, Mom, I have. And I'll hate you and Dad forever for it."

I snatch my pile of empty holsters, vest, knives, and a pre-packed emergency backpack as I head for the door. I don't stop to look at her face. I run.

CHAPTER 2

Niko

Maybe I'm looking for Lilith, or maybe I'm running until I feel like I can breathe again. Eventually, I emerge from the shadowy backstreets and into the dull streetlights, my tear-stained cheeks long-dried.

I'm just an asshole teenager, but full-grown, violence-prone men cross the street when they see me. I can't escape what I am no matter where I go.

Ashen barracks line the streets, but they're more like glorified boxes. If you're lucky enough to have a bush or two in your dirt yard, you're not actually lucky at all.

Top-end barracks are reserved for elite Department of Tactical Defense members working the deadliest combat jobs in the United States. They'll likely be killed soon anyway, so the Departments figure, "What's a little extra 'free' land for our nation's finest? But nothing more than a few bushes, of course." As if it's not stolen land to begin with.

Our "house" is different. My parents have enough prestige from doing god-knows-what horrible shit throughout their lives to have a secluded unit outside the main living compound. They're determined to keep Hana sheltered from the Departments out there—the only reason why I haven't fully hated them. But that also shows they know what we do isn't okay. Of course everyone is expected to enlist, but I can't understand why they *encouraged* me.

Before tonight, I didn't think about how trapped I am, but

Lilith's escape triggered a realization. Maybe Mom's right about more than I want to admit, and part of me wants to stay trapped. Or maybe the consequences of betraying the Departments are worse than death, so I can't let myself notice how trapped I feel. Subservience is the life I know, and change is terrifying.

But now I'm craving it.

I rush past Jay's barrack, not wanting my best friend to see me like this. We're getting shipped out to Japan in two days, and the last thing he needs is his infamous combat partner showing up looking like a cornered rat.

As the Department of Tactical Defense's dusty land ends, I reach the electric fence separating us from other Departments. Beyond all fences, the civilian world lies blissfully unaware. We're known only to the US Government—their weapons-for-hire. It's justified by loophole laws; sure, the government itself isn't executing our destructive jobs, they're just our indirect employers. Civilians must think we're Santa Desierto's secluded "military base" between the city and the forest, but we're so much more. This is a fucking paramilitary cult.

No one has to recruit Department cult members because we both breed and imprison them. Traitors are dead long before they take their last breath, and my parents are higher-ups who make sure of it. They don't talk about their jobs, but we all know the gist of what "executioners" do. Lilith, Jay, and I have seen the cannons launching our traitorous, soon-to-be-dead into the forest as part of our trainee initiation. The first time, we didn't sleep for weeks. Now the word "cannon" keeps us loyal.

There's no escape, not even socially. Visits to the civilian inner city are short and fleeting, our lives consumed by work. It's hard to understand civilian sentences, even if we're using the same language. I don't think we live in the same dimension.

It's past curfew. I'm not supposed to be outside, especially not outside my Department's fences, but I don't want to stop. I've seen no sign of Lilith, and I know she always goes this way. The dried-out, dying soil is all that can be seen for a few miles until our land encroaches on the forest. Our land's other half trails alongside downtown Santa Desierto, a hazy orange glow of lights washing out the stars.

Pulling military-grade rubber gloves from one of my many pockets, I make sure to only touch the electric fence with my hands and rubber-lined soles, hopping it without a sound. I repeat this fruitless search through every Department, the sky growing darker and darker as clouds black out the slim moon. Still no sign of Lilith.

Something tells me I'll never find her, like Mom said. Lilith and I have the same training. Once you know how to track people, you can figure out how not to be tracked. It's easier than it seems, mainly in the confidence of your steps.

I've already reached the Department of Health on the other side of the extensive compound. Standing in the darkness of a cushy backyard, I'm positive no one saw me, but I still feel exposed. My heart unconsciously dragged me toward someone's house. Someone in particular.

I'm grateful she lives in a place like this: a two-story, cookie-cutter American home, not a shoebox with a cement roof.

I remove my five-pound boots and tie their laces together, draping them over my neck. My socked feet are getting too big to grip her house's wooden siding, but I manage to climb it. One day soon, I might accidentally snap off a panel. Whether that inevitably gets us caught or something else, I'm sure life has plans to separate us yet again. I resent life for so many reasons, but our forced separation is near the top of my list.

It's like she knows I'm coming.

Throwing open her window, she greets me with a smile and open arms. I smile back as if I haven't noticed her red, puffy eyes.

On my way in, I bang my head on the half-open window. She slaps a hand over her mouth in suppressed laughter. Rubbing my head with the other, she shocks me with the first gentle touch I've felt in a while.

"Dammit, I'm way too tall for thi—"

Emmalee cups her hand over my mouth, tugging the rest of me inside. She locks her window with the tiniest click possible. Grabbing my palm, she begins to tap.

It's a simple language we created as kids, but we still talk like this when someone might overhear us. One tiny tap for each letter in the alphabet: one tap for A, two taps for B, and so on.

It's not worth the time unless it's a short message with someone you trust. We tap, rub, or scratch our own faces or legs—or, when we're lucky enough to come into close contact, on each other's shoulders or hands—playing it off as a natural fidget.

Sweep for me, Emmalee taps.

I'm tempted to laugh at myself. I should've done that to begin with, especially since the Departments force-fed me paranoia since birth, but this is how I act around Emmalee. My mind is too busy marveling over her existence to remember everyday tasks.

After sweeping the room for hidden cameras and mics, I find nothing of concern. Just in case, we settle in the safest corner, wedged between her wall and the bedside table I checked thoroughly. Her closet sits in the opposite corner, and it'd take forever to check every piece of fabric in the dark with how much this girl loves black.

"I knew you'd come." Her soft whisper tickles my cheek.

I don't understand how she could feel me coming, but I wholeheartedly believe her. We have a strange connection like that.

Taking a clearer look at her, I'm speechless. Her smooth brown hair is still wet from a shower, weighing itself into a subtle wave at the ends. The way it's cut frames her squishable cheeks. Even in the darkness, I can make out the softness of her overcast-gray eyes. In the 11 months since we last saw each other, she has grown up. I'm sure I have too, but this is different. Her shoulders are pulled back instead of habitually curled into herself, carving out her own respect in a world that has given her none. She's beautiful.

But she's hurting tonight, like I am. She digs out a note from her fuzzy pajama shorts, handing it to me.

Goodbye.

It's Lilith's handwriting. Lilith and Emmalee have been dating for almost a year.

"What?" I whisper. "Is this all she said to you?"

"Yeah." Emmalee's voice shakes in agony. "She told me she was making plans to run away someday, but I didn't expect it today. She didn't even take the time to break up with me first."

My heart sinks. If Emmalee has this note, Lilith doesn't want to be found. She'll make sure she won't be, not even by me.

The heartbreak in Emmalee's tearful expression yanks my heartstrings. I have to step up as her best friend in the world right now—while I still have a chance.

Stroking her soft hand, I huddle in closer. "Oh, Ems, I'm so sorry."

We spend a few silent minutes bundled up together. She sobs beneath her breath, not wanting to alert her parents that she's still awake. My arm stabilizes her shaking shoulders, even though this kills; she's hurting because she was in love with someone else, and my asshole sister was the one who broke her heart.

Soon enough, she presses her forehead into my neck, clinging to me in a desperate hug. I hope my jumpy heart doesn't give me away, but it doesn't need to. Emmalee can vividly sense people's emotions—a sixth sense the Departments deem "useful."

She's more than "useful" to me. I love her, and I always have.

But our deep connection has long been forbidden.

I cradle her head, rubbing her back until her breath evens out.

"Niko?" She traces circles on my chest, fluttering my stomach into my throat.

"Hm?"

"Will you be at the Christmas party?"

I grit my teeth. "Not this year. I haven't been able to tell you, but Jay and I are getting deployed soon for our graduation test. I'm sorry."

I expect her to be angry with me. The Department Extortion—I mean *Christmas*—party is the one time we're guaranteed to meet. To sneak away and be ourselves. And who knows if I'll come back alive from Japan.

Her classic, sly smile appears. "Then how about we continue our Christmas tradition? We have to be quieter than we are now, anyway. And if we're not *talking*, then..."

I gulp. "I-I don't know…"

"Oh. You don't want to?"

I readjust my legs to stifle my pounding heart. I'll never understand why this incredible girl always wants to make out with an asshole like me. "It's not that. You're heartbroken over someone else. I don't want to take advantage of that."

Emmalee smirks. "Pft. I was the one who asked for it."

I laugh beneath my breath, pushing a stray hair from her eyes. Despite being torn apart, we've known each other for so long that this friendly touch is natural. But tonight, it's different. The smiles disappear from our faces, and the hormones take over.

We kiss awkwardly and sloppily, which I can guarantee is 100% my inexperienced fault. It doesn't matter to us as long as we experience as much of each other's comfort in the short time we have. I love being close to her like this—close enough to re-memorize her faint, cozy scent. But when she reaches for the bottom of my shirt, I jerk backward and bang my elbow into the wall.

She gasps. "What's wrong?"

I never used to react like that, so I'm just as surprised. My core sinks in horror of what my reaction stems from, something I can't handle thinking about, myself. I shake my head to dispel Emmalee's concerns, not wanting her to know the truth.

"Sorry!" She holds my face. "I'm sorry. I should've asked first."

"It's okay, Ems. I just didn't expect it."

After she double-checks for the truth in my eyes, we smile and lean in close to continue. But then I hear something.

Emmalee freezes—alert eyes analyzing the sudden tension in my body. She doesn't hear it yet, but a parent's soft footsteps send me into extreme focus mode. I throw her onto her bed and slide myself beneath it in one swift movement, causing her to squeak in surprise.

A quiet knock at the door cues Emmalee into jamming her legs beneath the blankets. She takes a calming breath, calling out a soft, "Come in."

I almost forget to hide my backpack, yanking its strap to my chest just in time for the door to creak open.

Mrs. Richards peeks her head in, and I silence my breath.

"Are you okay? I thought I heard something and was surprised you're still up."

"Mhm, just dropped my phone, sorry."

"Okay, honey. Has she texted back?"

Emmalee sighs. "No."

"Oh, Emma… Are you too upset to sleep? Want me to sit with you?"

"I'm okay, Mom. I'm finally getting sleepy."

"Alright, put your phone away and go to sleep if you can, okay? We can talk things out again tomorrow."

"Okay. Thanks, Mom."

Mrs. Richards hesitates at the door. "You'll find someone again. Someone that'll stay, honey."

Emmalee sighs. "Thanks, Mom."

"I know you don't believe me, but anyone who doesn't see you for the amazing person you are doesn't deserve you. Okay?"

Emmalee chuckles. "Okay."

"Goodnight, Emma."

"Goodnight."

As soon as Mrs. Richards shuts the door, we sigh in unison. Emmalee whips her head over the bed's edge, peeking at me upside down.

"There's a monster under my bed!" She giggles.

I shake my head in dismay, chuckling. "More like *on* your bed. You dropped your phone, huh? Lying to your own mother—so smoothly too. Who knew I corrupted you so much?"

She jabs my cheek with her black fingernail. "Shut up. I'm pissed at you now. Who else am I going to make out with at the party?"

I want to laugh, but I hate the thought of her finding someone to replace me. My bitter expression raises a laugh from her, but a little too loud of one. We both rush to slap a hand over her mouth. This only makes us giggle more, and I decide it's probably safer if I leave.

But Emmalee doesn't let me leave through her window, hardly allowing me to pick up my backpack. She clings to me just as I slip one leg over the windowsill.

"Wait. Don't go yet."

I can't see her desperate hands on my back, but I can hear her distraught, muffled voice between my shoulder blades. A lump forms in my throat.

"I don't *want* to go. Ever," I whisper.

"But you have to. I know."

We stand in silence for a full minute. Emmalee can't let me go. I'm glad my back is turned, my eyes watering to the brim.

"Please come back," she whispers. "Don't die out there."

Shit. Now I really have to get my act together.

"I can't lose you too," she continues.

I duck back through the window to get one final hug in. Breathing in her damp hair's minty scent, I memorize her neck's softness beneath my fingertips and the way she still makes my heart pound by how she hugs me with her entire torso.

Drawing her chin toward me, I look into her crystal-clear eyes one last time.

"I'll be back before you know it."

With a shy kiss on her forehead, I slip out her bedroom window and run into the cover of darkness.

CHAPTER 3

Emmalee

It's been four months since my ex-girlfriend ran away without breaking up with me and my childhood best friend was deployed to probably go die somewhere. This shit sucks. Like I'm specifically 38 years old and verging on a mid-life crisis at 16.

That's why I'm extra surprised when Niko's father approaches me tonight.

A slender, black-haired man interrupts my Calculus homework. He looks apologetic in such a familiar way that I mistake him for a worn version of Niko; they make the same hurt-puppy expression if they upset or surprise you. And the last I knew, I wasn't supposed to talk to Niko at all, let alone his family.

"Hi. Sorry," Commander Yosuke Blackwood whispers.

"Hi?"

We're in the middle of the Department of Health's community library, which only makes this more confusing. He looks around before leaning in with a lowered voice. "Your parents told me last year at the Christmas party that you babysit after school. Is that still the case?"

"Oh." I turn to my textbook in disbelief. But yes, this is happening. I still have a shitload of homework, Commander Blackwood just admitted our parents talk, and he's talking to *me*. "Yeah, I still babysit. Or nanny. The last family came back from deployment recently, so I'm looking for another long-term job."

He sighs in relief, muttering something to himself in

Japanese. "I'm all out of willing babysitters. Niko is overseas, but you know how people are about him. They refuse to come near the house whether he's there or not." He scrubs his forehead. "Anyway, Clara and I won't be home until 8 p.m. on weekdays anymore, and I promised to find the next babysitter by tomorrow. I know your parents might disapprove, so you'll have to ask their permission and let me know what they say. I'll have to convince Clara too… But do you think you'd have time to watch Hana after school, or—"

"Of course!" I jump out of my seat, irritating the entire library with my obnoxious voice. I try again in a whisper. "I'd love to!"

After we agree on a time for me to arrive every day, Commander Blackwood disappears within seconds, leaving me in a daze over my half-finished Calculus homework. There's no way I can focus on it now, so I pack up my books and go home.

My heart and lungs threaten to kill me for speed-walking home, but I can't help it. I have to know what my parents will say—if they'll allow me to hang out with Niko's little sister as early as tomorrow. I love kids, and I've always wanted to meet Hana.

I might've brought too much enthusiasm to the table, both Mom and Dad wide-eyed as I toss my backpack down and struggle to catch my breath.

"Sweetheart, are you having an asthma attack?" Mom's palms press flat against the table, ready to burst into action.

"Nope! I just— Got a little— Ahead of myself."

"Okay, well, sit down at the table with us and breathe."

I do, plopping myself onto a worn, gingham cushion.

Then my nerves kick in. Both parents stare, expecting me to say something. I was so excited that I didn't think about the potential of this totally failing, but I'm definitely thinking about it now.

Taking a deep breath to harness my confidence, I begin. "I got an offer for babysitting tonight."

Dad rolls his eyes in recognition of my bargaining voice. He sighs, squishing his cheek into his palm. "We're listening."

Mom gives him a gentle push.

"What? I'm listening."

I blink a few times in simmering annoyance, then put on my best straight face. "Do you remember Hana, the baby Clara and Yosuke had a few years ago?"

Without turning his head, Dad knowingly eyes Mom.

Mom sighs, her golden-brown hair falling off her shoulder with a shake of her head. "Emma…"

"Before we get into it, I didn't agree to the job yet. I wanted to come home and ask you first." I chew on the inside of my cheek, silently thanking Commander Blackwood for helping me remember I should ask for permission in the first place.

"Okay, good." Dad straightens in his chair. "Because the answer is no."

My jaw tenses. "You won't even let me finish? This is Niko's baby sister. He won't even be there—"

"Emmalee, I said no."

Mom puts a hand on Dad's forearm, giving him a look I can't see with her head turned away from me. Dad twists his mouth to the side, sitting back and crossing his arms.

Mom pivots to me. "He's on tour, isn't he? How long will he be gone?"

I bite back every nagging impulse in me to say *thanks to them, I'm incapable of getting that information, or* any *meaningful information, about my best friend.* Instead, I say, "I don't know. Hopefully he'll come back at all. He could die any day now."

Their tense stares anticipate an emotional response.

I don't deliver one. "So, I haven't been able to find any other jobs yet, and I've always wanted to meet Hana. You were okay with me dating Lilith, right?"

Dad mutters, "Yeah, which was a major exception for me, by the way. And the rule was that she came *here* and you never went *there*. But then she broke your heart. Their family isn't exactly the shining example of— Well, anything."

I bite my lip hard enough to taste iron. This always gets Dad and me to fight, and that's definitely not what I want.

"If you're even thinking about arguing with me right now, Emma, the answer is no," he says.

"I *wasn't*," I say.

"But now you are."

We glare at each other. Mom kneads her forehead with the base of her palms. "Can we please have one normal conversation about this?"

Dad frowns. "What do you mean?"

"Emmalee hasn't asked you to see Niko. She asked for our permission about a job. He's not going to be there, and Emmalee already knows our stance on Niko. Don't you, Emma?"

I sigh. "I do. Even if I don't understand it."

"See?" Dad grumbles. "She's fishing."

My resting bitch face intensifies. "The interesting thing is, I also don't understand why it's bad to ask questions or to say I don't understand something."

By the look on Dad's face, I'm in for it now. But I can't help it.

"This could be resolved with a simple explanation, but no. You just *have* to assume I'm doing this to torture you every time, or that I don't care what you think, or something else ridiculous, but that's not true! I do care, Dad, and that's why you've made this so hard on me! I care about you both, and I care about him! You don't understand how this feels for me."

He grips his forehead, biting back anger. "Why are you so fixated on the Blackwoods, anyway? I mean, *two* siblings, Emmalee?"

My face grows hot. "It's not like there are a lot of options!"

Mom sighs. "Emma, of course there are."

I huff. "Alright, then, which is your amazing plan: would you rather I set my sights one of the guys who joke about how women are dogs to train, or one of the girls who will look the other way when those guys inevitably rape me?"

With Dad's jaw clenched, his mouth forms a thin line. "You can do the babysitting job, but you are *never* seeing Nikolai Blackwood again. Especially not with that attitude."

I stand from my chair. Dad said yes to the babysitting job. The rest of this conversation is a losing battle, so I better leave before I say anything I regret.

"Okay," I say. Dad raises his eyebrows, so I tack on a quick "thanks" and stride upstairs to my bedroom.

I rip open my art drawer, fumbling through a mess of paint tubes for a square artboard scrap. As for the paint, I grab a few colors I'm drawn to: deep burgundy, electric blue, and viridian green. Pulling out my palette tray, I begin to mix.

"Never" is such an impossible word. How the hell will Dad "protect" me from ever running into Niko for my whole life? What if we run into each other by mistake? Or if Niko needs my help and has no one else to go to, and I choose not to be a heartless bitch? Or if I ditch this place as soon as I turn 18 and do whatever the hell I want? "Never" doesn't exist.

I cling to the good news: I can tell Commander Blackwood I'm available to babysit tomorrow. I text the temporary number he wrote on my homework and get an immediate response, confirming my new job tomorrow at 1 p.m.—after my online classes end and I eat lunch.

But that's not enough comfort. I still have two more years before I turn 18. Even then, I'll be disabled for the rest of my life, relying on my parents. Regular working hours would kill me, a fact I've desperately avoided. But it's true; I'm not a person who'll grow up to be an independent adult. My parents know and accept this because they love me, yet they don't understand what they're doing to me otherwise.

A soft knock shocks me into swiping away my tears. I pause in my paint mixing, mumbling, "Come in."

Mom gives my irritated scowl a soft smile. "Can I sit with you?"

I scoot over so she can climb onto my bed beside my tiny desk. Mom leans her side against the headboard, crossing her legs and facing me like we're having a sleepover.

She smiles, shaking her head. "You two are so alike. That's why you clash."

I sigh. "I know I'm stubborn, but I'm not *that* stubborn."

She laughs. "Be nice."

"Sorry... I just need a better explanation. What I have now makes no sense."

"Okay."

I stop mixing. I didn't expect her to agree.

Mom smiles, brushing my hair behind my shoulder. "You don't have to stop."

"O-okay..."

The accumulation of paint looks black enough, so I make the first stroke on the square scrap board. Seeing it against the brisk white, I'm not satisfied. The last I saw his eyes, they were more of a violet-black, not a wine-black like this color. So I start mixing again, adding a bit more electric blue and a little less burgundy this time.

"Your father and I discussed it with the Blackwoods when you were children. We decided it was safest for you both to not communicate, at least not much."

"Right… So what's the deal with that? Are you and Clara, like, friends?"

Mom laughs. "Friends with *Clara?* No. But our husbands were friends."

My eyes widen. "Oh. When?"

"When they were in school. But Yosuke fell madly in love with Clara, who's bound to the DoTD, so Yosuke naturally became distant with your dad."

"Oh… Do they not like each other now or something?"

Mom settles further down, sinking into my pillow. She's silent as I rotate my palette beneath my desk lamp to get a more precise look at the color, but I can feel her contemplative energy.

"We're okay around each other for a short time, but our Departments definitely clash," Mom finally says.

I look over at her. "Because of your patients."

"Yes. The patients admitted from the Department of Tactical Defense aren't just physically injured, they're mentally… lost. They're so distorted that they'll never fit in with civilian life, and for you, we wanted you to socialize however you pleased. Niko won't be able to blend in with society. Ever."

My furious brush strokes threaten to ruin my synthetic brush, so I set the artboard down. "But what does that have to do with me?"

"What it has to do with you, sweetheart, is that you two are absolutely obsessed with each other and won't follow our rules. The more you talk to him, the more you involve yourself with his crowd. This isn't a crowd you want to be involved with."

"Then why are we here at all?"

My heart pounds as Mom gazes at the ceiling, growing a little too quiet. "We work here. This is our livelihood."

Her words edge me the wrong way. Whether it's an empath thing or my own irritation, I huff, shaking off her excuse. "I still don't understand."

"I know. But this is how it has to be. Clara and Yosuke did *not* want him growing up without learning how to defend himself. They enrolled him in the same combat training programs they grew up with, and that was that. If he was in another Department, it'd be different. But this isn't the Army. They're walking weapons of war."

My shoulders raise. "No, Mom, no. I *hate* when people call him stuff like that. He's a teenage, human boy."

"He's a very misguided one. You can't see it now, but one day, you'll understand how much we've protected you. We aren't doing this to spite you, either. We've lived through this longer than you and can see it from a wider perspective. One day, he'll hurt you or someone you love, and it's better to cut your relationship off before you get there. Spare yourself the pain."

I sigh through my watery eyes, painting the board's thin edges to finish off the violet-black swatch. "Well, I'm in pain now."

She pets my shoulder, but I can't even look at her. I turn away, tearing off a few pieces of my stickiest artist's tape and rolling them into little circles to stick on the artboard's backside. Once it's up on the wall next to my growing grid of vibrantly different black shades, I step back to admire it. It's still wet, reflecting a distracting shine from my desk lamp that makes it difficult to tell how it'll look once it dries, but it's already making the one to its left look a little less purple. This wall is the only evidence of him I can create in my life.

Mom finishes counting off the 4 x 4 inch squares beneath her breath. "Wow, 55 already! Like the end of your ID number."

"Oh. Yeah." I rub my back automatically, wishing I didn't have an ugly identification tattoo down my spine.

"Why do you paint these squares again? I can't remember what you said last time."

She awaits my response as I continue to stare at my work. The grid of paintings is black, but sitting in my lap, my limp hands are decorated with red, green, blue, purple, teal, indigo, and everything between. I turn away from the black grid, a rainbow of subtle colors no one else can see.

"No reason, really. I just like the color black."

CHAPTER 4

Emmalee

Within less than 24 hours, I'm on my way to the Blackwood household for the first time in 12 years. I'm a little hopeful. Maybe I can prove that Niko and I can handle ourselves—that "keeping us safe" by keeping us apart is pointless. If anything, it prevents us from trusting our parents.

I don't care what other people say about Niko. They don't even know him. I know him, and Niko is the only person I feel safe around in this fucked-up world.

It's weird to walk toward the boxy barracks after I finish my lunch, but I'm not complaining. Not even with the disgusting catcalls I get on the way there.

I haven't seen Hana since she was a baby, when we passed each other in the grocery store. Niko has shown me one or two Hana pictures throughout the years on Jay's phone, but we've all only seen each other a handful of times since Hana was born— just over six years ago.

Either way, Niko and I don't spend much time "talking" anymore. At thirteen, we created a tradition to celebrate our devious reunion. Every Christmas party, when the Departments merge for one night, I sneak him away… Minus when I dated his sister, in which the Christmas tradition paused for Niko, but continued for me.

Year after year, I'm overcome by the temptation to throw myself at him once we're reunited. If my mom knew, she'd be disappointed and tell me "boys love the chase," or something else outdated, and I'd tell her, "not this boy." I love seeing the blush rise to his increasingly sculpted cheeks every year. Lately, freckles swarm his naturally tan skin when he's had too much sun. They're as much of a tease as his full lips. Flustering a top-ranking combat trainee is a feat not many can flaunt.

Commander Blackwood swings the door open before I can knock, tugging me inside and slamming the door behind me.

"Sorry," he mutters to my terrified face. "I didn't want anyone to notice you coming in right before I leave you two here alone."

"Um… Okay."

He leads me down the empty hall. Their house feels frigid: bare and bland, minus the essentials. More of a convenient place to sleep than a home.

"Emmalee, please don't walk the barracks' streets next time. Walk through the back passageway. It's not safe in the streets, especially if you're not in the DoTD."

Commander Blackwood understands the dangers of navigating the Department of Tactical Defense better than I do, and I'm not about to question a Commander. At least not before I get paid.

"Niko isn't a good example of the Tactical Defense Department, by the way. Don't let his calm nature fool you into trusting anyone else there. He'll never admit it, but he has—Well, a heart."

I snicker. "Finally, someone agrees with me."

He hums in agreement, shooting me a quick smile. "But please don't tell Clara I said so."

"I won't, Comman—"

I'm too taken aback to finish my thoughts. A little girl with chunky strawberry beads stationed atop two pigtails peeks over the couch's edge, hiding behind it. From what Niko alluded to, Hana hasn't been around strangers much, so I wanted to be extra warm and welcoming when we met, but my mouth can't form words.

She has his dark eyes, his subtle spattering of freckles, and his bowed lips. If Niko was a little older, I could be convinced she was his. It revs up a biological need I shouldn't have yet.

I don't have to force a bright smile for her. "Hi, Hana! My name's Emmalee."

Hana dives back behind the couch. Her father eases toward her, holding out a hand, and they silently communicate. Even if he wasn't her father, the Commander could catch the fear I sense in Hana's emotions. He's like me: he's an empath.

Our sixth sense allows us to sense others' emotions without words—and to be used by the Departments. If I wasn't disabled, they would've used me as a Guide, my insight guiding unit members through otherwise impossible combat. Sixth senses aren't brushed off as fake here, but I'm not sure that's a good thing. The Departments' studies have found about 1% of any population have a sixth sense, but we're rarely combat-inclined, and we're valued as such. They use combat unit members as emotionless weapons, and Guides are mere weapon *upgrades*.

I'd imagine Commander Yosuke Blackwood is overshadowed by his combat-focused wife. He even took her Irish last name in exchange for his Japanese family name. Commander Clara Blackwood followed the Blackwood Lionheart family legacy—a long line of elite Department of Tactical Defense members. It's no surprise Niko is on track to do the same.

Clara never had a choice in the matter, and neither did Niko. None of us did. Just like Mom said, this is our livelihood.

The Commander speaks to Hana in Japanese, pausing to say my name with English pronunciation. This soothes her enough to take one teeny step from behind the couch.

I'm squatting at her eye level, my backpack on the floor beside me.

Hana does a double-take between her dad and me. "You're really Emmalee?"

"Yes! And you're Hana, right? It's so nice to meet you! I love your pigtails with those big strawberries. They're totally cute."

She gives me a shy glance, trying her hardest not to smile.

Commander Blackwood chuckles, bending to kiss her forehead. "You don't have to hide. She's safe, I promise."

"I-I know," Hana says. I'm a little confused as to why, but she's nervous. Not in an anxiety type of way, but a starstruck type of way.

With a smile in his eyes, Commander Blackwood says his goodbyes, assuring me he'll be back at 7:30, before Clara. We watch him from the window as he flails out the door, late for work. It's a torturous moment for us both to witness. For Hana, it's because of separation anxiety. But for me, it's because it's not a common sight to see a Commander losing his cool, so now *I'm* trying not to lose my shit laughing at him in front of his daughter.

"So." I gather the attention of her beautiful, obsidian eyes. "Is there anything you want to do first?" I'm met with stubborn silence. "A game? Book? TV show? Coloring?"

Her eyes light up at the last one, so I make my way to the living room. She follows, stopping at the hallway's mouth to watch me hunt for art supplies.

"Any idea where the paper is, Hana? Maybe some colored pencils? Markers?"

She hums in deep thought like Niko does when he has no idea what to say, so I continue my search alone. The first hint of personality in this house sits next to the TV: a school photograph of Niko. Even then, he looked striking. Composed. I have to laugh at his little frown, taking himself so seriously when he couldn't be much older than eight or nine. That's the Niko I remember best.

If this mini picture frame was in Niko's room instead of his parent's living room, I'd happily take it home like he stole my school picture. I hadn't noticed him stealing it with how dark it was when he last visited, but that guy is sly in all aspects of life. It wasn't too shocking that he could take something in the dark, but his unexplained reasoning surprised me. He could've just asked me for the photo, and I would've given it to him. But he didn't, and that makes me the most suspicious. I doubt he'll tell me why when—no, *if*—he comes back.

"We don't have paper," Hana mutters, suddenly by my ear.

I gasp, holding a hand over my thumping heart to keep it in place. My nervous system is annoyingly sensitive, another reason I didn't get wrapped up in Niko's Department.

"But we have *this!*" Hana gallops to the kitchen and snatches a black permanent marker out of a drawer.

My eyes widen in horror, thinking of the destruction I caused with one of those as a kid. "Um, yeah, let's stay away from the permanent stuff." Hana deflates. "It's okay! We can still draw! Let me grab some stuff out of my backpack."

Hana sticks to my side this time, peering over my shoulder in anticipation of these mysterious art supplies—apparently a rarity in this household. She gasps with every black or blue pen I pull out, gasps even louder at the graphite pencil, and finally, hops with a light squeal when I reveal my six colored pencils, grouped together with an old hair tie.

Hana bounces on my shoulder with her pigtails flying in every direction, and I have to laugh.

"Alright, little kangaroo! I'll set these on the table, okay? You can't run with them because I sharpened them before I left school, and I don't want you to get hurt."

"Okay." She calms herself into nothingness in an instant.

This worries me. I wouldn't be able to do that with how much of a fireball I was at six. Maybe Hana is just copying Niko, but this is a trauma response I've witnessed in him for as long as I've known him. It makes people think he's emotionless.

I hold out my hand, relieved as Hana grabs on and allows her smile to return. I mimic her bouncy steps to the table, stirring a contagious giggle in her as we skip to the kitchen. She's so cute, I could die.

As soon as she's situated with a cup of water, some apple slices, and her art supplies, I pull out my Calculus homework. I only write the first equation before realizing something feels off.

Hana isn't just zoning out, she looks… depressed?

I have no idea what behaviors are normal for Hana, so I try to appear as calm as I can. "Hana? Is something wrong?"

She continues to stare at her paper. After so much excitement, her emotions are frigid with panic, even more so since I noticed her behavior. Then she mumbles something into her hand.

"What's that? I couldn't hear you, little sprout," I say softly.

Hana looks up in surprise, beaming.

I smile. "Niko told me he calls you that—since your name means 'flower,' right? Do you like that nickname?"

She nods, although her eyebrows furrow. "When did he tell you? Have you seen him?"

My heart flinches. "No, little sprout. I'm sorry. He told me a couple years ago. He's still in another country."

"Oh… I know," she says, although it doesn't sound like she wants to accept it.

"He'll be back."

Her eyes widen. "He will?!"

Shit. Maybe I shouldn't have said that. "Well, he told me he would be, so he better."

"Are you gonna beat him up if he doesn't?" She eyes me.

I chuckle, tilting my head. "What? Uh, no. I mean, even if I wanted to beat him up, I don't stand a chance against your big brother, but I'd never hit him. That's not a nice thing to do."

"I know," she whispers. "I don't understand why Mom does. She's an adult."

I force down my shock as I stare at this grown-up in a child's body, clearly more mature than her parents. Then I calm the fire boiling in my gut. It's an inappropriate reaction, considering what I just told Hana, but I have the urge to hit Clara: a taste of her own medicine. It's such a vivid protection response that my arms twitch, anticipating a fight.

I quell my immaturity for Hana's sake. But I'm afraid of what this means. Does Clara hit Hana too? Thankfully, Hana overlooks my internal battle, figuring I'm giving her more space to talk.

"If you won't beat him up, what else do you do when you're angry?"

Her question is genuine, so I steady myself to answer carefully. "I wouldn't do anything to hurt him. Even if we argue, it's not nice to hurt people you care about. It's better to tell them how you feel so they can understand your emotions."

Hana's brows furrow, considering my words. "How would you feel, then?"

"What do you mean?"

"If he doesn't come back." She stares me down.

"Hmm. At first, I might be mad, but I think deep down, I'd just be very sad."

Hana's shoulders soften. "Me too." We turn our attention back to her blank paper, and her cheeks flush almost as red as the strawberries in her hair. "I don't know what to draw."

"Oh, is that what was wrong? That's okay!" I kneel by her side, setting my chin on the table. "What sorts of things do you like?"

"Um…"

"Hey, you could even scribble with your favorite colors!"

"Really? Isn't that for babies?"

"Nope!" I grin, grabbing a black pencil and slamming a paper in front of me for dramatic effect. As I furiously scribble, Hana's airy laughter eggs me on. I make goofy concentrating faces, pretending this scribble is the most difficult drawing I've ever made. Hana hops out of her chair and grabs my hand to stop me, and I find her silently laughing so hard that her face is turning purple.

I sort out her wispy hairline. "Okay, okay, breathe, kid. Don't die on me, now. At least not on my first day."

Hana sucks in a deep breath before letting out another infectious squeal, grabbing the sky blue pencil and scribbling chaotic lines all over my black scribbles. I join in on her laughter, holding the paper steady for her as she lets herself loose.

Once Hana fades into an exhausted giggle, I plop her back on her chair. "Alright, Little Miss Giggles."

"Little Miss Giggles!?" Hana fumbles through a laugh now that literally anything I say sounds funny to her. But then she gasps, staring at me. "I know what to draw now!"

"Oh, good! I can't wait to see it!"

She beams, and I can't help but pat her little head.

I play some soft music, and Hana jams out to it, bobbing her head as she draws. Keeping my laughter to myself so I don't pull her out of the zone, I focus on my homework while I can.

After the fourth equation, I get the sense I'm being watched. Looking up to find Hana's onyx stare, she gazes into my eyes for a hyper-concentrated millisecond before burying her face back into her paper.

"How's it going?" I ask.

"Fine," she says. Then she realizes I'm watching. Hooking an arm around her head and paper, she covers her drawing from me.

I laugh. "Am I not allowed to see?"

"Nope!" Her small, muffled voice cries out. "Not until I'm done!"

"Okay, that's fine. Just let me know if you need help—and don't forget about your apple slices."

She pops up, having forgotten about her snack out of excitement, as expected. I rest my chin in my palm with a goofy grin. I don't care if she's technically his "sister." This is totally Niko's *kid*.

Hana shoves an entire apple slice in her mouth at once, so thank God I was watching. I force her to spit it into my hand and make what I'm sure is a hideous face in disgust, sending Hana into another laughter fit.

"You're funny." She kicks her feet as she munches on a fresh apple slice.

I smile. "So are you!"

"Niko was right." Hana closes her eyes, nodding in feigned seriousness. It's a total imitation of her rigid mother. I have to cover my mouth to resist a sputtering laugh.

"Right about what?" I mumble into my palm.

"Huh?!" She gives me a mischievous grin. "Can't hear you!"

I laugh. "I *said*, Niko was right about what?"

Her smirk intensifies. "That you're very pretty."

My jaw drops, and we both sink into belly laughter. "Hana, did you just spill your big brother's secrets?!"

She swishes back and forth, scrunching her nose in a sly giggle. "Maybe."

"Oh, Hana…" I give her a look, *the* look. And she knows what she did wrong. The way she laughs it off convinces me of my suspicions: she's as much of a naughty little shit as I am. I shake my head, biting my lips to stop my spreading smile. The temptation is there to make her spill even more secrets, but on top of being a horrible influence, I shouldn't do that to Niko. Luckily, Hana saves me from my moral crisis yet again, uncovering her half-finished drawing. "Oh, wow! How beautiful! Did you finish?"

"Not yet." Her smirk is still glued to her face.

"Who's that? Your mom?"

"No!" Hana laughs. "It's *you*, silly!"

"Aww! How sweet!" I take a closer look over her shoulder. It's hilarious; she must've noticed the only color I wear and scribbled me a chunky, black triangle dress. She was kind enough to make my eyes blue, although I know they're an ugly, washed-out gray. "Why's there a crown on my head?"

"Because! You're a princess."

"Oh. That's cute."

"Hey!" She hangs on my arm. "Aren't you?"

"Um, I guess I can pretend to be?"

"But princesses are very fun, very pretty, and very cool. You *have* to be a real-life princess."

I laugh, rubbing her back. "That's pretty adorable. If that's all it took to be a rich princess, I'd try *much* harder to be all those things."

"But you are!" She's glaring now.

"Whoa, hey, sorry! Thank you, little sprout. That's really sweet of you."

Her frown softens. "Niko thinks you are too."

I bite my lower lip. "Hana, you can't share your brother's secrets like that. It's not nice."

Hana scowls. "He didn't say it was a secret. He tells me stories when I can't sleep, and he always names the hero Hana or Emmalee. You're just like the Emmalee in his stories. You're fun and pretty and cool, and you make everything better. A real-life princess."

My whole face flushes. It's so like Niko, leaving my loud mouth at a loss for words from the opposite hemisphere. "Thanks, Sprout. That's really sweet of you both."

Hana returns to her paper. "Sometimes, Princess Emmalee even has laser beams. Those are my favorites."

"Wow, that's… I think your brother and I have very different definitions of fairytales."

Hana pauses, looking up at me with furrowed brows. "Is that bad?"

I laugh. "Nope. His sound more fun."

She grins, rushing to scribble in some grass beneath my black circle feet and a neon sun in the corner. Shoving the paper in my face, she says, "Done!"

I take the fresh drawing in my hands, holding it under the pale overhead LEDs. Hana watches intently, awaiting my reaction. But I can't admit how I feel. I'm dying to smother her brother in affection—something I'll never be allowed to do. So I say everything I would've if she hadn't dropped a heart-wrenching bomb on me.

"Hana, the way you draw people is *so good!* Better than I did at your age! I can't believe you don't get to draw often. You're an amazing artist!"

She swings her feet at her chair's edge, lowering her head to hide a soft smile. "It's not too good."

"Hey, I mean it. I'm *so* impressed." Just like Niko, a gentle nudge of encouragement goes a long way for Hana. Her pride glows from within, expressing itself as a wide-eyed grin. "If you had fun drawing, you should keep going, little sprout! You'll keep getting better and better!"

She giggles, flipping to the next paper sheet. "Okay! I'm going to draw Niko now!"

I take a moment to admire this little energy ball lighting up the room with novel excitement. I don't understand why they've kept her from drawing, but it's nauseating how far her restrictions must go. I once made the mistake of asking Niko what hobbies he had; he didn't even know what a "hobby" was. The DoTD is his entire life.

But my parents aren't innocent, either. They're pulling us apart because we work well together.

Ever since we were toddlers, Niko and I have been drawn to each other. Our connection is irresistible, not a silly childhood crush. I've never gotten over him. He's the only person who really gets me, and I'm the only person who really gets him.

Maybe it's the bisexual rebel in me, but nothing can convince me that two people should be split apart for loving each other. Not only in a romantic way, but also loving each other as friends. And at the very least, I want to be his *best*-best friend. A part-time acquaintance isn't cutting it.

I have to find a way to tie us together permanently, or else I don't know how long we can survive like this. It's too painful.

And I'm already in too much pain. Chronic illness has kicked my ass for as long as I can remember, but it's settling in the past few years. After a long day at school, playing with Hana has my heart racing like it's on its last leg, and the night has only begun. I probably shouldn't have agreed to this job, but I need it. For the last of my sanity.

This has to work to bind us together, this time. I'm clinging to Niko for as long as I live, and unless it's his choice, I'm not letting him slip away again.

CHAPTER 5

Niko

"I think I've translated enough misogynistic bullshit this week to have some serious health concerns," I mutter into my hands.

Jay throws his head back and laughs, giving my shoulder a few hefty slaps. "Bro, I can't even imagine. I'm just along for the ride at this point. Enjoying the sushi while you do the heavy lifting."

I scoff, nudging him in the ribs. Jay knows I hate when he downplays how much he works his ass off. Which is exactly why he said it.

"You done for today, though?" He asks.

"Mm." I half-revert to Japanese. "I'm have done-ました。"

Jay snickers. "Um, what?"

"Shit, fuck. I don't know. I'm making up my own language at this point. I'm going to bed."

"Good. And I'm making sure of it."

We change into our civilian clothes and head to a worn-down, traditional Japanese inn that only takes cash. While Jay uses our tiny private restroom, I lay on the tatami and pull an old photo out of my pocket; it reminds me I have to live long enough to get home.

I prefer this benign type of mission: translating between some old white guys in our Department that we've never met and some fake-named Japanese guys, trying to take down an overlap in our countries' black markets. But by what I'm translating, I'm not sure we're much better. They're debating how to secure an injectable substance, but I can tell it's more than that. They won't let me hear the details, but Jay and I speculate it's a bioweapon. One that originated in the US and has been wreaking havoc on other countries, of course, so now we're mopping our own mess.

I don't want to think about it, but that's all my brain can do at night. Especially after six months of high-pressure vocabulary thrown around that I have to ingest both literally and culturally, then try not to make a mess as I shit it back out of my bilingually confused mouth.

Assigning some part-Japanese, asshole teenager to this mission makes no sense to me, but it's not my job to question what I'm doing.

We have to get through this to graduate. Jay and I were surprised they didn't choose a mission requiring us to play our usual violent, brutish roles. But we know *something* must be coming at the end of this that'll require that side of us. Something big enough to warrant our 16-year-old promotion into the actual Department ranks.

Footsteps march down the hall outside our room, so I dive into the open closet. Someone kicks through the door. My lungs stiffen when I see him through the closet slats; the intruder looks a lot like one of my Commanding Officers. Startlingly pale and tight-lipped, he has the same coercive blue eyes I know so well.

But he's not my Commanding Officer, I have to remind myself. Judging by his rifle, he's likely a European assassin. Everything in my training tells me to subdue or kill an intruder, but it also tells me to never defy authority—especially not *that* Commanding Officer. I'm so startled that I'm frozen for a whole three seconds. Thank god Jay's still in the bathroom and didn't have to see me fail after seven years of hardcore combat training.

The millisecond the intruder hears Jay turn on the bathroom sink and aims his automatic weapon at the bathroom door, I shake myself out of it. I'll never allow Jay to die.

His eyes are off me, so I make my move. Subduing him onto the floor in a single breath, I rip the automatic from the intruder's beefy hands and strap it over my shoulder.

Jay flings open the bathroom door, dressed in only a towel,

and says, "Goodnight!" He clocks the intruder in the jaw with a blur of a fist, knocking the guy out.

I laugh, shaking my head. "Why do you have to say something weird every time? You're going to be known as the foreigner kid that thinks he's in a spy movie. From the '00s. Formidable, but a freak."

Jay flicks his leftover toothpaste at me from his toothbrush, giving me a foamy smile. "Still formidable, though!" He spits. "You gonna call that in or what?"

I laugh. "You're ridiculous."

"You love me, though."

"Yeah, man. I do."

Jay gets unusually quiet, but he'll bounce back in a minute or two. I need him to get off my case before he notices my legs are jelly, straddling this doppelganger of my Commanding Officer, Dr. Sumner.

But I'm not a lucky person in general, so of course, Jay notices.

"That guy looks a lot like Sumner, doesn't he? Kinda freaky." He laughs, standing over the intruder's head. We sit in silence for a whole minute. Jay's depthful brown eyes tell me he doesn't need to ask to understand where I'm at. "So… You need help getting up?"

I try to wave Jay off, but he grabs my wrist, pulling me to my feet. My knuckles brush past his bare stomach on the way up, and my mind is definitely distracted now, although confused. I thought I was straight, but the more time I spend with Jay as we've grown older, the more I don't understand myself.

He grabs a hold of my head. Friendly, but showing off his exposed, flexing arms a little too much for me to speak. "Hey, what's going on, Ni? Something's… off."

"I… I don't feel too good," I whisper.

"Alright, let's get the danger stick off your back, first." Jay frees me of the rifle, strapping it onto his own back. Once we confiscate something as serious as an automatic, we keep it on ourselves so no one has a chance to use it against us. Still, it feels wrong, seeing Jay like this. Out of everyone I know, he hates rifles the most.

"Sorry," I whisper.

"Dude, stop. What kind of useless partner would I be if I couldn't take over for you now and then? You've been working your ass off. And you look like shit."

"*Thanks.*"

Jay laughs, pushing me onto the bed. "You're welcome. Now go the fuck to sleep, princess."

I throw my shirt off at his face, expecting him to laugh and seek revenge. But when he removes the faded black fabric draped over his head, his warm skin blushes an even darker bronze.

Something has shifted between us during this tour, and it makes me nervous. Especially because no one knows about my "classified" job after work, back at home. Even at our current relationship's strength, our closeness could risk Jay's life.

"S-sorry, I shouldn't distract you." I reach for my shirt.

Jay's his regular self again, whipping the shirt out of my reach. "No takebacks."

He ties the intruder like a packed sausage, then relays the situation to the Departments using our disposable work phone. The operator transfers us to the right stranger: someone who "cleans up."

Within an hour, the intruder is gone. The air feels breathable again. We move to a different room—one with its front door still intact—and go to sleep.

Men in full tactical gear barge in this time, thankfully from our own Department. Jay and I hardly slept, but we're awake now. The "deal" is unexpectedly closing, and so is our tour. Our final task is to betray the deal, capture our subjects, and steal their goods, removing their supply from the black market.

It's easy enough to breach the 50-story skyscraper after six months of rapport with the pharmaceutical company. We stride in with bulletproof vests beneath our plain clothes, guns, knives, and explosives packed flat into our inner jacket pockets.

But as soon as we step into the elevator, we're instructed to remove our trackers. Either someone caught wind of our heist, or their technology makes ours look outdated and can easily steal our chip data. And we don't want to be tracked by the wrong people. That's why the DoTD uses disposable chips to monitor our health and location instead of smartphones.

Jay whips out his knife, giving me a smug grin. "You wanna do each other or watch each other do ourselves?"

"Oh, fuck off." I laugh.

We dig into our arms, wedging the knife beneath the tracker implanted under a shallow skin flap. Then we pry it up enough to jab the blade's tip through an indent in the chip's center and pluck it out. This could leave a mess of blood in the elevator, but Jay and I have done this enough times to know how to keep the bleeding under control and bandage ourselves in seconds.

But then we're ordered to give ourselves epinephrine shots. This is a daunting change in plans, signaling there's no more "capturing" involved.

I give Jay a quick look, but he can't stand to face me. We figured out early on that the shots aren't only epinephrine, and whatever else is in there makes us rabid. Neither of us likes how things go when they want us to go berserk. We're trying our best to subdue or capture instead of kill anymore, and I think the Department is onto us. They want us to shut up and do as we're told.

And they want to watch.

That means I'll be forced to kill other Japanese people, and I know that's why they want *us* to do this job—the only high-ranking people of color in DoTD training. To show us what can be made of us if we disobey the United States of White America.

After seven years of loyalty-ensuring torture, *this* is their final test? Hazing us?

"Cheers," Jay grumbles, clinking our shots together before jabbing himself in the outer thigh.

I hate killing people, but I *really* hate being drugged to persuade me to kill people. For a split second, I consider ditching the shot entirely—retaining control over my breathing and heart rate when I'm in there, maybe faking a little extra energy as if I injected it.

The elevator dings, arriving at the last floor. Jay shoots me a terrifying glare. He's already boosted and violence-prone, so I know I should watch myself around him.

But I still haven't done the shot. I don't want to.

Mom was right; I've lost my mind, and I'll be killed for this.

As the door swings open, Jay rips the shot from my hands and slams it through my pants. We seethe at each other as a spreading web of heat burns my outer thigh, releasing adrenaline throughout my mind and body. Then the mystery drug takes over.

This isn't a single dose. Jay and I grew hyper-tolerant to that about a year ago. At this boosted dose, my blood feels like it's bursting from me, begging to be expressed through my twitching fingertips. It clouds my conscience and leaves a trail of destruction in my path. I do everything I'm told and more. And once I'm done with my orders, I turn to attack Jay for doing this to me.

Before I can tackle him to the ground and fight him hand-to-hand, he clutches my cheeks so hard that I'm concerned my molars will pierce through them.

"Don't fuck this up again," he says through his teeth.

The Communications members on the other side of our in-ears fall silent. They're waiting to see what we decide to do to each other before issuing further instructions.

They're probably anxious about losing such precious assets. It's not uncommon for DoTD unit members to kill each other. We're trained to. If someone goes rogue, no matter how friendly we are, we're supposed to kill them.

But Jay and I keep our mutual devotion a secret; it's the only taste of control we have that no one else has to know about. We know we'd die for each other, even if we have to pretend we'd kill each other. So they don't see the hurt in Jay's eyes. He's not threatening me; he's warning me. Terrified for my life, more than I am for my own.

We've seen what they've done to our friends for disobeying. They slaughter people, right in front of us. So we stopped making other friends. And we stopped disobeying.

Until now. I guess I'm even crazier than I thought. What would I do if Jay risked what I did, blatantly disobeying the Department in front of everyone? He's right to be upset. He's relying on me too. If I sabotage myself, I'll be leaving him behind. Just because I couldn't care about myself enough to care for him.

I have work to do.

I shove him off me. We distance ourselves, not wanting to do anything we regret. Or maybe it's embarrassment. The mess of bodies we've left behind makes me want to keel over from imagining their families' grief alone. They might have been "bad" people, maybe killers themselves, but they each had a life we stripped away from them. *This isn't us*, I wish I could say. But it is. This *is* us. Disgusting, ravenous creatures. No longer deserving of the title, "human."

The Department calls me the Wolf, but they fail to see what a beast Jay is. If I didn't have him rescuing my sanity and taming me every five seconds, I wouldn't be the terror I am. I could hate him for it, but I don't. He's both helping and hindering me, but with the best intentions. We're just trying to figure life out, and we haven't been handed the best examples. I would've never seen anything wrong with this life if Jay, Lilith, and Emmalee hadn't pointed out the Departments' manipulations.

They wouldn't have seen anything wrong with it either if Lilith didn't realize other women existed who were also attracted to women. Before then, we simply felt the Departments were "unfair," but that didn't matter; we were the problem for defying them. We never learned the word "discrimination," or any of its counterparts. Once Lilith learned discrimination existed, she announced she was not only a lesbian, but also a terrorist.

I still regret dismissing her revelation the first time I heard it, unwilling to process the horrors of what I've done. Jay took it upon himself to educate me—which is exactly why he might be taking too much responsibility for my epinephrine hesitation, thinking he made a traitor out of me too early.

I have to be patient. Someday, we can get out of this. Just not now.

They airlift us once we grab what we came for: a metal safe I'm positive is also a bomb. It's been chirping rhythmically ever since Jay and I removed it from the wall.

It turns out it *is* a bomb; a disarming specialist swoops in the instant I hand it over in the helicopter. We watch in a quiet calm, uncaring if it blows us all up. Everyone's expressionless faces surrounding a live explosive tempt me to laugh. Maybe I fit in better than I thought.

The safe reveals a set of unmarked vials. Our Superior Commanding Officer slams it closed, realizing Jay and I are still watching. Then we're all transferred to a DoTD private jet.

Jay and I try to hide our giddy relief. We're finally going home.

But then I see *him*. The Commanding Officer I haven't seen in months.

My previous life path is over. I've been complaining over digging through the topsoil, getting my hands a little dirty, but Dr. Sumner's molten stare drags me closer to the earth's core. Something in his frigid blue eyes threatens to bury me alive.

I'm ordered to deliver the unmarked vials to Dr. Sumner in the plane's sectioned-off, back half. Alone.

I don't understand how or why he's here, but after I'm given my orders in front of my best friend, I don't care what Sumner does to me next. Not after my mortification when Jay puts the pieces together: what I've been rushing off to do after work on the homeland.

The dreadful pain of Sumner's requirements never hit me until now. Anxiety seeps through my mental armor, and pure horror worms through Jay's eyes, shattering his stoic mask.

After Sumner takes thirty agonizing minutes to say his usual "hello," he injects me with a dose of clear liquid from the unmarked vials.

Sumner has a higher ranking than our mission's Superior Commanding Officer. It's an order to take the injection, so I can't say no. And I don't. Not to him.

As the mystery liquid disappears into my body, my heart pumps through my ears in anticipation, spreading it even faster.

But then I don't feel anything from it. I hope it stays that way.

Sumner warns me of potential side effects, admits he doesn't actually know most of them anyway, and that's why I'm helping him discover them. Then he stores the last remaining sample of my poison-free, pre-injection blood, summoning Jay for his dose. I can't stop Sumner from injecting Jay either. Even if

Sumner didn't have bodyguards, he reminds us, *this is what we signed up for.*

And he's right. This has been our designated reason for existing for as long as I can remember. And not just the Departments are at fault. Our own parents *bred* us for this job. Before, that was a fact of life. Now, it's an irrevocable insult.

And while my eyes have opened, they also see how deep I'm trapped. Tied to this reality, for life, down to my soiled blood.

I had my doubts about the Departments' intentions, but this is much, much worse than I realized. And I have a sick feeling it's just the beginning. That where we are now will soon seem like paradise.

CHAPTER 6

Emmalee

Civilians don't know it, but something bad is happening, and the Departments won't tell each other what. The Blackwoods are tight-lipped, defensive, and stressed to their limits. My parents stopped coming home until midnight, caring for a sudden influx of severely ill patients. People are also "disappearing."

Lilith once told me "Missing in Action" is a fancy title for intra-Department assassination. I've been checking the MIA announcements for her name. Eventually, I realized they must not know where she is, and it ignited a desperate hope in me.

She made it out. Someone actually escaped.

But no one is as skilled as Lilith. I'm not sure anyone else could escape.

After quitting the Departments' private school, Jay would update me whenever I'd run into him. He'd gush about Niko and Lilith being "silent tanks of human beings." People thought they were twins when we were kids—their movements similarly fluid and deadly—but they didn't appreciate that. They both hate their "skills."

Lilith had her doubts that "the enemies" are actually bad people. And I believe her. Even if she was shipped here as a traumatized child, her mind isn't as clouded as ours. She can see the toxicity we learned how to breathe through as infants.

But Niko is a master of erasing all expressions. That's why his cold exterior terrifies people: they think he's the no-mercy type.

But I know his outer mask only dams his pain from gushing out and breaking him. I know he hates this.

He doesn't have a choice. We expect him to come home alive, and if he doesn't obey, down to his facial expressions, the Departments will ensure he perishes.

So now I compulsively check that list for his name. I have a bad feeling that soon, nothing will be the same.

But I don't know how to help. Stress worsens my health, and the Departments don't know disability accommodations exist. If I want to work here, I'll have to pretend I don't have a disability and make myself sicker. I have my own mask, but sometimes my health plummets so badly, pain seeps through and I can't hide it. This is one of those times.

For now, I'm just a babysitter. And Hana Blackwood is a true gem.

My seventeenth birthday is coming up this month, and Hana is practicing her drawing skills to make me "the best card ever." Today, she drew me a picture covered in rainbows with us holding hands underneath. I smile and place it back on the couch arm beside me, careful not to disturb her. She's sacked out under my arm, her little breath huffing against my stomach.

The excessive lineup of door latches unlock, one by one, and I jump, ruining our serenity. It's nowhere near time for the Commanders to come home. Hana pops up in concern, and I cover her mouth.

Apparently, she knows the drill better than I do. With a stone-cold expression, she silently drags me into a bunker I didn't know existed beneath the kitchen floorboards.

We huddle into each other, Hana placing her little hand over my mouth to both soothe and quiet me. I'm tempted to cry. This is so unfair for her to need to know.

"Sprout?" A voice calls out above us.

My heart jolts. That's his voice, but…

No, it couldn't be Niko. Reality stomps on my hopes in an instant; it's much more likely this is a recording of Niko's voice to traffic his sister, me, or both of us.

The voice calls out again, this time in another language. Hana rises in excitement, terrifying me further. I grip the back of her shirt in an attempt to pull her back into my lap, but she gleams, wide-eyed.

"My brother is home!" She whispers. She answers the voice in what I now recognize as Japanese, waiting for his response before she unlocks the bunker. It sounds like they both have to answer the right thing to identify each other, and he passes the test. She flips it open, sprinting out before I can stop her and verify for myself.

Luckily, Hana's judgment was correct; Niko is really here, scooping up his baby sister. While Niko cradles Hana's head, allowing her to bawl her eyes out, I'm ready to pass the fuck out—my heart is still struggling to regulate, attempting to soak in this reality. I can't believe I'm lucky enough to see Niko again, alive.

"You said you'd be back three months ago!" Hana wails.

"I know." He's tangibly gentle with her despite her shrieking volume. "I'm sorry, my love."

"I was really scared, and mad, and sad!"

I press my fingertips to my lips, unsure how Niko will react, but so proud of Hana. We've talked about healthier forms of confrontation a few more times, something the Blackwoods have yet to realize came from me. Now she's better at emotional honesty than us all.

Niko tries his best to reassure Hana face to face, but she buries her head deeper into his collarbone. He releases a breathy laugh in defeat. Instead, he rubs her back in slow motions, whispering something into her ear until her heavy sobs turn into slow, hiccuping sniffles.

Then he realizes I'm here.

A chill ignites my spine; my body registers my imminent death before my brain. I should've made a point to say I was here to begin with, but I'm sure Niko didn't expect another person in the room. His default, predatory eyes shift into guilt from my terrified face.

"Ems?" His voice shakes. "You're really here? I didn't just imagine you?"

I want to rush into his arms and tell him how worried I was—to get the same reassurance as Hana—but it seems like he needs comfort more than I do. Dark circles dig beneath his jet-black irises. His skin is darker, but he somehow looks paler. I've never seen him like this before, not even after hardcore training intensives. He looks half-dead.

Something has happened.

"Hi." I throw on the best smile I can manage despite my quivering voice. "Can I have a welcome home hug too?"

His body language warms, loosening him into a Niko I recognize. We meet halfway in the hall, and I inhale his cozy scent, squeezing him until he lets out a heavy breath behind my head.

"This is surreal. Are you really in my house right now?"

I laugh, separating from him. "Yep. I'm the babysitter."

He lifts an eyebrow. "My mom allowed that?"

I laugh. "Well, it wasn't her idea, that's for sure. But when she found out, she was too exhausted to find another one. And either way, Hana and I are best friends now, so there's no way anyone would be cruel enough to split us up! Right?"

Niko and I share a knowing look, his grin widening.

"Yeah! She's *my* best friend now!" Hana wraps her arms around my thighs, sticking out her tongue at Niko. "You can't have her back, bro!"

"I guess I have some tough competition." Niko laughs through the exhaustion roughening his voice. He pops open his stale bedroom door to strip layer after layer of combat gear off his body. "You still sound just like Jay. I thought you'd give up the bro-ing by the time I got back."

"Never, *brooo!*" Hana deepens her little voice to mimic Jay, spurring us all into giggles.

Our conversation feels lighthearted, but Niko looks like he's in too much pain for me to ignore, his built back hunched and shaky.

I tuck Hana's stray hair wisp behind her ear. "Hana, I'm going to get your brother some water and a snack. Do you want to hang out with him, or come help me?"

"I'll come help!" She throws her hands in the air, marching to the kitchen.

Niko and I take one look at each other and laugh. But he can't hold my gaze like he used to.

My smile fades. "So… Meet you in the living room?"

He glances over his shoulder with a fake smile. "Yep! I just need a quick shower."

Niko looks ready to throw his shirt off, so I close his door behind myself. But the second I leave, I feel his mood darken into a startling level of hatred. Knowing him, it's self-directed. Its potency stops me in the hallway, forcing me to grip my panging heart. I'm torn between reopening his door and trying to help or giving him space to process his feelings. He decides for me, crossing into the bathroom behind me in a rush.

Hana and I change our minds from plain snacks to an early dinner, whipping up a quick spaghetti serving. It's ridiculously straightforward, but Niko still takes over as soon as he finishes showering.

I snort. "Thanks. My weak woman's arms couldn't *possibly* handle stirring spaghetti sauce."

Niko shoots me a shocked glare. "Did you just throw a sexist insult at *my* best friend?"

"Hey! She's mine!" Hana shrieks, rubbing her face into Niko's side.

He accidentally hip-checks me in an attempt to escape Hana's ticklish wrath, sending my unsuspecting, lanky body teetering like falling timber. Niko catches me by the arm, pulling me in close against his warm chest.

"Shit, sorry, Ems," he laughs, kissing me on the forehead.

Now *that* caught me off guard. Of course, he decides to look at me right when I turn bright red, my heart still tingling, and he giggles again. It's his first genuine laugh today.

Hana wedges herself between us. "Bro, you can't say 'shit!' I'm six years old!"

"Hana!?" I say.

"What?!"

"You can't say 'shit' either!"

"Oh! Oops!" She erupts into squealing giggles, nudging us all into a group hug full of laughter.

After some calming influence from Niko and me, we settle

down enough to eat our spaghetti without choking. Hana is glued to the animated movie on my laptop, kneeling on the floor between our legs as Niko and I slink into the Blackwoods' faded black couch.

Niko keeps sneaking a glance at me as we eat, thinking I don't notice. I wait for the right moment to catch him staring, and he jumps, splattering sauce across his lap.

I laugh, patting his back. "You good?"

He buries his face into his napkin and laughs away the redness burning his cheeks. Then he steals my hand away from me. Neither of us can continue eating with our dominant hands clasped, but I don't mind.

Do you feel sick? I tap onto his thumb.

He shrugs. *I just miss you.*

I giggle. "Present-tense?"

"Yup." He smiles. "I can't believe this is real."

"*Huh?*" Hana's irritation breaks us out of our bubble. "I can't hear the movie!"

"Sorry, that was my fault. I shouldn't have interrupted," I say.

Satisfied with my answer, Hana hops onto the couch, snuggling into my side.

"Hey, no fair." Niko pouts extra goofily when Hana looks back at him.

Hana giggles. "Told you she's mine."

Niko flops against us, wrapping an arm over a giddy Hana and tucking her into his chest. He lays his cheek on Hana's head, a hesitant arm settling around my shoulders. He brushes my hair off of my bony shoulder, tracing small circles with his thumb, and I can't stop smiling. I run my fingers through his spiky black hair, which has grown at least an inch since it was last shaved. It's a sign he hasn't been in combat for a couple months, but I have no idea what he's been doing since.

Niko's breath deepens beneath my touch. Suddenly, Hana squirms in discomfort between us.

"You okay, little sprout?" I whisper.

"Bro, you're— *Squishing* me!" She grunts, digging her elbow into Niko's sternum.

"*Ow.*" He drowsily laughs. "Sorry, sorry. I didn't mean to. I was falling asleep."

"Long day?" I laugh when Niko glares at my bad joke. "Week? Month? Year?"

"Something like that."

Niko drops his head back. I start to pet his hair again, but our eyes meet and I hesitate. Niko catches my hand, hugging it to his chest. We stare at each other, unable to keep a straight face. But with how worried I am, I can't smile for long either. He looks worse than tired.

"Go to sleep," I whisper.

He shakes his head no. I raise my eyebrows in response to his blatant defiance, and he laughs. "I want to spend time with you both."

"Hmm. I'll allow it."

Hana shushes us and we stifle a laugh.

I close my eyes as Niko reaches for my head now, brushing my bangs from my face. He's the only person I'll allow to do that, and he's so gentle about it that it lulls me into thoughtless silence. His emotions twist in a confusing blend of security and insecurity, so I open my eyes. He's looking at me with his eyebrows furrowed.

Niko rises off the couch, holding out a hand for me. "We'll be right back, Hana. Just going to talk in my room so we don't bother you."

Hana hums in response, still absorbed.

I never thought I'd be led by the hand into Nikolai Blackwood's bedroom with no one to stop us, but I'm eating this shit up. He might look tired, but his hands feel strong, wrapping me against his steady side once I worm my way beneath his elbow. We have a notable height difference for the first time in our lives—even though I've ended up taller than expected at 5'9", he's surpassed me by at least four inches.

Taking a seat on his bed's edge, I hook my elbow around the footboard post. My eyes linger on Niko's exposed arms as he shuts the door. I never remembered him having this many scars, and spot a fresh bandage peeking below his sleeve.

When Niko sits beside me, he leaves about a foot of space

between us. I look at him like he did the most ridiculous thing in the world and prepare myself to pounce.

He laughs, but hurriedly holds me back by the shoulders. Niko's voice turns sharp. "Wait, *don't*."

I pause and sit back.

According to the sudden turbulence in his emotions, that quick exchange meant something to him, although I'm not sure why.

He clears his throat. "S-sorry, I didn't mean for that to come out like that. I've been around aggressive assholes with no boundaries for nine months."

"Nine and a half."

He laughs softly. "I'm sorry."

"You better be."

"Ricky, I really am." He's not smiling anymore.

I touch his hand, my heart stinging; why did he use Jay's nickname for me instead of his? "I-I know, I was just joking. I'm not mad. I just... missed you too."

We draw each other in for a hug. I lay my head against his shoulder, the heat of his reddened ears against my neck.

"I'm glad you're back," I whisper. Niko giggles, so I sit up. "What? Did I say something weird?"

"No, never. I just feel like I've been with you the whole time."

I squint at him. "Because you stole my childhood photo, huh."

He giggles in a way he never does around anyone else, hiding his face on my shoulder. "Maybe."

"That's fine." I stroke his thick, soft hair at the base of his neck. "You can keep it if it helps. Don't know why you didn't ask, though."

"I didn't want to make it weird," he says. I can't see him, but I can hear his smile. "But I guess I did, anyway."

"Yep, classic Nikolai."

He laughs again, rising to meet my eyes. The air of sickness on his face looks strange, mixed with his smile. It's making me sympathetically nauseated. I never expected to see him so gaunt in my life, always striving to remain as solid as he can look.

Niko grows serious again, pressing two fingertips beneath my jaw by my left ear. "How's your heart?"

I sigh. "I don't know. POTS kicks my ass daily. Nothing new."

He continues to check my pulse, ignoring the annoyance on my face. "I brought you in here to tell you I'm worried. I could tell right away you're working yourself too hard."

I raise my eyebrows. "And you aren't?"

"Nope. This is just the right amount, can't you tell?"

I tentatively laugh, but I don't think it's funny anymore. "Niko, you have to tell me something about what's going on with you. Anything. Just to get it off your chest so you don't have to carry it alone." He considers my words, chewing on the inside of his bottom lip. "At least how you feel. You're sick, I can tell."

His eyebrows twitch. Then I get it. He's desperately trying not to cry.

"Niko?" I whisper, tempted to touch his cheek. But for the first time in our lives, I'm afraid to. Like he's cracked glass, one feather-touch away from splintering into piercing shards on the floor.

It turns out, he is. The second I smooth my thumb over his cheekbone, he clings to my shoulders, ducks his head between us, and sobs like I've never seen. It feels like someone died, but his emotions feel pressured. Haunted. Trapped.

I have no idea what to say or do. Niko hasn't cried from his core like this since he was eleven, and that was because… well, his training day wasn't the best. He was crying so hard at lunch that Lilith and Jay had to fill me in. Their shooting range instructor had a flashback and almost shot Niko in the face, executioner style. Niko hyperventilated until we cleaned the blood off—Lilith killed the instructor instead, giving Niko an unfortunate "shower." I didn't hate Lilith for it, although the thought of her being a murderer made me uncomfortable for a few years. We all knew if she didn't do it, Niko would be dead.

"What happened?" I ask.

He shakes his head in dismissal, gripping the bed at his sides. His whole body jolts in sporadic shivers, pulsing up and down like he's struggling to contain them.

"Niko, I can handle it."

He looks at me, and again, shakes his head no. Then he winces at the rising irritation on my face. "I'm sorry."

"I'm stronger than I seem. And I'm not letting you go through this alone."

He takes a few deep, shuddering breaths. "You *are* strong. Stronger than me. But if I tell you, you'll lose hope too. *One* of us has to still believe we can get out of here, or else we really won't."

I freeze. It took over a decade for Niko to admit the Departments weren't a normal place to live, but now he openly wants to leave. He's only been a silent observer of Lilith and Jay's escape plans before this: along for the ride, but not contributing. That was his survival method. Quieting himself.

But it sounds like that coping mechanism doesn't work anymore. Something pushed him over the threshold.

If I didn't have enough confirmation, this is it. Something big has happened, and not just to Niko.

"If you can't tell me the details, then just tell me how you feel." I scoot against his side, wrapping an arm around his shoulders.

He relaxes into me. "Okay."

A mechanical beeping suddenly screeches, echoing throughout the bare, long-unused room. Niko yanks his receiver out of his pocket, spiking it against the ground. I crumple into myself, drawing my knees back onto his bed with a shriek.

"Fuck, sorry. Sorry. I shouldn't have thrown that like a child." He stands, removing a knife from a different pocket.

"W-what are you doing?"

He doesn't hear me. He's too busy slicing his own arm open.

At first, I think he's cutting himself, and I jump up in a panic, but then I see he's jabbing his knife beneath something unnaturally square, small, and hard. Piercing it, he flicks it out of his arm. I'm stunned silent as he chucks the knife across the room with a skilled wrist snap, the blade's force chopping a microchip in half against the wall. The second it cracks, the receiver alert stops chirping.

I swallow a confusing mix of feelings in my chest. On the one hand, that was pretty badass, but on the other...

"Um, what the fuck just happened?"

Niko's frantic eyes scan my face for answers. Then he laughs. "Oh. That's not normal, is it?"

We laugh for a moment before falling silent to Niko's undulating current of thoughts.

"I can't do this anymore," he whispers. "That's how I feel."

As blood dribbles from his arm, I nod in quiet understanding. That's permission enough for Niko to cry openly again, allowing himself to be held in my arms. He speaks this truth to me until it doesn't hold the same weight. "I can't do this anymore. I just can't, Ems. I can't do this anymore," he repeats. When he eventually stops, he's calm.

I put pressure on his arm with a tissue to stop the bleeding. "So, what can we do to help? To change this for you, even if it's just step one of getting out of here together?"

My heart sinks before he speaks a word; the most fearless person I know overflows with terror.

"Ems, I don't know if we can do anything… at all."

CHAPTER 7

Emmalee

The Blackwood's front door flies open faster than my mind can process, but my nervous system certainly reacts; I scream, scrambling off the couch.

Thankfully, I'm greeted by a familiar face. "Yo, what the fuck? Who's screeching in—"

Jay and I meet eyes. I blink, gathering my bearings. I've been jumpy like this for two full weeks—ever since Niko broke down in front of me, confirming my suspicions about something foreboding happening within the Departments. But within the few seconds Jay and I have reconnected, my heart melts into just as pure of excitement as I feel from my dear friend's spreading smile.

"Jay!?" I throw my arms open, but Hana beats me to it, cheering as she sprints down the hallway.

Swinging her into his arms, Jay belly laughs. "Bro, you've got Richards as your babysitter?!"

Hana frowns. "*Richards?* That's *Emmalee*, bro!"

Jay and I laugh, squishing Hana into a group hug.

I watch in jealous awe as Jay makes the Blackwood home his, throwing open the fridge and carrying Hana around on his hip like an uncle. Our statuses in Niko's life are alternate realities.

Jay sets Hana down at the kitchen table. "Whatcha got going here, Ricky?"

"Oh, I'm teaching the Blackwood kids to paint."

"Both of them, huh?" He leans over the table on both palms to study the mess of paintings and supplies. "Is this one his?"

"No, that's *mine!*" Hana pouts.

Jay laughs. "Ah, okay. No wonder it looks good."

I scoff at how much of a jerk he is rather than joining in at Niko's expense, and Jay smirks wider.

"Good thing you covered this place in paper, or else there might actually be some color in this box." He drops into a seat with a thud. "So, how much for painting lessons? Five bucks? Nah, maybe two?"

I open my mouth to tell him to shut the hell up, but Hana's curious black eyes remain fixated on me. Jay beams, well-aware of my struggle.

"You are *so* lucky I'm on babysitting duty right now, Jay Olivas," I mutter.

He laughs. "I know. I'm just messing with you, Ricky. Sorry."

I hover over his shoulder, preparing a basic paint palette for him. "Uh-huh. Sure you are."

As I reach across the table for a fresh canvas, Jay takes his opportunity to tug on my ponytail, yanking me off balance.

"Jay! You fu— *Farting*— B-*butthole!*"

Hana cackles hysterically, but Jay's mocking grin makes me want to shove him even more than I did a second ago. Instead, I laugh, wrapping my arm around his neck and scrubbing my knuckles into his scalp.

Jay picks me up with one arm around my waist, and I scream in surprise. "Is that the best you've got, Richards? I thought you had the Wolf as your self-defense teacher!"

I grunt, trying my best to remember what Niko taught me the past two weeks, but resort to squirming around in the air. "Yeah, well, he doesn't treat me like *this!*"

"That's because—" Jay hoists me over his shoulder, striding toward the couch. "*I* see you as my sister. *He* doesn't, I'll tell you that much."

"Huh?! You're both my best friends!" I thrash my legs in the air.

Jay bumps his thighs against the couch's arm with a sigh. "God, you two are so dumb sometimes."

With that, he flips me over onto the cushions, far too fast for my heart to keep up with the change in position. My ears ring and I close my eyes, limbs limp against the couch as colors dance behind my eyelids. Multiple hands are on me, maybe even five of them, and I groan, trying to sift through a dark haze to respond to their muffled voices.

Once my ears quiet a little, all I can feel is my rabbit heart's rapid pounding, slowing into a heavy, struggling thump. I hate that feeling, but mainly because it means I've made someone worry about me.

Niko's furious voice appears above me. "Jay, how many times do I have to tell you not to shove her down? You're a ruthless brute, and she's a proper human being with a heart condition."

"I'm sorry! I'm so sorry." Jay sounds genuinely upset.

"Mmm… S'okay, Jay," I mumble, failing to open my heavy eyelids.

Cool hands grab my cheeks. They smell good—sweet and comforting. "Ems?! Are you okay?"

In my haze, I almost don't believe Niko is really back, but only one person calls me Ems. I grip his wrists, keeping my eyes closed. "Mhm… Tired."

He stays silent for a moment, audibly thinking between concerned huffs. "Do you need me to call an ambulance?"

I give a weak chuckle. "No, push forward."

Niko and Jay translate my delirium into English and drop my feet to the ground, laying my torso against my thighs. I hang over myself, catching my breath. Hana's tiny hand pats my back, and I smile.

"You okay?" She whimpers.

"Yes, Sprout. I'm okay." I lift my head to meet her eyes.

"Don't move." Niko's anxiety shows in his voice. He grips my shoulder to ensure I stay put. "Should one of us get you water?"

I sigh. "Sure."

"I-I've got it!" Jay scampers to the kitchen.

I chuckle to myself between my knees.

"Are you crying?" Niko whispers.

I laugh more. "No. You guys are so funny. You have no idea how many times this has happened. If I don't take a few minutes to sit up before standing in the morning, I wake up a second time for the day on the floor."

Niko says nothing.

"Sorry, that was funnier in my head." Sitting up, I take in everyone's worried faces crowding me. "I'm okay, really."

"Yeah, right. You sound terrible." Jay hands me a large water glass.

I laugh, swatting at him in the air as I take a swig. "Apparently, I'm terrible at self-defense too."

Jay's serious expression is so rare that it scares me.

I slump into the couch cushions, retracing the past few minutes. "Actually, I think Jay showed us something we're missing. If someone flipped me over like that, it'd be really bad. Knowing self-defense techniques would be useless at that point."

"Hmm." Niko's eyebrows furrow. "That *would* be really bad. I'll think of a few things you can do quickly, up close and in someone's arms."

I grab Jay's arm. "Hey, it's okay. Now we know."

Jay slinks into himself. I tug him closer, urging him to sit beside me on the couch. He only smiles after I belly laugh at the way he's flopping around like a doll, dramatizing his distress as I tug on his arm. Once he sits, he cuddles me in his massive arms. I close my eyes, content to huddle up in his warmth. Jay is a portable heater in every way. Our human-sized supernova.

"I'm sorry, Ricky," he mutters.

"It's okay. Seriously, Jay. I harassed you first, and you were just joking around."

I open my eyes to find Niko a foot away on the couch, his chin on his palm as he glowers into the distance.

I nudge Jay, pointing out Niko's quiet jealousy, and we snicker.

Niko eyes us, raising an eyebrow. I peel myself from Jay's arms, planting a kiss on Niko's cheek.

"Hey..." He breaks into a smile.

"*What!* What was *that?!*" Hana shriek-giggles. "You *kissed* him?!"

We simultaneously burst into laughter at her bright red face.

"I didn't want to leave your brother out!" I say.

"I wasn't left out. You guys can cuddle anyone you want." Niko buries his face in his hands. "I'm not jealous. I feel bad that this happens to you and that you even need to defend yourself from people here."

Jay reaches behind me to shove Niko into the couch's arm. "Yeah, right. You want in on this, bro."

"Yeah, bro!" Hana giggles.

I pull Niko on top of Jay and me, then reach for Hana. She launches herself at Niko, pelting him in the stomach with her knees.

"Ow." He laughs.

Hana giggles, squishing his cheeks. "Sorry!"

After a good minute of cuddly silence, Jay and Niko meet eyes over my head. There's a weirdly telepathic, combat partner communication ingrained into them, as far as I can tell. Niko checks my pulse first, then Jay verifies it with a nod. Before I can say a word, they lift me off the couch in choreographed unison.

With Niko's arms hooked beneath my armpits and Jay holding up my legs, I laugh so hard that I get lightheaded again, my head bobbing.

"Be careful with yourself," Niko says.

"I mean, I would, but two guys are carrying me like a dead body when one of you could probably lift three of me!"

They come to a stop in the hallway, giving each other blank stares.

"Bro, we're so dense," Jay says.

We all laugh, Jay gently releasing my legs. The boys hold me up to make sure I can stand on my own wobbly legs like an infant. This is just part of being chronically ill—and a great excuse to have Niko hold me in his arms and carry me to his bed.

Once he settles me beneath the comforter, he backs up a few feet. I hold back a smile, well-aware he's worried I'd be uncomfortable with him approaching me on a bed. Really, that's something I've always wanted him to do.

Before I can tease him, the new stack of fiction I left on his dresser catches his eye. The stack contains books I've kept all my life, returning to them whenever I need an escape. Niko never had that chance. So last week, I brought a few over, figuring escaping to another world might ease the mental burden of whatever he's seen. And he must be enjoying them, powering through one book every other day or so. He never asks for more, but I can tell how much he loves it, so I make a point of replenishing his book stack before he comes home. His spreading smile makes it all worth it.

"Hey, thanks, Ems." He says it so softly that my heart rate heightens.

"I was thinking…" I grip my right hand, fidgeting with each knuckle. "You can keep any of these that you want, you know. I've already read them a million times."

Laser-focused eyes zip to mine. "What?! No… These are yours. They're special books."

"That's why I want you to have at least one or two." I rub his arm. He allows me to touch him, but breaks eye contact, running his fingers down the spines of the books. "You didn't get to read anything like this growing up, and you're enjoying them, right? That's all I could ask for. Pick one you'll want to reread. It's okay, trust me."

Niko hasn't faced me again, but hugs my *Charlotte's Web* copy to his chest with hot cheeks. It's what I would've picked if I were him.

"Thank you," he whispers.

Jay barges in with Hana on his hip, setting her on the bed's edge. "Ricky, I really fucki— Uh, *really* missed you, dude!"

Niko gives Jay a soft shove, earning him a loud thump on the back.

I roll my eyes. "I can't believe I have to babysit three people for the price of one."

Jay readjusts himself, raising a few inches off the mattress to crash on the bed as hard as he can and send us all bouncing. Hana shrieks through her laughter, and Niko has to catch her from flying off the bed, earning Jay a glower. I can't help but laugh. We're finally all together again. Almost.

Jay squeezes my foot. "I'm serious, Ricky. It's been a long time since we caught up. I'm so sorry to hear you're single."

With this, Niko clenches his jaw and shoots the most terrifying glare at Jay that I have to cackle. "Yeah, I should've known no one *here* taught Lilith how to be in a relationship, let alone how to end one. But it's coming up on a year, so I feel good. I just miss having her as one of our best friends."

"Me too," Jay mutters.

"Me three," Hana says.

Niko's expression softens. "Oh, Sprout. Have you been feeling sad about it?"

Hana nods, but she's surprisingly calm. "Mom says big sis is okay, though."

Niko, Jay, and I exchange surprised glances.

"Oh, *really?*" Jay smirks.

"Actually, I believe that," I say. "I've been checking the MIA boards almost every day. I've never seen her name."

Niko and Jay's grins explode. Poor Hana is totally lost, glancing between us.

Jay slaps Niko on the arm with a laugh. "So it *is* possible to escape hell, bro!"

Niko sighs. "I hope so."

"Emmalee, what does MIA mean?" Hana asks.

"Uh—" I look to Niko for backup. He bites his lips and hums, struggling to think of an answer, so I say, "It means Missing in Action, but your big sister wasn't in combat when she ran away. She's not supposed to be on that list."

"Then why do you keep looking?" Hana asks.

"Because Emmalee is worried someone will report it incorrectly," Niko quickly says. "We still can't tell anyone Lilith is missing, Hana."

"I know," Hana grumbles. "Can you tell me a story about her?"

"Of course." Niko smiles, opening his arms for Hana. She climbs onto his lap right away, gripping his torso with all four limbs and a bright giggle. Jay and I snuggle in beside them.

"Alright, a story about Lilith." Niko sighs, closing his eyes and leaning back against the headboard.

Hana waits in his lap, fidgeting with his shirt sleeve. It reminds me of what I used to do with my dad when I couldn't sleep from feeling sick. He'd read me stories all night sometimes, and I'd fidget with his clothes or brush my fingers along his stubble as his jaw moved while he read.

Seeing the two of them like this makes my heart stir. I've known I've felt strongly about Niko for a long time, but this is different. I think I'm irreparably in love.

"Mom and Dad fostered Lilith about a year before Mom was pregnant with you."

"So I wasn't in Mom's belly yet?" Hana asks.

"Not yet. The first day Lilith came to school with Emmalee, Jay, and I, we were sent off to boot camp."

Niko sneaks a quick glance at me, and I smile. I'm tempted to play with his hair or trace his features like Hana is, but Jay is watching us closely. Sometimes Jay is thinking further ahead than any of us expect, and right now, his energy has a sad hint to it. Almost loneliness. I can't pinpoint why, but I don't want to accidentally exclude him.

"At boot camp, I did something not so nice, Hana," Niko continues.

"What? You got in trouble by the teacher?"

Niko laughs. "No, much worse: I was mean to Emmalee."

Hana gasps. I open my mouth to speak, but Hana scoffs like Clara, forcing Jay and I to bite back a laugh. "Why would you do that, bro?!"

"Because someone told me Ems was a bad person, so I started ignoring her. But that was the wrong thing for me to do. I should've given Ems a chance to speak for herself before I judged her."

Jay groans. "Well, then I pushed Emmalee down to the ground by mistake. Just like today."

"Bro?!" Hana gasps. "Why was everyone so mean to Emmalee?"

I rub her back. "It's okay, little sprout. Your brother is just trying to be nice. Niko actually thought he'd get in *huge* trouble for talking to me, no matter how badly he wanted to. I knew he didn't mean it. When Jay accidentally pushed me down while we were playing, Niko still ran to help me even though he wasn't allowed to talk to me."

Hana softens. "He did?"

I smile. "Yes. Then he was embarrassed that I caught him being nice and he ran away." Jay and I laugh, and Niko groans. "But that's where Lilith came in. I hadn't met her before, but she helped me up off the ground and became one of my best friends."

"Then what?" Hana asks.

"Then Lilith brought all four of us together no matter what anyone said," Niko says. "We knew we wouldn't get in trouble because Lilith protected us every single day, little sprout. She saved my life from a mean teacher one time, so when you were born, I could still be your big brother. She was the best big sister ever."

My gut burns. Niko is referring to the rogue instructor incident. As well as how Lilith never truly felt like she fit in with Niko's family. It wasn't just her name—how the Department suggested renaming her like a stray dog. It was worse than that.

Lilith is so traumatized that she doesn't remember which country she escaped from or how, and as a welcoming gift, the United States handed her to the Departments. The Blackwoods' Department captures undocumented "stray" children to raise free combat soldiers. We all know it's wrong, but our parents do nothing about it. But really, they can't. Trapped into subservience for life, like Niko fears.

These are only some of the *many* reasons Lilith left this place. Why her escape is all the more incredible.

"Was big sis strong?" Hana whispers.

"The strongest, Sprout. And I'm not joking about that," Niko says. "She was stronger than her teachers. Stronger than me—"

"And me!" Jay says.

Niko's sadness mutes his smile. "But that's not why we love her. We love her because she's our big sister. And if she ever comes back, we can remind her how much we love her and always have, okay?"

"Okay," Hana whispers.

She's on the verge of upset now, her lip quivering between deeper breaths, but she must not want to show the sorrowful ache in her core, desperately biting her lips. Niko's heart mirrors her emotions despite not feeling them like I can, which I find incredible. He just *knows* to lay her against his chest and let her feel.

"It's okay to cry, baby," he whispers. "I'm here for you, my love."

With that, Hana wails.

CHAPTER 8

Niko

I don't have to resort to anger around her. On the first day we reunited, Emmalee watched me dissolve into infantile tears, but afterward, she still looked at me like I had every shred of dignity intact. It was exhilarating. There was no punching wall to "get my aggression out," no forced sparring. Emmalee *sat* with me and *talked* me off the mental ledge within minutes. We even had time to catch up and hang out with Hana, hours before my parents came home.

At first, my parents were upset to see us together, but then they saw my face and shut up about it. I must look worse than I thought. And it makes sense, considering I've forgotten what "healthy" feels like.

Since then, I've been walking Emmalee home for *weeks*—the only miracle I've ever witnessed. We have no idea how long this will last, but we're taking advantage of every second.

She's fidgeting with my family's gold Lionheart crest, temporarily weighing down her neck on a steel chain. It's strange to see it on her, but it suits her far better than me. I've always wondered why the etched lion's head is turned in profile, *laying down*. For our fucked-up reputation, the crest is oddly calm. A "welcome to our pride," rather than "we exist to commit genocide." I recently asked Mom why the lion isn't standing, preparing to fight, but she only shot the question back. I guessed, "To catch prey off guard," knowing the Departments. Mom's stoic glance let me know I questioned too far.

"Your weird badge thing helped." Emmalee nudges me in the ribs. "I just flash the lion symbol, and everyone gives me a ten-foot radius. I can walk right down the middle of the barracks now like a badass bitch."

My mood sours, definitely not Emmalee's intention. When I saw the handprint bruise on her bicep last week, I nearly broke my no-killing-unless-absolutely-unavoidable rule. If she froze instead of retaliating—if she hadn't recently asked Jay and I for daily drills in self-defense—she'd have a shattering secret to hold instead of the story she laughs off. Her near-assault reminded me that the Wolf really does exist.

"You still haven't given me a description," I say.

Emmalee laughs, tugging on my arm. "Um, yeah, that's because I don't want to be responsible for a murder!"

"Well, the fucker shouldn't be pulling women into bushes and tearing at their clothes. The least I could do is scare him into never doing that to anyone else. Men need to be held responsible for their disgusting behaviors, or else they'll never stop."

She watches our feet as we walk, side by side in the desolate street. "You really think that's gonna stop these guys? If it's not him, it'll be another one."

Just before we hop onto the scuffed sidewalk, blackened by careless tires, I stop. My mind doesn't want to go down this topic's path, and I can't admit why. Within seconds, I bury it. I can breathe again.

"You okay, Ni—" She stumbles over the sidewalk edge and into her neighbor's grass, death-gripping my arm to keep herself upright.

God, I love her. She's ridiculously observant of other people but still the biggest klutz I know when it comes to her physical surroundings.

I smile. "Careful, Ricky."

"Sorry." She tucks her bangs behind her ear with a shy smile. Something has her all flustered tonight, and I can't figure it out.

"I'll forgive you." I wrap my arm around her shoulder. "Seriously, though. If anyone fucks with you again, find me. I don't care what I'm doing or who I have to disobey. I'll help you."

She rubs her lips together, thinking hard about something. But we're already in front of her house.

"Oh," she mutters. "We're in front of my house."

"...Yes."

She laughs, her face flushing again.

I smile, wishing I could kiss her forehead. But I can't. Not out here.

"I, um—" She peeks up at me, softening her voice. "Do you… want to come inside?"

I'm speechless for a few seconds. "W-what do you mean by that?"

Her face only gets redder. "Niko, stop making that face. You're embarrassing me."

I laugh. "Wow. I never thought I'd see the day where *I* embarrassed *you*."

She grabs my hand and darts for the door. "Well, I'll have to make up for that by embarrassing you hardcore in a few minutes."

"Uh…"

She unlocks the door, smiling over her shoulder. "I have something I want to ask you."

With those painfully vague words, I'm sent straight to anxiety hell. Emmalee laughs, kissing my cheek and scrubbing my hair as soon as we're safely inside, but it's not enough to calm my worries.

"It'll be okay, Niko, I promise." She laughs.

I think about it for a moment, then smile. "Okay, I trust you."

Other than her room, I don't think I've seen inside Emmalee's house before. It's colorful and warm, just like her. Fresh pink flowers sit in a vase at the entryway hall, there's a cozy, open-style living room with worn leather couches to the left, and ahead of us, an unlit kitchen with pale wooden cabinets still looks inviting in the dark. Everywhere I look, the walls are painted a soft grayish blue, making Emmalee's gorgeous eyes brighter than ever.

I can't resist staring at her baby photos in the hallway upstairs, covering my dorky grin. Her eyes were bluer then, and took up half her face. Baby Ems is the cutest, chubbiest doll of a baby I've ever seen, as huggable as baby Hana.

Emmalee tugs on my arm, begging me to keep walking, but she can't budge me, and she knows it. She resorts to flailing her arms around in my peripheral vision, forcing a laugh out of me. By the time I look over, she's dancing in the hallway, kicking her feet in random directions. We burst into heavy laughter. Poor Emmalee bends over in exhaustion, gripping her protesting heart.

I carry her to her room with her legs wrapped around my waist, but then she straps herself to me instead of laying back onto the bed, even when I hover horizontally over it. It makes me laugh so hard that I wheeze, plopping onto the bed's edge with Ems in my lap.

Our black clothes blend into her black comforter in the dark. I rub her heaving back, enjoying a peaceful moment with only the sound of her breath filling my mind.

"You okay, Ems? Sorry for making you overdo it."

She laughs shortly, still unable to breathe at an average rate as she pushes out her words in bursts. "Come on. That was— Entirely— My fault."

"Well, it was definitely cute."

She laughs again, leaning back to look me in the eyes.

I smile, tucking her hair behind her ear. "Was this what you had in mind? Getting me on your bed?"

I expect her to laugh along with my joke, but with wide eyes, she slaps both palms over her face.

"Ems?!"

"What?!" She laughs, revealing a blush that stretches across her upturned nose. "You're really surprised about this?"

"W-what do you mean?!" I laugh, taking her hand in mine. "W-we can't, we…"

"Hear me out for a second." She hops off my lap.

I shift uncomfortably in her absence, crossing my legs to cover myself. I can't kid myself, Emmalee notices. Her mischievous face is an even worse sign than it is on anyone else. She's almost always up to no good, and I love her for it, but this mischief clearly involves me. In a way I wasn't prepared for.

"We've been talking about me potentially getting raped all the way home," she says.

I grit my teeth, no longer smiling.

"Hang on, there's more to this." She leans against her window, only the glow of orange streetlights gliding over her round cheeks. "I know everyone tries to prevent it, but you're right. No one's holding rapists accountable, really. You and I know it's more common than not in the Departments. Especially for women, right?"

"Right…" I can't bear to hold eye contact. Emmalee doesn't realize who she's talking to about this. And actually, that's a major relief.

"So, I'll be working in the Department of Health soon, and— What's wrong?"

"Why *there?*"

"I don't understand why you're shocked, Niko. My parents work there. Isn't that why you're in the DoTD? Your family crest thing basically forces you to join, doesn't it?"

My stomach sinks. "Y-yeah."

I have to get up, walking off my anxiety in circles. It's true; the Lionheart crest means whoever bears the name Blackwood is a force to be reckoned with. But even us Lionhearts can't protect someone from the Department of Health. They run the country through pharmaceuticals like the Department of Tactical Defense runs the country through the overzealous military. And right now, they're melding into a deadly combination.

"Niko, is there something I should know?"

I take in her worried, exhausted face. She's perfect in every way, but she's already sick. She can't be hit with an injection dose too.

She'll die.

I have to tell her. "Yeah. Fuck it, I'm a fucking traitor."

Emmalee's eyes bulge. "Hey, okay, if it's like *that*, let's take a minute to breathe first. Don't tell me anything you shouldn't—"

"You can work there. Just don't let them inject you with *anything* new."

Emmalee stands to attention, unblinking. "W-what?"

I stop pacing. "Promise me."

Her eyes dart between mine, assessing the frantic severity in my voice. "O-okay. I won't let them. But what if they…"

"Force you to take it? I don't know. Will they? Is the DoH like that too?"

Emmalee looks ready to cry.

"Sorry, I didn't mean to scare—"

"I'm not scared for *me*, I'm scared for *you!*" She lets out a helpless little sound, and it guts me. "I-I didn't know they do *that* to you! Is that why you're sick, a-and why you guys don't like the DoH, and—"

I wrap my arms around her shaking shoulders, holding her until we both calm down. "It's okay. What's done is done. I'm okay."

Emmalee takes a few deep breaths, relaxing her hands behind my back and smoothing where she crumpled my shirt.

"Let's keep talking," I say. "I didn't mean to sidetrack you."

She leads me by the hand to sit beside her on the bed. I wipe the tears streaking her cheeks, and she smiles. It's a weary, strained smile, one I've seen more and more often on her throughout the years.

"What were you going to say about working in the DoH?" I ask.

"Oh." She clears her throat. "I'll be working with a lot of older men, and I just— I don't know."

"You're expecting the worst?"

"Yeah. But there's more."

I swallow hard as she meets my eyes. I have a feeling of what she'll say, and she was right; I'm totally embarrassed.

"I-it's just, you're my best friend, Niko."

"…Yeah?"

"And you're a cute guy. And I trust you."

"Ems…"

As she turns away to stare at her white carpet, her words come spurting out. "So I know losing your virginity is a bullshit concept made up by people who want to control people's bodies, but it still matters to me, I guess? I don't know! Not the losing it part—more like I want my first experience with sex to be with someone I actually *choose*, not some—" She waves her hand around, scrunching up her nose. "Nasty... asshole... dictator guy!"

I reach for her pillow, shoving my face deep into it with a heavy laugh.

She nudges my shoulder, urging me to sit back up. "Are you making fun of me?!"

"Mmf!" I say. It was supposed to be a no.

"Nikolai!?"

I pop up, revealing my red hot cheeks. "No! I'm wondering how *I'm* not another nasty-asshole-dictator guy!"

Emmalee bursts into laughter against my shoulder, snatching her pillow from my hands to fake scream into it. Hearing my laughter, she stops and beams at me. "You're *not* a nasty-asshole-dictator guy! You're not even rude."

"Are you sure? I *am* an asshole, sometimes."

"I'm pretty sure you don't know what being an asshole really is, Nikolai Blackwood."

I laugh, but I can't help but feel like we skipped over something huge. As I track our conversation backwards, I flinch.

Emmalee raises one eyebrow. "What are you—"

"Wait a second, I couldn't be your first. Unless you didn't— You know, already— Uh— With—"

I regret asking. Emmalee breaks into a devious grin. "No, I didn't sleep with Lili. We only kissed—"

Slapping my hands over my ears, I groan. "No, no, no. Please, stop. I don't want to know."

"Well, you asked!" Emmalee sputters into laughter, and I rub my eyes frantically as if it'll erase the image of my sister in bed with my best friend. Emmalee cackles even harder. "Stop picturing it, Niko!"

"I'm trying!" I laugh, rubbing her back as her adorable cheeks turn beet-red. "Ems, wait, I'm honestly really confused."

She straightens, wiping her tears of laughter. "I know. Let me try again."

I toss her pillow behind us, and she picks at her black nail polish.

"I-it's more like, if you're interested, I think you're the only person I'm... interested in doing that with."

"O-okay." I weigh a million things in my mind, but there's one I can't overlook. "As a friend, or as a—"

"As a friend." She's quick to say it, and I'm surprised by how much that hurts. She's not looking at me, so I can't tell if she rushed to reassure me because she thinks I don't want to be more than friends or if she's genuinely drawing a line.

I only realize I've sat in contemplative silence for far too long when she looks up, worried she's said too much.

I put my hand on her shoulder. "It doesn't matter if I'm interested. I'm not accidentally getting you pregnant."

She snickers, opening her bedside drawer. My eyes widen as she pulls out two condoms. These days, those are latex gold. And technically, illegal.

"Holy *shit*," I whisper. "How the fuck do you have those?"

"My dad. The DoH uses them for vaginal ultrasounds."

"Ouch."

She giggles. "Yeah. But he gave them to me in case of an emergency. The rapist kind, I guess. I try to keep one near me."

I have to take another deep breath to swallow that one. I would *not* want to have her reproductive organs in this world. Conservative white leaders banned not only abortions but also the use of *any* birth control a few years ago. If you slip up in the Departments, they'll require you to carry to term and often take your baby if you're deemed "unfit to parent," which is almost guaranteed in their Puritanical, whitewashed terms. I *never* want to force these realities on Emmalee.

"You need to save those for emergencies, then," I say.

She glares. "It's *my* choice how to use them."

"Y-you're right, sorry. It is."

"Okay. Well, this is how I want to use them." Emmalee's confidence terrifies me. "A-and if you're not cool with that, that's okay. I'm not going to force you or anything. I just thought you might like to— Um. Just— Say something. Please."

"Okay," I say. "I'm terrified of screwing this up."

"You mean our relationship?"

"Not that. You'll always be my best friend. No matter what."

We lace our fingers together, relaxing against each other's shoulders.

"I feel the same." She presses her cold nose into my cheek. "I trust you."

"I trust you too. But I don't trust the Departments. What if it breaks and I accidentally do that to you? Our parents will separate us again. Then you'll be forced to go through all that without me. That would be—" Emmalee's baby photo comes to mind, and my heart lurches in pain, thinking of her having a baby, *my* baby, without me. "I'd never forgive myself, Emmalee."

Emmalee giggles. "Why are you so red?"

"I'm serious, Ems."

"It won't happen."

"That's— *Emmalee*, you don't know that."

"Well, the alternative is that I have to experience sex a very different way for the first time. And I've thought about this for longer than you. I don't want my introduction to something that's supposed to bring people closer to be an experience that makes me stop trusting anyone."

I chew on the inside of my bottom lip. Hopefully she doesn't puzzle together my true emotions. God, I understand how she feels so well. But I can't tell her why. No one can know.

"And I thought you might feel the same way about me, and about firsts," she whispers.

My heart throbs. She doesn't know what she's saying. I close my eyes to hold back the panic. Please, *please* don't catch on, Emmalee.

"Since you haven't been with anyone in that way either, right?" She kisses my cheek.

I expect to find her ever-knowing stare. Expect her to know. But no. She's on her feet with her back to me, placing the condoms back into the drawer. Then Emmalee flops against the headboard with her knees tucked to her chest, leaving the silence open for me to decide what to do.

I think I get it. I've struggled with this trauma for so long that she thinks this is my normal. She still doesn't know.

She smiles. "What? Are you considering my ridiculous offer?"

I face her, one knee on the bed. "It's not ridiculous. I understand where you're coming from. And feel the same way."

She's still smiling, but visibly nervous. "S-so… You're saying you want to?"

"I want to, but, well, that doesn't mean we have to if you're not ready, and—" I pause. Seeing Emmalee's face light up sends a wave of relief through my body. I really hope I won't regret this. "I guess all I'm saying is, *if* we do this, you have to promise me you won't let me hurt you either. Don't push through any pain, not even for a second. Promise you'll tell me the second it's uncomfortable."

"Okay. I promise." She holds out a hand, and I take it.

"I'll still check in, but I want you to be honest with me. I don't want to be a person that hurts you at all, ever."

She nods, her face softening into an expression I've never seen on her before.

Crawling beside her, I lower my voice to a whisper. "And if you do get pregnant, you have to find a way to tell me so I can help you. We'll figure something out."

"Easy," she whispers, touching her nose to mine. "You'd be the first to know."

CHAPTER 9

Niko

My hands are shaking. We've mastered making out the past month, but we've never done anything further together in our lives. This is a relationship-altering leap, and we both know it.

She turns away from my lips, whispering into my ear. "There's no pressure, okay? You can say no too."

"I can," I mutter, almost reassuring myself.

"Yes, you can. I'm listening to what you need too."

Overcome by the freedom of choice, I realize I *do* want this. With *her*. And I want to pretend it's my first experience along with her.

"Ems, you're the only one I can imagine doing this with also," I whisper.

My face burns, probably bright red from saying something so direct for once, but I don't care. I want her to feel special.

And I think she does. When we kiss, something new is there. I'm enveloped in her fiery spirit, not just holding her; she's holding me. It doesn't take long for me to feel just as special.

She's beautiful, but she's also my best friend and first love. Once our physical intimacy escalates, the true depth of my feelings for her reveals itself. I love her so much that my heart hurts with happiness, marveling at her feeling so safe and vulnerable with me.

There's no way I'm confessing my love to her in this moment; I don't want her to think it's physical attraction speaking. That's secondary to me in general. I might not feel sexual attraction often, but I'm relishing in the fact that I *do* feel that rare attraction to her, and only her, because of our limitless emotional connection. A connection that never dies because we work our asses off to keep it alive. We always have.

Emmalee never fails to witness me. To be there for me, even if she's across the world, existing as a reminder of why I'm alive. Even if we can only see each other once a year. Even if we don't know when will finally be the last time we meet face to face before we're separated forever. She's fulfilling an unknown wish in my heart. I never thought I'd deserve the wholehearted warmth she infuses into my life, just by being Emmalee.

With her, life could be good. Simple and fun. Loving. And it is with her right now.

I want this deep connection to last. In fact, I can't think of anything else I *need*. Every future feels dark except forever with her crystalline eyes. It's not a possibility for us now, but she gives me more hope than I know what to do with.

Urgency stirs in me. I need to defy possibility and make a life with her happen.

After indulging in each other's affection, we stare into each other's eyes for a while in complete silence, already having said everything that needed to be said. I might not have expected this tonight, but I'll never forget it.

Combing through her wispy hair, I breathe through the heavy ache in my heart as Emmalee drifts off to sleep beneath my touch. I miss her already. It's agonizing to leave her, but I have to go home before my parents refuse to let me see her again.

It's Friday, so I won't be able to see her all weekend and almost can't bear it. Just in case I don't see her on her birthday Monday, I leave her a birthday card and a drawing from Hana and me in her bedside drawer. But not before taking the time to scribble down my current thoughts since a lot has changed since I wrote it. I think it's the most genuine, secret love letter I've ever written.

From the windowsill, I take one last look at her peaceful face, reassuring her to stay asleep when she stirs. She cuddles into the jacket I left behind for her, nuzzling in deeper beneath the blankets, and it's enough to reassure my raw heart it'll be okay to leave her. We'll be okay.

Once my feet touch the ground outside her house, something within me snaps. I collapse into the dirt, overwhelmed by my pounding heart in my ears. It feels like I'm crying, clutching fistfuls of dusty earth to reground myself, but I'm also smiling.

I didn't know my body was capable of feeling so good. It's so different from the reality I'm used to; Emmalee didn't hurt me at all. She wanted me to feel safe too. And I did. She didn't say the words, but I felt loved. I don't even know how to function in the aftermath, experiencing something monumental that doesn't make me want to die.

Eventually, I recover enough to stand, and I run. My mind threatens me, daring me to stop feeling happiness for the first time I can remember, and I'm trying my best to run away from any doubts. My best efforts to remain hopeful are crushed when a specific thought creeps by, so I lean into a sprint. I need to hear a raw, truthful opinion from someone I trust, as soon as possible.

It's painfully easy to break into Jay's battered bedroom window, but I'm not thinking clearly tonight and knock on the Olivas family's front door like a well-mannered person. By the time I realize how ridiculous that is, it's too late.

"Dude, it's ten-fucking-thirty at night, and my parents are—" Jay freezes, gripping his door. "What happened to *you?*"

I squeeze his shoulders, desperate to keep a hold on myself. "Help me."

He takes me seriously, dragging me through his house and reassuring his irritated, half-asleep parents with, "I'm just taking my freakish partner upstairs."

The word "partner" strikes a deeper chord. Yes, that's why I'm here.

Jay kicks a pile of dirty uniforms, armor, and plastic dishes out of the way, ordering me to sit on the one open spot on the floor with him, but I can't. I stand, still gripping his arm.

"What the hell is going on?" He asks.

"Jay." I stare at him, unsure where to start.

"Dude, you're freaking me out."

"No, listen. This is too much for me to handle alone."

He scoffs. "Fucking *finally*. Been waiting for you to say that for like, sixteen-and-a-half years."

"Jay, stop."

"I get it, I get it. This is serious. What happened, Wolf?"

I swallow the itching irritation that comes with hearing that name and decide to spew whatever comes to mind. "I just had sex with who I'm pretty sure is the love of my life, but she's not my girlfriend, and I don't think she ever can be, and I feel like a horrible person that doesn't deserve her, and therefore, it's the end of the world."

Jay's eyes bulge. "Okay, I—" He looks around his natural disaster scene of a room, collecting his thoughts. "Okay, yeah. This is a valid freakout moment for you."

"Y-yeah."

"Well, shit," he whispers. "What the fuck are you going to do?"

"I don't know. I think—" I grip my forehead, unsure if I should cross a line I've never crossed with Jay.

An anonymous letter was slipped into my pocket last week, something Jay and I have poured ourselves over to figure out. It's clearly a forged Department of Health letter, but there's no way to prove it. And if it's real, it implies they offer covert deprogramming therapy: a way out of the brainwashed, Department mindset. The only escape I can still see.

I touch my left thigh pocket, where Jay knows I've kept it on me ever since; if I die, he has to remove it. "I think we have to take that offer, Jay."

Jay freezes, and I gulp, even though I expected a stunned reaction. It's further proof I've let myself slip too far: not even my best friend knows the depth of my true feelings about the Departments.

I continue, "If our heads are clear, we can see what they're doing to us, enough to take the Departments down from the inside. The DoTD might frontline us soon, and if they do, we'll die before we turn eighteen. Even if we survive, the life expectancy for our next promotion is twenty-five. That's only a few more years left to live, Jay. And I... I don't want to die anymore. Not as *this* person."

Jay looks deep into my eyes. "Niko, listen to yourself for a second, okay? I'm happy you don't want to die, but this is a life-changing risk. Don't decide on impulse."

"I'm not. I've thought about leaving for a long time. And you were right. We can't stay here."

His eyes widen, taking in my words. "Are you sure about this, Ni? You were so paranoid about that letter before—"

"I told you, I was wrong, and you were right. What else can we do? There's no other way out of the Departments."

"Okay… But the deprogramming offer was for you, not me, and—"

"I'm *not* leaving you behind if there's a way out."

Jay bites his nails. "Fuck. Okay, what if *you* were right and it's a trap? That the deprogramming therapy doesn't exist and someone assassinates us?"

"That's why I've made the choice for myself first." I hold Jay by the shoulders. "I'll scope out the program on my own, then we can assess if it's safe for you to join too. Best-case scenario, we deprogram ourselves. Worst-case, the DoTD is testing us for cracks in our loyalties, so I'll say I was scoping the offer out to report it."

"That's… dangerous as fuck." Jay's eyebrows warp. Then his expression overwrites with resolve. "Alright, before this goes any further, I've gotta say: there's one thing I'm pissed about right now."

Shit. "O-okay, what?"

Jay's glare doesn't last long, his wide grin bursting at the seams. "You seriously think I'm gonna let you go in by yourself? Fuck that, man! I'm by your side, all the way!"

I laugh, unbelieving life could get better than it already has tonight. I tackle Jay with a heavy hug, and he's momentarily speechless.

With a slap on the back and a tight squeeze, we've made our own life-altering promise tonight. Something we won't be able to take back.

"Let's do this," Jay says beside my ear. "Let's end this demonic path our parents carved out for us, and their parents before that. Let's be the first to get out. To break the pattern."

My heart throbs with Jay's every word. Yes, this feels right.

"If anyone can manage it, it's us," I whisper.

Jay must feel it too. As we pull back to look into each other's eyes, he smiles wider than he has in weeks.

"Couldn't have said it better myself." Jay holds out his hand. "Let's be the ones to end the fucking cycle, bro."

"Let's end the cycle," I say.

We clasp hands, gripping each other's shoulders in confirmation of our pact.

From now on, we're traitors.

CHAPTER 10

Niko

Before we visit the Department of Health, Jay insists we burn my anonymous offer letter behind the Olivas' outdoor trash cans. Not because we need to, but to "set the mood."

"Will you stop rolling your eyes?" Jay hisses. "I'm living for this spy shit! You don't even have to kill anyone to be a good spy, bro! We should've joined the fucking CIA!"

I honestly have nothing to say beyond an unamused glare, which makes Jay cackle too loudly.

Before the smoke makes a scene, I slap the burning paper from Jay's hands and stomp it into the dry dirt. This earns me a bitter punch on the arm, and I don't argue with it. Jay grabs the paper's remaining corner, stamped with a faded pawprint symbol, and pops it into his mouth like charcoal-infused, dirt gum. He laughs at my disgust.

But I'm too busy fending off a panic attack to care; we're walking to our potential deaths. Jay agrees, growing quiet in the DoH hospital's shadow, its concrete exterior slathered in dust-stained white paint. If Jay wasn't a secret genius, his rare admittance of discomfort wouldn't terrify me.

The hospital fluorescents recolor our brown skin a sickly gray. Or maybe we're just sick. Neither of us wants to discuss Sumner's injection anymore. We just want to escape before he does something worse.

We're supposed to look so confident we're cocky, according to Jay. I didn't have the guts to tell him no one will question us regardless because I'm a fucking regular.

Jay smacks my finger out of the way in the elevator and presses the basement floor. He laughs, scrubbing my head to play it off as teasing, but we both know I just fucked up. I almost pressed the top floor: Sumner's watchpost. The whitecoats beside us just see us as DoTD brats and roll their eyes, thanks to my genius best friend. His grip tightens on my shoulder, urging me to wake the fuck up.

A lifetime of stealth training couldn't silence our clunky boots echoing down the basement halls. Blaring lights fuzz out the last door—what we're hoping is covert deprogramming therapy—but the official Department Mental Treatment Center walls us in.

"Treatment" is a weak cover-up for the Center's torture tactics, utilizing the promise of healing to re-establish loyalties in straying Department members. The guys we've seen return to our units from the MTC are shell-shocked beyond recognition, sunken-in eyes unable to meet anyone's gaze. None of them have told us what happens here, but it isn't hard to guess; the Department uses mental health diagnoses to claim anything said against the Departments is nonsense, threatening to remove unit members' autonomy if they speak out of line again.

No one wants to be sent to "treatment" here. I try not to look into the small window on each soundproof door, caging empty eyes as they're re-brainwashed. There's less of a barricade between us than it seems.

Jay opens the final door, winking as I pass him. I try to fake a laugh, but a familiar flier on the door catches my eye. Similar to my letter, it uses the necessary keywords to fake a Department flier, minus the faded pawprint stamp in the bottom left corner—definitely not an official logo—and the same "typo."

```
Reabilitation training.
```

The Departments don't make mistakes. We don't either.
We can't. We're not *able* to.
With my palm on the flier to draw Jay's attention to it, I hold

the door open for Jay, winking back. Jay cackles, patting my back in confirmation that he sees it too.

Bolstering my confidence, my Wolf mask is back on. But the receptionist doesn't flinch, probably surrounded by assholes like me every day. Or maybe she knows a hidden security camera perches above their front door, just like Jay and I do.

Before she has to ask, I recite my ID. "1, dash, 6, dash, 13, 56, 19, 33… 14."

"Affirmative, Fourteen."

Maybe she hasn't heard of the Wolf after all. She doesn't seem surprised by Jay's ID either. My shoulders relax.

But then she stares at us, waiting. "Well?"

I shift my weight onto the other foot, pretending like I'm not about to shit myself. "We're here for re-abili— re*ha*bilitation training."

She continues to stare, lifting one eyebrow. Wrong answer.

That was the only thing Jay and I could devise as a code. Now we have to rely on improvisation—and an entire childhood of lying off each other's lies to protect ourselves.

She sighs, holding out her hand. "Your rehabilitation orders?"

Jay laughs in that DoTD asshat way, leaning on the counter in her personal space. Really, I know it's to block the security camera. I have no idea what's about to come out of his ridiculous mouth, but then something literally does.

He spits his "gum" into his free hand. Unfurling it, Jay reveals the slimy pawprint stamp like a fucking boss.

"Sorry, lady. I was hungry."

The receptionist's neutrality doesn't budge. "Affirmative."

It fucking *worked*.

Jay tosses his "gum" back into his mouth and swallows it down. Even after spending a childhood beside him, he still surprises me; the stamp's ink must've been permanent, so burning the letter was his safety measure for our potential capture today. He's just been goofing off to stabilize my heart.

For the camera, we widen our knees, hogging as much space as possible in the waiting room chairs. When the receptionist calls us into the back, we only have to sign an NDA and be strip searched—things we do regularly anyway—before we select

which therapy we're here for. I rein back my hope when it's misspelled again on the tablet screen—*reabilitation training*—and I check myself off for it.

We stick close together, something I'm not sure they'll be comfortable with much longer. The soundproof cells look just like the surrounding Mental Treatment Center: stale gray interrogation rooms. But now that we're here, I'm no longer afraid this is a trap. I think this is fucking real, and we're about to start deprogramming therapy. With that out of the way, my core fears are all that's left.

What if we made it all the way here, and they don't believe us?

The second our retired instructor, Commander Díaz, meets my eyes, I lose all faith in myself. With what he's seen us do—my parents do—he'll never believe we deserve help. Believe what's been done to us. To me.

He's trying to split Jay and me up, something about a one-person-per-cell policy, but nothing will come out of my mouth. It's so bright in here, adding to the white noise in my head. No one will hear us behind those metal doors, a hazard for Díaz's safety as much as ours. But I'm not afraid of being hurt. Not physically.

What if he says we're too brainwashed to be helped? What if I'm trapped forever? *That* would hurt enough to kill.

Jay talks Commander Díaz down in rapid-fire Spanish, a whisper-blowout in the hallway. I wish Jay would just save himself and forget about me. Díaz knows I was born hopeless.

Before my mind fully fades, Jay's sharp whisper snaps me out of it, reverting to English. "Look at him. I can't leave him alone. He hasn't even said a fucking *word* to me today. *Help* him."

Jay's right. I hadn't even noticed. Only my fake Wolf persona could speak to the receptionist. I take a few sharp breaths, harnessing their attention as I struggle to speak. *Help us*, I want to say. *Not me, us.*

Commander Díaz doubles back to drag me by the elbow, requiring Jay's assistance to heave open a "therapy" room. He tugs Jay in behind us, and the soundproof door slams so hard that the echo stings. My muscles tense, preparing to fight for Jay's life, but the Commander sits me down and *holds my hands.*

I'm tempted to jerk back, but his sharp thumbs press into my palms, and it does something to me. I can suddenly hear my rapid breath, wheezing unnaturally, and feel the pounding migraine that's haunted me all day.

"Good," the Commander softly says, kneeling in front of me—which feels all sorts of incorrect. "Feel my thumbs on your palms, and your feet on the ground…"

I'm too distracted by his gentle eyes to hear the rest. It's the first time in over ten years that an older man looked at me like I needed to be cared for.

"First thing's first," the Commander continues, "My name is Emiliano Díaz. You'll call me Emiliano here. None of that 'Commander' shit. I retired for a reason."

After a disbelieving silence, Jay mutters, "Well, that's fuckin' weird."

"Language," I rasp, attempting to soften Jay's incoming punishment for disrespecting a superior.

But the Commander huffs out a laugh, clicking his tongue at Jay. "What did I tell you, *mijo?* That mouth of yours will kill you much faster."

"Hasn't yet." Jay smiles, draping his arm around me.

The second I relax against Jay's familiar touch, the Commander releases my hands. He steps away from what I now realize is a steel bench we're sitting on, bolted to the ground. Tapping the tablet awake on his desk, the Commander hums, relaxing into his leather chair like he's another DoTD doctor about to tactlessly call out our monthly STD test results to our entire unit.

"Alright, boys, we have our work cut out for us. Your rank and above rarely enters this office. They're usually in too deep. But I don't want this to dishearten you. You made it here, and that says a lot. Here's my only rule: as long as you respect my safety and practice, I'll respect you. You own yourself in my office."

Now *this* is heresy. I've never heard a Commanding Officer say something so loaded against everything we stand for, not even as a trick. This is real. I can finally take a deep breath.

But I can't stop thinking about these pawprints. The calmer my mind is, the more paws appear: embossed into his desk's corner, printed onto his tablet screen's corner, and the most subtle of all, stamped into the bench bolts at our feet.

"You look like you have questions already." The Commander stares straight at me.

I have plenty. How the hell I'm supposed to believe he won't turn around and report us, first of all, but also how he knew I'd understand that vague letter enough to find him. That I was traitorous enough to show up without killing him in fear. This was way too easy for people like us, and they know who they're dealing with.

But I can't let it go. Paws circle us, preparing to kill. Someone powerful enough to veil this program in genuine secrecy.

What if this really is a trap for potential traitors? What if I'm about to be executed by my Lionheart parents?

I grip my knees. "What animal is it supposed to be? The pawprint."

The Commander is at a standstill, and my fingers tingle with anxiety. Something is off.

If my parents are involved, there's no way this is real. I've watched them kill traitors with my own eyes. Friends. If they're ordered, they'll kill me too.

But it's rare to see a Commander confused, making this impossible scenario even more dreamlike. "Wait— You... What?"

Jay's forearms ripple as he clenches his fists; he can see it too.

The Commander expected us to know something we don't.

CHAPTER 11

Niko

An urgent pounding on the steel door sends us flying in different directions. The Commander doesn't seem to expect it either, shoving past us to rip open the door with bulging eyes.

"Urgent order: Blackwood." The receptionist blurts out.

"Behind the desk, Olivas!" The Commander drags Jay across the room before I can stop him. Then he hisses at me. "You, *sit*."

I do as I'm told, exactly what I hoped to train out of me by coming here. I might laugh about it later, if I live. But as Dr. Richards struts in, red-faced and furious, I'm not sure I'll want to.

Díaz exhales, tied between relief and exasperation, and I'm even more confused. "Oh, it's just y—"

"I wish it wasn't me," Dr. Richards snarls. After flashing an orange Commanding Order paper to silence Commander Díaz, Dr. Richards drags me out the door by the shirt collar. Except it isn't a regular order report: it's a misdemeanor report. With my name on it.

And Emmalee's.

"That's right, a fucking restraining order." Dr. Richards whisks us past the waiting room. "We didn't have to go here, Blackwood. Not until you put your filthy fucking hands on my daughter."

It adds up too fast for comfort: the last time I saw his daughter, the reason why I'm here for deprogramming. What this means for her too. I let out an involuntary cry.

"Shut the fuck up," he hisses.

I don't think I'll be able to speak again anyway. He's dragging me toward the hospital staircase, his enraged breath beating against my neck.

Once we're hidden enough on the stairwell, I snag the paper from his hands. I need to see it in all its horror. He tries to be angry with me, using his momentum to release me and indirectly throw me against the wall, but I've had worse. I halt where he lets go, evading his frustrated grasp as I read my misdemeanor sentencing. My eyes catch on the date just as I remember Hana, Jay, and my plans to make Emmalee smile as much as possible tomorrow, the deprogramming news part of our surprise.

"Right before her birthday?" I whisper.

"You're the one who defiled her on her birthday!" Dr. Richards tears at his hair, stifling his twitching hands. "If you weren't a fucking minor, I'd beat your ass unconscious! I don't care if she ever forgives you, or if she makes the worst decision of her life to ignore our protection and marry you. You're *never* welcome in *my* family."

I can't help it—I weep. This is it. She's torn away from me, forever.

He grips my collar, holding me close. "Wipe those fucking tears. I have no sympathy for rapists."

I did disobey him by entering his home, but I don't know what made him think I raped Emmalee. He continues to scream, spittle misting my face. If someone raped Emmalee, I'd do worse than scream, so I get it. But if she reported me herself, this misdemeanor charge wouldn't exist. They'd never believe her. And when someone does rape her someday, just like she's terrified of, they won't believe her without a man's testimony. Especially not if she's already reported someone once. He doesn't understand what he's done. They'll never believe her.

They'll never believe me.

He grips my shirt enough to yank it from my belt's grasp, and all I can focus on is how it violates wardrobe protocol, so I should lead him somewhere he can hurt me in private. My mind is thoroughly broken.

"Why are you crying?" He seethes, tears forming in his eyes. "Why are *you* crying?"

I love her. I wish it mattered.

Dr. Richards freezes, hurriedly smoothing my shirt down. I follow his anxious stare to find Amanda, my least favorite secretary. She's not shell-shocked into emotionlessness like Lilith; she genuinely couldn't care what Sumner does to me. He's the committer, but she's the orchestrator.

And if she's here, then…

"Benjamin," Dr. Sumner smiles.

"*Charles.*" Dr. Richards rolls his eyes, his back to Sumner. I guess I'm not the only one who thinks Sumner is an evil cheeseball.

"Funny we're all meeting here." Sumner giggles, patting Dr. Richards on the back. "I received your orders to tame a certain Wolf."

Dr. Richards clears his throat, avoiding my eyes. He turns his back on me, exiting the stairway.

Amanda follows after him, leaving Sumner and I alone. Sumner already knows I've lost it, so I allow myself to laugh through my sobs. They didn't catch Jay and I for being literal fucking traitors—they're punishing Emmalee and I for *loving* each other. I've never seen the Departments described so perfectly.

It stops being funny fairly quickly. Sumner begins to laugh too, his hand at its usual starting place: gripping the back of my neck. "I know you didn't rape her. You're too much of a perpetual victim."

Even the Wolf is unable to reply.

How do the ones who harm get away with the most? Who's protecting them? I guess I should be asking who *isn't* protecting them.

But who's ever going to protect us?

I've been tolerating long days with Sumner after Japan, trying to compensate for my traitorous hesitation in the crucial part of our mission. But I'm beyond the tolerable threshold now; just the relaxed huff of Sumner's breath makes me sick.

Sumner adopts a mocking, singsong tone. "Now that you've thrown another fuck-up in, you're making more work for me! If you don't complete my research tasks today, exactly how I wish, you'll leave me no choice but to let them frontline you!"

My heart feels like it's stripped from me, spliced across our feet. Frontlining will kill me, but so will having to fulfill Sumner's "tasks" one more time.

He drags me up the stairs, a slow climb to his office. I want to stop him, push him over the railing, fucking *say something*, but I can't. Defying him makes him angrier than anything. And whenever Sumner gets angry, I get hurt.

Unless this time, I hurt him badly enough to where he can't retaliate.

I can't speak, but I can fight under any conditions. People like Sumner made sure of it.

But I stopped fighting back with him years ago.

Sumner doesn't expect me to lean into him and land a swift backswing to his balls, putting my entire weight into it. His pained cry is cut short as he doubles over, crumpling on the top step. I hope I've sterilized him.

This is new. We don't know what to do, gaping at each other like total strangers from the stairwell's opposite sides. Maybe ripping everything away from me loosened my last screw. Maybe he got too comfortable with the feral animal he raised.

Maybe I've just had enough.

I grip my tactical knife's holster to do far worse, but his angry, bulging eyes immobilize me. Whether I want to move or not, my body goes on autopilot.

I forgot why this never worked. Every "punishment" he's ever committed flashes before my eyes, making me scramble down the steps in curdling, quivering terror.

After stumbling upright, Sumner chokes out, "You think you can defy me? Forget it. You're getting deployed, *today*."

I'm ready to scream-cry in the stairwell; in my panic, I forgot what this meant for Jay. We're combat partners, and we only get deployed together.

My only best friend left will die on the front lines because of *me*.

But crying will only encourage Sumner, so I suck my screeching fear back in until none of my emotional honesty is left alive.

"I have no use for traitors!" Sumner chucks me into his office.

He makes a quick call. I've fucked up enough for him to rescind his request to keep me home as his patient, the only thing preventing Jay and me from the front lines. All that time I spent with Sumner—buying our safety—was worth nothing.

Then Sumner turns toward me. His pale eyes scream vengeance.

Instead of bawling my eyes out, I focus on drowning beneath the power of nothing. Make my mind go far, far away. Until it goes black.

Eventually, I blink a few times in a very different location.

"Hello? Kid?" A nurse shakes me by the shoulders. "You lost?" He leans in to analyze my neck and falls silent. Slipping his finger beneath my shirt collar, he peeks at my chest. "Hey, do you need help—"

"I'm fine!" I shove him away.

With his hands up, he presses his back to the sterile white wall. "Hey, man, you're okay! I won't hurt you, but I can see you've been hurt. What's your name? I can go get another nurse to help if you're more comfortable with a woman, or—"

I shake my head no, my chest heaving. No one could want to help me here. Kindness is a trap.

Then I run. I'm yelled at a few times for it, but that's okay. Once I exit the Department of Health hospital, I make sure to take a separate block from Emmalee's street, costing me at least a 5-minute detour.

I've already taken too long. I have to find Jay. To explain before someone unexpectedly knocks on his door to deploy us. To beg him for forgiveness I don't deserve.

At the Department of Health border, I shock myself on the military-grade electric fence, grabbing it directly without thinking. Dropping to the ground in a deadweight plank, I lie paralyzed, grunting through the crushing pulses of my stuttering heart as it restarts itself.

Some geared-up guys jump off the watchpost, crowding around. They flinch when I lift my head to look at them, even though I can't lift it for long.

"Wait, that kid's not dead from this thing?"

"Shit, dude, isn't that the Wolf?"

They all take a few steps back.

"Whoa, that's creepy as fuck. He really is bulletproof."

One of them kicks me with his boot's rubber base. "Hey, you alive, man? Still volted up?"

I struggle to study their wobbling faces, my eyes unable to focus. They're from the DoTD, a few years older than me, but they sound like the usual assholes. And something they said stands out: I'm bulletproof.

Traumaproof. That's how I'm treated, and that's how Sumner sees me. And it's all my fault. Because I thought putting up with his shit, pretending it didn't hurt me, was the only way to survive. If I'd let myself crack, maybe a little, then maybe people wouldn't push me so far past my limits. Maybe I *have* turned myself into a perpetual victim.

It's so sad that it's funny. It starts off small at first, but then I break into a full laugh. The guys run.

I close my eyes, choking back tears. This only makes me laugh at myself more. Jay and I were *so close* to becoming better people, but we have to numb out—down to our souls—if we're deployed on the front lines as human weapons. Where we're going, having a conscience will only harm us.

By the time I can stumble to my feet, the guys open the gates, hoping I'll just leave. I wobble through the streets, breathing through the grief weighing down my entire body.

It's still a few minutes before curfew, so they allow me to pass through to the DoTD without lifting my shirt to check my ID on my bruised back. I lucked out this time.

Even though it kills, I jog to Jay's house. Multiple people freeze in the streets to watch me flail by, uncoordinated after bringing myself back from the brink of death, but no one says anything. No one asks if I'm okay, even as I trip and scrape my temple on the concrete. By the time I reach Jay's house, men crowd his door.

I have no idea how long I was with Sumner, but because I numbed out too much, I wasted too much time. Jay steps outside, meeting my eyes. He doesn't give me away and keeps it to a passing glance, but I'm sure he catches the guilt on my face.

So I run home.

My hands are shaking too much to open the door, but Mom flings it open for me.

I can tell she got a heads-up from a co-worker. She's glaring, her chest heaving and mouth tight. I tense to defend myself, but her eyes catch on my neck.

It must be extra bad today. I jerk away from her, but she's a long-time DoTD member—no one can escape her. She grabs my shoulders. Her eyes aren't angry anymore; they're horrified.

"What happ—"

"I finally fought back." I grind my teeth. "I'm sorry."

Her ashy eyes track mine, putting the pieces together. "Your second job?"

This is the last thing I want her to know, so I slink away, my knees weakening.

"Stop it! Stop hiding from me!" She's crying now. "I would've helped you!"

"I was trying to be strong!"

She covers her mouth, sobbing. Wrapping me in her arms, she holds me to her. I don't know how to react.

"I taught you all wrong, Nikolai. I'm so sorry."

This only upsets me more. It's too late for her to change her mind. To show me the exterior I've perfected was all for nothing. "No, Mom. It's my fault. Blame me."

She holds my face between her palms. "Tell me who it was."

"*No,*" I say. "Trust me when I say I *can't.*"

She exhales in defeat, sensing the finality in my voice. I don't have to explain that others will suffer if I tell; she knows how they work here.

Her eyebrows arch. "They wouldn't let me override your deployment order. I don't know if they ever will. So you have to survive. Come back home to me."

I tip my chin to the ceiling, unable to even look at her. She's asking me to keep playing the part, even if we both know it's wrong. At this point, I don't know what else to do.

"Okay," I whisper. "I will.

CHAPTER 12

Emmalee

My future died. It's been four months since I turned seventeen and had to go to the hospital. I didn't expect to feel hospital-level sick, but the stress of having Niko ripped away from me took a painful toll on my body. Even the hospital agreed I needed to be admitted for a week, when they often turn you away, half-dead. I can't even babysit Hana for comfort because I was promptly fired for getting their son in serious trouble.

I should've known better when I finally had Niko to myself. It was too incredible to last. Life is not that kind.

I'm killing my sanity by fantasizing over the night we shared. No amount of fantasizing will make it come true again, but sometimes I can't survive the waves of emotion washing over me. Without him, the black squares no longer help me feel better. Not even after I finish covering the entire wall.

So I close my eyes and picture it. How Niko cradled me like he was there to stay. How protected and safe I felt. How he suddenly knew how to kiss me until I was dizzy—like he finally read up on it, just for me. How he whispered soft reassurances against my lips and checked in constantly, ensuring he still had my full consent. For someone trained to kill, he was so gentle. So thoughtful.

We were so happy, it was almost weird. But I *loved* seeing him happy. It wasn't perfect—we had to laugh at how awkward we were a few times—but it was us. Finally free to be ourselves, even if it was just for each other.

I took a risk, asking for something so extreme compared to what we've done for years, but he listened and talked it through without judgment. That night, he soothed a horrifying dread in my heart that was drilled into me since I was a little girl. He showed me what sexual safety should feel like. Granted me my solace.

But it's time to grow up and shut up. My parents' toxicity heightens my disabilities, and I'd rather suffer in solitude than suffer with them. I have one year to work my ass off and move out. Then, if Niko doesn't hate me, I can beg him to forgive me for what my family and I have done.

I drag my heavy body out of bed for my first day of work in the Department of Health. I'm not sure what I'll be doing, but I haven't forgotten my promise to Niko. *No new injections.* Although, I'm not sure what that means now that I've had time to think it through. No injections, as in *no* injections? There has to be a certain one he wants me to look out for, so how do I know which is which? Maybe he doesn't either. Or maybe I'll know it when I see it.

"Ready for your first day?" Dad hops into the driver's seat of his car.

I can't even look at him. Maybe he has a point somewhere in his mind, but I can't see it. I'm staying in full-bitch mode for as long as I feel like it.

He takes my silence in stride, backing us out of the driveway without another word. We're about to have a painfully silent thirty-minute car ride into the city for work. Beyond our outer fences, the Departments have smaller factions all over the civilian area in downtown Santa Desierto. I'll be interning at Sumner Hospital—one of the DoH's partner hospitals—under my dad's co-worker.

But after a few minutes, the stale air becomes too much for my dad. "Are you going to act like this at work too?"

"I don't know, is my boss going to file a restraining order against my best friend and the only person I've ever loved for *raping me* with no grounds for it?"

He grips his steering wheel until it lets out a rubber

squeak. "Emmalee. The only person you've *ever* loved? What about Lilith?"

"The girl who abandoned me with little warning? Yeah, a great example of love."

"Well, is *he* a great example of love? The bred terrorist trying to get into your pants?"

At this point, I'm the type of angry that sends me into full-blown sobs rather than the tough girl rage I'm dying to convey. It makes me even angrier having to see his guilty expression from my tears.

"Emmalee, sweetheart, I know you don't see it yet, but you'll find someone else. Someone who'll take care of you properly and that you'll love even more."

"You don't even know what you're saying. You're so terrified that you won't even listen to me!"

"I'm not *terrified!*" He tacks on an unnecessary scoff.

Then Dad pulls over. To "talk." If I wasn't already feeling trapped in this life, I am now.

"Then what is it?" He lasers into the side of my face with his glare. "What is it I'm not understanding?"

"That it was *my* idea." My face turns a glorious shade of red, snot pouring out of my nose.

"Emmalee, I don't want those details."

"Then how can you know if he raped me or not? Why would you report him for something he never did, knowing it could get him killed?"

"Killed? Come on, don't be—"

I've channeled my rage, ready to face him eye to eye. "Dad! They could! No matter how much you deny it, you might've gotten the love of my life killed. Killed! How would you feel if your parents did that to Mom?"

His eyes trace mine. "I-I really don't think—"

"But you don't *know*. I've taken the time to talk to this 'terrorist' more than you, and I know. They put chips into his arms, Dad. He doesn't own a smartphone to prevent being tracked, but they track him in an even more obvious way, like he's their property. Scars cover his arms from where they taught him how to cut it out of his own skin, and if his receiver— Radio?

Thing beeps, he has to stop whatever he's doing and cut himself open because someone outside the Departments intercepted his chip. So basically, because the Departments don't give enough of a shit about him to protect him, he has to hurt himself. They're not even placing it somewhere hidden because they know he's not seen as a real person. Not by you, not by the Departments, not by anyone except his best friend, his baby sister, and me!"

"Come on, now, Emmalee. I know he's a human being. That's why I'm taking his power seriously. He shouldn't be allowed to disobey our household rules and use your body. I don't think that's much to ask for, on my part."

"That's not the point, at all." I grip my jeans. I'm struggling to calm my tears enough to settle my wiry heart muscles flexing out of control. "You don't want to talk about the actual problem."

"Okay, fine! Then let's talk about it!"

I can't meet his eyes. "Fine, I will! So don't stop me, even if you don't want to hear about your daughter's sex life."

"Oh, *God.*" He catches my enraged stare and sighs. "Okay. If that's really what you want, then go ahead."

I rub my lips together, thrown over the edge of tolerable upset. But I need to calm down if I want my dad to take me seriously. Right now, he sees me as an *overly emotional woman,* I'm sure of it.

"What you're not taking the time to hear is that *I* asked him." I soften my voice. "He would never use my body. The most ridiculous part of this is that he was walking me home to make sure I *didn't* get raped because someone pulled me into a bush recently after dark, and he wasn't about to let that happen again."

"What?! You never told me that! What did the guy do?!"

"Nothing. *Jay and Niko* taught me self defense. So the second some rando pulled me down, I jabbed him in the corner of the eye with my thumb, and he ran off, crying."

Dad fights back a smile. "You're amazing, Emma, but I'm still going to kill whoever did that."

"That's what Niko said," I grumble. "But I wouldn't let him. So he gave me his Lionheart— Insignia? Crest? *Thing* so I could protect myself while walking to babysit Hana. When I wore it, people stopped catcalling me, even in our own Department. I had no idea it was a precious family heirloom until his mom came to our door asking for it back when she fired me, but Niko did that for me."

"Okay, well, he should've."

"Yeah, because he's not an asshole. So when I asked him if—" I'm cut off by a sharp, harsh sob gripping my throat. I can't speak through my tears, remembering that night. How shocked and playful he was at first. How it flipped to instant concern for my future when he realized I was serious. How touched he was that someone chose him to be theirs for one night. How, like a coward, I crushed those hopes, insisting we were only friends when I haven't wanted to be "just friends," ever. I should've braved his potential rejection, even if it would've cost me my whole heart, but I couldn't bear the thought of losing him again.

And now it's too late to take it back. I lost him, no matter how hard I tried to cling onto him.

"Breathe, sweetheart. I'm listening." Dad rubs my shoulder.

I take a deep breath, my lip quivering. "When I asked him, he said no at first because he didn't want me to get pregnant. But I convinced him with the stuff you gave me, and maybe I shouldn't have done that, but—" I bury my face in embarrassment. "When I told him I didn't want to be raped the first time I had sex since I knew he wouldn't do that to me, he took my concerns seriously and said he understood what I meant. But I felt like— I felt like—"

"Keep breathing," Dad says.

I glance over to see if he's still pissed at me, and he's not. A wave of relief washes down my shaking limbs.

I grab Dad's hand, laying it all out there. "I felt like he was trying not to admit he'd already been raped before. Like he wouldn't dare say it, but something within him was crying out for my help. So when I said that, he genuinely understood why I didn't want to be raped for my first time. He's never dated or been with anyone else, which means he— He *was* raped his first time. But then I saw he still had bruises on his chest, like— God, it's too awful. I can't even say it."

"I'm a military doctor, Emma. I've seen everything. Let it out."

I swallow, knowing he's right. This pain is too heavy to carry alone.

"It was like someone had been holding him down, on multiple different days that week," I whisper. "He's been going through what I've been afraid of, all alone. And I'm so afraid that's who they're sending him to for his punishment. That I got a rape victim reported for rape, and now he's probably... I don't know. I don't know what to do, Dad."

Dad sits in silence for a while. I'm too overwhelmed to clear my head enough to read his thoughts or feelings—dizzy with pain and anxiety, wobbling in my seat, and holding onto the door for stability.

Finally, Dad mutters, "So he didn't hurt you at all? Pressure you?"

"No," I choke out, struggling to catch my breath. "He must've been thinking about how obnoxiously focused I get when my mind is set, no matter what it costs me. He could've used that to just do whatever he wanted, but knowing me, he made me promise I wouldn't push through any pain, and that I'd be honest whenever he asked if it hurt so he could stop. Then he proceeded to give me a ton of opportunities to stop him or change my mind. But I didn't want to, or have to."

Dad's eyes remain locked on his steering wheel as my heartbeat pounds into my ears. After an extended silence, his voice comes out soft. "And you really love this guy? You think he's safe?"

"Yes, and yes. I *really* love him, Dad."

"...Okay," he whispers.

"O-okay?"

My dad gets back on the road, speed-dialing the hospital. I listen in stunned silence as he says we're having a family emergency and can't come into work today. Then he makes a U-turn, heading back home.

"Dad?! Where are you going? I can't just *not show up* for my first day!"

"Emmalee, don't argue with me over this. You're not well... And I need to fix my mistakes."

I exhale, dropping my head against the headrest. I don't know if this is fixable, but I'm finally not alone in it.

Then a disturbing thought occurs. "Dad. Don't tell anyone he was raped."

"What? Why not?"

"You don't think it's his superiors?"

"I don't know, honey. What about his friend?"

"No. It's not Jay. Who would Niko let lay a hand on him? They train these guys to do as they're told, don't they?"

Dad twists his mouth in heavy concern.

"If we report it to his superiors and it turns out to be one of them, they'll punish him for snitching, and—"

Dad cusses beneath his breath. "Okay, you're right. I'll just ask for my report and restraining order to be removed from his record. Explain it was a misunderstanding."

"Do you think that'll work?" I shouldn't be filling my own father with doubt. I want his authority to help, but I don't know what to believe anymore.

After another uncomfortable silence, Dad strokes the back of my head. "Whether it works or not, I have to try. Or else my daughter will never forgive me. And I want you to feel like you can trust me with this in the future, even if it's awkward or about sex. I love you, Emma. I really do."

"I love you too." Tears gush from my buggy eyes yet again. "I'm a mess, aren't I?"

He laughs. "Yes, sweetheart. That's why you're taking a sick day."

Once we get home, I pass out asleep from emotional exhaustion. My nightmares are worse than ever, so I don't feel well-rested when I wake up.

I wander out of bed to find my parents huddled at their kitchen table, having a quiet, tense conversation with their hands clasped.

"What's going on?" I mumble, rubbing my eyes.

"Nothing, Emma," Mom says. "We're just discussing how to move forward from here. I'll bring you some food in a minute."

I stand frozen for a moment. Their emotions say something different than Mom's calming words. "Are you talking about me?"

Dad pulls out a chair. "Come sit."

I sit in silence as my world continues to crumble. They "couldn't" remove Niko's charge from his record since his punishment was already in motion. And he's not even here. He's been deployed. On the front lines.

Niko isn't dead yet, but my parents reassure me like he is, listing the philosophies of moving on from a loved one's death. I can't respond. I can't even cry.

I didn't get to apologize to Niko, not even for panic-friend-zoning him. He might die before I have the chance. It's all my fault.

CHAPTER 13

Emmalee

Everyone's so desperate to tell me what I "need" to do with my life lately.

It's been over a year, Emmalee. You need to find some new friends. You need to take better care of yourself. You need to date around a bit to get him out of your head.

You need to move on.

I don't know about "moving on," but I *am* sitting back and seeing where life takes me. The aimlessness overtaking me is my survival mode—relishing in every simple, quiet moment while it lasts. I'm still living despite my loss.

Our families still aren't on speaking terms. I haven't been able to ask anyone who might know if Niko's alive since it's classified, so I have to assume he's not. The front-liners who survive always come back after two to three months. That window is long gone.

I'm realizing grief never ends, so I should stop waiting for it to stop hurting before I can start living again. Everyone's shitty advice holds a bit of truth: maybe I should move *forward*, at least a little.

I've saved to move into a tiny Department of Health apartment, stacked on top of itself and sandwiched between hundreds of other units. The inside is stale, the walls patched and repatched from previous fist-rage damage. I don't have money to decorate beyond hanging my old, black and white skull scarf as a makeshift tapestry, but it's *my* place.

I'll admit, it's grueling to take care of myself with how sick

I feel, but I needed space. Turning eighteen was the best excuse I'd have to move out for a long time, so I took it. But after a few months alone, I don't want to admit I now have *too much* space—one that not even a hair dye and chop crisis could solve—so I'm driving to pick up a new friend today.

Fixing my chin-length, black hair in the rearview mirror, I spot Clarity exiting Sumner Hospital's automatic glass doors and instantly smile. We're both badass goth women with resting bitch faces, automatically making us friends. The day we met, I was filing paperwork for the DoH's civilian extension program, downtown. Clarity wasn't doing too well, but I wasn't either, so we bonded.

"Hey!" She smiles, hopping into my car. She's about six inches shorter than me and absolutely adorable, but sadly very straight.

"Hey, girl! How'd it go?"

Clarity sighs, likely adjusting to my car's quiet calm compared to a grossly overcrowded hospital. "It went… okay. They still don't know what's going on with me."

As we stop at a red light, I rub her shoulder. "I'm sorry, Clarity. They're so fucking clueless sometimes with chronic illness. It's infuriating."

"It is." She looks into my eyes. "I'm so sorry you've been through that too."

I smile. "Yeah, it's okay. At least I'm not alone anymore."

"Nope! You're stuck with me!" She giggles, pulling her long, dark brown hair into a ponytail.

"Well, good! I happen to like your company."

She laughs, doing a cute little happy dance.

I laugh. "So, are we still on for smoothies? Or are you too worn out after your appointment?"

"I'm good! I wouldn't miss it after our schedules keep clashing. I've missed you, Emmalee."

My smile widens. "I've missed you too."

Clarity grows unusually quiet. She notices me eyeing her a few times and shuffles in her seat. "Hey, I have one medical question before we talk about fun stuff the rest of the day."

"Oh." I'm a little surprised she brought it up at all; Clarity hates uncomfortable topics. "I don't mind. What's up?"

"You're trying that new experimental drug for autoimmune patients too, right?"

"Yeah. The clear IV bag treatments?"

"Yeah, those. Are they working for you?"

Reflecting on my violent trauma shakes during my last infusion, I decide it's not worth getting into the gory details.

With a shrug, I put the car in park. "Well, they suck ass, and I still feel like shit." We laugh, shutting our doors and meeting behind the trunk. "But these experimental trials pay well for once, and I'm kinda tight for money."

Her smile fades into a fake grin. "Yeah, me too."

"Are they not working for you either?"

She grows even quieter. "I don't know what they're doing, honestly. I think I'll stop after the trial period ends. Maybe *before* it ends…"

My heart rate spikes. Clarity isn't telling me something; I can feel it. "What's been going on? If you don't mind me asking."

"It's going to sound weird." She laughs. "I've just been having horrible dreams."

My shoulders soften. "Oh, yeah. Did your doctor diagnose you with Chronic Nightmare Syndrome too?"

"Yeah. From PTSD."

"That's from past medical trauma too, right? PTSD, I mean. Maybe if the treatments are making you feel worse, it's accumulating more trauma and making the CNS worse. That's what I think happens to me, at least."

"Yeah. I think you're right. It's a twisted cycle that feeds off itself."

We sigh, linking arms. Clarity lays her head on my shoulder while we walk, as if she could be any cuter.

The smoothie shop downtown is charming and homey, tucked into a half-store plot. Our noses are hit with a citrus breeze as soon as I crack open the door. Clarity has to help me wedge it the rest of the way open, and we laugh at ourselves, both too exhausted these days to open heavy doors.

We take our drinks to a shiny, pink retro diner table in the back corner, and I ask Clarity about her college classes and friends. We laugh and have a good time, but there's always a point where we hit a wall. Nothing ever goes too deep. And lately, she seems a little extra distant.

"Are you feeling okay?" I ask.

"Yeah! I'm good. I'm having fun."

"Okay!" I smile, unable to be the weirdo I am and say, *actually, I know you're not fine because I can literally feel your emotions.* Instead, I say, "If you're not doing well, I don't mind talking about it. Even if it's about health stuff, or anything, uh… deep."

She gives my hand a quick squeeze. "Thanks, Emmalee. I'm here for you too."

I take a large sip of my smoothie, preventing myself from saying anything I shouldn't. Within seconds, I have to smack my forehead with the base of my palm, groaning and drumming my feet from what we call a "smoothie headache."

Clarity laughs. "Did you drink too fast?"

"Ugh, fuck. Yes. God, I always do this to myself."

She giggles, reapplying her black lipstick. "You really do. Every time we come here, actually."

"What can I say, I'm a perpetual mess."

"That's what makes you fun," she says. Then something catches her eye across the room. Not once, but twice. "Hey," she whispers, leaning in close beside her drink. "Do you know that guy?"

A bulky guy with freshly buzzed, dark hair and a sharp jaw pays for his smoothie order. Clarity might not realize his black cargo pants are tactical pants, just like she might not realize this man is from the Departments. He meets my eyes with a half-smile, aware we're checking him out—and proud of it.

I whip back around, meeting Clarity's guilty cringe.

"Oops," she whispers.

We laugh quietly to ourselves.

But Clarity's smile drops. "Oh, my god, Emmalee. He's coming over here."

"What?" I hiss, looking down at my lazy outfit. "Oh, *God*, of course. What do I—"

"Richards, is that you?"

Taking a closer look at him towering above us, I gasp. "Wait— Andre?!"

He laughs. "This is crazy! I remember you from private school as a sassy little brunette, not a gorgeous *woman* with black hair."

I laugh, unsure if he means something more by that or if I'm being oversensitive. "A lot has changed, that's for sure. I hardly recognized you either!" I turn to Clarity. "Clarity, this is an old friend of mine, Andre."

Andre holds his hand out for her to shake. "Hey, Clarity."

"H-hey!" She says, her arm almost getting torn off.

I grip Andre's forearm, shooting him a glare. "Okay, big guy. Don't break her arm."

He laughs, releasing Clarity and brushing his hand over mine. I'm flustered for a moment, realizing I forgot to let go; Andre's arm reminds me of Niko's, chip scars lining the length of it. Andre was on track to join the DoTD when we were kids, and by how unruly he was then, I'm positive that's where he works now.

"Whoops. My bad, Clarity. I'm used to military guys," he says.

"Oh, wow, the military," she says. "What branch?"

I smooth the back of my hair, immediately uncomfortable. I try not to talk to Clarity about anything other than civilian life, and I'm not sure our stories will line up if Andre keeps this up.

Thankfully, Andre shoots me a knowing glance. "Marines." He brushes past it, leaning on the table's edge and looking directly into my eyes. "Hey, so do you want to— I don't know. Catch up sometime?"

"O-oh!"

I'm caught off guard, glancing at Clarity for backup. She's taking a *long* sip of her smoothie, eyeing me with a smile and subtle nod.

"S-sure!" I say. "Yeah! That sounds… nice!"

"Great." He smiles. "You still live at your parents' place? I can swing by and say hello."

"Oh. No, I don't actually—"

"No worries." He pulls his smoothie receipt from his pocket, scribbling his number onto it with his fingernail. "Text me, and I'll pick you up for dinner sometime."

"O-okay! Sounds good." I force my best "confident" smile.

"Awesome. See you later, then. Bye, Clarity." He gives us what I call a bro nod, backing out the door.

I'm frozen, gawking at Clarity's increasing smile.

She bursts out laughing. "He *totally* wants to bang you."

I slap my pink cheeks. "Oh, my God, no… Do you think?"

"Are you kidding? Did you not see him checking you out? I mean, I get why. I'm not a lesbian, but if I was, I'd say you were hot too."

I laugh off my irritation. "Thanks, but you don't have to be sexually attracted to someone to think they look nice, right?"

She shrugs. "I guess you're right. Well, anyway, isn't this what you wanted? Aren't you a little… touch-deprived?"

"Shh!" I laugh, gripping Andre's number and leaning in closer. We're collecting stares in such a tiny shop. "I mean, yeah. More like touch-*starved*." Clarity and I giggle to ourselves. "But are you sure that's what this is?"

She gives me a picturesque goth smirk. "Text him. You'll see."

So I do.

And he texts back, asking for a time.

Then I drop Clarity off, sending Andre another quick text in her driveway. I'm too nervous to wait to see what he wants from me, so I ask if he's free tonight or tomorrow. I don't know if that's considered too forward, but I'm a forward person, so he'll have to deal.

Apparently, he *really* likes "forward."

He shows up at my apartment within an eager hour. It's already dark, so I decide to straight-up ask if he was planning to have sex with me tonight. He's even more flustered and comes inside. We skip dinner entirely.

By the time we've made out and stripped, the nerves spike. I haven't slept with anyone except for Niko, and as I've told Clarity multiple times, I'm horrendously touch-deprived. It's probably clouding my vision since Andre isn't exactly my personality type, but he looks like he could pick me up and throw me with one arm, which, for some reason, appeals to me today. He also has that brisk, DoTD seriousness—an intense, analytical nature that reminds me of Niko.

"S-so," I say, grabbing a condom from the small stash I've

wishfully accumulated at work throughout the past year. "I-I'm not sure how far you want to go, but—"

"Oh, I'll take it." He snatches it from my fingertips.

I watch him casually put it on, right in front of me, and can feel my cheeks turning bright red. "U-um, I'm a little—"

"Nervous?" He leans in to kiss me square on the lips. "Don't be. You're hot."

Not the most eloquent person I've ever met, but as he shoves his tongue in my mouth, he certainly makes me feel good with his hands. The heavier we kiss and touch, the more relief I feel. The weight of life lifts off my shoulders, momentarily replaced with pleasure. I hadn't realized how much pain I was carrying until he pries it off me with his body. I crave more of him, even if he makes a weird scrunched-up face when he's aroused. That's fixable, though: I just close my eyes. Numb to the world except for his powerful hands on my thighs.

I expect him to last longer than I do, but as soon as he's done, he gets up and puts his pants on.

"Oh, um, are you leaving?" I comb my wrecked hairstyle with my fingers.

He shrugs. "Sorry, Richards. I have to get up for work in, like, one, two... Yup, six hours. If I don't go home now, I'll be dead tomorrow." He laughs. "Maybe literally. You know how the Tac. Department is."

I cringe for too many reasons to process, not exactly turned on by how often unit members die. "Um, okay..."

He smirks, bending over for another quick kiss. "What? You want more?"

"Well, I— Yeah? You didn't even ask if I was done—"

He might not have asked if I was ready to stop the first time, but he takes my words seriously now, sticking his fingers into me and finishing what he started. He's a very gruff person and we have zero emotional connection, but I'm still touch-deprived enough to not care. This time, I'm left dizzy under his touch. His eyes glaze over with a hunger for my reaction, daring me to ask for more.

But then we're left in a strange silence.

"Should I come back this weekend?" He smiles.

I nod, still struggling to stabilize my heart muscles.

Then I'm left all alone again. I steal a blanket from the couch on the way to the toilet, brush my teeth, and climb into bed in a daze. I curl up on my side, too exhausted to fix my bedsheets strewn across the floor, and huddle under the small blanket I took from the couch.

Tucked into myself, I'm hit with an emotional downpour: a severe emptiness eating away at my core, making my stomach ache.

He didn't hurt me. He actually did what I asked for... once I asked. I'm not bothered by social or romantic awkwardness, and I've happily dated people who show little emotion before; Lilith didn't realize she had to continue to tell me she loved me after saying it once. But tonight wasn't like that. It was purely physical.

And that's okay. For many other people.

But what if Niko's gift to me was more of a curse than the blessing I've seen it as? Nothing compares, and I don't think it's teenage idealism distorting my memory of him.

I think he was *it* for me. I'll probably never love someone like that again in my life. That thought kills me, sending me into guttural sobs as I cling to my pillow.

CHAPTER 14

Niko

The fifteen minutes of deprogramming were lovely, but now Díaz's reassurance haunts our sleep. Our accumulating guilt is unavoidable, and our nightmares remind us we'll never fully atone.

Either that, or nightmares are another side effect of S817. Every time Sumner's medical crew reexamines us for "side effects," they grill us about our nightmares. Eventually, they diagnosed us with Chronic Nightmare Syndrome from a thick load of PTSD. But that's normal in the Department of Tactical Defense, so we don't do anything about it. Jay almost strangled me in his sleep once, but other than that, they're just nightmares.

If I'm honest with myself—and these days, I'm not—I hate that I created this reality for us. They saw through Jay and me as traitors from the second I hesitated to inject myself with epinephrine in Japan, and our fate was set.

We love to joke about our imminent deaths now. We don't know what else to do.

Jay sits at my side in the back of a clunky transport van, surrounded by other front-liners.

"I think," he whispers, leaning in close. "If I don't get blown into Jay stew in a few minutes—" Jay pauses, waiting for me to crack a smile. "My life dream should also include chickens."

This almost gets me to laugh. "*Chickens?*" I hiss. "As a pet?"

"Yeah, man. They're fucking cute."

He says this a little too loud, earning himself a long-winded, personally insulting scolding from our Commanding Officer. Jay and I have to curl our toes to keep from laughing since the Commander's chicken anger just made our conversation about ten times funnier.

We've survived longer than almost any front liner in history—eighteen whole months—and I don't think that's an accomplishment. If you survive the first one or two units, they consider you a top-level DoTD unit member, send you home, and promote you directly to the top. Usually. Twelve units later, they're clearly waiting for *us* to die, using us for impossible jobs no one wants to do.

The day I left, Mom admitted a front-liner future was why she didn't allow me to see Emmalee. She explained a rare power-couple would've been placed on the front lines for life, but I don't see how that adds up. Emmalee's parents refused to let her join the DoTD. That should've been enough protection from this life.

Worst of all, I wouldn't have tried so hard to make something of myself in the DoTD if I realized my parents wanted me *off* the front lines instead of *on* them, but they failed to make many things clear. I thought I was making them proud, ensuring I'd at least be a good person in one or two people's eyes.

But really, I'm only bitter with myself. I totally fucked up.

We're somewhere in the midwestern farmlands "to break up internal conflict" in the newly developing Civil War II. Identity-less mercenaries, we're disguised as cops, Marines, or National Guards. Our authoritarian presence alone escalates the violence until everyone either dies or flees, so I guess we *do* "break things up" in a way. A pointlessly violent way.

I think we're almost to today's destination. I can feel it in the slowing wheels and the brakes nudging me into Jay's shoulder.

Closing my eyes, I picture Emmalee's school photo in my left breast pocket, Hana's in my right. Just to humor Jay, I snatched his childhood photo for my left hip pocket too. I don't know if I can qualify the photos as a reminder to survive anymore. I've accepted I won't.

I'm just hoping to stay connected. Hopefully Emmalee remembers my birthday letter and can move on from me in peace when I die. She deserves to live a full life. To find someone else who loves *all* of her, no matter how much the thought kills me.

I shouldn't be thinking about this right now. I was doing so well, numbing out to my core. Apparently, even worse rumors exist about Jay and me because we don't respond to death anymore. Well, according to our unit. They don't see my nightly meltdown, or Jay's nightly guilt fits. Death still hurts like the first time. But because of our heartless exterior, our Commanding Officers assign the most gruesome tasks; we're "the only ones who can handle it."

Honestly, I think Jay and I are only okay because everything is so bad that the mundane feels like the best shit we've ever experienced. So right now, in the back of a piss-smelling van, wedged in with ten other brainwashed sixteen- to eighteen-year-olds, and laughing about chickens, we're high on life.

They dole out our protective gear, staging a "mix-up" with the new tech. It's obvious they want us to have the old, weaker gear so we'll off ourselves already, but Jay and I don't give a shit.

Jay winks at the hunkiest guy in our unit as we step out, and I drop my tinted helmet visor so I can silent-laugh in peace. I've been standing guard for Jay during his sexcapades with various men, and I don't mind. He might as well get some final pleasure in.

Protecting him from rampant homophobes is the least I could do. I single-handedly ruined his life.

"Tonight's target?" I ask as Jay returns to my side.

"Bro. That's not funny. I'm holding a danger stick right now. I wouldn't piss me off if I were you."

I laugh. "I feel bad for the Comms that have to overhear you calling their precious new toys a *danger stick* mission after mission."

"Oh, come on. They probably love it. Everyone loves me."

We hear confirmation in our headsets that our communications members, in fact, don't love it, or love him, and we laugh our asses off.

Just to piss everyone off, we rarely kill anyone we're supposed to. I used to think it was unavoidable, but Jay and I have had a year and a half of hands-on experience. We can trap or subdue anyone or anything in the most impossible circumstances. Everyone's so reliant on their long-range automatics that they can't defend themselves close-range. Their overconfidence allows us to recklessly charge and disarm them no matter what they're holding.

That's exactly what we do this afternoon, and no one in our unit dies. I thought there would be more civilian deaths; we ran into white supremacist Christian extremists this time, bloody crosses on their foreheads and all.

Civil War II has boiled down to white supremacists vs. everyone else, but that's hardly a fair summary. White supremacists are the ones that can access the "best" ammunition—and the only ones who mow down swaths of civilians in blatant genocide. It's them destroying society while making themselves out as victims, there's no "versus" about it. They know they have no consequences in a country that caters to them. The Departments are biased toward them too. I think the DoTD recruits them; they're perfect brainwashing fodder. People like that think they're God's only favorite and will do anything to prove it.

"Bro!" Jay yells, gathering my attention across the empty field.

He's next to what looks like an abandoned barn, splintering into swordlike fragments and miraculously upright. My senses heighten. Something tells me Jay isn't safe there. No one has swept the barn yet.

I jog to a speaking distance, but Jay still yells, "There's fucking *chickens* here, bro!"

I laugh. "Bro! No way!"

"Bro."

"...Aren't you gonna have to eat them eventually, though? On your farm?"

Jay flings up his tinted visor to shoot me a glare, scooping up a chicken. "Don't threaten my new son. I'm going *vegan* after this, bro."

"Bro... I literally could *not* imagine that. Plus, that chicken is a girl."

"Uh... He's trans."

"Oh." I turn to the chicken. "Sorry, little bro."

Jay nods at the chicken as if he's listening. "He says he doesn't forgive you."

I laugh. "Add him to the list."

Jay eyes me but doesn't comment further. He releases the chicken into the air, quickly realizing chickens can't fly and apologizing profusely.

Then our in-ear communications disconnect.

Jay and I rip out our trackers habitually, both in our arms and helmets.

He meets my eyes, hiding his fear behind a smile before snapping his tinted visor down. "So, what's next to add to your life dream?"

Planes hum in the distance, so Jay makes a run for the barn.

He shouts over his shoulder. "I've got the chickens in my barn, a hot fiancé, three sports cars, a mansion, and a job where I don't have to fucking kill anyone for a living. You've gotta give me something new this time, man!"

My instincts are still on high alert and sending me huge red flags about that barn, especially considering the plane's trajectory. I catch Jay by his armored vest collar, thrusting him backward.

"My dream—" I say, sprinting away from the barn at top speed. "Is still the same." Jay effortlessly catches up to me, groaning in annoyance. "I just want to marry someone I love—" We jump a half-collapsed wooden fence. "And live a quiet life with them."

"Bro," Jay huffs, overtaking me. "Your dream is starting to sound boring as fu—"

The first bombs drop in the distance, so I tackle Jay to the ground. "Yes—" I rip out armfuls of three-foot-tall weeds to lay over our bodies. "*Boring* is the point."

Praying to what I'm convinced is a non-existent God that the planes can't see us from overhead, I flatten against Jay's chest, wrapping my armored arms around his head to protect him.

The weeds work.

A few silent minutes pass without ear-splitting blasts in the distance, but we know better than to stand right away. Jay lifts his head from beneath me to catch a quick peek, looking over my shoulder.

"Nooo," he whines. "My chickens, bro! The barn's totaled!"

"What?! They even got the fucking chickens?"

"Yeah, man!"

Jay and I burst into wild laughter.

Then I pause, wondering who's listening. "You think they still can't hear us on the mics?"

"Doubt it. Probably not for another thirty minutes. Wait—" Jay raises my tinted visor and grips my helmet, looking into my stinging eyes. "Bro… Are you gonna cry over my *chickens?!*"

I sob against Jay's shoulder, half-laughing and half-crying. "Yeah. They didn't deserve to die, either."

He slinks his gloved hands beneath my helmet, hushing me between spurts of laughter. "You're sweet, kid."

"I'm not…"

He lifts my second visor, wiping my eyes. Then he covers my helmet camera with his palm, planting a heavy kiss onto my lips.

I don't know why my two best friends have been so tempted to kiss me platonically throughout my life, but I'm finding Jay's new habit especially confusing. He thinks I fit the "demisexual" description pretty well, and I agree with him. But then it took me even longer to understand why I find him so romantically attractive in a non-platonic way, dare I say sexually attractive.

The only other person I've felt this consumingly attracted to was Emmalee, so I knew I couldn't be *only* attracted to men. But I've always felt someone like me didn't "count." I never explored who I was alongside my best friends as they came out, and maybe a part of me was scared of what the consequences could be if I did. That maybe, if I looked too closely, I might find something I'd regret—or that in being attracted to men, what if that meant I enjoyed Sumner's "attention?"

The thought makes my guts curdle, tempting me to shut down every last emotion and pretend I'm incapable of love.

Yet there has been no denying the heavy pit growing in my stomach, standing watch outside Jay's door at night.

I pull back, looking into his ruby brown eyes.

He smirks. "*That* got you to stop crying."

Emmalee and I have no chance together, and Jay and I might die any minute, so I think I'll finally ask him tonight.

"What is it? You're not saying anything," Jay whispers.

Or maybe I'll ask him now.

I muffle Jay's helmet mic with my thick glove, and he quickly does the same for mine, getting the message; in case the signal reconnects, what I'm about to say can't be heard by the Departments.

Although, I don't know if I'm afraid of the DoTD's physical punishments anymore. Saying the truth aloud to Jay's curious, sweet gaze is what scares me the most. What if I tear us apart, making him hurt even worse than he does every day? Maybe I should keep the status quo—protect him from the broken disaster I am.

But then it hits me: how badly Jay needs these nights of comfort with other men, and how none of it seems to fill his soul.

What if we die before he realizes he's always been loved?

With a shaky breath, I soften my voice to the faintest whisper. "Do you like me?"

Jay is miraculously speechless, his eyes widening. "I— What?"

"Because I love you like a best friend, but this is also nice. And we're going to die, anyway, so I might as well be honest: you're ridiculously attractive, and I feel closer to you than I've felt with anyone. I think I like you. More than a friend. For a long time."

For the first time since we've become official combat partners, Jay's eyes well up. "Why didn't you say that sooner?"

My heart pangs. "I'm sorry. I'm so ridiculous. I know people who are bi, but I didn't think *I* could be bi because I was told I was straight and I do like girls. And—"

"Niko, you don't have to explain *that*."

"I know, but I'm sorry. I've been doing everything I've been told for so long that I didn't think to question myself. But thanks to you, I finally got a chance. We're ending the cycle—*all* of them—right?"

Jay readjusts his grip on my head, sinking into my gloved touch as I dry his tears. "Right." His lips quiver, and it tugs on my heart. "So I can finally tell you I *really* don't want you to die? Because I really like you too."

"Jay—" My voice cuts short with a hitch. We're both crying now. "I don't want you to die, either."

I gather the courage to kiss him, myself. His fresh stubble brushes against my chin, and I lean into his weighty lips kissing me back.

For a few seconds, I'm elated. Convinced everything will be okay. Our feverish desperation to cram in every touch we can muster brings me right back down. This is it for us. It's not the start of something, it's the end of everything.

Jay flips me onto my back, reversing our position. At first, I panic at the mercy of a man's control. Even after all this time, I'm still broken.

Jay pauses, slowing his approach as he draws me close. He removes our helmets—not ideal, but the bombs have already passed, so our eardrums won't need protection. And more importantly, neither of us cares about getting reprimanded anymore.

Whispering into my ear, Jay cradles me to him. "Don't feel pressured by me, Ni. I know you're afraid of being touched."

My heart flinches, unsure if he's joking. But I have a feeling he's not. Sumner stalks us too frequently for Jay to not know anymore.

"I know someone broke your trust, but I won't," he whispers, pressing his nose into mine. "Ever."

I cling to him, tears rolling down my cheeks and into my ears. Whether he knows the depth of his words or not, no one has helped me carry this weight before. My debt to him grows.

"Can I?" His eager fingers pry up my vest's edge.

I laugh through my nerves, looking around us at the empty field and pushing our helmets farther away. "Only if I can too."

Jay strips his gloves and makes his way down to my waist, but I don't panic. His heavy touch is all I can focus on or care about, entranced by him. I have an urgent need to relish in our last moments, soaking up every second with him.

Jay is now the second person to show me sex doesn't have to

be violent. But midway through, we're forced to pull ourselves together and run back to the van, giggling like absolute dorks.

"Fourteen!" Our Commanding Officer calls me out directly.

"Yes, Sir."

"What the fuck is in your hair?"

I scrub at my fuzzy, shaved head, realizing Jay *really* helped me enjoy myself, embedding the entire back of my uniform and hair with crushed weeds.

"We hid in the weeds, Sir." I glance at Jay's uniform.

He eyes us up and down, analyzing Jay's covered back to match mine. After an agonizing silence, he says, "Nice work. You're the only survivors."

We sit across from each other in silence the whole empty van ride back.

I realize there's nothing we could've done to save anyone else in time since we were so spread out, but I don't understand why we're here at this point. Not just from a practical standpoint.

Why is *this* what we came into this world to do? What the fuck was my soul thinking, agreeing to this life, and how could anyone relish in a higher power that lets them live just to die a horrible death like this? I don't understand anything about life anymore. I'm a helpless newborn wobbling naively towards a hopeless future, setting myself up to be hurt.

And I am hurt. Even with Jay's comfort, life feels irreparable.

We can't hold each other together anymore.

I can laugh off our deaths all day, but when I'm alone in my own head every night, I really don't want to die. I don't want this to be the end.

I don't want this to be me.

CHAPTER 15

Emmalee

A dark presence stalks my nightmares: a black fuzz that hurts to the touch. Whenever it arrives, something terrible is about to happen.

All week, I've dreamt I'm lying in front of Sumner Hospital, staring at its glowing red sign. The longer I stare, the more I find it weird: why is a covert government faction collaborating with a private hospital?

But then I remember the United States government has run on pharmaceutical money for decades. With that thought, the black fuzz burns my skin off until I wake up, panting.

So I research the name "Sumner."

Dr. Charles Sumner owns an entire hospital branch in his name, but he didn't start with the hospitals; he started with pharmaceuticals. Everything leads to three basic facts: one, he owns a hospital in every major US city. Two, he owns Sumner Pharmaceuticals. And three, it's an inherited family business.

But that's *it*.

It's strange—someone so influential with minimal information online. The only other thing I can find is a financial tabloid gushing about his business savvy and "charming smile," the article climaxing with his sponsored drug advertisement.

He's the one connected to the Departments, I know it. Searching him online is useless.

It's only 10 a.m., but my head hurts too much to stay awake. The second I nap on the couch, the black fuzz gnaws on my spine until I lose every sense except touch. The presence is so invasive that I jolt awake, shaking like I'm experiencing physical trauma.

I think it doesn't want me to know the truth.

But I don't have absolute proof Sumner is involved.

At my pitiful rank, my Department database is pointless, only displaying my manager and immediate co-workers. My parents still overwork themselves, so they haven't asked me to visit outside of birthdays and holidays, but they're the closest people I know with DoH databases.

I think it's time I visit home.

Dad buys my movie marathon excuse. On his next day off, we binge the sci-fi trilogy we rewatch ritualistically. I know it by heart, but when an alien stabs the main character with a glowing, neon syringe, I flinch.

Dad warily chuckles. "Are you okay, Emma?"

I laugh it off. "Sorry—empath."

Dad buys that too.

For the rest of the movie, I have to force my enjoyment. The campy sci-fi feels more realistic than my ridiculous theory, but I *believe* it. Sumner is drugging people, and no one seems to care.

Am I losing touch with reality?

While Dad's in the bathroom, I open his database app and search the Department of Health's member list. With "Dr. C—" alone, "Dr. Charles Sumner" appears at the top: the highest rank.

That's expected by now, but I'm finding it hard to breathe. The guy's *name* has bad vibes, and it's hard to ignore my empathic senses.

I don't want to tap on Sumner's name and save the search in Dad's history, but I don't need to; as I scroll further, I find my proof.

It also stations Sumner under the Department of Tactical Defense:

```
Chief Executive Officer of
Pharmaceutical Research.
```

Backspacing my search and closing the app, I return Dad's phone to its exact, original position and focus on slowing my tight breath. I don't even know Sumner, yet he's suffocating me.

The bathroom lock snaps, and I gasp. Thankfully, Dad's too busy whisper-rehearsing something to notice.

When we meet eyes, he smiles. "Don't go in there. I've contracted a dangerous case of *feces magma.*"

He giggles at his own dad joke, so I burst out laughing, grateful for the distraction.

But a piece of my heart hurts to look at him. What the hell has *Dad* done in the DoH?

After the last movie, we cook our favorite gluten-free mac and cheese recipe, but I can't eat. My stomach burns like it's on fire.

I curl into a ball on my childhood bathroom floor, unable to move or speak. Dad's energy spikes with worry, and bitter nostalgia strikes; I hate feeling like a burden. I hate losing control over my health. I hate thinking Dad could take my independence away, blaming my worsening symptoms on my living alone.

But Dad doesn't question me. He covers me with a blanket, kissing my head goodnight.

How am I supposed to hate my loving father once I find out what he's done?

All night, I study the old bathtub caulking, too afraid to close my eyes and find the black presence.

I'm assuming Niko was recently injected when he told me to avoid "*new* injections," and I never saw him look so sick. But my symptoms have also worsened ever since Niko left—and I had to go to the hospital. Sure, my emotional heart was A-bombed with his loss, but something else is wrong with me. Something that hasn't left.

But I wasn't injected in the hospital.

I don't know why I feel so sick.

Civilians like Clarity aren't Department brats, but she's extra sick too. We've joked we have the same symptoms, yet no one can figure out why. That's not funny anymore.

Scrolling through social media, I'm horrified; *everyone* has the same dark circles under their eyes. Like they hardly slept.

Something is making *everyone* ill.

I don't want to believe it. Are my parents involved with Sumner, or is he running his own sealed-off unit? Do the papers I'm filing at my shitty desk job contain the answers?

I spend weeks zoning out, watching my back. Avoiding work and taking extra sick days.

Then the DoH job opening list has a new addition:

```
Requesting applications for an
Empathic Assistant to assist in
research development under top CEO,
Dr. Charles Sumner.

Job requirements consist of:

  · Prior experience in the
  Department of Health.

  · No charges on personal records
  for Department misdemeanors.

  · An enthusiastic interest in
  exploring exciting new fields of
  medical research.
```

I was doing a decent enough job preventing myself from vomiting on the tablet screen at the sight of his name, but the "medical research" line inspires a genuine gag.

Everyone chronically ill knows experimental drugs are a long shot. Anyone interested in "exciting" medical research is only excited to see their name on the patent for a mildly successful drug.

So I apply for the job.

Maybe I've lost my mind, but if my ludicrous theory is true, I want to take Dr. Sumner down from the inside.

I've had enough of people thinking I'm a failure. I dropped out of the Department private school at ten because my parents were scared of me being used as an empath—especially when I'd experience every second of death alongside the people I'd be ordered to kill, leaving me to writhe until their last breath. But without my empathic abilities, the Departments couldn't see how a chronically ill *girl* could be worth anything.

After I grew up a bit, I could see it was a blessing not to work in the Department of Tactical Defense with my best friends. My parents made the right decision, but a part of me still sees myself as a below-average failure, growing up labeled as such by powerful adults. Not just once. Time after time, all because I was disabled.

I want to do something substantial, not be forced to sit on the sidelines while my friends die. I want to *actually* help Niko, Jay, and Lilith, and everyone else like them. We were raised as weaponized profit, and someone needs to put a stop to it.

I'm someone Dr. Sumner would least suspect.

Within three days, the DoH requests a formal interview. My interviewer is a quiet woman, her features as fierce and stealthy as her emotions. I only know her as "Amanda," and she asks unusually basic questions for a Department position.

That night, I get the job.

Even if a long line of superiors precedes me, that means Dr. Sumner, or whoever makes decisions for him, had to sign off on *me*.

I start having heavy panic attacks—heavy enough that I'm terrified I'm about to die alone in my apartment. I haven't used my emergency inhaler in years, but I recognize the feeling when my bronchial tubes snap shut. My body burns, losing oxygen by the second as I dig through my bedside drawer, but my vibrating hands drop my emergency inhaler. I scramble across the carpet for it, but by the time it reaches my lips, my airway is too restricted to suck in more than a baby's breath of medicine. After the second puff, I watch my lips turn purple in my bedroom mirror, my eyes bulging wider than I've ever seen them. The millisecond I ditch my prescribed dose, sucking in a third puff, it grants me back my life.

I suck in a heaving, clear breath.

And I think.

Sumner has no idea of my intentions. No one does.

But why does it feel like my health is deteriorating more than ever? Normally, I only need to use my emergency inhaler during bad colds.

For now, I can breathe. I press my forehead against the cold mirror, and I inhale. Exhale. That's all I can do.

Until the next morning—my first substantial shift at Sumner Hospital.

It's fairly simple: I visit patients, write down how they say they're feeling, and note what I feel empathically.

But I never make it so simple. I hold their hands, encouraging them that they're not alone—until my manager scolds me and ushers me to my next patient.

I'm not sure if I'm helping or harming by spreading false hope, but for some, I'm their only visitor. *All* of Sumner's patients are bedridden, forced to spend every day alone in a blank, echoey hospital room.

The loneliest patients disappear first. I have to assume they died or were transferred to the ICU; their charts are confiscated, and no one explains why. It's only been one week, but I've seen five vanish this way.

I couldn't feel worse. Waves of others' trauma rub off on me a bit more every shift.

I'm used to illness, but this is different. Every gaunt smile peels a piece off my heart, knowing the pain it hides.

Something is eating away at our hope.

By the second week, I sob so hard every night that it triggers daily asthma attacks—an extreme shift from my usual trigger-focused attacks—and my doctor prescribes a daily maintenance inhaler. But the inhalers never fully work, leaving me with a subtle tightness in my chest all day long. I'm slowly drowning.

One could argue I'm misreading Dr. Sumner. That he's a good guy taking on severely ill patients no other doctors will—since they don't want a liability on their hands. But that's a flaming sack of bullshit.

This is not for the people. This is for the money.

When patients complain of dangerous symptoms, they're sent other heavy-duty medications… made by Sumner Pharmaceuticals. Then *those* medications create side effects that force patients to pay for *more* medications… made by Sumner Pharmaceuticals. Insurance covers none of it. When did they ever?

This process is familiar to disabled people like me, but these days, it's even more extreme. Now that "Civil War II" broke out over white supremacy, it doesn't matter if the literal warzone is in the Midwest—our hospital overflows with hate crime victims until we hardly have space to walk. No one has time to address their health when we're all just trying to *survive*.

People rely on Sumner's experimental drug trial compensation, so they keep coming back. I can tell they hope to heal in the process, but I haven't seen a single case improve. The fatalities are at a whopping 40%, to which I've been told, "Well, 60% live, and most of them would die, anyway." But would they?

Even with this disgusting behavior, I can't dethrone Sumner. Under federal and state law, he's not doing anything wrong. Even if he was, his company funds multiple politicians, granting him a free pass.

And his patients sign his experimental drug contract. I'm not sure anyone reads it—or if they can with how tiny the text is— but the side effects are written out, including death.

Everyone says the same thing: this is normal. "All powerful drugs have scary side effects."

And honestly, it *is* normal. Sumner or not, pharmaceuticals have handed out "treatments" with fatal side effects for centuries. For some reason, everyone has accepted that as okay.

But I won't.

I'm ending this cycle of suffering, even if I have to do it alone.

CHAPTER 16

Emmalee

"Will you be my girlfriend?" Andre asked one day from across the room, throwing me my shirt to put back on.

"Oh. Sure. Okay."

And just like that, I got myself into deeper shit.

I'm sitting across the table from him, my cheek resting on my palm, with a dinner plate that's been empty for about eight minutes. He's glued to his phone, wiping his nose every so often and sniffling instead of fully blowing. I've tried clearing my throat, shifting positions, and even blowing *my* nose for the hell of it, but I've settled on glaring for the past… three minutes. No reaction whatsoever.

But we have fun in bed, I guess. At least *he* does.

"Oh, by the way." Andre finally looks up from his phone. He doesn't care that I'm glaring and stares me dead in the eyes. Maybe he thinks that's just how my face looks with how much he brings it out. "You're running out of condoms."

I sit back, crossing my arms with a sigh. "Okay… I'll steal some more. I can only take one once a month or less from work without someone noticing the stash is *dwindling away*."

"Dwin-dindl—?" He raises an eyebrow. "I have no idea what you're saying."

"Sorry." I wince. The Departments cheated so many of these guys out of education, and I keep accidentally doing this to him. "I meant I don't want someone to notice the hospital stash is slowly disappearing."

"Gotcha. Anyway, I was gonna ask you if you want me to pull out instead. You know, spare you the trouble of stealing, and all."

I burst out laughing. Until I realize I'm the only one who finds this funny. "Oh, fuck. You're serious right now."

He tenses. "Why are you being so rude?"

"Are you kidding me? Pulling out basically doesn't work."

He scoffs. "How do *you* know? Have you tried?"

"Oh, my God… No, Andre! I know because I know how my body and your body works. I've read all about it. You don't know if anything will travel down early, or be left inside after the first time, or plain come out too early, or—"

He shrugs, returning to his phone. "Suit yourself."

"Just look it up. Please."

He doesn't respond.

I grab our plates, toss them into the dishwasher, and lock myself into the bathroom.

I wish I could shit this whole relationship into this toilet.

Clarity laughs at me over text, sending me a photo of herself crying from laughter in response to Andre's suggestion.

I laugh a little. It *is* pretty funny, in a way. I totally brought this on myself by keeping him around.

Washing my hands, I find Andre still on his phone. Marching up to him, I grab him by the cheeks and kiss him.

"Whoa, hey." He holds me by the waist with a smile. "What was that for?"

"Just trying to get you to look at your girlfriend instead of your phone."

He smiles. "Okay, fine. Are you tired?"

"Yeah. Are you?"

He nods, heading to the restroom.

He's not the worst person in the world, just not the best. But I'm a little worried about potentially breaking up. He can be stormy, and I'm nervous being here alone when I do it. Dumping him in front of Clarity seems like it could be taken offensively, so I'll have to suck it up and do it myself someday soon.

Especially because something else has been eating me up inside.

I received an anonymous note under my doormat:

GET OUT OF IT WHILE YOU CAN.
       -A FELLOW WOMAN

If that's not a *bucket* of red flags, I don't know what is.

But I don't have anyone else to spend time with. Andre hasn't done anything dangerously wrong besides irritating me, so maybe he's grown up a bit between this relationship and his last. He just had his 20th birthday, and I know I'm far different at 19, even from when I was 18.

He crawls into bed next to me, tucking me into his chest. I'd really miss having someone to sleep beside like this. When he's not sleeping over, my insomnia and nightmares are far worse. Now I know it's because of Sumner, not PTSD.

My heart throbs, thinking of Niko's warning. How if I actually used my head, I could've sleuthed everything earlier and helped him find a way out of the Departments' hands. Before it was too late.

I've been too nervous to ask Andre if I could search for Niko in his DoTD database, but maybe I could just ask *him* to research Niko's status for me. I'm his girlfriend, after all. Maybe I'm too afraid to hear the news that Niko died. Or maybe I know that question could set off a bomb in my weird relationship.

Luckily, Andre seems neutral tonight despite our bickering at the table.

"Can't sleep?" He whispers.

I sigh, turning onto my back. "No."

He rubs my hips to coax me, but I scoot them away so he doesn't get the wrong idea.

"Hey, I have a question," I say.

He sighs. "You don't wanna get some goodnight-exercise in?"

I laugh, rolling my eyes at that painful phrase. "We already did earlier. I'm exhausted. Let's save our stash."

"Okay…" He mutters. "What's your question?"

I bite my lip, looking into his hazel eyes. Running my fingers through his buzzed hair to keep him relaxed, I whisper, "It's kind of a favor, actually." He blinks a few times, waiting for me to continue. "I haven't heard from a friend who was deployed. I have no idea if he's still alive, and I'd really like to know. Do you have clearance to look people up?"

He props himself on one elbow, thinking. "Probably not. But maybe I've heard of him. What's his name?"

"Nikolai Blackwood," I whisper. His name sets my heart into motion.

Andre's eyes widen. "The *Wolf?*" He laughs. "You're worried he *died?* So you haven't heard much about him, clearly."

I can't speak. If I heard Andre correctly, Niko isn't dead.

"That crazy bastard is still on the front lines," Andre continues, crushing my hopes for Niko's survival. "People are betting he has someone on the inside covering for him and Olivas, his combat partner. But in my opinion, man, he's fucking bulletproof or some classified, supernatural alien thing—those are always creepy as fuck. Anyway, if someone was really vouching for him, they'd use him in the top DoTD unit. Everyone knows the front-liners are new weapons test subjects. If they're keeping him there, he's as good as dead."

That kills me to hear. I try to say something ordinary, but all that comes out is, "He's… alive now, though?"

"Yeah..?" He eyes me, confused. Then a spark of recognition flashes across his face. "Shit, that's right. You guys were friends when we were kids, huh?"

I nod, pressing my knuckles to my mouth.

"Whoops. Didn't think that one through. I told Commander Blackwood I had no idea what she was talking about when she approached me because you never mentioned him before. I figured you didn't know him."

I shoot upright. "What?! *Clara Blackwood* was looking for *me?*"

"Uh, yeah?"

I'm speechless. Have I totally fucked everything up by distancing myself from both of our families? But as Andre's shoulders rise, I have something more pressing to deal with.

"What is he to you anyway?" He grips my thigh.

"Hey, it's okay, Andre. He's just a childhood best friend. I thought he died, so I was upset."

He jumps out of bed. "But you're *still* upset. I told you multiple times now, he didn't die. Why are you so obsessed with him?"

"H-he's my best friend! Of course I'm worried about—"

"*Best* friend now? You're in love with him, aren't you?" He snaps his shirt on.

"What?! He's been gone for like two years, Andre. I'm not in love with him!"

He grinds his jaw. "You're not *now*, but you *were*, huh."

I stare into his frantic eyes. If this were Niko or Lilith, I'd tell the truth, no matter their emotional state. "When I was a kid, sure. But that was long before you and I— Wait, Andre?!"

As he stomps away, I can still hear him talking to himself. He makes sure of it.

"In love with the fucking Wolf," he hisses. "Stupid bitch."

He storms out of my apartment, slamming the front door. The walls shake with his exit's impact, and I'm left alone in the dark.

CHAPTER 17

Niko

Last night, Jay pinned me against the bed with a thousand kisses. Today, he's pinning my blood-splattered face against an abandoned, flipped truck, trying to force some sense back into my brain.

I have a nasty habit of running into crossfire. Yesterday, it was for a fallen old man, seconds before he was run over. Last week, it was for a limping dog. That's what pisses Jay off the most: risking my life for people or animals who will soon die.

Anyone "inferior" looks the same to white supremacists, an "easy target" to prove a point. Authority figures aren't willing to turn their backs on their white supremacist fan base to admit the truth: Civil War II is a business strategy worth our "inferior" lives.

Saving civilians only extends their suffering, but I can't help myself. Jay and I argued over it many times on the front lines, eventually clearing our biggest misunderstanding: this isn't a hero complex, this is a scramble to retain the last of my humanity.

Jay understands. Genocidal horror, day after day, eats away at Jay too, although he'd never admit it—leading to my misunderstanding about his paranoia's severity.

We're in a new type of love, but we've always been in love, even if it was initially platonic. It runs deep. Maybe too deep; Jay's vicious perseverance of my life has only escalated. He's always seen his job as stopping me from hurting myself, even if that means forcing me into submission.

At first, I created a false expectation that this aggressiveness would change with romance added in. We clarified that misunderstanding right away; it couldn't be avoided in combat the very next morning. But I've since struggled to compartmentalize Jay—where his aggression fits into his love, and how that differs from Sumner's violating aggression.

I don't know if it's the blood on my face, reminiscent of the first death I witnessed when Lilith's bullet whizzed over my head, or the now-dead man in the street that looks startlingly similar to my father—the one Jay wouldn't let me save. Either way, Jay's forceful hands mean something different to my brain than the truth of who he is. I know him, I trust him, and I love him. But he's supposed to be my boyfriend, and most people don't enjoy their boyfriends pinning them down against their will.

Maybe I'm way too fucking sensitive. Jay says he loves it about me, but I'm struggling to stop my mind from seeing him as a threat in his furious arms, rightfully upset with me for almost getting myself killed. He misunderstands this as me trying to escape his grasp to continue my recklessness, when really, *my* PTSD turns me into a petrified rabbit, and I'm straining to flee.

My heart thunders so loudly that my vision vibrates, and Jay isn't seeing it. He couldn't save that man either, and *his* PTSD is a guilt monster that we can't figure out how to control at its peak. It morphs him into everything we hate. Usually, we rough it out by sparring—like Mom expected me to need. Jay takes complete responsibility for any out-of-line behaviors afterward, insisting mental health never excuses aggression. Although, I've never felt he crossed the line, especially considering we've agreed ahead of time to work it out this way.

But after his tenderness last night, our usual struggle catches me off guard. I'm aware of my misunderstanding, but I can't stop my mind from going there. From seeing the ways I've been pinned down by Sumner, struggling beneath my obligation to the hands on me.

I must be making a scene. Jay tears my helmet off, and I misunderstand it as further aggression, cowering into the truck's wheelhouse. I watch him rip our communications from our helmets so the DoTD doesn't have to see me at my most vulnerable, but it doesn't register. My brain sees an angry man. And not just any man: I'm writhing on the ground in front of the only man I thought I could trust. It's not until Jay kisses me that I realize I can't breathe; he's using our old tactic to shock me out of hyperventilation with a surprise kiss. But it couldn't have come at a worse time, further painting in memories of Sumner I've kept hidden under a deadbolt.

Jay feels horrible for it. He's no longer furious, his face so contorted that I swear we've aged twenty years in the three we've been frontlined.

For as long as I can remember, he's been the one that makes me laugh, so I never wanted to make him sad. But Jay never wanted to make me afraid. I think we just shattered our own hearts.

For the first time, he doesn't reach out to comfort me. It shocks the flashback from my system. I lunge for Jay, cradling him on the crumbling sidewalk, but he doesn't return my embrace. Maybe it's because I'm wheezing uncontrollably and he thinks he's the cause, so I force my lungs to take slower breaths. I kiss him, trying to force us to fit back together. He doesn't kiss me back.

Jay waits until we're home to cry.

It's a silent cry, and that almost makes it worse. I don't know what to do or what to say, a flaw Jay always remedied with his boisterous hilarity. But tonight, he won't even look at me.

"I can't be what you need," Jay whispers.

Everything in me wants to disagree. He taught me how to understand myself in so many ways, for so many years. I'm positive he's vital to me, and I to him. But I think I understand what he's saying. I'm not the *boyfriend* he needs either. As we meet eyes, I know we're breaking up, and we'll probably be better for it.

We excel as work partners, pushing each other to survive even if we have to get aggressive to save each other's lives. While Jay also wants that firmness in a romantic partnership, I think I *need* peace. He needs me to shove him out of the emotional crossfire to safety, but I need to feel safe to let myself love.

I try to let him finally be the one that cries. He's whimpering, grieving us, but I don't want it to end like this. I kiss him back into the pillows, massaging his body into relieving the emotional pain. But I'm scared I'm misreading him again and he'll leave me afterward. I can't resist being the one that cries.

Jay smiles, sucking back snot. "There's my crybaby best friend."

Being friendzoned on his lap forces a wet laugh out of me. He nuzzles into my mouth, kissing me as softly as he can. I know it's the last kiss we'll share, but as long as he still calls me *his* best friend, I can manage whatever we become.

Before I can realize I'm still clinging to him, Jay strokes my arms into relaxation. "I'm leaving the boyfriend *label* behind us, but I'm *never* leaving *you*."

Relief floods me. I hadn't realized how obligated I felt to please him, but Jay always knows how to free me. He must see it on my face. Jay huddles into my chest, smiling despite his shaking shoulders.

We hold each other all night, whispering reassurances of our relabeled companionship. I've never loved him more.

CHAPTER 18

Niko

Dr. Sumner is so obsessed with me that he's living in a bunker out here, in the middle of asscrack nowhere. Now I never get a break.

Jay and I have our own bunker; they gave up trying to move us into a complete unit since the rest of ours kept dying. We're our own unit now, stationed somewhere in Montana where the Department of Health can experiment on outcast Department of Tactical Defense members in peace.

Our place is a cramped cube. We can't own anything other than the clothes on our backs, a single spare uniform, and a toothbrush, so we've secretly collected small bits from every mission to make it feel more like home: A tire rim bolt that popped Jay in the forehead when an SUV blew up once—thankfully, Jay was wearing his helmet. A surviving chicken feather from the abandoned barn, almost a year back. A tiny plastic dinosaur some kid handed me when I disobeyed orders, yanking him from the crossfire.

A bunch of useless items that only mean something to us. History we won't be able to pass on.

We trade off storing them in our pockets each time we leave the bunker, in case one of us dies and they excavate our room. Maybe, by some impossible circumstance, we'll live to tell the tales.

Jay grips my wrist, stopping me at the door.

"I have work," I say.

"I know, but…"

Soulmates must be real, but not in the way people think. I've realized we can have multiple, and not all soulmates are romantic. Jay is one of my soulmates.

I can't lie or hide from him anymore, and I don't want to. So as Jay begs me not to return to Sumner in the gentlest way he can manage, I can't look at him. I've never felt more connected to Jay, which makes my work with Sumner even more agonizing. But I can't avoid my second job if I want us both to live. I won't make that mistake twice.

"Let's… I don't know. Run away," Jay says.

I meet his thoughtful doe eyes. We burst into laughter.

Running away is childish. Impossible. Especially if we want to live. The only way that'd work is if the Department *wants* us to run away. But we're abominable creations they took too far—their responsibility to destroy.

"How about I—" Jay stops himself.

I know what he's thinking. He wants to go instead of me.

I've told Jay everything: how if I don't indulge Sumner, he'll threaten to kill our unit members or family. How Sumner was the one who deployed us when I finally disobeyed him, as well as the one shielding us from assassination. Now that his experiments are changing our entire government's course, Sumner ranks higher than my parents. He can have *anything* he wants.

He experiments on Jay and me together sometimes, but I think he gets bored with medical-only experimentation. High-maintenance is an understatement. He's drained my entire soul, drinking it all for himself.

It's confusing, but I feel like this is my burden to bear—protecting people I love by submitting to Sumner—and I don't know who I am without it. I hate that thought, but that doesn't stop me from feeling its weight.

I absolutely disgust myself.

I wrap my arms around Jay. "I *never* want you to go through this. It's fine. I'm used to it now."

He returns my embrace, twice as snug. "Are you going to black it out again?"

"Yes. Every time."

"Good. I can't stand that you have to—"

It feels like I blink, and I'm in Sumner's office. The clock sets my head straight; two hours have passed since I was talking to Jay.

I don't know what I survived, but I survived it.

"Oh, you're back." Sumner tightens his disheveled tie in the mirror. "How do you feel?"

I glare at him through the mirror after getting a good look at myself, bruised and exhausted. "I can't feel anything yet."

He smiles. "Are you sure you feel *nothing?*"

I smile too. It's not a happy smile. "Are you asking me if I still have a deep urge to kill you?"

"Yes."

"Of course I do." I stare deep into his eyes—a grating blue. "Always."

"Then why haven't you?"

He faces me. My whole body freezes. I almost slip back into nothingness, but I can't. I have to remain coherent if I want to walk home tonight.

"I asked you a question, *Nikolai.*"

I have no words. His white hair, white grin, and hollow, white cheekbones order my brain to submit. To evacuate control. Because I'm not mine to control. I'm his.

He laughs. "Look at you! I haven't even come near you. Calm down, kid."

Sumner sticks wire after wire onto my head, plugging me into a machine that analyzes brain activity. I try to convince myself he's kind sometimes, just to survive it. He must be with the gentle way he's placing the probes onto my head. ...Or maybe he just cares about his equipment.

"I'll answer for you. You *can't* kill me, Nikolai—" He takes a few steps back to double-check he placed every wire correctly. "Because you need me."

I nod mindlessly. Dissent isn't an option.

He pats my shoulder.

"Did you give me a sleeping pill already?"

His eyebrows furrow. "Yes. Thirty minutes ago, remember?"

I believe him. That explains why I'm ready to slip into nothingness—or maybe a nightmare.

I don't "dream" anymore; something Sumner does worsens the Chronic Nightmare Syndrome. But these aren't regular nightmares. What I can't explain is how every nightmare seems to be in the same location. Not necessarily the same room, or even the same general area. It has the essence of the same *world*—no, *dimension*. One with different universal laws. Which makes Sumner and me infants, fumbling around and unaware of our significance—or lack of it.

I close my eyes early this time, hoping he'll let information slip. He knows I block things out, so he'll talk my ear off, pretending I'm pleasant company. Sometimes I'll manage to catch a bit before I fall asleep, slowly gathering pieces over time.

One day, I'll sabotage him with his own pet project. End the cycle.

"I think you'll be the ticket, *Nikolai*," he says. "Maybe we can go home soon."

This rouses a hopeful mumble from me, but it's nothing more than a quick groan. Dammit, I'm already drowsier than I thought. I don't catch anything else he says.

My dream world stabilizes.

It's the same as it looked yesterday.

I'm in Sumner's bunker. It's startlingly vivid, maybe even clearer than my drugged, awake mind could see. He's not here, but I'm still tied to a chair like I was minutes ago.

I free myself with a shrug. The loose ropes are a psychological boundary, even in real life. But *he* put him there, so they hold weight. I'm truly his domesticated wolf.

I do what I'm supposed to, approaching his front door. The knob chills my fingertips, and for a moment, it's unclear if I actually fell asleep.

Swinging the door open, I find a swirling black mass buzzing past me just outside the doorway. It spirals around the bunker whenever I dream here, trapping me inside no matter what we change. He wants me to touch this black, smoky substance for as long as possible. I stick my arm out the door, allowing what feels like molten lava to sear my hand.

He wants me to tolerate it for longer this time. To "stop being such a pussy about it." So I do all I know how.

I numb myself out, pushing my entire arm in.

The black mass shifts as my mind shifts. It's like we're playing chase, undulating in unison; I numb, it slows. This development is new and exciting, so I stop numbing out to test if the black mass returns to its typical spiral. To pull myself out of numbness, I pay close attention to my arm. It's covered in bright red, stinging irritation, threatening to claw its way to my throat.

But I'm paying too close of attention.

I haven't let myself feel, really *feel*, in so long that once I finally do, I can't stop. Not until I'm spiraling out of control— and so is the black mass.

My thoughts overcome me, pain erupting from every corner of my life. Pain spurred by everyone I've come across, including myself. I'm buried so deeply in terror that I'm suffocating in silence.

Then something new happens.

The black mass injects itself into my body. It digs and digs, forcing me to writhe on the ground and scratch at my own skin. It wiggles around every intestinal nook, worming through my brain's ridges. My consciousness switches off, reverting to my primal core. Instinct overwhelms me; a desperate need to purge.

I curl up tight and picture it: forcing the black mass out.

The black smoke ejects in every direction, exploding from my back. And it kills, ricocheting off the walls and scorching me all over.

I scream my throat raw, unable to shut off the sensation. The pain is so severe that panic swallows me, making me dart around the room in ways I can't control—a wild animal unleashed from its cage only to discover it's trapped in another one.

The black mass coagulates. I freeze, assessing it for danger. It's taking a human form.

Not just any human form.

That's… me.

But not me. *He* looks demonic, the searing smoke radiating from his eyes as they flit around the room. I've seen people look distorted like this in these nightmares—usually people that died in a way I hate to remember—but I've never seen *myself*.

"Hello!" *That* "me" giggles.

His voice penetrates my ears, daring me to cover them. But my primal brain urges me to hunch down and track his movements, sensing he's plotting something.

I don't know if we're connected somehow, but I can feel it in my blood: *that* "me" wants to kill me. I'm immobilized by it. He struts over, slamming the bunker closed behind me. Despite my panic, I evade him with swift, steady bounds.

At least, I thought I did.

Pinning me off my feet with one hand, he strangles me against the wall. His laugh sounds like nails in a blender, relishing in my struggle.

I'm reeling. How the hell did he catch me? I've spent literal years dodging bullets.

But my shock is another mistake; he grins wider than I ever have, warping his imitation of my cheeks.

I know how to escape him, but—

"But you can't convince yourself to try, I know." His smirk disappears.

I can feel my eyes bugging; I'm running out of air.

"That's because you're only good for one thing."

He wields my favorite combat knife, swirling it around my Adam's apple in gentle circles.

"You're not just a perpetual victim, Ni—"

It's surreal to see a copy of myself digging into my throat, just between the clavicles, splashing hot liquid down my torso and legs as they fall limp. It makes it hurt in more than one way.

He sneers. "You're a useless sex doll. That's all you're good for."

I jolt upright—awake, but greeted by Sumner's exploding grin.

Holding my sweaty, tear-stained cheeks, he kisses my forehead, throwing my head back against the chair. This peppy mood of his always makes me nauseous.

"You did it!" He jabs the monitor with a violent finger, screeching in delight. "You figured it out!"

"What?"

I sit up, squinting past the sleeping pill haze. He fetches another pill, shoving my head back until I give up trying to stay upright. Sumner's bony thumb forces the pill down my throat, and I swallow uncontrollably.

"There's more of you to study now," he whispers. "Do it again."

CHAPTER 19

Emmalee

Andre and I broke up. Well, I've been break-*ing* up with him. Then he comes back, begging for another chance. We've hooked up because of it—he always catches me when I'm agonizingly lonely, and I'm afraid of how he'll react if I reject him too many times—but I'm sick of his tantrums. I can't handle seeing him for more than an hour.

He did leave me with one blessing, however. Thanks to him, I reached out to Clara Blackwood.

She claims she contacted me to "repair things." Knowing her, I seriously doubt that. But I want to know if she can tell me something, *anything* about Niko, so here I am at our rendezvous point, in the middle of Santa Desierto's Downtown Park. Hoping the jet-black SUV swinging by hasn't come to murder me.

I'm ordered inside by a helmeted DoTD unit member, but all she cares to do is wave me into the SUV with a single hand flick. I don't hesitate; I don't have a choice.

As I step in, Commander Clara Blackwoods nods through her rearview mirror's reflection. "Good to see you again, Richards. Thanks for agreeing to meet us here."

Sliding across the black leather backseats, I'm too distracted to answer; the unit member slides in next to me rather than in the front seat with her Commander. Then she pulls off her helmet.

For a second, I wonder if they killed me in the park. Meeting her in the afterlife seems more believable than sitting next to my runaway ex-girlfriend in her mom's SUV.

"Hey, Emma," Lilith mutters, peeking over.

I throw myself at her, knowing she'll catch me. The second she wraps her sturdy arm around my back, I burst into tears like I did the day she left me three years ago. I didn't realize it still hurt so badly.

At first she pats my back, allowing me to cry. But she's holding her breath every few exhales—her thinking breath.

"Why are you so upset?"

Her question leaves my eyes wide and unblinking, especially when I feel how honest her energy is. She has *no* idea what I'm feeling.

But her worried eyes prove she didn't mean to upset me. Actually, she's terrified of it.

She *can't* understand. Trauma hijacked her emotional wiring so severely, she lost more empathy than I realized. I'll have to explain how her sudden disappearance was hurtful, especially without officially breaking up with me, but I'm too overwhelmed to mention it.

"We broke up, right?" She blurts out.

I swallow hard. "Yeah, we did."

Her anxiety spikes, eyes flicking from our hands to the lack of space between us.

I smile, wiping my tears. "We're still friends. I'm just relieved you're still alive."

Lilith softens, patting my shoulder. "I am. Did you get my note?"

"I did. I wanted to believe it meant you were okay."

Lilith settles against the backseat with a slow exhale.

I thought I'd be pissed if I ever saw her again, but in person, it's clear this is the deepest connection level she can manage. More than anything, I'm happy to have one of my best friends back. I can't stop smiling, snuggling up to her sturdy side.

"I thought you might like to see her again," Clara mutters.

"Not true. You thought she wouldn't believe you if you told her alone," Lilith announces.

Clara shoots Lilith a frazzled glare, and I stifle a laugh. This is *exactly* why I love Lilith.

"We're deprogramming traitors instead of executing them, and the Departments have no idea." Lilith tightens her vest straps as if she didn't just drop earth-shattering information. "We thought you might like to join us."

I'm no longer laughing. Lilith never lies, and I know she's not lying, but this *sounds* like the worst lie I've ever heard.

My shoulders tense into a cramp; we're right in front of Clara, the Lionheart executioner, infamous for killing people who say these exact things. I'm not sure if that's why Clara is bulletting through Department roads, forcing unit members to scramble away, or if that's just Clara.

But when guilt permeates Commander Blackwood's smile, I know it's real.

"Well, it's out there now," she chuckles.

For the first time in a long time, I have no idea what to say.

Clara clears her throat. "I know how it sounds, but bear with me. We have our own deprogramming therapists in the DoH's Mental Treatment Center, using the Center's bullshit 'therapy' as a coverup for actual therapy. If traitors accept our underground escape offer, we do everything we can to rebirth them. And if they don't, well…"

"No one's taking a Blackwood threat for granted," Lilith says.

My heart drops. I hoped they meant their executions were also an act, but apparently not.

Overwhelm doesn't begin to describe the marathon my mind races to catch up with their confession—how it recolors everything we've experienced together, and how I'll feel about it once it registers.

Before I can come even close to grasping the situation, Clara clears her throat. "If you join us, we'd send you carefully selected traitors for emotional support. I'll tell you more about it inside."

My jaw gapes as I take odd, short breaths of air. I dig into my purse for my inhaler, just in case.

With Clara's lawless driving, she's already whipping into the DoH parking lot. "Alright girls, say your goodbyes."

My chest tightens, squeezing Lilith closer. "*Excuse* me?"

Lilith flashes the tiniest smile, staring at my fingernails gripping her biceps. "Hmm. I don't think she'll let go of me, Blackwood."

"Well, she has to," Clara says.

For as much as I love them, the Blackwoods might kill me. "This is brutal, Commander. I haven't seen Lili for years, and you think my heart wouldn't have emotional whiplash from just saying 'hi' and 'bye?'"

Clara's shoulders tighten as her energy stiffens in defense, but she doesn't say a word.

I huff, turning to Lilith. "You really aren't coming with us, Lili?"

"I can't." Lilith pats my hand, softening my heart.

Which means it's once again breaking. "Why not? I miss you so much."

"The Department thinks she's our classified 'escapee traitor hunter,'" Clara says. "They want us to keep an appearance that she's nonexistent until she comes to bite. You'll still see each other, but she mainly lives in the forest."

My stomach lurches. Everyone knows the forest kills human life within an hour—a swath of unclaimed land that emits brain-melting electromagnetic radiation.

"How the hell—" I rasp.

"We had someone design a life-saving radiation blocker, creating a true vanishing act," Clara continues. "The Department has promoted us for years, thinking we're ruthless, loyal dogs, leading traitors to rot in the forest. In reality, we've housed a hidden army who hates the Departments as much as us."

The elation in Clara's soul grips my heart—honest, pure joy I've never felt from either of the Blackwood parents. This is real.

I can't stop my tears. At first they're happy, but then a bitter sadness strikes me in the gut, making me shake. This is decades too late, attempting to repair trauma we'll never unlive.

Niko would've loved this.

I hug Lilith as long as I can, not sure if I'll ever see her again.

She squeezes me tight. "I have the best job in the world, Emma," Lilith whispers. "I bring traitors home. Hopefully, one day soon, I'll bring you home too."

Biting back tears, I neaten her silky, long hair. "Goodbye, Lili."

"For now." With a renewed shine in her eyes despite her flat expression, Lilith dons her helmet, leaping over the center console to the driver's seat.

Outside the car, Clara doesn't let me track Lilith's exit, sharp fingers at my spine urging me ahead as she marches too quickly for my stuttering heart. I'm so overwhelmed that the DoH main floor whirls by.

It doesn't hit me until the elevator.

If the Blackwoods had a way out, why the hell didn't they save Niko? Or *any* of our traitorous best friend group, begging the universe to one day be free?

Rage explodes in my chest, blurring my vision. I'm not sure how long my heart can keep up, and it must show. Clara pulls me to her side, keeping me upright with a nervous glance. Neither of us can speak, aware we're being watched, but I'm dying to confront her.

And I intend to—once we pass through this murder-story-esque basement, lined with torture cells. I don't have to look in the windows to know it's happening; I can feel their panic, only adding to my spinning heart.

Storming into the basement floor's final door, we bypass the waiting room, jetting into an open room with a monstrous metal door.

I don't wait for Clara to close it before I whisper-scream, "You let your son be sent off to die!"

Her wide eyes flicker with pain as she whisper-sputters. "He was indoctrinated! I thought he'd kill us all!"

I seethe, knowing she didn't pay attention to who he really was. "You didn't bring me here to apologize at all. You're *still* lying to us."

When her energy plummets into severe guilt, making me dizzy, I realize why she's been rushing me through so many revelations.

She blames herself for Niko too. Nothing can fix what she's done.

But she can still fix her future choices.

"Why won't you bring him home?" I ask.

Her voice croaks, shattered and wet. "I *can't.*"

"Emmalee Marie Richards, that's enough." Dad's voice interrupts us.

Sure enough, he's slamming the metal door closed behind himself. Behind *us.*

My heart has had enough of my anxious bullshit. I stumble as the room tilts. Searching for something to catch myself on, my hands fall short.

Guilt overwhelms Dad's energy as he lifts me by the armpits like I'm five, placing me into the therapist chair. "Hi, sweetheart."

Gazing up at him *here*, nowhere near his office in the DoH top floors, is so surreal that my dizzy heart muscles compete with my rapid inhales. I've never seen a therapy office with meaty deadbolts before, but sandwiched between Clara and Dad in full uniform, I figure it's necessary; a single glance at this impossible combination is too mind-boggling to be normal.

"You're welcome to give me a hard time, but cut the Blackwoods some slack," Dad says. "A single, traitorous instance will set the Departments against them, and if the Blackwoods get caught, we all do."

This is too weird to respond. Dad doesn't approve of the Departments either. Dad *agrees* with me for once. Even weirder, he said *"we."* I look to Clara for proof of their alliance, but she's busy shoving down her emotions in the corner.

"I administrate the therapy space here, but it wouldn't be possible without Clara and Yosuke," Dad continues. "I'm so sorry I had to keep it from you too. If you didn't give me absolute proof of your mindset with your—" Dad glances at Clara, softening his voice. "*Shenanigans*, then I couldn't have risked it either."

My throat tightens until I lurch through a swallow. He's talking about my secret sabotage, screwing with Sumner's experiment records: traitorism galore.

Dad sighs. "You're lucky I keep tabs on your work account. Empaths don't get executed, they get tortured. You need to be more careful next time, young woman."

He's been covering for me.

I sputter through tears, flinging my arms around him. I've

been fighting against him all this time, not realizing he was protecting me.

Like the Blackwoods, Dad's secret courage reverses his image in my mind. They could be killed for this, risking their lives for others' safety. It's horrible to hear that as I suffered my childhood away, the exit I wanted and needed from the Departments was so close all along. But the more I process my shock, the more I recognize the dread in Dad's energy. I can assume it's due to what I'm realizing; Dad is still here. So are the Blackwoods.

The only true way out of the Departments is death. If not a literal death, then a faked one, forcing us to kill every last connection we have to the rest of the world. Sorting through everything I'd have to let go of—people I love, our memories, and my favorite places that have shaped me—I can't help but feel like their escape plan is a form of death in itself. Otherwise, the Departments will hunt us for the rest of our lives.

It's impossible to truly leave.

And I can't blame Dad or the Blackwoods without blaming myself; every single one of us has contributed to the Departments' cycle of abuse.

But as I shut my eyes, feeling into Dad's rapid heartbeat against my cheek, my heart finds peace; I'm happy to witness my true father.

"I'm so sorry, Emma." Dad's voice cracks. "You don't have to forgive me. Just know I love you. So much."

When I let out a pathetic sob, Dad kisses my head. Clara turns her back, unable to even *look* at our embrace.

No matter how angry I am with her, my heart aches. I wish Niko could know his real parents too.

Swiping his tears away, Dad smiles. "So, are you in?"

"Yes. *Absolutely*," I breathe.

Dad chuckles, scrubbing my hair. "That's my Emma."

But Clara doesn't seem convinced. "You don't have any questions?"

"I don't think you want me to ask five billion things at once, and I can't handle more anyway. Tell me how and where, and I'm all in."

Clara drops into the bench in relief, her emotions threatening to bob back to the surface. But when Dad smiles just like his wedding picture, I have a question after all.

"Dad, what about Mom?"

As his smile fades, the hint of dread I've been sensing in his energy skyrockets into chaotic shame. Then anger.

"This program is classified. Don't *ever* mention it in my household, or thousands of deaths could be on your hands," Dad snaps, his face glowing red. "Do you understand me?"

"Yes," I whisper. A growing pit in my stomach tempts me to be sick at my feet, but I know better than to move. Dad's message is clear: Mom isn't part of this, and she never will be.

This makes a lot more sense than "needing proof" I wouldn't turn my dad in. They weren't afraid of me. They're afraid of my *mother*.

I was right to leave home.

CHAPTER 20

Niko

Sumner never starts with *medical* experimentation. For years, I've blocked out Sumner's "fun" experiments before the medical experiments, but something shakes me back to earth today.

Jay stands before me, eyes wide. We've seen our unit members, friends, and civilian children blown apart, yet the sight of me stripped and bound to a chair is what's terrifying him. The humiliation hurts enough that I'm positive it'll suffocate me.

"How—" I gasp; my eyes catch on Sumner, motionless on the floor.

Jay verges on tears, easing the loose ropes off my wrists and legs. "You know how to get out of these, Ni. You're not even tied down. I don't understa—"

"Why would you do this?!" I yell. "I'm trying to keep us alive!"

He doesn't yell back. He holds my face close, his touch so soft that it feels unfamiliar. "You… want this?"

I grip his arms, ready to fight. He plucks my hand off him, revealing how limp I am. I can't bear to hold myself up, slumping against his chest.

"No, you don't want this. You're shaking so badly." Jay's face contorts as he sits me upright. "I know I broke my promise by doing this, Ni. But you're fucking killing yourself. I couldn't sit back and wait anymore."

He hoists me to my feet, and we're reminded I have no control over my body. The fear of my sessions with Sumner makes my body check out as much as my head, forcing me to crumble without a chair's support. Jay doesn't point it out this time, swinging me into his arms and holding me chest to chest.

My exhausted head rests on Jay's shoulder as I gasp for air, in my anxiety's climax. Sumner is still on the floor. Part of me hopes he's dead. The other part feels guilty he's lying in a heap, like I've made a world-destroying error.

Jay strokes the back of my head. "Where are your clothes, bro?"

"I can't remember anything." I scrunch my eyes shut, trying to track backward before I saw Jay standing over me. Sumner's face, inches from mine, comes to mind. That's all I can manage before I begin to sob, clinging to Jay like I'm struggling not to fall off a cliffside.

"I've got you! I've got you." He squeezes me tighter. "Alright. Fuck clothes, everyone's gonna have to deal with seeing your sweet ass."

I laugh softly. "Please, no."

He kisses my temple, kicking the door open. "I'm just kidding, bro. I won't let a single soul see you."

My breath huffs from my chest with every hit of Jay's boots against the asphalt. "Did you kill him?"

"Unfortunately not." Jay's jaw tightens against the side of my head. "*That* would make them assassinate us in a heartbeat. I just… scared him a little."

Jay struggles to unlock the door with me in his arms, missing the keyhole at least five times. I worm out of his grip to help, and he gives in with a frustrated sigh. Jay protects my bare back, blocking us from potential onlookers as I steady his shaking hands. Finally, the key is in the lock.

Jay can hardly wrangle me inside as panic hits us both. He doesn't know what to do once we slam the door behind us, pressing against it like that'll keep *these* people out. I can tell my explosive emotional breakdown terrifies him; it's worse now that no one can see us, my sobs coming out more like screams. I'm throwing us off our game, but I can't help but cry like Jay has already died.

I know they'll come for him for doing this. It's too late. As I look at him, my best friend, one of my soulmates, is dead.

And it's all my fault.

Holding my face, Jay whimpers, "Niko, Nikolai, I'm here. It's okay."

I can't even get the words out, gasping for air as I mouth the word "no." Jay buries his nose into my shoulder, clutching me close to soothe me. I'm so relieved to be home with him in our shitty bunker, but I feel guilty for this relief. So guilty that I'm angry. At him, but mostly myself.

"They're gonna fucking kill you." The words burn on the way out, scraping my raw throat. "Why did you do this?"

"Hey, we're alive, aren't we?"

I try to push him off me, but I can't hold up his weight. He eases up, taking a step back until I can't stand how far away he is. Soon I might not have him at all.

I grip his hand. "You *have* to escape."

Jay prepares himself to laugh, but then he sees my face. "Are you fucking serious?"

I cup his jaw in my palms, urging him closer. "Yes, I'm serious! You better save yourself! You broke our promise!"

"I told you, asshole, I'm never leaving you behind! Just like I'm not letting you meet with that freak anymore."

I'm audibly shuddering. "I can handle it."

"No, Niko. You can't. And that's okay."

I cough, sobbing harder. "It's not! I'm going to lose you now, and it's all my fault."

"This was *my* choice!" Jay tears me off him, steadying my shoulders instead. "I can do whatever the fuck I want."

"We're supposed to be partners! We're supposed to decide these things *together*."

"This is different." His eyes look so sad that I can't respond. "You can't see it from the outside, Niko. You're in too deep. You need help, and no one else in this world is gonna help us. It's just you and me, bro."

I grip my forehead. "So what am I supposed to do when you're killed? How the fuck will I live with myself?"

Jay's eyes dart to my bare feet, his brows furrowing.

"I know you're trying to help, and I'm grateful for what you were willing to risk for me." I step closer. "But I'm also fucking pissed. I don't *want* to survive without you, Jay. I need you. You have to survive too."

He smirks. "Well, I already did it, so..."

I try my best to tackle him to the ground, but it turns into a heavy hug. Jay backs us against the bed, dropping us onto it and throwing the blankets over me.

"Shh. You're okay." Jay bats off my angry hands.

"I'm not at all," I rasp through tears. "You have to promise me, a real promise this time, if they come for you and I'm not around to protect you, you run. And trust me, I'll make sure they won't follow." Jay sighs, and I give myself half a second to swallow my fear. "He'll listen to me. That's the benefit of this bullshit I'm bringing onto myself. So the second you feel that target on your back, you run, and you don't stop until they stop looking."

Jay smiles, ready to brush me off, but I cover his mouth, desperate to show him I'm serious.

"You didn't give me a choice, so I'm not giving you one. You *will* run when they come for you. Don't let them take you down." He isn't convinced, and I hate it. "Why the fuck would we make it this far together if you're going to die without me?"

His eyes harden. I release his mouth, praying he'll at least pretend to promise me. But he doesn't say anything. Jay huddles into me, holding me in silence for what feels like hours.

He falls asleep first. I stare at every mole and discoloration on his face from the brutal sun. The exhaustion under his eyes from what he's sacrificing for us to stay alive. The scar on his cheek from when mini Jay accidentally cut his own face during knife practice. I soak in all his glowing beauty. Eventually, I can't stay awake beneath the soothing heaviness of his protective arms.

When I open my eyes, he's gone. He left our weird memorabilia stash on the windowsill, so I know he's probably just in the communal bathroom; there's really nowhere else for us to go.

But a sick feeling gnaws at my core. I throw on the only uniform I have left, making a run for the front-liner barracks bathroom.

It's nighttime already, and a new moon obstructs most visibility. The perfect hunting hour.

He's not in the communal bathroom. Not in the showers. Not anywhere.

I run back to the barracks, suit up, and hide our memorabilia in my breast pocket. With my helmet on and communications wiring disconnected, it's time to hunt the hunted.

Curfew is in five minutes, so no one else is outside. I evade a Commanding Officer exiting another front-liner's barracks, crunching between two compounds with less than a foot between them. No one hears me because I make sure there's nothing to be heard. Not even as I shuffle between the barracks, squirming out the back before the Commander crosses the front.

If Jay and I excel at anything, it's evasion. Jay could survive for a while on the run, as long as he stays out of reach. He can outrun anyone—even Lilith.

The problem with running away isn't our capabilities; we'd have to run forever, tracked, stalked, and brutalized until we obey or die. We may as well be trapped beneath their feet here instead of unfamiliar territory.

So if an assassin came for Jay tonight in the bathroom, his escape is worthless unless I prevent them from chasing him. Beg for Sumner's forgiveness in the way he loves most.

And I will. If Jay isn't already dead.

The sky turns a deep navy, signaling it's almost sunrise. After five hours of searching every inch of the compound, I return to the barracks.

Within that time, Jay never came home. His gear isn't here, so maybe he had a hunch. He's smarter than I gave him credit for last night.

But he's gone. With each passing minute, it becomes more real. I can't hold still.

I didn't even get to remind him how much I love him. If that was our last shitty conversation, I yelled at him over things we can't control. My body physically rejects this reality, shaking like I'm freezing.

He's the only person I have left on my side—the only one who has ever done something about Sumner.

I'm completely alone.

At 5:30 a.m., I open my door to two rookie unit members. They hand me a note.

> Unit Member Jay Olivas has been declared Missing in Action as of 7 p.m., August 17th. Unit Member Nikolai Blackwood will not be assigned a new combat partner at this time.

The messengers await confirmation that I acknowledge their message. I look them in the eyes, struggling to contain myself. These guys have no idea what I just read, but I do. I'm forced to return the note, surrendering the evidence of its declaration: the Departments want me to know they killed Jay. We weren't in battle. This was a MIA *order*.

Our tiny box of a "home" suddenly feels like an empty warehouse. I expect myself to freak out once I shut the door, but I stand there in silence for a moment. Thinking.

Something is off. His time of death couldn't have been at 7 p.m. because the sun currently sets around 6:50, and I was awake after sunset. At 7, he was holding me, asleep. The MIA declaration must've referenced that the *order* was put in at 7 p.m. I only have confirmation they're *trying* to assassinate him.

Jay didn't promise he'd run, but he didn't disagree, either. I'm positive he did everything he could to evade them. But evasion is different from escaping the compound, and it's been many hours since then. Once he crosses the wall, unit members have to be painstakingly assembled and ordered to exit the compound and chase after him, buying him a chunk of time to really *run*.

But if he didn't manage to hop the border, even Jay could've died by now. And I can't believe that. Not yet. I want to believe he escaped.

My paranoia fights me, taking over. As well as rage. Jay's past behavior proves my hopes wrong. He's as stubborn as Emmalee, refusing to split up unless one of us was dead.

But we both knew he was as good as dead if he stayed. Maybe he realized there was no other way.

Denial or not, I refuse to believe he couldn't end the cycle with me. I'm going to make sure Sumner calls off the assassination, and give Jay a chance at freedom.

Then I'll end the cycle in Jay's stead.

Today.

In Jay's way.

CHAPTER 21

Niko

I undress down to my casual uniform. Stuffing my knives and our memorabilia into my pants, I head to breakfast. I speak to no one. Eyes scour every inch of me. I allow them to see I'm unhappy, let them think I might've given up. It's the first time I've eaten alone in years, left to battle my overbearing thoughts without Jay's incessant distractions, so distress isn't hard to fake. Then I head back to the barracks and wait until it's time for me to work with Sumner at 12 p.m.

I don't mind that a few Commanding Officers watch me strut down the Commander barracks' hall. They've seen me walk into Sumner's room every day for months. As expected, they turn their backs, pretending as if Sumner's *habits* are unknown to them.

Swinging open the door, I find Sumner's distorted face at his desk. Luckily, Jay left one of Sumner's eyes untouched. Now Sumner can see my smile.

Sumner brushes off my ferocious expression, but only after halting mid-breath, forgetting what he was about to say. I shut the door behind myself. Then I stand there, beaming at his bruised disaster of a face. Waiting for him to realize *today is different.*

"Sit down, *Nikolai*," he hisses, irritated he has to command me.

I don't move. He gawks behind the chair I usually sit in, eyes darting from my smile, to "my" chair, to his security camera-less room. It's rare to see *Charles* confused, but I'm loving it.

Sumner laughs. "I thought you'd like the present I gave you last night, but you actually did love it, huh? You're more of a sick fuck than I thought."

I laugh. He just confirmed he's entirely to blame. It's valid to kill him.

Sumner's eyes bulge. He clears his throat, struggling to keep his cool as I step toward him. I stop about two feet away, and he squirms.

Terrorizing people usually makes me hate myself, but yes, today is different; I'm loving his shaky reaction. I'm as sick in the head as Sumner wants, but not in the way he intended.

"I'm not even touching you." I mock his voice and words. "Look at you, I haven't even come near you." He swallows hard. "So, kid, are you *sure* you don't feel anything?"

Gripping his face with a single hand, I pinch his cheeks between tight fingers. His jaw feels like glass, begging to be shattered in my palm. For once, he's speechless.

I laugh. "You wanted to see what would happen when you killed someone I loved, huh? You thought I'd just sit down in your chair?"

"I—" He ruffles his shoulders, attempting to make himself look bigger.

"You're how old now? 70? 75? No wonder your jaw is creaking like it's ready to bust in two." I give it a test squeeze, making him cry out beneath the pressure. "Can't imagine what that sounds like in your head, but I can feel it verging on snapping. You're fucking fragile. What's the word I'm looking for? You say it a lot... Oh, yes. Expendable."

When I release his jaw, his teeth chatter. For a moment, I feel horrible for becoming this person. But the guilt doesn't come close to the all-consuming emptiness washing over me, knowing Jay could be dead. Sumner was gloating about it, minutes ago.

Yes, he deserves this. All of this.

"S-sit down," Sumner says.

I place my hands over his on the chair's back, leaning in until he's less than a foot from my nose.

"No. *You* sit down."

The second he sits, I laugh again. It was this fucking easy.

Which means Sumner continues to be right: I've been too cowardly to fight back. A perpetual victim.

"You're the patient today. Your turn for some good ol' 'Merican healthcare." I laugh to my heart's content.

It's the first time Sumner hasn't smiled in years, other than when he's about to punish me. So I take my time tying him up, making a show of it, but with genuine military-grade knots instead of the weak shit he ties me in. He'll never wriggle out of these. And he tries at first, so I mock his voice again. "You remind me of myself, you know? When I was twelve years old."

"I-I'm sorry, I—"

"You're *sorry?*" I empty my pockets onto his desk, taking the time to lay out my weapon stash, one by one. "Oh, really now?"

"I'm paying you well, remember? I can compensate you even better for your loss."

I freeze, my heart dropping to the vinyl beneath my combat boots. But I have to be careful. Not allow him to see I'm wondering if Jay's assassination succeeded or not. To dig for information while he's scared, I have to pretend I know more.

"Oh, my *loss?*" I lean over him, raising his pasty chin so I can look into his eyes. "I'm not losing anyone. You'll call the assassination order off, Jay will run free for the rest of his life, and you'll send me home."

"I-I can't, I—"

My smile grows. Jay isn't dead. Not that Sumner knows of, or else he'd rub it in. He was hoping I assumed the worst, and now that he knows I haven't, he's screwed.

He has no leverage left.

"Aww, you can't? Doctor CEO, master of fucking the entire country in the ass, suddenly forgot how to function? That's too bad."

All I have to do is hover over my favorite tactical knife. Sumner pants, choking out his words. "G-gi-give me the phone!"

"Good boy," I mock.

He scoffs. "Untie my hand."

I laugh in his hopeful face, and he visibly shrinks. "I'd say nice try, but that was kind of pathetic. *I'm* dialing the number for you, *Charles*, and you'll do what you do best and talk out of your ass."

His face reddens, vibrating in both anger and fear.

"Hmm… Let's take a minute for you to calm down."

I crouch on his desk, glowering down at him for a whole five minutes. The longer I stare, the angrier I get. I've lost control of myself to years of pent-up grief. Grieving all he has taken from me while I sat in that chair, silent.

And he can feel it. Instead of calming down, he shakes harder.

I sigh. "Alright, let's get this over with since *someone* can't stomach responsibility for his actions."

I swipe through his Department database. On my way to his contact list, I send out an order for a few pivotal research files to be permanently destroyed. As I sift through them, familiar titles come back to mind. He must've told me about them while I was mentally numb, which means memories of every fucked-up session must be hiding in my mind, somewhere. But now I don't have to remember them. With one tap, they're erased forever.

He's starting to notice I'm doing something other than dialing, so I say, "Hey, buddy, listen. You won't tell a single soul about this. In fact, I could imagine a rapist like you fantasizing tonight about me tying you up."

"I'm not a *rapist!*" He whines, offended enough to *cry*.

I suck in a gasp, then I laugh so hard my stomach aches. "Aww, poor baby can't handle being called a rapist? Everything else you've done is okay, but not that, huh? I bet you're not racist either." He gulps, struggling to stay quiet. I sigh, finding a few more files to destroy. "You white supremacists are all the same. And guess what? You *are* a rapist. So when you've done everything I want, I'll sit down in that chair, and you can do whatever the fuck you want to me like the rapist you are. Do you see how doing what I want benefits you?"

His white, un-gelled bangs bounce with his rapid nods.

I hover over the call button for my barrack's Commanding Officer, but something doesn't feel right. Sumner isn't convinced enough for me to be comfortable.

I lean in close, slipping my favorite knife against his jugular. "Oh, and did I mention, if you don't say the right thing, you'll bleed out in 5-15 seconds? You know what this vein is, right, Doctor? You seem to. You use it to choke me out every week.

I would pierce your throat and sever your brain stem from the front, but that's too easy. In your final seconds of life, you'll have to watch me standing here as you gush blood. Your money can't patch a neck leak, bud. Got it?"

He gasps a little, so I step back, smiling. The knife dances around my fingertips, and his veiny eyes track it back and forth, up and down.

"*Hello?* I asked you a *question*," I mock his ever-impatient voice.

"Y-yes! I understand. I'll do it."

He doesn't look like he's lying, but dread gurgles in my guts as I tap the call button.

"And you'll do anything I want after, right?" He whispers.

An unspoken struggle for power ripples between us, leaving me to fight to retain my smile as his reappears. As the dial-tone chimes, Sumner somehow regains dominance.

"I'm the one asking questions today, asshole," I hiss.

The call's receiving end picks up.

After seeing Sumner's caller ID, my barracks' Commanding Officer gives Sumner a gruff, "What *now?*" and I nearly burst into laughter.

Sumner sighs, sweat beading down his tear-stained cheeks. "You work for me, you know."

"Y-yes, Sir."

"Call off the order to hunt that Jay kid."

"Yes, Sir."

"You didn't kill him yet, right?"

"No, Sir. We've… lost sight of him."

"Useless sacks of shit…" Sumner ignores my wide grin. "Alright, whatever. If he ever shows up again, he'll be an interesting subject for S817. I'm requesting future use of both unit members in Santa Desierto. Send an order to return Blackwood for now."

My smile fades. We're still trapped, and Sumner is about to get away with it.

I touch the blade's tip to his neck. My palm is at the knife's base, ready to hammer the knife into his throat after all—a change of plans. Sumner huffs in panic, forcing me to cover his disgusting mouth. "I *said*, let Jay run free," I hiss into his ear.

"But for now," Sumner says. "Let the Jay idiot run free. You have better things to do with your time since you can't even do that correctly."

"Sir, I can erase Unit Member Olivas from the database, but… I cannot authorize the use of Unit Member Blackwood."

"*Excuse* me?"

My stomach twists, hearing my barrack's Commanding Officer shake at the thought of defying Sumner. "Unit Member Blackwood is scheduled for an MIA Mission run tonight. We have men lined up until tomorrow. We have to dispose of him before the Lionhearts find out he's alone. These two are unkillable. It's fucking ridiculous."

Sumner twitches, seething in rage. "That's exactly why *I want him!*"

A nauseating chill slithers through me.

My barrack's Commanding Officer sits in silence for a moment before muttering, "That's above my authority, Sir. The order is already sent from above for the mission toni—"

"I don't give a shit," Sumner sputters. "He's *mine!*" His glare swallows me with a possessiveness I've never experienced before. I lose all blood in my face. "And if you kill him, you will *pay* for the losses." He mouths to me, "Hang up."

"Sir, you're the closest contact to… You'll have to use other means to override—"

I hang up, as instructed.

For a moment, Sumner studies my face. He's protecting my life, but I never thought I'd be repulsed by having my life saved. I'm trying my best not to fuzz everything out. Not to let him gain the upper hand since he's somehow so close to it, even though he's the one tied to a chair.

He smiles. "So, what's this about you sitting back down in *your chair?*"

All logic in my mind turns off. I untie Sumner, making him think I'm listening.

Then I watch him run.

He's shrieking, darting all around his bunker as I simply walk after him, holding my favorite combat knife. It must be some type of primal communication letting him know I'm a predator, not prey today. That his life is coming to an end.

It's painfully easy to pin him to the ground. He's so afraid, whimpering and wriggling beneath me, that my heart starts to hurt.

Even if it's Sumner, I'm not a killer at heart. I could flip him onto his stomach so I don't have to see his face, stab him a few times in the back and let him bleed out. But the longer I stare into his frigid, terrified eyes, the sicker I feel. I've never chosen to kill anyone without being ordered to.

"I-I'm going to call your parents and tip them off!" He screams. "I'll tip them off on the assassination, and you'll be set free! You can go home!"

I picture going home. To Hana. Mom. Emmalee. The person I'm about to become doesn't deserve to see these traumatized women.

"I'm sorry, Nikolai!" His sobs sound genuine, so my grip loosens. But then he yells, "I'm sorry you hate me so much!"

I laugh, beginning to cry. I don't know what I expected. Leaning my head back, I numb my mind and body with the blaring fluorescent lights.

Jay didn't kill Sumner, either. If I kill Sumner and the power he represents, the Departments will target me full-throttle until I'm dead. And Jay ran. If I die, Jay risked his life for me for no reason.

If I don't obey *now*, Sumner will hurt everyone worse. He's proven that theorem enough times for me to know better.

I don't want anyone to get hurt. I never have.

Sumner *does* have leverage; I'm just too immersed in it to remember it exists. This is my life. My fate.

I stand, soaking in Sumner frozen on the floor beneath me. He's struggling to breathe, eyes tracking me for my next move. I'm sure I've never hated him more and he can see it on my face. But he's not much to look at, either. His pants are wet. He looks horrible from Jay's scare tactics yesterday, swollen and undignified.

But this sad sack of shit won tonight.

I walk my pathetic ass to the chair.

"Yes, yes! That's it!" Crawling over on his hands and knees, he grips my thighs, allowing me to glower down at him. "Now, you're going to forget this. All of this."

He shoves a plastic mask over my face, flicking a knob on an unmarked gas tank. I promised to do what he wanted in exchange for Jay's life, but I don't recognize this game.

"You have to forget, or else everyone you know will die because of you. Jay will go first, and you'll only have yourself to blame. You never should've told him about me. I can't even stomach how weak you are." My eyes roll back, struggling to remain conscious, and he giggles. "Nuh-uh, not yet! Listen closely before you sleep: You're going to suffer for how you misbehaved tonight, even if you forget it. And you *will* forget something."

He extracts a pale yellow file from his desk drawer. Inside, he stores endless photos of other unit members' dead bodies. They're not just dead; they're dismembered.

Sumner selects a particularly gruesome image, shoving it against my nose so there's nowhere else to look. "When you wake up, you'll think Jay is dead. Memorize this photo. Believe this is what you did to him, and what'll happen to you if you're assassinated. And now I'm going to save your life. You'll never be able to repay me. You owe me, forever."

I find myself nodding, losing the truth as my knife slips from my fingertips, clattering against the floor. It sounds like it's worlds away, the blade's last *tink* just a whisper.

I enter my dreams—the alternate dimension where I'm a playtoy to not just Sumner, but myself.

"Welcome back," the Wolf grins, black smoke billowing from his teeth. "You finally almost let me win."

CHAPTER 22

Emmalee

"Hey," Lilith says. "You're zoning out."

"I know," I mutter.

Lilith stays in the forest most days, but no one gives her shit if she disguises herself to meet me at my favorite smoothie cafe downtown because, well, she's Lilith. No one can stop her.

So far, she's remained as straightforward and emotionless as ever despite deprogramming therapy. But as she devours her sandwich today, something in her energy feels different.

"How was therapy?" I ask.

Lilith sets her sandwich down. "I finally remembered how the Departments decided they wanted to use me as a child terrorist."

I freeze mid-slurp. Frantically glancing at the cafe patrons around us, my head spins as my heart rages. No one heard Lilith's deadpan confession, but she's never said anything like this to me about her past before. I almost don't know how to react.

Leaning in, I can barely choke out a whisper. "Oh, my God, Lili. How?"

With a massive sandwich bite stuffing her cheeks, Lilith shrugs. "I killed the head of a trafficking ring while he was raping me. Stabbed him to death over me. I forgot it all."

My gut twists in horror, leaving my jaw agape. Lilith was only 10 when she came here. If I experienced anything like that, I wouldn't want to feel ever again either.

I swallow my shaky voice. "How are you feeling after processing that?"

Lilith frowns. "I don't like small talk."

I blink a few times, struggling to catch up with her train of thought. "Oh. Because I asked some version of 'how are you?'"

"Yes. I told you I hate answering that. No one means it."

"I realize that. We don't have to keep talking about this, but I figured your session was kinda deep, so this 'how are you' isn't exactly casual conversation."

"Oh, well, yeah. If you're genuinely asking how I am, then I feel fine now."

"...Are you upset with me?"

Her black eyes don't stray from mine. "Yes."

"Okay. Do you want to talk about why?"

She stands, brushing herself free of crumbs. "I don't understand what happened to Niko after I left; something's off with everyone's story. And you're still working in your mom's department. How do I know you won't fuck us over?"

I rub my face, probably smudging my eyeliner in every direction. "Okay, wait. What about her department? If you could actually explain what you know, that would help."

Lilith cocks her head. "You're working in the DoH, and you don't know what they're doing to people?"

My eyes widen. "No, I don't. What are they doing?"

"I heard it from other traitors. They're making people sick. They have chronic nightmares at first, then most people's brains rot. They forget things. *Important* things, like family. But if they become useful instead of braindead, they become *very* useful to the DoH." She tosses her food in the trash. "I can't talk about this without wanting to throw up. I'm going to take a nap. I'll tell you the rest later."

"Lilith, wait." My knees shake as I stand. Luckily, she stops. "*That's* what the injections are? If you're worried I'm involved, I'm not administering anything. Only helping people cope with treatments and writing down how they feel."

She scoffs. "Jesus Christ. So you *are* part of it. It's not just injections anymore, Emmalee. If you've been in the hospital the past few years, you've probably been 'treated' with it too. We're all fucked."

With that, she storms out of the cafe.

I guessed *everything* right. But I never wanted to be right about this.

I drive back to work in a haze. Like most workdays, I run to the bathroom to bawl.

During our blissful evenings together after his first deployment, I only saw Niko fall asleep once. He scared Hana and me shitless, screaming in his sleep. Once we woke him, he spouted gory details, like he couldn't stop his dream repeating in his mind. Something about a unit member chopping pieces off Niko's body until Niko was forced to kill his unit member to make it stop. The worst part was that his unit member recently died during training, so Niko felt incredibly guilty. It was just a dream, but it sounded hyper-realistic. Too realistic.

I have those nightmares now. Was the drug trial Clarity and I participated in somehow connected to the Departments? I don't know if that's what Lilith's talking about, but if my parents have anything to do with the original injections, I don't know how to feel.

And what if, on the ridiculous chance Niko doesn't die in combat, he'll come home and die of "brain rot," anyway? What if he forgets me?

Or what if he comes back and survives the injection, and while he's "useful," *my* brain rots?

I exit the bathroom stall, sighing at my shaggy hair in the mirror; its black dye has already faded to a hazy dark brown. It takes me a whole fifteen minutes to fix my eyeliner and settle my hair around my jaw in an orderly enough fashion. Nothing, however, will fix the dreary circles under my eyes. Outside of work, my main focus is staying upright. I've been passing out almost every day—like I used to before I started getting weekly hydration IVs. I can only hope it's not a sign of brain rot.

Just as I touch the door handle, I'm face to face with Clara Blackwood—mainly because she nearly swings the door into my nose.

We stare in tense silence, then she sidesteps to allow me to pass. In a split-second change of heart, she catches my wrist.

"Emmalee, wait."

"I still don't want to talk, Commander."

"Okay." She releases me. "I understand."

She might be on Dad's good side, but we still haven't made up. I consider leaving, as I always do, but this is the first time she's acknowledged she's done something wrong.

Whipping around, I look straight into her beautiful face. "No, you do not fucking *understand*."

She leans over the sink. "Alright. Lay it on me."

This is a shock. There's so much I could say that I don't know what to say at all.

So I say the one thing only I know.

"You used to hit him!" I yell. It feels hot, like stomach acid coming up.

"What?! Who said that? Did he?"

"No! Hana. As a six-year-old child, not understanding why her mother would hit her big brother when she was angry."

Clara's eyes dart with such rapid speed across the tile floor that I'm terrified of what she's recollecting.

She scrubs her face. "Oh, that girl is going to give me a heart attack. This is a huge misunderstanding."

"Uh, huh. I'm *sure*," I hiss.

"You don't have to believe me, but this really can be explained."

Her anxiety feels honest. I cross my arms. "Okay. Go ahead and try."

"The Department of Tactical Defense trains us to build our anger and keep it there, heightened like a live fuse until we're ready to set it off. That's one way we can upkeep our adrenaline to behave in superhuman ways. My brainwashed son would come home agitated, so I tried to give him an outlet by letting him spar with me. I wanted to keep him from doing anything worse. He didn't have a choice, he—"

Clara freezes beneath my glare.

"He didn't have a choice," I repeat, enunciating every syllable. "Which means you forced him to hit you *and be hit by you.*"

"Okay... Maybe I didn't think about that. But he knew I loved him, and it wasn't like that."

My eyes well up. "It wasn't what you *intended*. But you did. You hit him when he probably only needed comfort. Anger isn't his only emotion. And Commander, I'm saying this as a family friend who wants the best for you and your family: *you* need to be deprogrammed too."

Clara's entire body tenses. "Okay, kid, that's taking it a little too far."

For a moment, I'm afraid for my safety. But then I feel how she's actually hurting. She needs someone to take her seriously—to look past the anger she uses to mask her underlying sadness, and allow her to finally show her pain. I can absolutely relate.

"Yeah, well, I hate this as much as you do. But even if I'm upset with you, I hate watching you suffer. That's why I want you to get the help you deserve. I love Niko, and that also means I love you and your family. I care about you, Commander."

Clara expels a steady breath, gawking like I've handed her the biggest reality check of her life. Then she frantically paces. "Okay, then what else are we not clear on? What else am I missing?"

I close my eyes. She's making me dizzy. "Commander—"

"Is it about separating you two? Because the four of us parents decided together. We realized the moment you two seemed to just *click*, you'd be a target for the top DoTD unit... Like Yosuke and I were. I didn't want you to live the life I did, Emmalee."

My whole body is shaking. "Yeah, I get that. *Now*. But why? Why not tell us directly so we could avoid it? We weren't senseless."

"Because you couldn't control yourselves around each other, and we had to protect you. If they saw how *instinctually* close you two are, they'd put you together whether we rejected the offer or not. They could've easily stolen you from us, and you two just did *not* get the terror of it! When you went to your first boot camp, where Nikolai got paired with Jay, they saw you and—"

"Wanted to partner Niko and me instead, until my parents pulled me out of the camp. I know."

"But you don't know. The life you two would've seen on the front lines is much worse—if you even lived to see it."

I let out a weird gasp for air, unable to contain my sobs anymore. "But that's what happened to him, anyway."

"I'm so sorry," she whispers. I can't see her face, but she

doesn't sound okay, either. "I genuinely thought I lost him to the killer mentality we were raised in. It took Yosuke and I decades to secretly, safely set this place up. And in the meantime, we did play executioner, as promised to the DoTD. The thousands of people we had to kill to gain the Departments' trust? Unforgivable. And Niko saw his parents do that. But we had to. We didn't mean to get pregnant before we were ready to be traitors. They've been watching us—watching *him*—since the day they knew I was carrying a Lionheart fetus. No matter what we did, we knew they'd get ahold of him."

My legs wobble, struggling to soak in the gravity of her words. Of what Niko has seen, as a *child*. How indoctrinated he was, yet still had so much compassion left in his sensitive heart. So much love.

All this horror was for the sake of finding a way out. If killing our way to the top is what it *really* takes, I can't tell if it's worse to stay or leave.

Clara can see it on my face, covering her embarrassment with shaking hands. "I know, Emmalee. But I'm telling you the truth: before Lilith left, he gave me *zero* indication he was looking into deprogramming behind our backs, or I would've sent him the letter to test him sooner. When he answered, but then was deployed that day, I never hated myself more. I'm a horrible mother."

Everything clicks into place, leaving me in a sudden tranquility. "You didn't know because he's so goddamn good at hiding everything."

"He is." She finds the courage to peek at me again.

Standing in exhausted silence, I swallow down this reality. My voice comes out soft but strained. "Thank you for finally telling me the truth, Commander."

I try to be strong as she wobbily smiles, but bitter sobs rip from my core.

I wasted so much time while Niko was home—those precious, insignificant moments I'll never get back. I should've talked to him more, spent time with him for no reason, snuck out to see him—anything to just plain be with him a second longer. Before he was taken from me, possibly forever.

Clara snatches a paper towel to dab my eyes. "I know, honey. None of it is fair."

I don't think this is what this woman signed up for when we decided to have our confrontational chat in a grungy bathroom, but with a single comforting touch, I can't stop myself from slurring through snotty tears.

"I should've told him I love him."

Clara pulls my head to her shoulder, rubbing my back. "You two gave us a hell of a time trying to protect you because you were determined to be together. That's love, even if you didn't say it out loud."

Thank God I'm in too much emotional pain to be embarrassed, crumbling in front of my confidant, Clara Blackwood, of all people. "But do you think he knew how I felt?"

"Yes, sweet Emmalee. He knows. And he's always loved you with all his heart. He told me he loved you the first time when he was four years old."

We brace each other by the elbows, a mutual snotty disaster, and Clara groans.

"To this day, I feel guilty for telling him he was too young to know what love is. He threw the biggest tantrum I've ever seen, telling me he isn't a baby, he knows what love is because he loves Emmalee Richards, and refused to stop being your friend. I thought he was being overdramatic, but time proved me so, so wrong."

I laugh, then cry, really cry, stooped over my teardrops on the linoleum.

"Emmalee, you need to breathe and remember my freakish beast of a son is somehow still alive. We have no idea if he's going to die or not, okay?"

"I can't live with myself if he dies."

She squats below me, taking my face in her hands. "Yes. Yes, you can. You just stood up to a top Commander in the most powerful organization in the US. We need you. You're terrifying in the most loving way, and he would *not* want you to die. Especially not for his sake."

I huff a few times, streaking my eyeliner all over my face again with the back of my hand. I think about everyone healing in our program—people like us. Niko didn't ask to be sacrificed, but I'm relieved he was finally heard.

I nod. "Okay… Okay."

The only bonus about widespread chronic illness is that I don't have to explain my debilitating exhaustion anymore; everyone's sick, so everyone gets it. Clara holds my burning body upright as I wash my face and painstakingly reapply my makeup with shaking hands.

She walks me all the way back to my apartment, pausing when I grab her hand and don't let her leave. We hug it out in silence over the edge of my bed, and she leaves me to nap.

CHAPTER 23

Emmalee

My nap is interrupted by a gentle but frantic tap on my shoulder. Yosuke Blackwood is at my bedside, once again puzzling my brain into thinking I've time traveled to see future Niko. I quickly realize that's impossible, and it hurts my heart.

Then I jolt upright. Yosuke Blackwood is in my apartment.

"What is it?! Is he dead?"

He shakes his head no. "Please stay as calm as you can and come with me."

I swing my feet out of bed, and Yosuke whispers as I slip my boots back on.

"Someone with a higher authority has blocked our requests to end Niko's tour for four years, until today. I don't know what changed, but someone must not want him to die."

My heart flinches. I don't know whether to be hopeful or scared.

The Blackwood security entourage is waiting outside my apartment, "helping" me into a car with an urgent shove. As soon as I strap in, Commander Blackwood hands me a phone.

"For you, Miss Richards."

I give him a weird look for calling me that, but then I realize we're surrounded by his coworkers, and whatever *this* is, it's work. He's working right now. *I'm* about to work right now. For the Department of Tactical Defense.

"*What* is going on?" I whisper.

"Focus on being completely calm." He steadies the phone

in my hands. "Do you remember how to empathically connect through the sound of someone's voice? You've done this before with Niko, but it's been a long time, right?"

I chew on my bottom lip, treading through a thought avalanche. "Yes, I have. Only a few times. That was like... ten years ago."

"Try your best. Hearing your voice might be enough to calm him, but if you can guide him out alive, I'll be in your debt forever. And if you two still want to be together, I'll fight for your relationship too. Until the day I die."

I gape at Niko's father, his words' meaning sinking in. Niko and I were good at this exact job, the real reason we were forbidden from contact. We were incredible, in fact. The inseparable way our minds, bodies, and technically, our *souls* link allows us to communicate beyond all limitations. Including physical distance.

I never realized how ridiculous that is. Our parents were right; this power is a terrifying weapon. The Departments would've leached us dry.

"But I only have the phone?" My voice sounds so mousey that I'm irritating myself.

"We're transporting you to get a visual from his helmet. So before we get there... I need to warn you from personal experience." He leans in. "You'll see things you'll never forget, no matter how much you want to. But for me, if it meant keeping Clara alive, I was always willing."

My breath shudders. "Yes, I understand."

"We have one of our people on his communications team, and— Well, there's no easy way to say this: you have to prepare yourself to potentially watch him perish. This was an unexpected attack. Oh, and don't ask him about Jay. I've been told that's what's throwing him off; Jay went MIA less than two days ago and Niko hasn't mentally recovered. But he won't listen to anyone's orders and specifically requested your ID number as a Guide. So whenever you're ready, dial."

I expected to freak out, but a powerful calmness encompasses me. From the mere mention of Niko needing me, I already feel our ghosts trying to connect.

I dial.

An operator answers instantly. "Verify your ID, please."

"O-oh—" I blank out. How the hell did Niko remember my ID number *in combat* when *I* can't remember it?

I lift the back of my shirt for Niko's father to read the tattooed number on my spine. Luckily, he catches on quickly and reads it off.

"Uh, 6— 26… 99… 22… 57… 55," I repeat.

There's a brief pause.

"Affirmative, Fifty-Five. Access granted."

When it connects, all I hear is white noise.

Then his ragged breath.

My stomach flips. I close my eyes, tuning into Niko's individual sound and feel. He's so alive, it washes goosebumps down every inch of my skin. His terror runs through me, but also his focus. He's unbelievably analytical, whereas I'm all feeling. We usually have to meet halfway because of it. But not right now. We're perfect complements, filling in for each other's insecurities like we were hand-crafted to interlock.

"Fourteen?" I haven't called him by his ID number in so long that it feels wrong.

He gasps in both relief and horror. "Fifty-Five!"

I steady my voice for him. "I'm here. I'm here as your Guide."

"They—" He grunts, avoiding something loud. Explosive. "They're trying to kill me. Jay's gone, and I— I have a feeling they killed him."

He whispered that last part. Commander Blackwood and I lock eyes in horror. Niko's gut feelings are usually spot-on.

"I don't want to die," Niko continues.

"You won't."

I don't mean to guarantee it; it just comes out. Like I was whispered the secret truth, and delivered it from the universe. I dive deeper into him: his surroundings, his health, all threats for his life. Then I see immediate steps he needs to take to survive.

"Turn to your left, and run."

CHAPTER 24

Emmalee

Niko and I are out of sync because he's not himself.

"Where is he?" he asks for the fifth time.

Like every time, I'm as honest as I can be over a shared communications line. "We don't know where Jay is. Keep going. He wouldn't want you to die, so you have to keep going."

Thankfully, he listens… to *me*. If anyone else chimes in, he calls them a slurry of expletives and names like "terrorist breeder" or "happiness killer." I have to laugh. He seems to enjoy making me laugh, slowing his running heart rate from a panicked 170 to a healthy 120.

I cling to these small victories; everything else is pretty damn nauseating. They even gave me a trash bag in case. We reached the Department of Tactical Defense Communications Center about fifteen minutes ago. I can see what Niko sees, through his helmet camera. People are blown apart everywhere he turns—all over him—and there are no signs of it stopping. I don't understand what they want him to do out there, but he's pretty much defenseless against whatever weapons they're using. When the opposition fires against Niko's unit members, it looks… unnatural. Like a rippling pop of flesh. These weird weapons clearly intend to botch body evidence.

"They're testing this bullshit on us." Niko reads my mind. "We're severely outmatched."

I glare at his Superior Commanding Officer, who's unwilling to meet my eyes. "And no one's giving an order to retreat yet. I'm giving your SCO a staredown for you."

Niko huffs a tiny laugh. "Thanks."

Then my head whips back to the screen. "Fourteen, I'm sensing something."

Niko slows his steps, understanding my voice's severity.

I cup my hand around my mic. "There's someone… to your right."

He gives a quick glance. "T-that's— He's in my unit."

"I know. But…"

There are whispers amongst the Comms behind me. Commander Blackwood pushes his way through to the SCO, prepared to argue for his son's life. We're catching onto something nefarious.

Harming his unit member might make Niko a traitor, but the only alternative is far worse.

"He's going to kill you," I whisper into the receiver. "I can feel it."

Niko takes an extensive look at his unit member this time. The guy is bulked out and ungrounded in a way I can only describe as rabid. "Fuck," Niko whispers.

The guy senses him, latching onto Niko's eyes. His unit member's piercing, hollow eyes make my skin shiver from three states away. The two men circle each other, hunching like prowling animals—which might be the closest thing to the truth.

"Watch out to your left," I say.

Niko turns his attention back to the crossfire, dodging a smoking, white-hot ball. I gasp as it narrowly whizzes by. That was the same weapon that blasted his unit members apart into indistinguishable pieces. That was almost him.

When Niko refocuses on his unit member, he's tackled like prey.

Niko grunts beneath the beast's force. Ripping off the attacker's helmet, Niko attempts to punch him square in the jaw and knock him out.

But it looks like the guy is drugged.

"Get on top of him. Get yourself off the floor," I say.

Niko struggles beneath the guy, probably half the man's weight. I can't help but notice this unit member is perfectly untouched. They're both no longer being fired at despite being stationary targets, and *everyone else* is mincemeat.

Glancing at Niko's Superior Commanding Officer, I'm met with a ravenous stare. This man *hates* that I warned Niko. This man wanted him dead.

Just as Niko's father starts a literal brawl against his co-worker for trying to assassinate his son, Niko flings himself in an arc around his unit member. He uses backward, rolling momentum instead of wasting energy by heaving the guy up and off him, and it works: Niko scurries out from under him like a spider. I'm awed, remaining perfectly silent to allow Niko to concentrate. He's focusing so heavily on pinning the guy's limbs down that I can literally *see* his action plan in my mind's eye.

Niko's focus comes with great reward. But the blazing look in his unit member's eyes hit me full force.

"He has a gun," I say.

"I— Know!" Niko grunts, struggling to contain the man's arms, preventing him from attaining the handgun in his vest.

I close my eyes, not wanting it to come to this place. But I can feel it. This man is drugged. He won't stop until Niko is dead, or he is, himself.

"You have to do it," I say.

"Fuck. I know."

Niko's dread hits me like a semi. Part of me is relieved he hasn't become bloodthirsty after years of forced bloodshed, not even beneath the excuse of self-defense. But then I feel just as guilty for assuming he could be.

This is *not* the life Niko ever wanted or needed. It's clearer than ever, his agonized reluctance gnawing at my heart's walls.

"D-don't think about it too much," I mutter.

But Niko still struggles with the decision, his hesitation nearly allowing the man to escape. Then Niko zeroes in on the man's gloves, ripping at the straps like he's tearing open a present.

"What are you doing?! Protect yourself!"

"I am! Mentally!" He claws at the second glove, digging his elbow beneath the man's jaw while he analyzes the guy's freshly exposed skin. "I'm looking."

"For *what?!*"

"A good motive. Bet you he's a fucking Nazi."

My eyes go wide. Niko presses his knee into the guy's face now, arresting his arms over his head as Niko tears at his sleeves with a knife, ripping them into shreds. Then we all see it. A clear neo-Nazi symbol tattooed onto his unit member's skin.

"Okay." Niko wheezes, flipping upright. "Don't feel bad now. Look away."

The guy reaches for his gun, his hands finally free. Before I can scream—pressing both hands to my forehead in an instinct to cover my eyes but unable to look away—Niko dives back in with a fistful of knives.

He makes quick work of the neo-Nazi, but that doesn't mean it's pretty. Niko lacerates multiple arteries before I can blink—a frothy mess. I try not to look, covering my mouth to hold powerful gags back—and physically jerking in agonizing pain as the unit member dies in front of us—but I *want* to look. I want to be there for the one I love. This is the reality he's forced to live. I want to witness it. To understand his trauma.

Just as he finishes, a putrid energy tightens my every muscle—another white-hot shot incoming. I croak my words out. "Get out of there!"

Niko sprints away without another word, his narrow dodge of the glowing projectile leaving me gasping for air.

The firing suddenly stops.

I turn around to find Commander Blackwood at the head desk. After winning his fist fight, Yosuke dethroned the Superior Commanding Officer leading Niko's mission, speaking into the receiver. I shudder with the realization that by hijacking the operation, *Yosuke's* command stopped the "enemy's" crossfire.

Our hunch was correct; this was a setup. Like Andre said, they wanted to test new, horrifying weapons against incredibly skilled targets—arguably the best test subjects in the world. But this was more than a test.

If someone hadn't tipped off the Blackwoods, we'd receive news of a very different outcome tonight. Deep in my heart, I know they set this up to kill Jay and Niko.

They wouldn't have stopped until Niko was dead.

I scramble for scrap paper at my temporary desk, desperate to craft a message no one else will understand: 9 taps for "I," 12 taps for "L," and 25 taps for "Y." Maybe the acronym "I.L.Y." is cheesy compared to the depth of my love for him, but it's the best I can come up with in the mere seconds we have left to communicate.

"Fourteen," I whisper, interrupting Niko's panting to mash those numbers together. "Ninety-one thousand, two hundred twenty-five."

His exhausted brain struggles to take in my words. "Wha—"

Someone on the ground with Niko cuts our signal. I'm not sure he heard me, let alone understood. My heart hurts.

Yosuke, who never wears his upset, demands they fly Niko home with shaking, bloodied fists. His threat is clear with the simple phrase, "Lionhearts euthanize for lesser treasons." The Departments scramble to appease their favorite executioners, ensuring Niko will be home in about five hours. Unfortunately, however, he's still under the DoTD's command. We still have no word of who tipped us off from higher up.

The Blackwood security entourage drives me home in complete silence.

It really hits me in the car ride home; Jay is probably dead. Our lovable goofball, one of my favorite people in the world. He survived for so long just to die for absolutely *nothing*.

I begin to cry so hard that Commander Blackwood stops his driver, rushing into the back seat to give me a dad hug. Sobbing heavy tears, I lean against him as his arm remains stationed on my shoulder.

"You did it," he says. "I'm forever in your debt."

"I want Niko to live, so I would've done it no matter what. But we— We couldn't save Jay."

He says nothing.

I've been grieving Niko and Jay for a long time. This is only confirmation of what I've grappled with for four years, but it still fucking kills. If Niko's father weren't comforting me, I wouldn't know how to breathe.

When we pull up to my apartment, I groan; Andre's car

is parked on the street. We all notice him stepping outside, watching us from the balcony like a hawk.

"Do you know him?" Yosuke mutters, still gently patting my back.

"Yes. A regrettable ex. I've tried to break up with him three times now."

Niko's father grows quiet. I can feel his irritation no matter how much he suppresses it. "Do you need me to remove him from your apartment?"

I chuckle, pulling myself together. "It's fine, thanks. I'll deal with him myself. He'll leave after I break up with him a fourth time."

"A *fourth*? Emmalee. I'll go with you."

"N-no, really, Commander. It's just… This is too embarrassing. I'll get rid of him myself."

Yosuke understands the power of an empath's reassurance, so rather than disagreeing, he looks away. "Clara and I are here if you need us. We'll protect you, no matter what."

I hug him, earning me a respectful pat on the back. "Thank you, Commander. As soon as Niko's home, I'll be there. Please let me know."

As I hop out of the car, he genuinely smiles. "I will, Emmalee. Thank you. For everything. Thanks to you, this isn't the worst day of my life."

I wave, biting back tears and waiting for his car to pull away. But it doesn't; he's still nervous about my ex-ex-ex boyfriend in my apartment and won't leave until I'm safely inside. I laugh beneath my breath, beeping myself into my apartment complex and rushing upstairs.

My front door swings open before I can find my keys.

"Who was that?" Andre's forehead is covered with nervous sweat beads.

"Andre, I'm the one who should be asking questions. Why are you inside my apartment?" I duck beneath his arm to slip past, setting my keys on the table with a clatter. Then I exit onto the balcony, giving the Commander a thumbs up. "Breaking into your ex's apartment isn't appropriate, pretty much anywhere else in the world."

"You've never had a problem with it before. And I… I missed you."

I whip around to face him. "You just miss the sex."

He drops his head to avoid my gaze, leaning against the sliding glass door. "Have you been crying?"

My heart aches even deeper; it's more real with every passing second. "Yes."

"Oh…" He says. I can tell he's expecting something more.

I grind my teeth in an effort to contain myself. "An old friend of mine died."

"Oh." He meets my eyes again. For a moment, it seems like he expected me to say something else, although I can't imagine what. But considering the awkwardness emanating from him, I figure he's unsure how to respond to grief.

He opens his arms for a hug.

I instantly bawl. Andre wraps my exhausted body in his arms, carrying me to bed. He's grown more thoughtful over time, but someone else will love him in the way that I can't.

I can't handle his explosiveness. Or name-calling. Or subtle manipulation. Okay, maybe he's more toxic than I realized while we were dating.

But as I lay here and cry in his arms for *three whole hours* until I have no more tears left, my mind numbs. And he worms his desires back into our discussion.

"Can we make love just one more time?"

My guts churn. How will he react when I say no this time? "Andre…"

"I'll leave you alone about it forever. This can be goodbye."

I sigh.

"Just so I don't have to leave you like this. Let me make you feel good one last time so you don't have to cry yourself to sleep."

I prop myself up, feeling into the ache in his eyes.

If I don't focus on my present surroundings, either I see a bloody, dying neo-Nazi, or my heart seizes in pain over memories of Jay that are too raw to face. If Andre wasn't here, I'd be having full-blown panic attacks.

And after all we've been through, keeping each other from agonizing loneliness the past two years, I think I didn't let him down soft enough. Deep down, he wants to be loved. Then there's the dose of male entitlement clouding his mind. He can't wrap his head around rejection without thinking he's a failure.

Being a failure is something I relate with, down to my core. I don't really love Andre, but I do care about him and don't want to make him feel like another washed-up reject.

"Listen to me," I whisper. "I'm still your friend, but we are *not* together anymore. I don't want to hurt you, and that's not what this is. I'm trying to tell you the truth so you can live a better life with someone who will appreciate *everything* about you, okay? You'll find someone else who will love you right, I promise."

Something shifts between his eyes. It's the first time I've felt him getting in touch with his emotional heart. "Is that a no?"

"Yes, Andre. That's a no. We broke up."

After an agonizingly long pause, he says, "I know. This is really goodbye."

Eventually, I cry myself to sleep. When I wake up a few hours later to Yosuke texting me about Niko's incoming arrival, I also wake up to a sobering object on my bedside table—and no Andre.

My heart screams in my ears, knowing exactly what disastrous, plastic omen I'm looking at with no idea of how to react. My mind exits my body.

Then I'm sent into a rage. I call Andre, something I never do, but of course he doesn't answer. I'm forced to text him, asking why the hell he left a "thing" on my bedside dresser and bolted before explaining himself.

Waiting for his response, my whole body quivers as I stare at the unused pregnancy test. This is worse than ominous—it's a threat. I can't write out what it is over text, let alone use it. A text is evidence, the test is even better evidence, and Andre knows it. This is another manipulative tactic to control me. It has to be.

But he confesses—over text—to what he's done.

"I haven't worn a condom since you broke up with me, and I feel kinda bad about it," his text says. At least I think that's what it says with how blurry my tears make my eyes.

He assured me he wore one, every time. He definitely didn't use his ridiculous pull-out method either.

Then he texts, "I just couldn't let you go."

His energy feels honest through the screen, no matter how twisted his logic is. I don't think he intended to hurt me, but rather to tie me to him with a pregnancy. To keep me from breaking up with him, permanently.

"But now I know I have to let you go," he continues. "There's money in your drawer in case it's positive. Goodbye."

I've never felt this type of hurt in my life. I don't know what type of violence this qualifies as, but I know it burns a raging fire in my gut. The curious look in his eyes from a few hours ago makes perfect sense now, but I don't want it to. I want to pretend this text never existed, ripping open my bedside table and chucking what must be Andre's entire savings across the room.

When I call Andre again to scream at him, he sends me straight to voicemail. Again and again, until Yosuke texts me that Niko's flight lands in forty-five minutes and I have to run out the door.

I trip on the apartment stairs, slipping down a step before gripping the railing like a lifeline. Struggling to contain both the grief and disgust boiling inside me, it feels like hot, angry tears are all I own. My life was just getting good, but this could change everything. If gutting me to strip me of my power was Andre's goal, it worked.

CHAPTER 25

Niko

Opening my eyes, I'm met with an unfamiliar face.

"Oh, my God," this woman whispers, swishing her long, dark hair with a turn of her head. "Emmalee!"

Hearing Emmalee's name, I jump out of bed to find her, but this unfamiliar woman stops me. I pause to process her black lipstick, highly intrigued. I haven't seen anyone wearing makeup in a while, and this look is striking to the point it's surreal. I thought it was dried blood painted on her lips. Maybe I'm still in Sumner's nightmare dimension.

"Niko?!" Emmalee's breathy whisper makes my heart hurt. I can *feel* her pain.

Sure enough, her eyes are bright red. They're prominent against jet-black hair dye, chopped above her shoulders with feathered bangs. She's stooped over, clutching her stomach.

"Ems, you're hurti—"

I was attempting to run to her, but somehow I ended up on the floor.

There's a clunky, protective boot on my right foot. The sting wasn't noticeable at first, but now that I think about it, I was running on a fractured foot for hours—the absolute least of my problems.

Emmalee gasps, kneeling at my side. Her black lipstick friend trails behind her, covering her gaping mouth.

Flopping back against the floor, I burst out laughing. I can't stop.

"Niko?!" Emmalee half-laughs. "What the hell is going through your mind right now?"

I roll onto my side, only laughing harder. "After all that, only my fucking *foot* is broken?"

She laughs with me, squinting against swollen eyes. "What do you mean *only?* Three of your ribs are too!"

"Eh, that's fine. They usually are."

We cackle even louder, clinging to each other's hands. Her friend gawks at us, only making us laugh harder.

Emmalee dives for my chest, burying her nose into me. Her warmth is real. This is *real.* Then she really starts to sob; her whole body trembles violently in my arms.

I whisper, "I'm so sorry, *so* sorry. I'm never leaving you again."

"I was so scared I lost you." She clings to me. "Nothing felt right without you."

Her words sink into my chest, flushing a sob out. With Emmalee's friend meeting my eyes, I'm reminded I can't talk about the Departments. For now, I bury my nose into Emmalee's ear, whispering as quietly as possible. "You literally saved my life, Ems. You're the most incredible best friend in the world."

She squeezes me, feeling my head, back, and shoulders like she's making sure I'm real. I take a few deep breaths, stroking the back of her head. Soon, her breathing levels out, especially when her friend helps me comfort her with whispered reassurances.

Then I analyze our surroundings. "Has anyone checked that camera?"

Emmalee's friend points to the security camera eyeing us from the corner. "You mean that janky thing? What are we checking for, exactly?"

"It's alright, Clarity." Emmalee gets extremely serious despite her adorable runny nose. She steadies my cheeks with soft palms, gazing straight into my eyes. "Niko, listen to me closely."

"O-okay."

"This is a safe place. You don't have to do that anymore."

I furrow my brows, glancing at the camera. Checking it feels compulsory. "You really aren't going to check it?"

"Nope. This is not a warzone. This is a place for you to heal. And keep looking at me, okay?"

I gaze into her gorgeous eyes, as instructed.

"Let me take a turn. I'll protect you and keep watch. Your work is done."

I grip her arm, sighing in relief and preparing to thank her. But who was protecting me all this time? I wasn't alone, was I? My heart throbs. I've forgotten something important. Someone.

"Jay," I whisper.

Emmalee draws a shaky, tearful breath. "What do you remember about Jay?"

I think about it, long and hard.

She's staring expectantly, but I honestly have nothing. I have no idea where Jay is or what happened to him. I don't know how I got here, what city I'm in, or if I'm wrong and this isn't real.

"I'm sorry," I whisper. "I don't know."

Emmalee wipes her eyes, still holding my hand as she stands. "That's okay."

The quiet woman touches Emmalee's shoulder, her confused eyes darting between us.

Emmalee clears her throat. "Sorry, Clarity. Let me introduce you both properly."

"Wait, let me get up." I rise to my knees, and have instant proof that, yes, this is very real. And my foot is very broken. It's probably just a hairline fracture since I can still move it, but my body is screaming at me to stop putting weight on it.

"Are you okay?!" Clarity rushes to help Emmalee pull me to my feet.

"Yep." I grit my teeth as I plop on the bed's edge. "I'm *great*. Nice to meet you, Clarity."

Emmalee laughs, and I stare in awe. Her laugh is sweeter than I remembered.

"I really am great," I mutter. "I'm alive. And with you."

Clarity and Emmalee smile. Then they help me lay back in bed. I don't have much to say yet, so I listen as they tell me all about how they became instant friends in the hospital, helping each other through a rough time. Multiple red flags raise, notably how ill they are. Their pain is no longer concealable. I force myself to smile, biting back the knowledge that it's too late for any of us to be free from Sumner's experiment.

As they speak, I can gauge how much is wrong with me. I keep waiting for the parts of their stories with mission instructions, giving me a command on what to do next, or who to kill, or who not to kill, or how to act when I get there. Or worst of all, expecting them to snap and turn on me, forcing me to subdue or kill them. I'm shocked at how free they are to walk around and hang out. To speak about things openly and laugh about something other than their own deaths.

"Are you... okay?" Emmalee mutters.

"I'm fine."

Clarity stands, taking her cue to leave. "It was so nice to meet you, Niko. I hope you feel better."

"Thank you, it was nice to meet you too." I sound robotic.

I watch Clarity exit in silence. Then I look over to Emmalee. She's absolutely devastated about something. I brush her bangs from her eyes, and she smiles.

"Are *you* okay?" I ask.

She nods. "How about you?"

"I'm... confused. Where are we exactly?"

"We're in Sumner Hospital." Her expression shifts to mirrored panic as my anxiety spikes. "What? Is that bad?!"

I sigh, sinking into my pillow. "Pretty much the worst. Especially with that camera."

"What? But I work here..."

"Do you ever see him? The CEO?"

"Um... No..."

I exhale. But when I close my eyes, I see something. Sumner. Me. *Jay.*

My breathing rate soars beyond my control.

Emmalee jumps up. "What's wrong?!"

"I— I see— His— Body." I have to pant out each word. "In— My— Head."

Emmalee searches my eyes, not understanding. Then she takes an empath's guess. "You saw how Jay died?"

"Yes," I gasp. "Can't— Breathe."

Multiple agonizing minutes pass until Emmalee tracks down a nurse who isn't already dealing with a crisis.

Two figures race in. At first glance, I see unfamiliar, attacking forms.

Jerking upright, I reach for my combat knife to defend myself, only to find my thigh bare—and that the "attacking forms" are just civilian nurses. Something about my face must show how instinctual it has become to fight back, even when I can't breathe; the nurses backpedal, bumping into Emmalee in the doorway.

"No! Help him!" Emmalee rasps alongside my desperate gasps for air, her petrified, wide eyes tearing at my heart.

The nurses share an uneasy glance before rushing back into action.

Their first solution is to hold a paper bag over my mouth, which I'm unable to say never works for me. Only Jay knows how to help me when this happens, and he's *dead*.

One nurse tries to inject me with something without telling me what it is, and I grab her wrist forcefully. The poor woman shrieks. The vial flips out of her hands and shatters, convincing two nurses to pin me down while another runs for a new vial.

"Don't hurt him!" Emmalee says. "He's double triggered; someone injec— sorry, someone drugged him without his consent once. You have to actually *explain* what you're doing to your patients."

"Oh…" A nurse softens her grip.

"Can I do it?" Emmalee asks. They look at her like she's speaking backwards. "The injection part, after you put the needle in safely?"

The nurse returns with a new vial. "I *guess* that's okay?"

"Will you allow me to do it instead?" Emmalee leans in, stroking my cheek. Her voice is a soothing lifeline.

My focus darts between her hands and the vial, unsure about this "help" even if my lungs are drowning themselves. But I can't stop seeing what became of Jay. It genuinely feels like I'm about to die.

"Niko. Would I ever knowingly hurt you?" Emmalee asks.

I shake my head no.

"Then you can trust me when I say… you'll probably like this high, to be honest." She smirks, and I melt.

I've missed that smile. Her childhood picture could never compare to the real thing, no matter how attached I've become to that photo.

I nod, giving everyone my approval.

Resisting all urges to snap the syringe in half in the nurse's hand, I tense up instead, bouncing my knee.

"You're okay." Emmalee rubs my arm, reminding me to stay calm. "We're just trying to help you."

She takes over for the actual injection part. True panic hits when I stare at the syringe itself, watching the liquid disappear into my body.

But then I'm suddenly calm.

They surround me in silence as the room starts to feel like jelly.

"Oh, he's definitely feeling good now," one nurse chuckles.

They all laugh, tidying the disheveled room. Emmalee waltzes around everyone, not letting go of my hand for a single second as they work around us. Her mesmerizing black hair swishes across her pink cheeks. I'm dying to run my fingers through it. I'd kiss her until she also couldn't breathe, but my body is so heavy. So relaxed.

"Ems," I mumble. "Are you my angel?"

She turns, surprised. Then she throws her head back and laughs like her and Jay always do: with their whole hearts. I chuckle softly as she runs her hands through my ugly, buzzed hair, her black fingernails sending tingles down my spine.

I flip onto my side, reaching for her. She leans over the hospital bed guard rails, giving me a stable hug.

"I never wanna leave you, ever," I say.

She chuckles beneath her breath, nuzzling into my nose with hers. "I'll make sure you won't have to anymore."

"Really?"

"Yes, really. We're going to get you feeling so much better, okay?"

"Okay."

She smiles, kissing my forehead. I fumble for her hair, desperate to pet her head.

Emmalee laughs. "You are *so* high."

I frown. "No, you're just pretty."

She giggles, biting her lower lip. "Don't say anything sober-Niko wouldn't say."

"Sober-Niko says you're pretty too."

Emmalee laughs, but I'm not joking. "I'm sorry, don't be mad! You're just so... adorable."

I sigh. "I'm serious. Your heart is the prettiest."

She tears up again. Emmalee squishes her cheek against mine, her breath tickling my ear. "Your heart is beautiful too, pretty boy."

"...Emmalee?"

"Hm?"

"I love you. Do you know that?"

She freezes. Pulling back, she studies my face. I try to seem as sober as possible to make her believe me, but that only makes her smile.

"Yes, I know. Do you know I love you too?"

I grasp in the air until I find her hand. "You do?"

Kissing my cheek, she whispers, "Yes, I do. I always have, and I always will."

I bury my embarrassingly huge grin into my pillow with a groan.

"Niko? What are you doing?"

"Mm... That made my heart feel *really* good..."

Stroking my head with a laugh, Emmalee beams. "Oh, you are *so* not going to remember any of this tomorrow, huh?"

I laugh along with her, searching for her hand again. She places it into mine.

"I'm sleepy," I say.

"Go to sleep. I'll be here, on duty."

That's right. Emmalee said she's my new protector. I wish I was sober enough to express how much that means to me. The best I can do is mumble, "I want to protect you too."

"I know," she whispers. "But it's my turn right now. I'll keep you safe, no matter what, okay? I'll watch over you while you sleep."

I stare at her incredible see-through gray eyes until I can't keep my eyes open. "Thank you, Ems."

"Thank *you* for coming back."

CHAPTER 26

Emmalee

Niko had to be transferred to the locked-down psychiatric ward at Sumner Hospital—where they "treat" immense pain with a dose of medical neglect. I hate this for him. Whenever they let me visit after a shift, I find him pacing around his tiny hospital bed with his crutches. It's like he's been running for years and doesn't know how to stop.

His wounded mind cycles over something in particular, and it's freaking me out. Chronic Nightmare Syndrome—that Clarity, Niko, and I have been separately diagnosed with—isn't an accurate diagnosis, according to Niko. He says it's a symptom of a biological weapon called S-8-something-I-can-never-remember that was tested on the DoTD.

Of course, no one believes him but me, but even I'm unclear on the level he's seeing reality. I think I hurt his feelings because of it.

I can believe the Departments would toy with a biological weapon. But does that mean it's the reason behind everyone seeming ill, experimental drug trial patient or not? I almost don't want to believe it.

No matter what, I can't wrap my head around one part of Niko's theory: that S8-whatever is "creating a whole new place." Niko is *insistent* on it.

Whenever neighboring psychiatric patients have an episode, Niko reverts to pure paranoia. At its worst, it takes him a long time to come out of combat mode, but the poor guy doesn't do anything wrong. Yet, if he even flinches, three or more buff people barge in to restrain him. Despite Niko's skills, it still feels like an overreaction. He's never hurt any of us.

Although, they might be seeing what I'm seeing and responding accordingly. If I leave to pee, when I return, there's a split second where Niko deciphers if he's supposed to kill me—hunter eyes that whip your soul out of you. His resulting guilt is so potent that it stings my eyes and exacerbates my nausea—something that's increasingly worse this week.

I don't know how to be close to him anymore when we do talk. And I don't know if he's protecting himself or me, but he's distancing himself more every visit. Then I go home and, of course, cry.

It feels like all I do is bawl. Maybe I'm PMS-ing, but it's never been this bad. My emotions are sky-high until I'm physically nauseous from upset, my swollen chest aches, and I'm so tired that I can't stand for longer than a few minutes at a time.

It scares me. I usually never track my period, but I tried counting back on the calendar at least twenty times. I'm guessing it's about five days late, which isn't that big of a deal.

Okay, maybe it is. The other option is that I've been so busy with my second job at the covert deprogramming operation that I didn't realize I missed my period last month, in which "thirty-three days late" makes me want to shit myself in fear.

Let's go with five.

But no matter how much I've tried to bury it, I haven't forgotten Andre's drastic betrayal. What one day late could mean, let alone five. I'm not dating Niko, but if I'm pregnant and forced to tell Niko why, I think guilt might strangle me.

Terrified is an understatement. I'm mortified I let this happen to myself, that I didn't *notice*. I feel so unbelievably naive and ashamed that I haven't told a soul.

Andre truly meant "goodbye." I can't find that worm anywhere. I'm assuming he'll show up to claim me if I end up visibly pregnant, but for now, I've been completely abandoned and devastated. Even the thought of touching the test strikes terror into me.

And the most terrifying problem of all: I've always wanted to have a baby, but only with one person.

"Emmalee, did you hear me?" Niko asks.

"Sorry, Niko… I'm *so* tired."

"I was saying, maybe you should go home early to get some rest. You look exhausted."

He's right, but it pisses me off. He's pushing me away, but we're finally together. Not only that—I'm angry I'm physically unable to be strong for him. My shoulders raise, and I can't hold back. "I came here to be with you. Don't you want to spend time with me?"

Niko says nothing at first, knowing this is a losing battle. Then he smiles. "I always do, Ems. That's why you should rest so we can spend more time together tomorrow."

My cheeks burn. Even when he's this sick, he's more level-headed than I am. I grab his hand and draw it to my forehead, trying my best not to break into tears.

"Emmalee?"

"Just give me a minute."

I've sent multiple deprogramming therapists to scope out his case, but only one is willing to work with "the Wolf." It's all so frustrating.

On top of that, Dr. Sumner is visiting the hospital today. I *can't* go home and rest; I have a CEO to destroy.

It's a colossal undertaking I've kept to myself, and I'm dying to spill it to the person I trust the most. Especially because it sounded like Niko hates Sumner too. He probably has information I could *really* use.

But Niko isn't fully present. When he is, he keeps me at a distance.

So I have no one.

"Hey, Ems," Niko whispers.

I look up to his puppy-dog expression verging on tears, and my chest constricts. I was so focused on myself that I didn't notice his energy plummeting.

"I'm sorry, okay? I want to be close to you, but I'm a weapon, not a person anymore. It's not safe for you here."

Tears flow. Hot, angry ones. "Nikolai Blackwood. You are a

human being, even if you've been told otherwise. I'm going to be here for you, but I need you to put in the work to survive this, okay? Do *not* give up on yourself. Or us."

His bottom lip quivers, tears streaming down his cheeks. "Okay, Ems. I'll work hard. I'm sorry."

I open my arms for him, warning him of an approaching hug instead of diving straight in. Once he opens his arms to show me it's okay to touch him, I squeeze him tightly until he lets out a soft sob.

"It's not your fault," I whisper. "You don't have to work hard, just try your best. You can do this. You can feel like yourself again someday soon."

He nods. Then he shudders at the door creaking open. It's not his usual defensive reaction, so it startles me when his emotions spike in a relentless fear. And I *feel* why.

A vile presence appears behind me.

It's the first time in my life I've felt such severe instincts burst inside me, demanding I shield my abdomen and run— startling evidence of something I can't think about right now. But I shouldn't make a scene, so I bottle my adrenaline flood. I'm Niko's protector too.

Wiping my eyes, I whip around to greet the foreboding footsteps at the door.

And there he is: Dr. Sumner.

"Oh, who's this?" He smiles. It's not like the tabloid described; as his grin stretches wider, raising my shoulders with a flash of Niko's doom in my core, it's the furthest from "charming" I can imagine.

My stuttering heart begs me to run. But that's not what I came here for.

I hold my hand out, putting on my best smile. "Hi! Emmalee Richards."

He shakes my hand, studying my face. "Richards, Richards… Oh! You're the empath, yes?"

"Yes!" I hope Sumner can't see my knees shaking. He recognized my name.

"I see you've met one of my vital patients. Are you working today? Where's his chart?"

Turning around to find his "vital" patient, I realize he's motioning directly to *Niko*. And Niko looks like a terrified baby bunny. Not just of Sumner. Of *me*. I look back to Sumner and find him smiling in the face of Niko's fear.

I'm way in over my head.

The floor threatens to meet my skull, tugging at my eyes and making me see a rainbow flurry amongst a black sea. I drop into the visitor chair at Niko's side with a thud, keeping my cool as the blood returns to my brain.

Finger-combing my hair, I steady my voice. "I don't have Blackwood's chart yet. He's still new. We were just talking about a mutual friend who passed away, so I'm sorry I've obviously been crying."

Sumner *laughs*. Even after I glare, his unaltered expression says he believes his reaction was socially acceptable. Maybe in the DoTD crowd, but nowhere else. I *definitely* wasn't joking about my dead friend.

Niko gives me what-the-fuck-are-you-doing eyes, and I pat his hand.

"So? What do you think?" Sumner asks.

"Excuse me?"

"About Blackwood. We've worked closely for years. He's a good friend of mine. A little weird, I'll admit, but very helpful."

Niko's breathing speeds up double-time behind my back, but I keep calm.

I'm not sure what he's done outside of horrific experimentation, but Sumner isn't ashamed. He's *gloating*. I monitor his eyes, absorbing his emotions. He's immersed in Niko's reaction. *Craving* it. He knows what he's saying will upset Niko, and that's why he's saying it.

Now I don't just want to take him down. I want him to suffer at the hands of his own game.

I "impatiently" cross my arms, my excuse to tap a subtle message to Niko: *sabotaging him*. As I tap, I put on my scariest, scolding babysitter face. "You're asking me to talk about my patient, right in front of my patient? A little inappropriate, don't you think?"

Niko huffs out a short laugh. His energy has less betrayal

coursing through it in my direction, but his hatred hasn't lightened toward Sumner.

Dr. Sumner cackles at the top of his lungs. I'm tempted to cringe at its ratty tenor, but he looks me directly in the eyes to say, "I *like* you!" I shudder. Waving me toward him, he cackles again. "Challenging a CEO in his own hospital! *You* are *hilarious*. Come! Tell me about yourself."

I hesitate. There's no choice but to follow Dr. Sumner. If I don't, he'll ask why and see right through me. He just seems like that type of guy.

So even though this might hurt Niko to watch, I follow Sumner out the door.

I'm a little spacey, drowning beneath the onslaught of Niko's upset. It's all I can focus on, calling out to me like he's screaming. In reality, he's fallen silent.

Sumner catches on, checking over his shoulder at Niko's locked cell. "Oh, is he distracting you? You can feel his emotions, right? Don't pay him any mind; it's always such melodrama with him. He's an interesting case, though. Predictable, but also not."

"Really? Well, I'm still getting to know him."

He stops walking. "That's interesting. I read you had a restraining order filed against him."

My fingers are numb from how thready my heartbeat feels. Sumner has definitely looked me up, and has been asking leading questions *this whole time*. From now on, I'll have to stick with vague bits of truth. Just enough to hold up on paper.

All I can do to recover from my blatant lie is to laugh off my anxiety, urging him to continue walking by strutting ahead like nothing happened. "You can thank my overprotective father for that. It was ridiculous, really. I made my father overturn it."

"Really? So my patient didn't actually hurt you? He *is* the violent type."

"I'm seeing that now." I internally cringe at my hurtful lie. "If you *really* want to know what's up between Blackwood and me, my parents were obsessed with keeping me separated from the dreaded Wolf growing up. So by 'getting to know him,' I mean I'm getting to know the *new* Blackwood. We met years ago in school, and he's, well, not the same anymore."

Sumner hums, still smiling. He hasn't stopped smiling since I met him, really. "I see, I see. So, what about you, Richards?"

"Me?" My focus zips down the hall for something safe to latch onto. But we're alone. Still in the psych ward, where everyone is buried behind doors. "I'm not that interesting."

"That's *exactly* what makes you interesting."

I give him a staredown. Up close, I can see he's wearing makeup to cover old bruising. But I'm too unsettled to be satisfied with the thought of someone kicking his ass. He's smirking, attempting to either flatter me or crack my composure. If my forward nature amuses him, I'll work with it.

I sigh, rolling my eyes. "You're trying to butter me up, aren't you?"

He blinks a few times in surprise before letting out a hearty laugh. "You caught me. But I do want to know. It seems we'll be working together." He looks back to Niko's cell, snickering again. "I was planning on working closely with one of my local assistants, and I might've just found my girl! We should get to know each other!"

"*Your* girl?" I bite back the urge to tear his eyeballs out, giving a light scoff as a compromise between my safety and sanity. "Watch it, CEO."

He lets out another noxious cackle.

"But you're right," I continue. "We *should* get to know each other."

CHAPTER 27

Niko

I don't think I've felt this confused for a long time. Emmalee was the last person I expected to turn on me, but she claimed to be "sabotaging" Sumner. I don't think she realizes that doesn't exist with him; she's ultimately sabotaging herself. I'm upset she's trying to stay involved with someone like him, but I'll do my part to erase Sumner's thoughts on Emmalee's connection to me. She'll have to decide what to do with the rest.

When my door opens next, I expect to see her again, ready to sort things out, but I'm reminded life isn't that kind.

Sumner smirks. "Hello, you little shit."

Without Emmalee here, I'm no longer shaking with shame as his power reigns over me. I've had a full day of anger boiling beneath the surface for this man with little left to live for. I know what I have to do before he takes another best friend's life.

"What the fuck do *you* want, old man?"

He steps closer, expecting me to flinch. I shove him backward once, and he almost loses his composure. So I hop off the bed and shove him again, and again, and one more time until he's pressed against the wall.

"You don't own me anymore," I hiss.

He doesn't take the opening I leave to respond. He's frozen, struggling to retain his smile.

I laugh. "That's right. Nothing has changed since we last 'worked' together. You held up your end of the deal, and I held up mine. Now that I'm dishonorably discharged, you don't have the authority to order me around. I'm just another fucking traitor."

Sumner traces his thoughts. His smile fades, and my body tenses, taught to brace itself at the sight of his straight face. But he doesn't lash out right away.

He looks sad. "You didn't hold up on your end. You still owe me."

"Excuse me? What the fuck do you call what you did to me after, rapi—"

He slaps a heavy hand over my mouth, cursing my nose with antiseptic stench. "Don't call me that ever again, thief."

"Mmph?"

"Yes, *thief.* I saved your life, and what do I get? You stole my research like a starving dog. I should've known what you were really after."

I suck in an ecstatic breath. This is the best bait I've ever been handed; something finally upset him enough to feel like he's losing. I pull myself together, continuing to play the character of his waking nightmares. Just like I play it in mine.

Rolling my eyes, I snort against his hand before tearing it off me. "Why the fuck would I want your *research?*"

His chin juts back in wounded shock.

"Your precious life's work is as useful as my own shit. I didn't steal it. I permanently *deleted* it."

Sumner's entire body sinks before my eyes, and I burst into hysterical laughter. The more I laugh, the more his face falls blank.

He sputters. "Y-you— You'll—"

"I won't *anything.* I'm not your starving dog anymore, buddy. Go the fuck home and leave everyone I know out of your bullshit."

He turns to leave without another word, and it's enough to startle my stomach into an anxious gurgle. He's doing it. *He's* obeying *me.*

But I'm not convinced he's scared enough.

I catch his wiry wrist just as he brushes the doorknob. "You want to know the real reason why I didn't kill you?"

With a tense swallow, Sumner's curiosity peeks through fearful eyes.

"That's what you raised me to be—a killer. But I won't be

what you want anymore. I'd much rather kill your research than waste my time killing you. Your social experiment in keeping me tethered to you failed. And guess what, *Charles?*"

His bottom lip quivers. "What?"

"You created a monster you'll never be able to kill." I grip his wrist until the joint crackles. "If you go against my wishes at any point, *no one* can physically stop me from breaking back into your office and sending out more orders to delete *everything*. So you leave my friends and family alone, and I'll leave you alone. Got it?"

After studying my eyes, he only grows more scared. I'm not smiling either. We're dead serious, and I can feel him mentally shrinking away. My threat is valid this time. His research is worth more than his life.

He nods rapidly.

With that, I let him go.

My punishment for my behavior isn't as bad as I expected. I'm strapped to the bed now, but what else can I do here except find images in the textured ceiling tile, anyway?

I lay here and think for a while, mostly about how I'm finally seeing Hana tomorrow. I'm afraid to see how much she's grown. How much I've missed.

All for nothing. For *research*.

Sumner didn't realize it, but my leverage against him is useless. If I delete the data, he's powerful enough to do anything he wants without medical grounds for it. At this point, "proper" scientific research is his excuse to justify his sick pleasures to his colleagues. He's fooling no one but himself, something I'm counting on to make sure he leaves Emmalee and our families alone.

Hopefully my threatening act was enough. Enough to scare him into irrational thought patterns surrounding what's most precious to him—a torture tactic he's proven works on me. Now he'll spend his energy keeping me out instead of pulling me in.

It's the only thing I could think to do. At this point, killing Sumner or exposing his research will turn everyone who follows him against me.

No one would believe *me*. Even Emmalee doubts me.

Sumner's influence has grown to an uncontainable infection rate, burrowing its way into too many lives to be killed at the source. He's no longer a single person. He's everywhere I look.

Eventually, my spinning head aches enough to knock me out, and I sleep straight into the next day. They're convinced by midday that I'm behaving myself again and set me free from my bed straps. I continue to lie here anyway.

Until my dad walks in, my baby sister trailing behind him.

I hop out of bed, kneeling with my arms outstretched. But it's an unnecessary gesture. Hana is already a foot taller, up to my chest's base.

"Oh, my gosh, little sprout, you're not so 'little' anymore!" I smile.

She doesn't even look at me. Taking a seat in the visitor's chair, Hana tucks her chin to her chest and crosses her arms.

"Sorry, Hana. I'm not making fun of you—I'm excited for you. You always wanted to be tall like Mom and I, right?"

No response.

Dad pats my shoulder, urging me backward until I plop back on the bed. "You can't walk on that foot, son."

Up close, his drained face pits my stomach. It's the expression he used to get when Hana would have toddler tantrums. She's been giving him hell, and I'm pretty sure it's because…

"You don't want to see me, huh?" I mutter.

"*No,*" she says.

I swallow the poisonous, acidic surge in my veins from her forceful words. A piece of my heart dissolves.

I soften my voice the best I can. "Okay. That's okay. I won't force you to see me, but I'm genuinely so sorry, Hana. I never in my life would choose to leave you."

She meets my eyes with red-faced, rageful tears. "Well, you did."

I'm left gasping like a helpless child as my ten-year-old sister hops up to leave the room. Dad blocks the doorway, and he doesn't need words to express how angry he is with her. She faces him directly, unfazed like a true Lionhearted Blackwood, and fits the name far better than me. No matter how upset she is with me, I love her conviction. She won't take shit from anyone, and we all made sure of it.

She'll be okay. She can survive this world. Without me.

English or Japanese doesn't dissuade her, but Dad tries his best in both. Eventually, I can't stand his temptation to yell at her—a rare occasion for my gentle father—and grab his arm.

"It's okay, Dad. If she wants to go, she can go."

He's frozen in place, torn between us. With a short huff from his nose, he knocks to notify the guard and guides Hana out by the shoulders, telling me he'll be back tomorrow with my mom.

I make sure to seem outwardly calm in front of the guard so she'll let me watch my family disappear down the hall. I cram my cheek against the door's window—smaller than a picture frame—catching the back of Hana's long, flowing brown hair just as it slips out of view. No matter how hard I squish myself into the door, I can't even hold on to the sight of her.

Stumbling back to bed, lying down doesn't feel right anymore. It's one of the rare times I can tell I'm trying to numb out something dreadful because of how much I'm failing to do so. The ache reverberates through me in a low rumble at first, but the moment I pay attention to it, it surges. I bite my arm to keep as quiet as I can, wanting at least one moment to myself before someone drugs or restrains me, but my cries quickly morph into agonized sobs.

I failed her, but I promised my parents I'd protect her with my life. She always felt more like a daughter than a sister, but life kept her from me too. It's no wonder she can't stand me. She thinks I abandoned her.

Mom was forced to have me. She'd never tell me this herself, but earlier this week, Dad used his roundabout analogy method to imply she cares about me but doesn't know how to show it. He told me how hard she fought to hide her pregnancy— to protect me from this world—and how much she still hates herself for getting caught. My existence submitted us to a life of surveillance; a Clara and Yosuke clone was worth more to the Departments than anything they could buy.

But Hana was different, a rainbow baby born a little less than six years after Mom lost the twins. I've learned to appreciate that my parents liked me enough to choose to have a baby again when I was four years old. However, I still remember my mom's face as she struggled against fate on the kitchen floor. It didn't matter how young I was; that moment hurt enough to burn permanent stains in my memory. How she snapped at me, telling me I wasn't allowed to call for help in case the twins could stay inside her and survive. How she shoved me away, accidentally knocking me on my butt. And how disappointed she was that I called for help anyway.

I remember Emmalee's face that day too. She was the only one who didn't look at me like she pitied me—although, she did force me to wash my hands from my mom's blood. Mini Emmalee sighed like I was a silly child and she was a full-grown adult, a whopping four months older and already five.

Dad always told me to find Dr. Richards in case of a medical emergency. Although Mom resented me for years, I'm glad I chose to save her life over the twins' fading chances. I know she blamed me out of her own torturous pain, but deep down, my siblings' loss still feels like my fault. I wanted to redeem myself with Hana.

For a while, I did. At ten years old, I learned everything about raising a baby, skipping a month of school to cradle her tiny body while Mom was recovering and Dad couldn't skip work. She never wanted to be put down, but I never minded. The first time I saw her swollen face, I loved her more than I loved anything, desperate to give her the world. It only made me fight harder. I wanted to shoulder our burdens so she'd never have to be like me, to struggle enough for us both so she'd be forever blissfully unaware.

But I failed at that too. Hana looks as depressed as I was as a child. I wasn't around for her to reach to me for help anymore.

By trying to protect her, I hurt her.

I don't resist the beefy nurses assigned to me today, allowing them to pin me down in fear that I'm hurting myself. They're stunned silent as I sob. It's the first time I've *fully* cried without Jay at my side, so I can't stop. Especially when I remember he'll never be there to stop my tears again, and I wasn't there to ease his fears either. He died all alone.

After they're certain I won't hurt myself, they leave me alone again. I feel like a total weirdo, but I can't help myself. Wadding my bedsheet into a bundle, I hold it to my chest, imagining it's Hana. Imagining I'm worth relying on again.

CHAPTER 28

Emmalee

This is bad, *really* bad.

Oh, I got to know Sumner. Quickly. I pictured Dr. Sumner to be money-driven, but I think it's much, much worse. He's particularly hungry for sadistic pain.

He smiled and smiled. Patient after patient, his smile only grew. He smiled when they wept in my arms. He smiled when I warned him certain patients didn't seem to have much longer to live, directly due to his experiments. He smiled when I got angry with him for smiling. And he smiled when I said I wasn't feeling well and needed to go home. His smile only dissolved once I said I saw what a disgusting piece of shit he was and I plan to quit. That his greed is all he has—not even a mother could love a slimy bastard like him.

Sumner ultimately brushed me off. I'm disposable. He doesn't have to hide his sick power-pleasure because he's protected.

I ran home and puked my guts out for three hours, tainted from standing at his side all day. After witnessing his reaction to the chaos he created, I'm not sure how I'll find the stamina to take him down.

And today, I don't have energy to spare on assholes. I waited all weekend to visit Niko again; his family took the visitor hour for both days.

Today, I have to repair my relationship with Niko.

The guard opens the door from the other side. This is the point where she usually lets me in behind her, so I trudge ahead by habit. But the guard catches me by the arm.

"Sorry, sweetie. He doesn't want any visitors today."

I freeze. I'm not sure if this is an order from higher up or a request from Niko, himself.

My palms sweat, wondering if Sumner returned to harass Niko after I went home, probably to say something about me. I don't know how Sumner hadn't filled his misery quota by the time I left work.

Or maybe Niko truly didn't understand what I'm attempting. Maybe he's mad at *me*.

"Did you tell him it was Emmalee Richards who—"

The guard nods. "Sorry, hun. You'll have to try again tomorrow."

I stand there, quivering, not wanting to leave him alone and verging on panic. "Can you give him a note for me?"

"I *can*." She glances down the hallway to make sure we're alone. "Or you can just, you know… Check in with your badge and make a 'work' visit."

I gasp, tears stinging the corners of my eyes. "Oh, my God, thank you!" I dig into my bag, retrieving my badge with shaky hands. "I'll try to be quick."

"Be careful, sweetie. He's not having a good day."

I swallow the nausea in my throat.

Despite the guard's warning, I gasp when Niko lurches at me the second I walk through the door. Then he melts into his hands, trembling as he grips his hair.

His despair is so potent that I'm already choking back sobs. "I'm so sorry."

"No, *I'm* sorry," he says through his teeth. "Everything is ruined. He's onto you because of me. I can't forgive myself, but they won't let me die, Emmalee. They tied my wrists as if that could somehow stop *me* from hurting myself. And they're watching us on that camera."

With a feverish stare, he urges me to look up at the camera. But I don't. I stride toward him, seething.

"What happened to never wanting to leave me again? I can't do this without you!"

His eyes widen. "I hurt you by tying you to him. To help you, I have to save you from me."

"Stop it!"

He walls off in an instant, eyes falling flat.

I'm really sobbing now. "I'm sorry, I shouldn't have raised my voice. You're still sick, and I need to remember that."

He shrugs, and I chew on my lip.

"This was my choice to get involved, Niko. I'm trying to help everyone survive, okay? You have so much to live for. And I don't want you to die, so… Please don't. Even if you don't want to see me again."

Niko doesn't respond at first, his brows furrowing. "I thought I wanted to see you, but I don't understand your intentions anymore. You're working with him?"

I kneel at his bedside, tapping on his knees. *I'm sabotaging him,* I tap. "Yes, you could say I'm working 'with' him. *Beneath* him is more like it."

"I don't like this," he whispers. "You don't know what he's like."

"Why do you seem so defensive?"

"Because, Emmalee. This is not the game you think it is."

"Wow, that's rude. That sounds like every other man I know. You think my hard work is a *silly* game because I'm a *silly* girl, don't you?"

"No, what? Ems, I'd *never* say that. If you continue to chase him, he'll tear you apart and everyone you love until you've got nothing left of yourself anymore. Not even your own clothes." He thrusts his bound wrists out, struggling to gesture with his hands.

I study his bleach-frayed hospital gown, and it sinks in; Sumner wasn't lying when he emphasized his connection to Niko.

Niko is less delusional than everyone else thinks. He's just another abuse survivor no one believes.

"God, I'm pathetic," he hisses, unaware of my internal freakout. "But I don't think you're a 'silly girl.' You're a powerful woman. And where you use your power matters. If you're truly joining him—helping him do this to me and all those other people—then you're not who I thought you were."

I swallow hard, feeling the weight of his disappointment.

"I never once intended to do any harm to my patients. Yeah, I wrote down how people felt as I comforted them, and I knew the research was fucked-up, but a lot of DoH research is like this! I didn't know what Sumner was truly like until we met, either. I had to guess his intentions behind his research like a conspiratorial freak, then brainstorm alone about how to safely, covertly mess with him. But after meeting Sumner the other day, I couldn't keep pretending. I called him a piece of shit to his smug fucking face and gave him my one-month notice. ...Although, I'm not sure the DoH will actually allow me to quit."

Niko's eyes widen. But then he's entranced with a faraway thought, his energy darkening. He's keeping so much from me when I'm the only one who might understand.

"Niko, what did he do, really?"

He shakes his head no.

"Tell me, please."

"I said, *no*," he snaps.

I shrink into myself. I've never seen Niko's eyes pierce me in distrust like this, let alone hear his voice so sharpened. "I'm not trying to hurt you."

"You already did by helping him."

"I— I didn't know he was targeting you."

"He's the one fucking around with the bioweapon, which you probably have in your system. He's *already* hurt you, Ems, and I can't stand it."

"Niko, what—"

"He killed Jay."

I press my back against the wall, sliding to the floor in shock. No, Niko's not delusional. He's telling the raw truth; I can feel it.

He gets up, approaching me slowly. Crouching in front of me, he looks at me in reflected agony. I cover my mouth, trying not to disturb the entire psych ward with my whimpering.

My mind keeps cycling back to the experimental drug Clarity and I tried for our autoimmune diseases, leaving us with Chronic Nightmare Syndrome. I didn't have the insight to ask the nurses which company created the drug at the time, and it was mixed into saline IVs, so it's not like the bags were marked.

All along, was Sumner's "drug" actually this biological weapon? The S-8-something Niko keeps talking about?

I have no idea if Sumner's cruelty was behind it, but at this point, I think it's safe to assume. Lilith's "brain rot" warning haunts my chronic nightmares—that I could lose all functioning and thought overnight, or worse, forget everyone I've loved. Every night, I dream I'm trapped with other brain-dead patients in animal cages, basements, or jail cells—a confinement roulette.

If Niko's bioweapon theory is true, so is my dream's metaphor. Sumner's experiments were a trap. The experiments *I* participated in, as an empathic researcher, were testing biological weapons on immunocompromised, desperate people. And I was unknowingly on both sides.

But now our best friend is gone because of Sumner. I don't understand why anyone would cause such purposeful suffering, and to so many people. I'm not sure I ever will.

"I'm sorry," I breathe. "I'm so sorry I hurt you and others by doing this."

Niko loops his arms over my head, his bound wrists resting at the crook of my neck. He pets my head the best he can, leaning into my nose. "Fuck, no, I'm sorry for being so harsh and suspicious of you. I see your intentions now, and I believe you."

I'm only able to speak through a pained breath. "I didn't know. I just knew he was hurting people, and I didn't think he'd suspect me, so maybe I could be the one to help save everyone, and… I didn't know."

He kisses my head. "I believe you. You're incredibly brave, and you always have been. I just got paranoid that he somehow distorted the Ems I knew, but I'm relieved to be wrong."

I huff, rubbing Niko's back. "Why? Why would he do this?"

Niko gives me a sympathetic sigh, shaking his head. "I can only guess for the money and widespread control. He's patenting it soon."

I groan. "Yeah, that sounds like every research-obsessed doctor I've ever met."

Our foreheads bump together as we sigh in unison. Luckily, I'm still able to smile at our synchronicity.

But not for long. "What the hell do I do now? Have I

made things worse for you by letting him walk in on you and me hugging?"

"I'm not worried about myself as much as you, Ems. Just stop all association with him so you don't die, please. You're scaring me."

"Okay. But I don't want you to die, either. Especially not by choice."

He takes a deep breath, contemplating my words like I'm asking a cumbersome favor. "Okay. Fine. I won't."

We gaze into each other's eyes for a moment, deep in thought.

"Can I tell your parents you need to be separated from him?" I ask.

"It won't work. His authority is almost at the top."

My stomach drops. "Of the Departments?"

Niko shakes his head no, his eyes bulging to say it goes much further than that.

I gulp. "I had *no* idea… What would I do without you?"

He smiles. "Apparently, try to take down one of the most powerful figureheads in the entire US, all by yourself."

I laugh through my tears. "Shit. Can I at least use your parents' authority to discharge you?"

"Everyone keeps saying I'm too dangerous to go home— lunging at everyone uncontrollably."

"They don't know the Niko I do," I huff. "How about this: if we say we're sending you to their therapy program on a strict schedule, I bet they could convince the DoTD and DoH to let you out early."

A flash of hope hits Niko's eyes for the first time since he's been back, tightening my chest in awe. The Blackwoods told me they hinted at sending him to deprogramming therapy, but he wasn't as relieved as they expected. Then he flat-out rejected their offer. I'm determined to find out why.

"Niko, do you still want to be deprogrammed?"

He drops his gaze. "Do you think… there's still hope for me?"

"To get treated?"

"*Successfully,* yes."

My heart shatters. I feel it in Niko's aching soul; he believes what everyone is saying about him. "Absolutely, Niko. You're not broken. You're mentally, emotionally malnourished. It might be hard to learn how to support yourself, but I *know* you can do it. You just have to take the offer, and we'll be there to help."

He nods over and over again. "Then, please. That's what I want. I'll do the work."

I kiss his cheek. "Okay. Consider it done."

I call Clara Blackwood right where we sit. The Departments are still in damage-control mode when it comes to the Blackwoods, so it's easier than anticipated. Within an hour, we discharge Niko from Sumner Hospital.

CHAPTER 29

Niko

Seconds into my dad and his men escorting me from *Sumner-fucking-Hospital*, a plane approaches.

We're downtown with an airport nearby—something I should've thought about before tackling my father to the ground, sheltering him "before the bombs arrive."

I've made a spectacle of us. People stop to stare.

But it only makes me feel like the whole world has lost its mind.

"What's everyone doing?! The bomber planes are—"

"Shh, not so loud." My father's lean, bruised hands lift me off the ground, pressing me to his chest. He hasn't done that since I was at least half my size.

His right-hand security guy, Max, hands me my crutches. I rush to regain my balance, shoving the crutches under my armpits.

"Slow down. Look around you," Dad says.

So I do. Everyone has already minded their own business, uncaring. I grit my teeth as the plane passes over, revealing itself as a large commercial jet.

I'm met with a horrible sadness I've never seen in my dad's eyes. It makes me uncomfortable.

Then he speaks to me in Japanese. The language has a soothing effect on us both, unwavering in its even pace.

He tells me I can completely leave our security to them. After I go to my first deprogramming appointment, they'll take me home, and, apparently, I'll never have to worry about these things again.

I doubt that.

But I try my best to accept his words, relaxing into the back seat of his car. I can't believe Dad punched my Superior Commanding Officer so hard that his broken hand is *still* green and blue, but I admit it improved my trust in him.

It makes me sick how involved Emmalee is now. She probably *could* take Sumner down, considering she uncovered so much hidden truth, alone, and still had the guts to berate him. But I don't want her to live that miserable life. I don't know how deep she dug herself, but I want to help her escape the hole Sumner traps everyone in. I need to, for us both.

Until the second day, I genuinely had no idea I was in the psychiatric ward. I asked why I was admitted overnight for a hairline fracture in my foot, earning me a pitied look from my favorite nurse.

They admitted me not because I've lost my mind, but because I killed a neo-Nazi assassin in my own unit without being ordered to. Even though it was reported as self-defense, I'm unofficially classified as a traitor. And traitors aren't welcome in the DoH hospital.

The DoTD dishonorably discharged me before they'd be held responsible for my future "unwieldy" behaviors. Especially with my parents incessantly chomping at their necks for the MIA order.

Now they can't order me around. I'll be watched for the rest of my life, but at least the Departments can't stop me from living anymore. They don't have a say after all our family has offered them. How much internal damage we'd cause if we spread the news of their betrayal, after how heavily they've used and advertised me. My dishonorable discharge is both an insult and a blessing.

But no one erased my reputation. Everywhere I go, I'm treated like a live explosive.

We drive onto Department land, headed straight for the DoH.

I sit at attention, watching the pale gray "Medical Strategy" buildings pass. The Department of Health never fails to heighten my paranoia. It's far worse these days, and coming here directly makes us closer than ever to Sumner's grasp.

I don't think I can tell anyone what he's done, ever again. I'm terrified he'll target the people I love. Kill them, like he killed Jay.

Jay's death is *my* fault. I can't stand to live beneath that agonizing weight for much longer.

I've fought for years to live, only to come home begging to die.

"Niko, relax," Dad says. "This is not the same Department of Health you know. Mom and I aren't the only ones with secret disloyalties, and it isn't just a few people anymore. We're an entire *organization* helping people like us feel less… loyal."

"Wow…" I slink back into my seat.

No matter how many times I convince myself that my parents' deprogramming operation is real, it's still a shock to hear my father defy the Departments; I learned my unfaltering loyalty from him, long before I realized my loyalty was misplaced. I thought Dad got his *military* loyalty from his parents, and their parents before that. All along, Dad's loyalty was to the greater benefit of all, no matter what brutal actions he was forced to take to achieve it—even if it meant giving up the family name that gave life to his loyal heart. I always wondered if it felt like he rejected a piece of him in doing so, but his choice finally makes sense; the Lionhearts' killer reputation is also what opened the door to a new, free life for us all.

After years of hating everything he and Mom forced upon me, I'm now more grateful than ever to share their loyal blood.

My slow exhale comes out shaky. "There's a lot I've missed."

"Mm. But I think you'll like this."

Dad exits the car, opening my door and helping me out. I'm a little on edge, not used to all this touching.

He notices, taking a step back to give me some space. "Before we go in, I have something to say."

I peek at him, afraid of what he's thinking. I'm not exactly someone to be proud of.

"Niko." He bends at the waist in a deep bow. "I'm so sorry.

I've failed to raise you in a safe way, and I'll regret it for the rest of my life."

This feels so wrong. I wasn't born in Japan, but I absolutely understand how much silent gravity his gesture holds—too much, if you ask me. I try to bow lower than him, but he doesn't let me. "It's oka—"

"It's *not* okay." His insistence startles me. "I've wronged you, and I'm sorry. You haven't lived the life you wanted to, and that was all I was supposed to give you as a father." He breaks eye contact, shifting his focus to my broken foot. "That's all I'll say for today. I don't want to overwhelm you; the therapy program is already a lot to process, I'm sure. But please know, if you have anything else you desire that'll make your life less painful, I'll do *everything* I can to make it happen."

I clench my teeth a few times in stunned silence. I try to bow at him, thanking him in Japanese, but that's incredibly difficult to accomplish with crutches.

We chuckle to ourselves when he has to catch me. Up close, I study his black irises. The rich black he passed down to me—the color Emmalee always tells me she loves.

I hug him. It's weird, and not something we really do, but I want so many things to change. This feels like a new, undeserved chance at life.

Dad hugs me back.

I'm emotionally exhausted by the time I hobble up the wide cement staircase, attracting extra stares as my dad, a high-ranking Commander, helps his dishonorable son up the Department of Health steps.

We travel the DoH hospital basement's uncomfortably white halls, eventually reaching the Mental Treatment Center. It's no accident they built it in the basement, in the very back. This is supposed to be the walk of shame. But here, I see I'm not alone. The Mental Treatment Center halls bustle with vibrant voices, no longer rigid and eerie like it was four years ago. Familiar faces, old and young, are here to better themselves.

"Fellow traitors," Dad whispers. "And proud of it."

I smile. "I see why you think I might fit in here."

Dad breathes out a soft laugh, the most I can ever rise out of him.

But he doesn't know something else about me, and this is the only individual time we might have for a while.

"Hey, Dad?"

He turns expectantly. We stop in the hallway, leaning in to speak in hushed whispers.

"I'm not just a traitor. I'm also bisexual."

He blinks a few times, taking it all in. Eventually, he asks, "Are you saying you have a boyfriend?"

I shake my head no, my cheeks flushing hot.

"Oh. Well… Okay. Thanks for telling me."

He pats my head, I nod, and that's that: the most boring coming out story in history.

I see a few more familiar faces inside, but I'm generally not well-received. And that's okay. I just need to do better. Be better.

But then I see Dr. Richards, and my hope liquifies.

I whip a U-turn the best I can in crutches, speed-hopping to the entryway's automatic door.

"Nikolai!" Dr. Richards calls out. "Wait!"

I freeze. He's technically a superior, so I correct my posture, dropping my crutches and standing at attention like a flamingo.

Dad collects my crutches this time as Max steadies me by the armpit. I'm verging on heavy panic, face-to-face with the man who probably still hates my guts for "breaking into" his daughter's bedroom.

Instead, Dr. Richards pats my shoulder. Opening and closing his mouth, he looks like he's hesitating on what he wants to say and how he wants to say it.

So I take my chance to say, "I'm sorr—"

"I am so—" He pauses.

We both spoke at the same time, now awkwardly waiting for one another to continue.

I glance at him. I thought his eyes were bloodshot, but he's… crying?

"I'm so sorry—" He chokes up before he can continue. "I didn't mean for you to get deployed, or— Or any of it. I misjudged you."

I sigh in relief. "Dr. Richards, Sir—"

"Please, call me Ben."

"Ah— Um… Ben?" I look to the floor to tame my nerves. "This is the result of my own behavior. I'm sorry for my careless actions when I was a teenager. I disrespected your household and am working as hard as I can to become a better person."

Dr. Richards laughs. "So you're very different from my daughter, after all. *I'm* usually the one who has to apologize to *her*."

I smile. "She's always ten steps ahead."

Dr. Richards guides us to his office, revealing a detailed set of deprogramming plans to choose from. I'm struggling to comprehend that Dr. Richards is working with my dad, let alone that I have the power to choose my own treatment program. Their system is so efficient, Dad and Dr. Richards explain I can start as early as today.

By the end of their explanation, I'm desperately suppressing tears. They've thought of me, about what I might need coming home, when all I really wanted was to plain *come home*. It's almost too much; I'm ready to refuse this help I don't think I deserve, but Dr. Richards and Dad both insist.

I can't argue with one dad, let alone two dads, so we create my therapy goals for this first month: reacting a little less when someone enters the room and carrying cohesive conversations. Apparently, these problems are more pressing than I noticed. I'm humiliated to think about what I've done to help them discover that, but I'm told this is "normal abnormal behavior" for DoTD veterans.

Before I know it, I'm in front of another ex-instructor. The Commander—who insists I call him Brayden—has a psychology degree now, but thankfully, he still looks like he could beat the shit out of my out-of-control ass.

"Do you have any questions about how this works or anything you'd like to start with?" Brayden asks.

I haven't said a word yet. I'm so shocked this is happening. That I'm here. "Is this… Is this like regular talking therapy?"

He shrugs. "If I say yes, is that a problem?"

I reach for my crutches.

"Leaving already?" He sighs, pausing for his heavy smoker's cough. "Take it from me, kid; it's best to just throw yourself into the deep end, head first."

I stare at him for a moment. He's grayed far past his years from what I assume to be as much trauma as I've experienced. I agree with him, but… "Can I at least pace back here? I can't sit still."

"Pace if you need to, but don't leave before you give yourself a chance."

After a pause, I settle on pacing. Except it's not really pacing, it's a clunky hop that clogs my thoughts more than helping them flow. I end up dropping my crutches without thinking, standing flat on two feet.

"Doesn't that hurt?"

"No. I haven't been able to feel things for a long time."

Staring at it, we give my broken foot a moment of silence.

"Welp. That's not good," Brayden says. "You need to feel."

My heart pounds wildly, and I'm not sure why. "Sometimes you don't." I'm surprised by how much I snap at Brayden, like I snapped at poor Emmalee.

But Brayden doesn't take it to heart. "That's true. I used to do a bit of that too. Numbing out until it all piled on top of me and I felt like I couldn't move, breathe, or live beneath its weight. I know you feel trapped in this room, but I'm sure you feel trapped no matter where you go. And that's exactly why I'm trying to pull you out. I'm here to help un-trap you, but I can only do that with your permission."

"Sorry…"

He looks at my foot again. "Alright, just take a damn seat, kid. You're stressing me out with that foot."

I laugh, sitting on the reminiscent, pawprint-bolted bench. "Sorry. I *do* want to do this. I'm just… not used to anything therapeutic other than joking about dying."

His sudden, contagious belly laugh escalates into a booming ring throughout the bare room. "That's not therapeutic *or* a fucking joke, kid!"

I have to laugh along with him. "I know. That's why it's funny."

"You must've wanted to live if you survived that long out there."

I nod.

"So why joke about dying?"

"Because that's how Jay and I made death feel less scary. He's still my combat partner after all these years, and he— Um…"

It's too painful to correct myself from "he is" to "he *was*," so I fall silent.

I wish I could cry in front of someone other than Jay or Emmalee. Today, I can remember Jay died. My insides feel like they're ripping apart under my skin. I can remember everything leading up to his brutal death, but my brain has a deadbolt on the details the closer I get to the end. I'm not sure which parts are missing. I could say this is Sumner's fault for targeting us in revenge, but it's really my fault. For staying involved with Sumner and letting Jay in on my secret, compromising Jay's safety. And now…

"I'm so fucking angry," I whisper.

It's terrifying to say. I don't like being angry. It makes me think of Hana—when she was so small that my mom and I must've seemed like rageful giants. I hate being that person, but it's true. I'm so mad.

"I'm so angry he died."

Brayden leans in. "Because he left you behind?"

My face contorts, so I hide it behind clasped fists. "No. Because Jay isn't just my combat partner. He's been my best friend since childhood. Fuck, no, he's one of my—" My throat tightens like I'm choking. I still can't accept that I lost one of my soulmates. It can't be real. Willing the thought away, I clench my teeth, hard. "I told him not to protect me, not to risk his life for me, but he did, and they targeted him for it, and—" I clear my throat a few times, forcing down burning tears. "And he died the *day* before we could've finally come home! That's fucking ridiculous! What the fuck did we survive *together* for if he was just going to die without me?!"

The air ices over with my agitation. Brayden gets very quiet.

Then he takes a seat beside me. "Niko, your lifelong friend died this past *month?*"

I nod. My whole body violently shakes, and I'm desperately hiding my face as I try not to hyperventilate again.

"I'm so sorry to hear that. I remember how close you've always been, and I can't imagine how hard this must be. It's okay to be upset. You need to let this out, and you're doing great so far. Keep letting yourself feel."

The second the tears flow, I shake my head no, not wanting this to be real. "I don't want to feel. I just want him back."

"I hear you, this is heavy. I'm sure it hurts so deeply. Especially if you're not used to feeling." His validation helps me breathe deeper, even if the anguish doesn't stop. "Did you say he died protecting you?"

"It's my fault."

"Risking his life for you was Jay's decision. That's not your fault."

Everything within me wants to attack this man for not blaming me. I look into his eyes, absolutely seething. Then I immediately feel guilty.

"I'm a monster," I say.

"You're ill, not a monst—"

"*I* should have died!"

We stare in silence. I feel childish and small—so small—cowering deeper into the couch cushions.

But Brayden doesn't budge. "What makes you think that?"

My gaping black hole of a heart threatens to absorb me whenever I think about why I should've died instead—*really* think about it.

Jay was only deployed because I couldn't withstand Sumner's abuse anymore. No matter how much I logic away everything else I've done, I can't forget this. None of this would've happened if I didn't let myself slip.

But I can't tell Brayden. Telling the truth about Sumner killed Jay too.

Brayden softens his gravelly voice. "Niko, I know you want to live, and you *should*. You have people who love you and need you. It sounds like Jay gave you a second chance to be with them. You have to take it."

"Fuck," I whisper, rocking myself in reassurance. "You're right. You're right."

"What do you need right now? Some water and a walk? A hug? A punching bag?"

I shrug. "I don't think anything will help."

"Why not?"

I consider brushing Brayden off, but he might be the only one who knows what to do with me. With this unused energy trapped in my body. I can see it in his scars and honest eyes—the kind that have lived mass death.

"It feels so weird being home," I mutter. "I'm not used to the calm, and I'm definitely not used to going through horrible shit without Jay by my side. I keep wanting to tell him what's happening, to hear his excitement that would make this all feel real for me. I'm dying to let him get treated here first, for him to finally feel okay in his life before he has to go out, but I *can't*. I feel like—" My voice softens to a breathy rasp. "I feel like I'm lost."

Brayden sits in a heavy silence with me, only interrupted by his deep, gentle hum. "Well, let's just start by getting through today. That's all you need to do right now. It won't get better instantly, but in bits and pieces over time."

I'm still shivering uncontrollably. Brayden offers me a tissue. I hesitate before grabbing it, still feeling like an out-of-control child.

"Are you uncomfortable receiving help?"

My jaw locks. "Why do you ask?"

"Because you look and sound like you need support, but the second someone offers it, you're pushing it away. Is there something about it that's making you feel unsafe? Maybe we can work around it until you feel safer to receive my help."

I take a few deep breaths, realizing no one is forcing me to do this at all. "It's more like… I'm afraid of hurting you if you come close to me."

He hums in understanding. "Have you ever hurt someone you weren't ordered to hurt?"

His effortless question mentally knocks me off my feet. I think about it for a long time, desperate to find an example. To prove to Brayden I'm a monster. But even if I regret the harm I've caused, I haven't gone rogue to hurt people on my own—other than to defend civilians from white supremacist terrorists. My shoulders relax.

But then I remember one person.

"My Commanding Officer," I whisper.

I just admitted I'm a different type of traitor, but Brayden doesn't skip a beat.

"What did you do to your CO?"

I bounce my knee a few times. "I just scared him a little. For ordering Jay to death."

"Did you physically harm him?"

I shake my head no.

"Well, that sounds reasonable enough."

I look up at him, tempted to laugh that this is the advice a *therapist* is giving me.

He laughs. "What? We aren't your average human beings. It sounds like you practiced major restraint considering your superior was baiting you, how upset you are now, and everything you've been taught."

"I guess. But my restraint was still selfish. I didn't want to be killed for killing him." He raises his eyebrows, likely knowing that was a half-truth by my stifled voice. I laugh beneath my breath, turning away. "Okay, I didn't want to become that type of killer either. He's hurt me a lot, but I felt kind of... bad. For scaring him. I know it sounds ridiculous, considering I've done so much worse to far less horrible people."

"I've been there, kid. We need to take responsibility for the lives we've taken, but that doesn't mean you're a monster. We all know how they work. You don't have a goddamn say. And you could've bought into their mindset, but you didn't. You didn't want this life. If you did, you wouldn't be here, trying your damn hardest to start over."

His worn eyes are comforting, an example of enlightened survival, and a growing part of me is desperate to receive his help.

"In order to heal, you also have to let people love you, and to love openly," he says.

Looking at him is too much to bear anymore. I bury my head

in my hands, thinking of Jay. He died because of our love, but we also survived for so long because of it. It's so confusing for me, as confusing as coming home and being terrified of Emmalee's love for the first time.

"Maybe we don't need to talk more today," Brayden says. "How about I just sit with you while you let yourself be as upset as you need to be? I can show you I trust you not to hurt me until you can trust yourself a little more too. Would that be okay?"

I bury my forehead into my knees, gripping my bruised body. "Yes. Thank you."

CHAPTER 30

Niko

After two weeks of full time outpatient therapy, I'm comfortable enough to ask Emmalee to visit me at home. I miss her so much. We waited over four years to reunite—and over a decade to freely visit each other—but now I'm painfully anxious around her. I can't stop worrying things will never be the same.

She feels like herself, maybe a bit quieter than usual, but I know *I'm* not the same person. I'm not the strong, calm force she knows as her best friend. I'm a fucking wreck.

Amazingly, the memorabilia Jay and I collected made it back to me. It took me weeks to stomach lining them on my windowsill, just like we'd do every night in our barrack. But I can't bear to look at them today. There's no one to laugh with about every fucked-up memory attached to these bits of junk, and there never will be again. Our story together is over.

There's a knock at my bedroom door. I don't know how to respond; I can't remember a time where my family didn't barge in. I hop up, thinking it must be Emmalee, only to find Mom's tense hazel eyes staring back.

"Hey, kid. Can I come in?"

I continue to stare, waiting for her to let herself in. Eventually, I realize she's not budging without my permission. "Yes?"

The second I stand back from the doorway, she gives a quick smile, brushing past me to sit on my bed. I don't know whether to keep the door open or not, so she nods to tell me to close it.

Once I sit beside her, my shoulders rise.

"Sorry." She covers her eyes, squeezing her temples. "I'm not trying to make this uncomfortable."

My badass mother looks frail. My arm hesitates above her shoulders, tempted to curl her into my chest and let her cry.

But she pops up. "I'm sorry."

"Um, it's okay, I guess? You don't have anything to be sorry for."

"Yes. Yes, I do. I wanted to tell you before Emmalee arrives. She helped me see what I had to apologize for."

I'm still struggling to process. "What did she say?"

Mom smiles. "Oh, she said *plenty*. She sure knows how to tell someone like it is, no matter their status or rank."

This almost convinces me to smile, but the tiredness tugging beneath Mom's eyes still twists my heart.

Mom doesn't seem to know where to place her hands, eventually clasping them in her lap. "All this to say, I really did raise you wrong, and—"

"Mom, no—"

"Yes. Yes, Nikolai."

Her sharp seriousness freezes me. I'm a little relieved our dynamic hasn't entirely disappeared; I can recognize her now.

But she softens again, cupping her face in her hands. "I'm really afraid I didn't teach you it was okay to be loved."

With this, she's fully in tears. I rush to rub her back, but she pulls away.

"I'm not trying to get you to comfort me." She stands, startling me with a bright red stare. "You should be mad at me. *I* should be comforting *you*."

"I— Well, I'm not mad at you."

Her eyebrows twitch in pinched confusion.

"Really, Mom, I'm not. I've had years to think about it, and I'm not an angry teenager anymore. Everything that happened is just as much my fault."

"No, it's not. I'm just— Ugh. I'm not explaining myself right."

Mom takes a seat, grabbing me by the shoulders. After a few quick inhales like she's about to speak but changes her mind, she closes her eyes.

"Your dad and I wanted you to be able to defend yourself

from the Departments. That's why we pushed you to join the DoTD. Not because of my family's Lionheart Blackwood legacy like we've always told you, but because we wanted you to be the first generation to *fully* get out. But we took the facade too far, and the DoTD pulled you in too deep, and far earlier than they did for us, forcing you to become someone you never wanted to be. And I'm so sorry I've contributed... by hurting you. Physically."

She opens her eyes to find my stale silence. I have zero clue what to say or do in response, and I can tell that's not what she had in mind.

"Say something." Hot tears rim her eyes.

I look down at the space between us. "I... don't really understand what's happening."

"I'm apologizing to you."

"I know, but— It's different. I don't know how to act."

Her brows furrow. "I'm not telling you how to act anymore. Just be yourself."

As I stare into her eyes, I realize I don't know *how* to be myself because I don't know myself. I don't know what I like, or who I'd be if this wasn't my reality. I've never felt safe enough to contemplate it—exactly why it took me fifteen years to realize I was also attracted to boys, even with a gorgeous boy right in front of me. Now I don't know how to catch up to everyone else. I'm my own unsolvable mystery.

To appease her, I smile softly. "Thank you for taking the time to apologize, even though I understand your intentions."

"But... you shouldn't." Mom's arms fall limp. "That's the problem. You shouldn't have learned to tolerate that treatment under any conditions. And I can't let myself treat you like that anymore."

"Okay, then I'll try to unlearn that too."

She pats my shoulder.

"Are you disappointed?"

She shrugs. "Don't worry about me, kid."

"You *are* disappointed. You want me to blame you."

She clasps her hands in her lap again. "I mean, you *should*..."

I sigh. "I don't want to, Mom. I'm tired. *So* tired. And I'm especially tired of being mad."

She peeks up at me. I jump when she bursts out crying again, curling into my chest for the first time I can remember. I wrap my arms around her, my heart throbbing against her forehead in an embarrassing display of discomfort.

We're immersed in a raw, unmapped limbo in our relationship. I know she's trying to do the right thing, but I feel obligated to stop her tears. Even if I have to lie that I'm fine. But I know that's not the right thing for *me* to do, so now what?

Her sobs are interrupted by a knock at the front door. Mom jolts upright, wiping her eyes. I try to keep holding her, but she brushes me away. Her rejection hurts my heart more than I remember it hurting growing up.

"That must be Emmalee," she mumbles. "I thought she'd be a bit late from work, but I guess not."

"Mom, should I tell her to come back later so we can continue to talk?"

"No, please, no. Don't let me keep her from you a single second more. I've already fucked *that* up enough."

I stand. "I'll tell her to come back tomorrow."

"No!"

There are no more words, only quick glances toward the door. By the time I fling it open, Mom blocks the exit with her entire body. We grapple in my bedroom doorway, fighting to keep the other from answering the front door. Eventually, I burst into laughter at how ridiculous we must look, but my mom isn't amused.

"Here I am, physically fighting with you again!" She wails.

I cup her cheeks, unable to stop smiling. "You look *just* like Ilana right now, I swear." I kiss her forehead, and with a tiny gasp, she falls silent. "I'm fine, Mom. *This* is harmless fun. And you're cute."

Emmalee knocks a second time. Mom is still stunned, gingerly touching where I kissed her forehead. I chuckle to myself, slipping out the doorway to offload the front door from its one million locks.

Once I swing it open, Emmalee is halfway down our front steps with her back to me, thinking I'm not home.

"Ems!" I call out.

She turns, unsteady on her feet.

My smile fades, much to her dismay. She probably wanted to hide it from me, but I know that exhausted face. The lights in her brain are flickering, threatening to go out. I give myself a head start in case I unexpectedly have to catch her. It's happened before, and the last thing she needs is a concussion. But as soon as I approach, she stumbles away, tripping down another step.

"I'm— Fine," she slurs through her words. "Don't."

I cross my arms. "You're not going to let me help you?"

She sighs. "I don't want to bother you. I shouldn't have come while feeling like this, but I wasn't thinking clearly, and— Well, I didn't know where else to go."

"Then please, Ems. I want to help you."

She wobbles a little. "I don't know… I'm fine to take care of myself."

"Uh-huh. *Very* convincing."

She doesn't laugh along with me, so I take a few steps toward her. My heart hurts, looking at her in so much pain.

"It's not weak to receive help. We all need extra support sometimes." I stop in front of her, softening my voice. "And that's coming from me. I know it's hard to accept help when you're fighting so fucking hard to be strong, but you're still as strong as ever in my eyes. I want to be there for you too, okay? Rely on me."

She finally meets my eyes. "Okay."

Scooping her off her feet before she tries to hobble back up the steps herself, I ask, "Are you about to pass out or throw up?"

She laughs. "Hopefully neither, but probably both."

"Okay. I've got you."

It's strange. Emmalee weighs nothing to me anymore, and she's finally about six inches shorter than me. I didn't realize how much I'd grown apart from her in every way. It's starting to scare me.

I shift her higher against my chest to open the front door, and she swallows hard.

"Shit," she whispers.

"You can throw up if you need to. I'll try not to scream and cry because of it like I did when I was 7."

She huffs out a breathy laugh, her head bouncing in dizzy exhaustion with our steps. "No."

"No?" I laugh, pulling the door closed with my foot. "Mom? Can you lock the door? Emmalee needs help."

Emmalee groans. "Don't bother her too."

"Shh. I can 'bother' her for you, and I will."

Mom runs out of her bedroom, her eyes still red. "What's wrong?!"

"*Nothing*," Emmalee blurts out.

I sigh. "She's not feeling well at all. Can you help me get her some water? And a leak-proof trashbag?"

Mom stares in puzzled concern for a moment, then scurries off to the kitchen.

I slow my steps in my bedroom, trying to signal to Emmalee it's time to release her death grip on my torso. But she only clings tighter, nuzzling into my shoulder and taking heavy breaths.

"You okay?"

"Trying to stay conscious."

"Can I lay you on my bed?"

She shakes her head no.

"Oh. Will that make it worse?"

She shrugs, burying her face into me until all I see is her fading black hair dye.

I bite back a smile. "You just don't want to let go of me, huh?"

She puffs out a muffled laugh. Her hot breath through my shirt sends goosebumps down my arms.

I sit on the bed, holding her like a ridiculously tall baby. Then I cradle her huffing torso, adjusting her legs so they're bent and closer to her heart to make circulation easier. She suddenly unburies her upturned nose and squishes her cheek against my chest, revealing reddened cheeks with desperate gasps for air.

"Emmalee, please don't suffocate yourself on my body."

She laughs between pants, cuddling into me. I can tell she genuinely feels horrible, and it's making me sympathetically nauseous. I smooth her hair from her eyes, her dewy skin sinking into a translucent, gray paleness. But then her breath slows beneath my touch. I trace her gorgeous facial features, one by one, until the tension in her legs releases enough to bump against my side. Her coloring returns—her heart is stabilizing. The worst is over.

We huddle into a cohesive ball, her gentle scent wafting over me. My cheeks flush when Mom walks in, pausing in the doorway to take a look at us. She mouths her words, asking if Emmalee is okay, and I nod. Mom sets the water on my bedside table as gently as possible, but Emmalee still stirs.

"Oh, thank you. Sorry, Commander."

"It's still Clara, sweetheart. Don't apologize. Do you need anything else?"

Emmalee smiles weakly, her discomfort more apparent than ever. "I'm okay."

"Wow, that was a huge lie," Mom says. "What are you feeling like?"

"Uh… Just dizzy, lightheaded, and nauseous. I'm probably just dehydrated, and— I don't know what else."

Mom pats Emmalee's shoulder a little too hard. I instinctively cradle Emmalee tighter until she lets out a soft grunt.

"Well, don't *squish* her!" Mom scoffs, making Ems and I laugh. "Alright, Emmalee. I'm going to the civilian store to get you some things that helped me feel less nauseous and dizzy when I was pregnant with Hana."

"Oh," Emmalee breathes, suddenly chewing her bottom lip. "Thank you…"

Mom has already rushed out of my room, so I'm not sure if anyone else saw the dread flash across Emmalee's face. I don't understand why, but I can only guess she doesn't want to inconvenience us.

"I've still got you, Ems. You can accept our help."

She curls tighter against me in silence. Tears slip down her cheeks, but she doesn't make a sound.

I breathe out the pain from seeing her so upset, combing my fingers through her hair.

Suddenly, she giggles. "Your scent is making me less nauseous."

"W-what?" I laugh.

"Yeah. I'm weird, I know."

Her smile throws me over the edge; I can't resist smothering her with affection a minute longer. I kiss her forehead without a second thought, and her eyes spring wide open.

"Oh. Sorry," I whisper.

"Don't be. I just… don't want you to feel pressured to do that stuff."

"Oh… I don't…"

Emmalee lifts her head. "You sound hurt."

"I'm okay," I say. She glares at me. "Okay, I don't know why you're suddenly saying that. I thought that extra affection was normal for us. Since we were like, thirteen."

She bites her lip. "It *was*."

My heart sinks. "So I was right. Our relationship has changed for you."

"No, I— You— That's not it! I feel even stronger about you emotionally, but you feel farther away."

I can't bear to look at her. The losses I'm accumulating are too much to withstand, sending sharp pains through my chest.

"I'm sorry," I whisper.

"I'm not trying to guilt you. I'm telling you I *want* to be closer."

"O-okay, but… I don't know what I'm doing wrong."

"You're distant," she says.

"I don't know how to fix that anymore. You've been feeling horrible and won't tell me why. We've hardly spoken."

"Because I don't want to pressure you when you have enough to deal with."

"Are you sure it's not because I'm not the same person anymore?" I mutter.

"What? Nikolai, you're still you. I don't understand."

"No, it's my fault. I need to try harder to be normal."

"I don't want you to be 'normal.' I want you to feel free to be *yourself*."

With that, I sigh in frustration. And Emmalee's forehead wrinkles in upset.

"Oh, no… Don't let me make you cry too," I say. "It's my fault.

I don't know what to say to anyone, or how to act around anyone, or who to be because… I don't know who I am anymore."

Her features soften. "Well, right now, you're my protector. And it's hard to admit, but you're right; I've been trying to protect you from my emotions, so I've been distant too. Maybe I can force myself to step down for today and let you take your turn."

Her gray eyes look bluer than ever from crying, and my heart melts. I can't contain my smile as I bury my fingers back into her hair, allowing her to relax. And she does. She trusts me; I can feel it. It makes me feel like I'm finally doing something right. Like I can stop running.

"Thank you," I whisper.

"Huh? For what?"

"I feel a little more like myself already."

She tucks her nose into my chest, but she can't hide her faint, satisfied smile.

We sit in silence for a few minutes, breathing each other in. Not long after Emmalee's face relaxes into my chest, her arms slip off me. I suppress my adoration enough to bite back a laugh and lift her sleepy body. She clings to my shirt, keeping her eyes closed as I nestle her into the sheets. But she won't fully lay down, squinting against the light and groaning in discomfort.

"What's wrong, Ems?" I whisper.

"I'm cold without you."

I have to laugh now. I lay down beside her before returning her to my arms. But all my giddiness falls when I see her crying again.

She grips my hand as soon as I attempt to dry her wet cheeks. "Sorry. Just ignore me. This is exactly what I meant; I'm an irrational, emotional mess."

"You can cry in front of me. What are you thinking?"

She nuzzles into my neck to avoid the truth. Her hot tears slide down to my collarbone, and I have to look up to prevent myself from crying with her.

She sniffles. "It's been so long since someone has taken care of me that now I can feel how badly I needed it. Not that they should, but— I don't know. No one has held me like this. And it's not just that. No one even asked if I needed them to. I'm not used to your kindness anymore."

"Oh, Ems, I'm so sorry. You didn't date or hang out with anyone that was there for you while I was away?"

Maybe that was the wrong question to ask. She only cries harder. "I did date someone, but he definitely didn't take care of me. I didn't realize how bad it was until— Well, it's sinking in more every day."

She's still clinging to me, so I rub her anchored fingers and set them against my chest once they finally relax.

"Well, I've got you now," I whisper. "Like you said, it's my turn to be your protector this time. You can go off duty."

She attempts a smile. "Thank you. So much."

I can get used to this. The sound of her gentle breath, slowing with every beat of my heart against her cheek. Yes, if this is life, this is manageable.

But after a few cozy, silent moments, Emmalee lifts her head. "Niko, what do you have lined up on your windowsill?"

"Jay and I collected some—"

I try to think of every explanation possible for our memorabilia—our history—but nothing sounds quite right.

Somehow, I find myself smiling. "Well, to be honest, we collected some really weird shit."

Emmalee takes one look at me, hardly stifling a laugh. "Thank God *I* didn't have to be the one to say it."

With that, we sputter into uncontrollable laughter, which is eventually accompanied by tears at the thought of our goofy best friend. But our laughter is proof of something more.

Our story isn't over yet.

CHAPTER 31

Emmalee

The rift between Niko and me has been drilling a hole in my gut. But it's unfair of me, watching how hard he's trying to be comfortable around people again while I sulk like a spoiled brat. For a month and a half, we've been in a back-and-forth battle of trying to support each other without opening up for the other to help. Last week was an improvement at his house, but we're still not our old, inseparable selves.

I'm at a loss. Jay's death clouds my brain, and I can't hold my biggest secret alone anymore. Especially if Niko knows something about S817 that could be harming this secret.

Gentle hands settle on my shoulders. I jump awake and shove them off me, hunching over to protect my abdomen.

"Sorry!" Niko backs up two feet.

I must've fallen asleep past our meeting time; I'm still on the DoH's creaky break room couch, face-to-face with Niko's puppy-dog guilt. I reach for him, ready to bawl for accidentally pushing him away when all I've wanted is for him to reach out first. My emotions are an uncontainable mess.

Something Niko said last week struck a chord. With a novel mix of powerful hormones coursing through my body, I'm also not myself anymore. We're *both* having to figure out the updated version of "us" as a unit, *and* our individual, altered identities.

But I need his help.

Thankfully, Niko understands without me saying a word, bundling me in his embrace.

"I'm sorry, Ems, I'm so sorry." He holds my head to his shoulder and cuddles into it with his cheek.

Every time we separate, I fall back into thinking he's gone. And before recently, we hadn't hugged like this for so long that I still feel an irresistible itch to cling to his back today, letting out a heavy cry.

"I don't want to lose you," Niko says. "I keep thinking about what you said last week. I didn't mean to distance myself from you, Ems. I didn't realize how much I was, but I see it now, and I'm so sorry I hurt you like that."

My breath slows, leaning into his soothing touch. "Thank you. That's all I needed to hear."

God, he smells so good. I nuzzle into his neck, inhaling as much of him as I can. Smells have been so much more intense, but mostly in a gross way, unlike Niko's sweet, comforting scent. My nose is begging me to indulge in him.

Niko brushes my hair from my eyes, the strands wet with tears and sticking to my cheek. "Ems, I want to make an effort to communicate better with you from now on."

"Oh, Niko... I want to too." I gaze into his beautiful, overwhelming black irises. He finally smiles up to them—a *real* smile—and my lungs swell in joyous relief. "You're working so hard. Your voice sounds so much clearer every time I see you. I'm so impressed."

He shakes his head, dismissing my compliments. "I need to do this, and I need to do better."

"Well, you made me feel better in, like, two minutes. That's an accomplishment these days." I rub my eyes, squishing them into my skull. Niko stops me with a grimace, and I laugh. "What, you still don't like that?"

He smiles. "No. I don't want to see you get hurt at all. Which is why I came here to ask... Do you want to go to therapy with me tonight? So we can work everything out?"

I cup his cheeks in my hands. We're not officially dating, but my best friend is determined to communicate with me better than anyone I've known. Like he's my true life partner.

He wipes a stray tear from my eyes. "Oh, Ems... Did I overwhelm you?"

"No, I want this so much. It's just so sweet—that's why I'm crying. I *really* want to be close to you like this."

He presses his forehead to mine. "I want to be close to you too. I missed you for way too long. Especially when I wasn't supposed to."

I'm dying to let our fears melt away between our lips, but leading him on would be unfair; I want to explain my situation to him before moving forward. If he isn't upset with me for what I let Andre do, I'll tell Niko how I really feel. With words, not my body.

We walk hand-in-hand through the Department of Health's Mental Treatment Center. It's surreal, having permission to be together. I think most of our problems stem from this sudden freedom we don't know how to use. We built our initial relationship around secrecy, even with saying hello.

"So, do you want to get dinner, or should we just hang out for a bit?" Niko asks.

"Mhm, yeah."

He laughs. "Ems, I was asking a question with two—"

Niko does a double-take, sensing my continuous stare. But I can't stop beaming at him. These days, worry is etched into my face, so maybe it's only temporary, but I'm legitimately *happy*, just from being by his side. We smile, and he pulls me to a stop.

Leaning against the wall, Niko draws me into his chest. I soften against his touch, cuddling into him. He gives me a tight squeeze like I usually love, but it *really* hurts, so I wince backward, reflexively covering my chest.

Niko completely releases me. "Oh, sorry! Did I hurt you?"

I sigh, irritated with my shrinking bra, and bend forward to ease the pressure. "Sorry, I'm just... PMS-ing. Don't squeeze my boobs."

He gasps. "I did *not* squeeze your *boobs?!* My hands were on your *back!*"

I blink a few times, confused by the blush competing with his dark freckles. But then I think about what I just said and burst into heavy laughter. "Oh, I meant squish! You squished, not squeezed!"

"D-did I?!"

We giggle. Niko covers his giant grin with his palm, laughing despite his confusion. My heart aches. His skin is so tan that he's at least three shades darker than when we were 17, spotting his cheeks and nose with a beautiful arrangement of freckles. But wow, he grew up. Without me. And now I did this. Without him.

I grasp his hand, ready to keep moving. "You didn't mean to, pretty boy, but you did."

"Sorry." He drops his head, attempting to hide his smile. "I'll be gentler with you this week."

My throat catches. I didn't think this through. About what Niko might say if, in one week, my "PMS" doesn't get any better. Lying to him is pointless, but telling him the truth will kill me.

"Emmalee?" Just from witnessing my expression, Niko's eyes match mine: two terrified, dilated pupils. "Are you okay?"

"I-I'm a little dizzy."

Niko guides me to sit with him in the hallway. He strokes my hair and back as I put my head between my knees, taking deep breaths. Thank God I gave up on buttoning my pants this week, or else I wouldn't be able to sit like this.

"Niko?"

He scoots forward until his nose is only inches from my face. "Yes?"

His soft, unsuspecting voice against my ear makes this that much harder. But I can't do this alone. I don't know anyone else that won't judge me for this, although I feel like I genuinely deserve harsh judgment.

I'm humiliated that I enjoyed Andre's sexual attention. It feels like I don't deserve to be upset because he didn't physically hurt or restrain me. Honestly, if this was from the last time I slept with him, I felt great—for once. Which is why my pleasure no longer feels positive, and all I'm left with is grief. It feels like I betrayed myself too.

I clench my teeth, steadying myself with a few more breaths. "I have to tell you something I haven't told anyone else. Something I did."

"Okay. I'm here."

I lift my head to peek into his thoughtful eyes. They stare back, focused and present. Free of judgment.

I'm washed over with a knowing that everything will be okay, before he even understands what he's helping me with. No matter what separates us, I have faith we'll always come back around like this. Creating our own safe space.

And safety is what I need. Every time I think of how Clara described her pregnancy with Niko, I feel like I'm moments away from being hunted. It makes my stomach lurch.

"I need to tell you tonight, when we go back to my apartment," I whisper. "I don't want *anyone* else to know."

He strokes my hair. "Okay, no problem. We'll do that."

I close my eyes, taking a few breaths to steady myself before we have to walk all the way home. I'm ridiculously nauseous from anxiety, my heart pounding past its limits.

"Hang on, Ems, don't get up. I'll carry you to your car."

I laugh. "How are you going to carry me all the way there, Boot Foot?"

He looks down at his broken foot, shaking it in the air a couple times. "It's just a hairline fracture. I don't even feel it."

I raise my eyebrows, well-aware he was just prescribed to wear it an extra two months from not giving it proper rest.

He huffs out a laugh. "Okay, fine. Give me your phone. I'll just call Jay to help carry you."

I cover my mouth with a sharp inhale, really wanting to puke now.

Niko's mind catches up to his mouth, and he shrinks. "Fuck, sorry... I'm so used to working with him with everything I do that sometimes, I..."

I hoist myself to my feet with a grunt, startling Niko with a tackle. We hold each other gently until I can't help myself; I have to squeeze him fully against me, no matter if it hurts.

"B-but... Your boobs?" He whispers.

I burst into a heavy cackle, cuddling against his head on my shoulder. I continue to laugh so hard that he laughs with me, rocking us back and forth. We must look delirious; people stop in the hallway to ask if we need anything. Niko asks for a wheelchair for me and wheels me out of the Department of Health hospital.

"Niko, we have to return the wheelchair now." I drop my head back against his stomach to look up at him.

He keeps his eyes straight ahead. "Nope, you need it. The least these Department fuckers could do is lend us a fucking wheelchair once in a while."

I laugh. "That's just a fancy way of justifying stealing."

"Yes, Ems. Yes, it is."

We laugh. Niko's smile widens the second we meet eyes. He stops us in the middle of the street, bending over me with the intention of planting a kiss on my lips. I'm so eager for it that I catch his cheeks on the way down, urging him closer. Just before he kisses me, we freeze, realizing we were expecting the same thing. Like this was natural for us. Part of our everyday lives, when we haven't kissed for years, let alone seriously dated. We never had a chance to.

"I-is this okay?" He whispers against my lips.

A smile spreads across my face. "Please."

He giddily *beams*, wheeling me back against his stomach to get a fuller reach of my lips. We kiss, and my whole body flushes with a comforting warmth. This feels so right, even though everything else has gone so wrong.

An armored DoTD utility vehicle honks at us, causing me to jump in my seat. Niko jolts upright, and at first, I'm scared that honk could've set off a flashback.

But a devious smile grows on his face. One I've never seen him allow in public; when we were kids, he'd panic whenever he thought he did something wrong. These smiles were reserved for collaborating with *my* deviance.

Now, Niko gives the vehicle a middle finger with a soft snicker.

I scream-laugh. "Nikolai Blackwood! You better wheel me out of here before they mow us over!"

His supercharged eyes meet mine. "You got it, Commander."

He thrusts us forward, lurching me back into my chair. I curl into it, gripping his arms to hang on. Laughing my heart out with the wind in my hair.

We make it to my parking spot in less than a minute and still

can't hold ourselves together. I sigh through the end of a laugh, and Niko reorganizes my hair.

"Sorry, Ems. I'm still used to being a total dick to those guys."

"I don't blame you. They're dickier than you."

Niko feigns a hurt scowl, holding his hand open for my car keys. I giggle at him as he holds back a laugh with tense lips.

I allow him to help me into the driver's seat, snatching his shirt collar on the way in and kissing him a little too hard.

"Mm!?" He says in surprise.

Once I release his lips, we both laugh, but Niko scoops his hand around the back of my neck, kissing me softly once more. Its simple, slow ease makes my heart flutter like when we were teens.

He giggles at my dazed eyes. "Looks like we're doing pretty well without therapy, after all."

I laugh, knowing full well he's joking; we have a ridiculous number of things to talk about. He closes my door for me, putting the stolen wheelchair in the trunk and hopping into the passenger's seat.

"Ah, fuck," I whisper.

"What?"

I look over, guiltily chewing my lip. "I really have to pee."

"Again?"

I fake-glare, suppressing a smile as I pull out of the parking spot. "Yes, *again*. It's okay, though. I'll just pee when we get to wherever we're going."

Niko chuckles. "I figured we're going to that smoothie place you're obsessed with."

I freeze. "Is that okay?"

"Of course, Ems." He laughs, tucking my hair behind my ear as I drive.

I keep my eyes on the road, but I can feel his heart and thoughts wholly focused on me. It makes me blush, unsure of what to say. But then he rubs my neck and shoulder so softly that I want to burrow into his arms and sleep for a week.

Thankfully, the smoothie place is quiet today. We settle in the back at my favorite spot, tucked into a cushioned corner booth.

Honestly, I don't know what's happening to us. It's like all the nightmares fell away, and it's just us enjoying life. Giggling for no reason. Gazing into each other's eyes. Scooting closer and closer until our thighs practically overlap and we realize this is probably too much PDA for the other customers to handle.

By the time we're in front of Brayden for therapy, I'm more in love with Niko than I've ever been.

Which makes me extra nervous about this conversation.

"So I know Niko has things he wants to talk about. But is there anything you'd like to start with, Emmalee?" Brayden asks.

I chew on my bottom lip, meeting Niko's expectant stare. He's smiling from across the couch, which I honestly can't stand.

"Can you just… sit closer to me?!"

Niko laughs, scooting against my side and resting his arm across my shoulders. "Is this better?"

I sigh. "Yes. Now I don't feel like we're fighting."

Brayden belly laughs. "You two sound the same as when you were in boot camp. I can't believe it."

Niko fidgets with my hair's ends, giving me space to talk, and I smile. "Well, we definitely weren't allowed to be this close back then."

"Is it a strange adjustment now? To finally be able to be close?"

Niko and I look at each other for a reaction, but neither of us speaks.

Brayden chuckles. "This is a neutral discussion where we're sharing our feelings openly. You don't need to look to each other for approval. Just share how you feel."

To my surprise, Niko speaks up right away. "It *is* a little weird, to be honest. I'm kind of freaking out internally whenever we're outside."

My heart drops. "Really? I'm sorry, Niko. I couldn't tell."

"It's okay. I still have a good time with you." He smiles, and I'm warmer already.

Brayden switches his focus. "How about you, Emmalee?"

Now that Brayden's eyes are on me, I wrap my arms around my stomach. He notices, but it's too late to move now.

"W-well, I think I have to get used to it too." I turn to Niko, instantly empowered by his onyx stare. "But I really do love it. Being by your side."

Niko softens into a gentle smile.

Brayden chuckles again, leaning forward. "Alright, great! So you're at the start of a new phase in your lives, and you're making an effort to communicate. Niko, do you want to talk about why?"

Niko takes a deep breath, quivering at the edge of his inhale. His energy warns me of far worse nerves than he's letting off.

"I—" He takes another deep breath, then looks me in the eyes. "I wanted to talk about why I was distancing myself from you so you can know it was a me-thing and not because I didn't want to be around you. Because I *do* want to be around you. Which is why I distanced myself."

I'm tempted to respond, but Brayden raises his hand. "Let's let Niko finish what he has to say first."

Niko clams up, his hand curling off my shoulder. This must be the most challenging part of what he has to tell me. I wedge my arm between our huddled up sides to hug him, and he snaps out of it, giving me a grateful but pensive smile.

"Jay was targeted because he was doing reckless things… to try to protect *me*." Niko squeezes his eyes shut, his voice shrinking. "At first, I was afraid you'd also be targeted as my best friend. But when I realized how involved you already were, I—" Niko bites his lip, swallowing back tears. "I got so scared it was about to happen again. I wanted them to stay as far away from you as possible, so I pushed you away. But then I saw I was hurting you, and it was all for nothing because it didn't protect you either, and—"

Niko shakes his head, not knowing how else to continue. Everything makes more sense now: that's a very Jay thing to get in trouble for. I only wish it didn't get him into *fatal* trouble. I used to marvel at the impossible he'd get away with. What feels impossible now is that he *didn't* get away with it. Niko must be struggling to rationalize this shock just as much as I am.

I rub Niko's back. "I had no idea. My behavior must've been so triggering for you, and I'm *so* sorry. Thank you for telling me."

"There's also something else. About feeling out of control?" Brayden asks.

Niko's forehead warps. I reach for a tissue, wiping a few tears off him as he tries to laugh off his emotions.

"It's okay. Let it out," I whisper.

He rubs my back in slow circles, dissolving into agony. "It was just so sad, Ems. Seeing your face every time I'd automatically lunge at you. Even if it wasn't intentional, I could tell it hurt you. And I never wanted to be that person around you. I'm so sorry."

"Dammit, now *I'm* crying." I grab myself a tissue, laugh-crying with Niko. "Listen, I know how hard you're working. And those instincts are what literally kept you alive and brought you back to me. I'm grateful for them, and I'm also worried about you. You've fought for so long just to *live*. You must be *so* exhausted."

He drops his forehead against my shoulder, letting out a soft cry. "Yeah. But still. I'm really sorry."

I comb my knuckles through his short hair. "It's okay. I've already forgiven you."

We both take a few deep breaths to settle ourselves.

Brayden sits in silence for a moment with a sad smile. "Is there anything you'd like to communicate, work on, or apologize for, Emmalee?"

My heart rate spikes. "Um, probably, yeah."

"Sorry, didn't mean to put you on the spot. We can come back to it."

I look into Niko's reddened eyes and know that's not a productive option. "No, I want to try talking about some of it now. I just didn't have anything prepared, exactly."

Niko smiles. "It's all okay, Ems."

I grasp his hand. His expression grows solemn with mine, so I look at the glass coffee table in front of us, reflecting the bright overhead lights.

"I've never talked about this out loud."

Brayden says, "That's okay! Is there something easy you can start with?"

I picture Niko's shut-down expression in the psych ward. "Yes. I've been overly emotional lately, and I took it out on you a few times while you were sick, Niko. I'm so sorry about that. I don't like snapping at you, and I especially shouldn't have done it when you were feeling so awful."

Niko shakes his head. "That's all I've been doing to other people. It just happens when you feel trapped."

I swallow hard, my voice growing small. "Yeah…"

Niko leans in, massaging my back in concern.

I don't know how to form the right words, so I stop thinking and just speak. "I just wanted to make a difference for once."

"*For once?* Ems, you—"

Niko is cut off by Brayden's raised hand. "What do you mean by making a difference, Emmalee?"

I force myself to stop chewing on my lip. "I've had multiple chronic illnesses for a long time. This place doesn't accept people like me. Well, us."

Brayden laughs. "Oh, that's for sure. Physical or mental illness, they've put us all in the gutter."

I relax into Niko's embrace. "Right? Well, I found something that maybe I could take part in *because* I had no record of accomplishments in the Departments. It was risky and more reckless than I thought— Sorry, Niko." He sighs, and I smile. "But I was tired of being put on the sidelines. Growing up, the Departments labeled me as a failure because I wasn't able to do any physical labor. I'm sick of being treated as unimportant. Having to sit back and watch people I love go off to die somewhere, and unable to be anyone's protector, only the protected. Like my disabilities make it so I'm never the reliable one. I feel like I *am* reliable inside, but I don't know how to prove that to anyone."

Niko's eyes widen. "Oh, Ems… I didn't think about that before, but I should've. I'm so sorry."

"It's okay, really. You have enough to worry about."

"Now hang on a minute," Brayden says. "This is what he *wants* to worry about. You both want to communicate better, yes?"

We give a simultaneous "yes."

"Then you *both* have to share the load of worries and responsibilities in your relationship. What you're describing, Emmalee, is a critical perspective within your relationship that

Niko needs to take the time to understand. But he can't do that if you don't speak up. Just like you can't support him if he keeps hiding his emotions."

As Niko and I turn to each other, we sigh in unison. Then we laugh.

"He's right," Niko says.

I groan. "I know."

Niko giggles, and it's the cutest thing ever. I nearly kiss him right on the mouth without thinking. Niko laughs, sticking with a shy hug.

"Okay, there *is* something I want to say about this, though," Niko says.

"O-okay."

We extend our hug, holding each other as he speaks.

"I do feel awful for leaving you behind. *And,* I actually think you're key to people's healing, Ems. You have a clarity about life that we have to be deprogrammed to see, and you've dragged me out of hell more times than you must be aware of. I'm so glad I didn't have to force you to come out there with me and suffer more than you do."

Niko peeks into my eyes, and I nod with a sigh.

"And since I was gone for so long—" Niko swallows hard, his dread seeping into me. "I don't want you to feel like you're obligated to me because I'm sure you've met other people, dated other people, and experienced many things that I missed."

This sends me into a heavy sob.

Niko tenses. "W-wha—"

Brayden leans forward. "What's coming forward for you, Emmalee?"

I shake my head in denial. It scares me to confess my feelings before I can gauge Niko's reaction to my secret, but I doubt he remembers confessing his love for me while high. I think he needs to hear it from me first. Just as much as I need to say it.

"I *really* regret dating some guy when I thought you wouldn't come back home," I say. "I know you and I were never officially dating, but I still feel guilty for it. Because… I love you, Niko. I always have."

Niko's eyes widen.

He jumps off the couch, separating himself from me. It feels like a microtear, splitting open my physical heart.

But then I see he felt the need to pace. He never does this when he's upset with me, but upset with himself.

Brayden motions for me to stay seated, on high alert with his eyes trained on Niko. "What's going through your mind, kid? Do you need to talk to me alone?"

Niko walks faster now, struggling to control his breath. "Everyone I love and who loves me back gets hurt because of me."

After a moment of deep contemplation, Brayden asks, "Are you saying you and Jay were a couple?"

I stiffen in shock, waiting for a response from Niko's frantic back and forth motions.

I can't believe my bisexual ass never considered Niko could be bi too, but if he dated Jay, it makes *complete* sense why he's afraid to love me. Pushing me away as our connection grows stronger.

"For a short time, yes," Niko mutters. "We broke up quickly, but we loved each other more than ever as friends. Friend soulmates. That's why Jay saved me from him."

"Who's 'him?'"

"My… superior." Niko faces away from us and grips his neck. "Jay didn't like that he would… do things to me."

My eyes widen as horror punches me in the gut. The pieces suddenly fit, and they point directly to Sumner. I whip my attention back to Brayden, who looks more unsettled than I've seen him yet.

"What type of things?" Brayden asks.

Niko takes a pained breath to speak but decides against it, shaking his head no.

"Can I guess it for you?" I ask. "Would that help?"

Niko's shoulders rise. Then he nods.

"Did he rape you?" I whisper.

Niko stands frozen for a moment, his back still turned. Then he paces again.

"Yes, that," he mutters. "Many times. Since I was 12."

My heart sinks. I left our private school after I turned 10.

Niko and I hardly saw each other for years after that. Niko must have felt so alone… Like I do now.

Since he was that shy, scowling kid, Niko has been labeled a monster. In some ways, he's grown into one; there's no denying he's a masterful, lethal force to be reckoned with. But what other choice did he have? The Departments forced him to become a monster, but maybe a part of him also decided he had to become one to survive. How else could he outmatch the largest predator he's ever met—one that none of us could ever outrun?

I open my arms for Niko, approaching slowly. He covers his face, not wanting me to look at him. But he stops pacing to allow me to approach, so I hug him, drawing his head to my shoulder.

"I believe you. I absolutely believe you," I say. He lets out a weary sob, but the relief in his energy floods my heart. "Please don't be ashamed, Niko. That was *never* your fault. You were a child, and he abused his power. That's all on him."

Niko doesn't stop shaking, but he wraps his arms around me, careful not to squish my chest again.

"I'm so proud of you for telling us," I whisper. "And I'm so sorry you had to live through that alone for so long."

Niko nuzzles into my neck. "You always helped me. You just didn't know."

"W-What?"

"You'd always pick up on how I was upset growing up, even if you didn't know why. But you cared enough to ask, and you stuck by me regardless. I never felt truly alone because I knew you were out there somewhere. I always knew I at least had you on my side."

Tears spill down my cheeks. Niko doesn't realize he's been returning the favor. I hold his head in my hands, desperate to meet him face to face. It's a challenge for him, but he does it for me.

"You don't have to hide anymore, okay? Not even your love. You deserve this love I have for you, not more hurt."

Niko gradually soaks in my words. "I want to accept it. And I want to say the same words to you, but… not in association with him. Not now."

Now I understand why he thought I needed an open choice to stay or go: *he* needs one to feel safe.

I give him the best smile I can muster. "That's okay, Niko. You're not forced to say or do *anything* with me."

With these words, Niko fully relaxes into my arms.

Brayden gives us a weary smile. "You two will be just fine together. You're making an old man cry."

CHAPTER 32

Emmalee

We made so much progress.

Which means I'm terrified. After how close we're becoming, what if it's stripped away the moment I confess my entire life is turning upside down?

Niko's physical comfort provides much-needed reassurance for now. We take a long walk in the local park at sunset. I'm normally unable to take a walk with how sick I've become, but Niko walks me around in my stolen wheelchair, making sure I know I can fully relax. I didn't realize how much I needed this. We point out birds skating over our heads, the cleanest clouds we can find in the wispy California haze, and the sweetest scented flowers—settling into each other's quiet company after heavy therapy. Sometimes we stop in the middle of the trail and he bends over, easing our lips together with slow precision. We breathe in each other's warmth against the chilled wind, not wanting to separate.

But as Niko unlocks my wheelchair-inaccessible apartment complex in the dark, he has to leave me a couple feet away on the sidewalk. My panic attacks lessened after giving my one-month's notice, but with the accumulated stressors today, Niko's turned back hits just right.

It feels like I'm suddenly alone. Like I can't fend for myself, utterly lost as the future pummels ahead like a stampede. On top of that, my body is energy-bankrupt. Every ounce is used for something else. *Someone* else. I can't do this alone.

I clutch Niko's shirt, nearly tumbling out of the wheelchair.

"Emmalee?!" Niko lifts his arm, looking down at me in shock. "What's going on?"

"I feel *so* vulnerable right now."

He bends over me to soothe me, rubbing my back with sweeping, circular motions. "Is it because you can't control yourself in this type of chair?"

"Not exactly. Something bad happened."

He pulls back to look me in the eyes. I must seem more panicked than I know because his eyes reflect dire urgency. "The thing you need to tell me about in private?"

"Yes. I really don't feel good, Niko."

He gives out a distressed sigh over seeing me in pain, cupping my cheek. "Do you need me to spend the night and take care of you, Ems?"

I nod furiously, clinging to him. Everything within me wants to burrow into him—a primal *need*. He feels like the only safe place to be.

"Hang on to me, okay? I'm going to lift you." Niko scoops me up, one arm under my butt and the other lifting the clunky, metal wheelchair like an empty briefcase. "Is this okay?"

"Yes, but… I'm sorry you have to carry me again with your foot," I mumble into his neck.

"Ems, I carried so much equipment on my body for almost four years nonstop, usually with broken ribs. This doesn't bother me at all."

I huff through a laugh, closing my eyes against the comfort of his sturdy torso supporting my full weight.

"You're going to be okay, Ems. I'm here," he whispers, unlocking my door.

"I hate feeling helpless like this."

He closes the door behind us, shifting my weight to his opposite arm. "You're not helpless. You just need some support like we all do sometimes. I'm *so* relieved you asked me for help—and so proud of you, Ems."

Niko doesn't remember I can *feel* how desperate he is to help. It's the reason I can accept his healing comfort without a second thought.

Everyone else shies away from my disabilities, treating me

like a burden. But I think I'm finally ready to stop treating myself like one.

Especially with Niko. He stares my pain in the face, no matter how afraid it makes us both.

By now, I'm sniffling on his shoulder, staining his shirt with tears. He carries me to my room without a single comment about my disastrous apartment, covered in days' worth of messes I physically can't clean.

Laying me on the bed, he pauses to brush my hair from my eyes, kissing my nose, forehead, and cheeks until I can smile through my tears. Then he helps me remove my jacket and pants, tossing me some loose pajama bottoms. I don't have to tell him my clothes are making me feel worse. He must remember the one or two times I've explained what happens when I'm in a lot of pain; even the weight of clothing hurts.

When he turns around, I try my best to cover myself. From my chronic illnesses, I've been losing a dangerous amount of weight the past year or two, shrinking me into a shriveled version of myself. But right now, my lower abdomen extends far past my hip bones. The tank top I wore beneath my loose work shirt is tight around my belly, showing off its newfound pride. I'm positive ever-observant Niko will notice, but I don't want to freak him out. It's honestly freaking *me* out.

Of course, this only gives me away. Niko freezes, holding up a loose T-shirt and attempting to decipher why I've drawn my knees up awkwardly and crossed both arms around my hips.

"Do you… want me to look away?" He looks me directly in the eyes and nowhere else.

"Just… don't look too closely."

"Okay." He kneels at my feet. "Is it too painful to put your pants on?"

"Yeah…"

As he focuses on my legs, I change shirts. Unhooking my bra inside a giant t-shirt, I release a loud, relieved grunt. Niko doesn't look, but he smiles, sitting back onto his feet. Placing my left foot into his lap, he shuffles the left pajama pant leg to the base, slips it over my toes, and repeats with the other leg. He's so gentle and meticulous that I'm already starting to relax. After dragging the waistband to my knees, he braces my torso. I lean into his chest to finish hoisting up my pants, burning my final energy shred.

"Emmalee, what do you feel like?"

I choke up, letting out a weird sob. "Nauseous. Exhausted. Ridiculously emotional."

He eases me back into the pillows. "It's not ridiculous. You're upset and scared, I can tell."

"I am. I fucked up so badly."

He lifts the covers over me, but I stop him halfway, tugging on his shirt to coax him into bed. Niko huffs out a soft, doting laugh before removing his jacket, as usual, for me to cuddle later. Sliding in beside me, Niko eases the blankets over us, encasing us in each other's heat.

I don't know what to feel. This is exactly what I've dreamed of, but in all the wrong circumstances.

"I've ruined my life, I think," I whisper.

"There's always a second chance. You and Jay really drilled that one into my head." Niko smiles softly. I struggle to contain whimpering, annoying tears, but Niko leans into my ear and whispers, "Don't hold it in. Let yourself be upset."

He kneads my back and shoulders as I cry into my pillow. His delicate, slow breath against my cheek relaxes me despite how much I'm dreading this conversation.

"What happened, Ems? Tell me. I'm here."

"I'm afraid it'll hurt you if I say."

He hums in thought. "As long as you're not about to say you suddenly hate me, I can handle it. I mean, not that you can't tell me if you do end up hating me. You can tell me anything, but I— You know. That would suck."

I sniffle through a laugh, massaging his built chest with my knuckles. "I don't hate you, but I feel like *you* could hate *me* for this."

Niko stops my hands. He's doing his best to stay centered for me, but his anxiety is kicking in. I should know better than to be vague with him, but this is the final rift left between us. I don't want it to be the one that destroys us.

He props himself on his elbow. "Do you remember the letter I wrote you for your 17th birthday?"

I blink up at him. "What letter?"

"Oh... Maybe you never saw it." He smiles to brush my worries away, but I can feel his disappointment. "It's okay. It just said a few things, one of them being no matter what happens, I'm always on team Emmalee. You can tell me *anything*, Ems, and I'll still have your back."

His tan cheeks have darkened a shade and he can't bear to look at me as he says it, but it certainly has an impact. My heart wallops against my ribcage as I absorb his loving words, knowing his emotions verify it: Niko's whole heart is behind me.

This is it—the right time. I have to tell him.

"My period is over a month late. I think. Maybe two. I kinda lost track," I blurt out. "And I feel like *total* shit."

His eyebrows arch like he wants to cry. But then he seals it away.

Niko smooths my hair off my shoulders. "Okay. I— Do you think you're— Could you be...?"

I cover my mouth, sobs erupting full-force. The bed feels like it's on fire with the thunderous stress reverberating through me. But I have to tell him the truth.

"I think I am, but I can't create evidence by taking a pregnancy test. I'm scared the DoH will find out. That the— The guy will find out. I don't want anyone to track me down, Niko. I have to keep it a secret from everyone."

"Oh, Ricky... What— What happened? I mean, I know this is a big deal, but I can tell something... *happened*."

He swallows hard when he looks at me. I can guess what he's thinking, using Jay and Niko's friendly nickname for me instead of *Niko's* nickname for me; he doesn't know how he fits into my life anymore. I can't stand that thought.

I'm not sure what he sees beneath the panic clouding my vision, but he breaks from his fear in a heartbeat. Niko cradles my head, wedging an arm underneath my back to hold me against him.

"Breathe. Keep breathing," he says.

I can feel the pain rippling through Niko's heart, and it's

searing my own. "I didn't mean for this to happen, I didn't choose this, he was the one who— He didn't—" My words are cut short by a heavy gag.

Niko jolts away from the potential splash zone. Wide-eyed, I clench my jaw shut and manage to barricade everything down.

After he's sure I won't throw up all over him, Niko hovers over me, testing my forehead's temperature and checking my pulse. "E-Emmalee, I need you to take deeper, slower breaths. You're over-stressing your body. I don't hate you, so don't worry about that. I'm here to help you figure this out, okay?"

I try my best to match his lungs' steady pace. We breathe deeply together, an exercise he's been practicing in therapy and teaching me.

Then he slumps on the bed's edge in silence. Niko is as nervous as I am; I can feel it. We're adding to the collective nausea in the air as we sit and stare at each other, suddenly a foot apart and unsure what to do next.

But Niko can't contain himself anymore. "What did he do to you?" His voice is quiet, but has a tight edge.

I close my eyes, gripping the sheets. Niko wriggles his fingers into mine, replacing my terrified grip with a stable one. Taking one huge breath in, I decide to tell him everything.

"He told me he was wearing protection, but he didn't." My chest heaves in relief as the truth finally lifts off me. But then it bites back with a vengeance when Niko squeezes my hand even tighter.

He looks *so* upset.

Desperate to hear his reaction to the complete story before I crumble in agony, I blurt out everything: the lonely, horny disaster-relationship I tied myself to, how breaking up felt impossible, but then it actually was, and Andre's final bullshit confession text.

By the time I trail off, panting for air, Niko is *seething*.

He stands to pace. "Before you say it, I'm not mad at you. Please don't think that."

I gnaw on my bottom lip, covered in sweat at this point. "O-okay. But what are you thinking?"

"That I need to be there for you, not run off to murder this pathetic piece of shit—or at the very least, break his face—but that's all my brain is telling me to do."

I laugh.

Niko comes to a halt, whipping his head toward me in irritated surprise.

This only makes me laugh harder. "I'd pay *big money* to watch someone beat up that asshole."

"Emmalee, I'm literally going through treatment to not be a violent person."

I shrug, smirking. "Didn't your therapist also say violence has a place?"

Niko sighs through a weak smile. "You have just as much of a fucked-up sense of humor as I do."

I snicker, wiping my nose before resorting back to tears again.

My head loops in the same cycle these days: aching to enjoy Niko's company, but realizing my life is changing dramatically and Niko might not want to endure it with me, and worst of all, realizing I've fumbled this baby's future. They're a ridiculously small little thing, but I'm still responsible for them.

Admittedly, I feel something for this baby already. Something powerful, uncontainable, and far out of my control: a love too deep to describe. Their soft energy keeps me company at night, relieving the day's loneliness. We're all each other has.

Niko settles his hand on my forearm. "Do you love him? Even if he's a fucking asshole?"

I let out a weird laugh between tears. "No, I don't. That's what's so fucked up."

He nods, staring at his limp hand in his lap.

"Not just because I don't love him, but because—" I stop to chew on my bottom lip some more. I don't know if this is the best time or a right time exists. But as Niko meets my eyes, our collective sorrow hits me full force. "Because I've always wanted to— Well, ever since I realized I was pregnant, I felt so guilty. Like I ripped our future life away."

I've never seen Niko so still.

"Your future life with who?"

I gather my courage. "I-If you want it… Then my life with you."

His forehead twitches, which I recognize as his trying-to-be-strong face.

"I'm so sorry I ruined this for us," I say.

Niko dives for me, burying his nose into my shoulder as I cry out in heavy sobs. Soon, my neck and collarbones are wet with Niko's tears. I pet his short hair to try to soothe him.

"You didn't ruin it, Ems." His voice is jagged. "I should've been here."

"Well, I shouldn't have slept with him, no matter how convincing he was."

He juts back with a no-nonsense stare. "*Convincing?*"

My stomach flips. I shrink into myself, mortified. "I— I don't know, I was just worried he would do worse if I said no, and—"

Niko sucks in a harsh breath—before his forehead warps in agony. "Emmalee. Stop blaming yourself right now. You never agreed to have unprotected sex and get pregnant against your will. That's domestic rape, even if he wasn't scaring you into giving fake 'consent,' but even more so if that's the case. Your ex is completely to blame. This is *not* your fault."

All words escape me. For some reason, Niko's firm declaration relaxes me, even if the truth is horrible. I had no idea what to call what happened to me for so long. I was too preoccupied, scrambling to survive the aftermath.

As he validates it for me, I close my eyes, letting out a long exhale. Niko senses my relief, stroking my hair and cheeks. I settle deep into the pillows, my breath slowing.

"Thank you for telling me," he whispers.

I can tell he's still crying, so I open my eyes and stroke his exhausted cheeks. "Niko, don't feel pressured to help me with my bullshit. I know this has to hurt for you, and I'm so fucking sorry."

"*I'm* sorry this happened to you. I should've been honest with you about how I felt sooner. But I didn't want you to feel stuck waiting for me, feeling worse than I'm sure you did, and now—"

"Hey, it's okay. I'm okay. Just a little lost right now."

He lifts my hand off his knee, pressing my fingers to his lips.

I open my arms for him, so he cuddles against my side. His hand hovers over me, unsure where to lay his arm on my torso.

I laugh, holding his hand for now. "I'm not suddenly fragile."

"I-I know, but—" His eyes dart between mine. "How do you feel? About… being pregnant? Not that you have to decide yet, but have you been thinking about what you might want to… do?"

I chew on my lip, avoiding his worried stare. "I've always wanted to have a baby, Niko."

"I know, Ems."

"But that was before I saw how horrible this world actually is. Now I feel guilty bringing someone here and, on top of that, not being prepared."

I have a feeling he's catching what I'm embarrassed to admit. He hums, taking in my words. "It's a lot to think about. But this is entirely your choice, and I'm here to help with anything you need."

My eyebrows arch. I habitually cup my bloated stomach, taking a deep breath. I haven't done this in front of anyone yet, but an overwhelming bond forms when I hold the baby. *My* baby. I wasn't given a choice to carry them, but since I've experienced everything alone from the start, they've never felt like Andre's. When I'm lying in bed at night, simply carrying them—nurturing them, and nothing else—my heart finds safety.

"What's wrong?"

I turn to face Niko. "Is it weird to already be attached? Especially with how it happened?"

He sighs, tucking a hair behind my ear. "No. If that's how you feel, it's just how you feel."

I shuffle under the covers, uncomfortable with what I'm finally about to ask. A question I've feared so deeply that it's made me physically ill multiple nights.

"Do you think that they—the baby—will… make it? If I was given S— S8…"

"S817?" Niko thinks hard, and I grow more terrified by the second. "I wish I knew, Ems. But I know he was experimenting on how to create as much suffering as possible, *without* killing people. Population control is just a conspiracy theory. He wants people to be more vulnerable. Moldable, not dead. I'd assume killing fetuses wouldn't do him any good, right? Maybe it won't even pass through in utero."

I groan, not ready to trust optimism when it comes to Sumner. I hate what he did to Niko, to me, to everyone I love. It wouldn't be surprising if he also harmed my unborn baby before I had a chance to protect them.

With that agonizing thought, fresh tears pour down my cheeks. "Is there any way to detox S817?"

"Oh, Ems, I'm *so* sorry… I don't know. We might just have to ride it out and see what happens. Unless—"

An anxiety swell rushes over me at the hint of fury in his eyes. "Niko. Don't ask Sumner. Don't even go *near* him or those fucking evil experiments again. Not even for me."

He chuckles, bottling away his thoughts. "Wow. How did you read my mind *that* accurately?"

I shrug, unable to laugh. "Promise me."

Niko sobers. My resting bitch face is useful for promise-making; Niko has no question about how deadly serious I am.

He squeezes my shoulder in reassurance. "Okay. I promise."

I try to breathe off some stress, but nothing calms the undulating ocean of anxiety in my gut, and Niko can tell. He huddles in closer at the sight of my knotted forehead, massaging my neck.

"Did you use singular-they pronouns for the baby?"

I'm aware he's attempting to distract me, but it's still effective by how softly he brushes his fingertips down every stressed crevice of my face. "Yes. I want their life to look different than ours. To give them space to be anyone they are."

He bites his lips, complex emotions stirring within his midnight eyes. Neither of us speak other than energetic exchanges, something new bubbling between our lingering stares. It feels like he's reading my energy too.

Niko whispers, "You love this baby already, don't you, Ems? Really *love* them."

I'm too scared to admit the truth, but his adoring smile tells me he already knows. He can feel how much I love them, and I can feel how much *he loves that*. For some reason, his approval reassures my twisting heartstrings.

"I'll tell you what Brayden says when everything feels impossible, okay?" Niko continues. "Let's just get through today,

Ems. Just today. Tomorrow, we can work on tomorrow. And guess what? I'm here for you now, all the way."

I was afraid my emotions were too big to tell, but his sincerity convinces me to share what's making this pregnancy so hard.

"I wish—" I hesitate. Niko is staring right into my heart. "I wish this baby was yours. Then I wouldn't have a single worry."

Niko turns into a statue again.

"N-Niko? I'm sorry, I—"

He kisses me firmly. I huff out my nose in surprise, so he releases me. Our emotions are both flustered as hell now. Niko hesitates over the hand cradling my stomach, unsure if he's allowed to touch me there. I place it onto my belly for him. Something happens between us that I can't put my finger on, a lightning strike so powerful, I almost feel like I have to run from it.

"M-maybe they *can* be mine," he says.

My pounding heart makes my voice breathy. "What?"

"Well, I care about you, Ems. So if you care this deeply for this baby, I care about them too."

My lip quivers; I'm run over by emotion. Niko nuzzles our foreheads together, staring into my eyes. He slips his hand beneath my shirt, running delicate circles on my abdomen with his fingers before settling over my swollen belly. I close my eyes, inhaling his soft scent. The warmth of my dearest friend's hand reassures me the world is full of good surprises too.

I let out a heavy sigh. Niko's gentle, protective energy communicates to my rampaging parental instincts that we're finally safe, and my eyelids droop. It's like my body knew to run to Niko for help, and this is exactly where it wants to be.

This is beautifully different from what I'm used to. Niko settled my lost heart *with* me—a true partnership. When I was with Andre, I'd cry and cry, never feeling any better.

But Niko is so warm, even when he's silent. I don't know how I got so lucky, but it's clearer by the second: he accepts me. All of me. He doesn't need to speak to express it, showing me with his actions and emotions.

This is love.

I snuggle into him and fall deep asleep in the first true rest I've had in years.

CHAPTER 33

Niko

My brain is far too overloaded to sleep. I'm holding my best friend and the love of my life in my arms, but she's pregnant with someone else's baby and in more pain than I can fathom.

I thought I'd be upset, but I'm mostly terrified for her. I don't know how to help, so I'm using one hand to look up everything I can about pregnancy on Emmalee's phone while holding her with the other. She's nuzzled into my chest, safely hidden from the screen's dim glow.

I vividly remember Mom's exhaustion from carrying Hana, but she wasn't too open about it. It's far more strenuous than I took the time to think about, crafting another body inside yours.

Now I'm even more worried. Emmalee will need more help than she probably knows. I don't think I can leave her alone in good conscience, but I definitely don't want to force my presence on her after what she's been through. She didn't answer if she'd like my help raising an entirely new human being or not, but I was dead-serious. Especially when she has no choice but to suffer through childbirth now, no matter if her baby survives or not.

After I read multiple articles about the next few weeks for Emmalee, she suddenly wants to lay on her opposite side, so I click the phone to sleep. I help her roll over, settling against her back to spoon her. With my hand on her lower abdomen again, she falls completely still.

Her belly is delicately round, so subtle when she stands

that it only grazes against a loose shirt. She used to wear tight, button-up blazers for work, so I was wondering why she started unbuttoning it and wearing loose undershirts. Now I know. It's much more pronounced when she sleeps on her side like this, distending her abdomen without care. She's cuddling her pillow against her chest like I've seen her do with my jackets, absolutely *exhausted* from carrying this baby alone. And from what I looked up, she'll rapidly grow from now on. I don't know how she expects to hide it, but I'll do my best to help.

The moment I held her tiny bump in my palm for the first time, her whole body slackened in relief. She looked so scared earlier, her unfailing strength cracking enough to cling to me in desperation multiple times. She must have suffered for *weeks*. Alone. Terrified she couldn't defend herself if anyone finds out she's pregnant. And that's all while her body grows a whole extra person, totally dependent on her health to survive? It's no surprise she felt vulnerable. It breaks my heart in two.

Ems flips to huddle into me, unsatisfied from facing away. If I remove my hand from her belly, her forehead knots in protest. I delicately brush her sides, arms, and whole abdomen with my fingertips, and she slips back into peaceful bliss, huffing against my chest.

For an hour or so, I teeter between crying and smiling. Emmalee said she wants to spend her life with me. It's almost my dream come true, but she's right; our dreams have been muddied by two disgusting men.

And whether Emmalee realizes it or not, she's trusting me with her baby's safety. I'm still terrified I'm a hazard, afraid I'll lead her straight into Sumner's arms. Scared that I already did, and S817 could be hurting her baby like she fears.

But Brayden and Emmalee were right. I can't let Sumner prevent me from loving wholly. Moments like these are what I want to live for, providing a safe space for Emmalee while she rebuilds stability in my life, just by being herself.

This situation is honestly terrifying, yet a sugary peace warms my core. I don't think I've felt this sensation before, but my body *knows* this is where I want to be. Who I want to be with. True safety.

I must've fallen asleep, opening my eyes to the dim morning blue. Emmalee whimpers on her bedside's edge.

"Ems? Are you okay?" I whisper.

She rolls over to face me, teetering upright with her hair a mess, tiny belly exposed, and eyes still shut. "Niko?"

I barely contain a laugh. "Come here, Ems. You're still sleepy."

She groans, scooting closer. Then she bodyslams me, draping over my chest and legs like a wet rag.

I have to laugh. "Oh, my *god*, be careful with yourself!"

Her limbs sprawl across me in a full-body stretch. "Huh? I'm awake."

I laugh. "Good morning, my Guide."

"Morning, my protector." She jams her knuckles against her eyes, and giggles when I cringe. After a few spacey moments, Emmalee's talkative brain turns on. "Did I bother you while I slept? It's been so hard to sleep lately, but it felt so much better when I was laying with you."

My smile gushes. "You definitely didn't bother me. You were ridiculously cute."

She grins, combing her short hair with her fingers. Her dazed eyes can stay open a little longer now. I've imagined the day I could finally spend a full night at her side, but I didn't realize how adorable she'd really be in the mornings. I'm dying to nurture her sad, sleepy eyes.

"Are you hungry, Ems?"

She groans. "You have *no* idea."

"Is there anything I can make you or go buy you?"

"*Anything?*" She thinks hard for a moment. "A new bra."

I laugh. "I meant food, but I can do that too. You'll have to tell me what size."

Her cheeks burn against her smile. "Sorry, I'm *so* tired and have the worst brain fog of my life. But if I could have anything, I really want a grilled cheese and french fries."

It takes everything within me not to laugh. "Okay. Grilled cheese and fries for breakfast in 30 minutes or so."

Thank god Mom forced me to cook and clean before I became a front-liner. I sort through the dirty dish mountain in Emmalee's kitchen, scrub a pan and the small counter spaces in her apartment, turn on the oven, and get to work chopping potatoes.

By the time I have the potato slices in the oven and heat up a pan, Emmalee scurries to the bathroom with a blanket draped around her shoulders. She exits twenty minutes later in a tank top and pajama pants, no longer hiding her stomach.

My adorable best friend has somehow become so regal, even in pajamas. Her features are sharper, but elegant. Something about her emanates reassurance that makes me believe she can accomplish anything. Others haven't taken the time to see her true strength, but I've never doubted her.

I forget everything I was doing, in awe of her. Emmalee turns beet red, hurriedly burrowing into my back.

"God, you're cute," I mumble.

Emmalee giggles, her breath puffing into my back, and I'm glad I'm not the only one still feeling shy.

"Go lay down. I'll bring it to you in a minute."

She grumbles, so I poke her forearm over and over again until she unwraps her arms from around my waist.

"Fine." She slinks in feigned annoyance down the hall, and we both laugh.

I have no idea if she'll like this carbohydrate hell—or if she can stomach it—but the second I walk in with a hot plate, her eyes spring open.

"Oh, my God. *Thank* you." She releases my jacket she was cuddling, reaching for the plate.

I hand it to her, and she furrows her brows.

"Hey, I was reaching for you!" She laughs. "To thank you."

"Oh." I smile against my hot cheeks, sitting beside her.

Ems hugs me hard before diving into her food. I'm amazed as she devours it. She's always been nauseous, so I haven't seen her enjoy food for most of our lives. I actually didn't notice the difference until now: she's *really* enjoying it, groaning and thanking me multiple times. All I can do is laugh.

Her eyes grow serious. "Hey, where's yours?"

"Um, I didn't exactly want *this* for breakfast."

She cackles, nudging me with her elbow. "Hey, it's not *that* weird! It's actually glorious. But go get yourself something boring then and eat with me!"

I laugh, doing as I'm told. I return with two apples and some extra fries, in case Emmalee wants some of each.

But as soon as I see her, I hold my breath, realizing most of her plate is cleared, and she's sobbing.

And smiling?

She beams up at me with massive tears in her eyes.

"E-Emmalee?"

She whimpers with her cheeks full. "You made me the best food ever."

I laugh, wiping her cheeks. "I want to help, Ems, and this is pretty much the bare minimum."

Her breath hitches as she continues to chew, taking another bite. But she can't seem to stop crying, so we laugh.

"Did you think I'd ever bawl unironically over food?" She giggles at herself, still whimpering.

I smile. "Not like this, no."

Emmalee sighs, staring off into the distance. We lean into each other as we chew, contemplating what's ahead.

After I finish my apple, I stretch my arms above my head, and Emmalee looks up in deep concern. "Are you leaving?"

I kiss her cheek. "Not for long. What else do you need me to pick up?"

She grasps my wrist, giving it an affectionate massage. "Wait, what are you getting so far?"

"Just a bra and more food since you're running low."

Emmalee wells up again, and we laugh. Kneeling on her bed's edge, she throws her arms around my neck, kissing my cheek.

She pauses in front of my nose. "Can I kiss you on the lips, even if I smell like grilled cheese?"

I laugh. "As long as you don't puke in my mouth."

She pinches my arm, letting out a loud, rambunctious laugh.

I kiss her until our smiles fade. Our eyes lock, throwing my heart into overdrive. I can't bear the thought of letting go of her, so I pull her closer, softening my voice.

"Ems, you're just—"

She interrupts my doting sigh with kiss after kiss. As we lean into each other, her eager fingers grip my back. I almost can't believe how heavy her breath becomes, my heart restarting itself with each of her desperate kisses. I'm enjoying it too much to remember anything I wanted to do with her today, content to absorb every second of her existence. But as soon as my heart soars, my mood plummets.

This is wonderful. Too good for me to trust it'll stay okay.

"What's wrong?" Breathless, Emmalee pulls back, holding my face. "Talk to me."

"I feel like something horrible might happen at any moment."

She hums in understanding. "I have that sometimes too. After you were deployed, that was all I felt for a long time because it actually *did* come true... But then we ended up together again, right?"

I stare into her cerulean eyes, bright with hope. They weren't like this yesterday. I don't want to agree since my doubt has been my survival, but maybe I should allow her to fill me with hope too. At least for today.

"Right," I whisper. "I'm so thankful for this time with you that it makes the thought of losing you extra horrible."

She kisses me so softly that my heart aches. "I know. But it's going to be okay. We'll protect each other from now on."

I close my eyes and exhale, rubbing her sides. "Yes. We will."

"Okay, how about I save up some energy for a couple days until we can go to the mall together? Let's not leave each other's side anymore until we're comfortable with it."

"Like... at all?"

She shrugs with a sly smile. "I mean, yeah. You're welcome to stay over as long as you want. Move in, even. We can keep an eye on each other."

My entire body settles with her words, sinking into a deep sigh. "Okay, *yes*. That sounds *much* better."

Emmalee chuckles. "Come here. It's my turn."

I know exactly what she means, and allow her to wrap me in her arms; right now, she's my protector. We curl up on her bed, spending wordless time together with no limit in sight.

CHAPTER 34

Niko

Instead of kids selling cookies outside of convenience stores, white supremacist "truth-spreaders" harass customers. There's no question if the cops will stop them; cops loudly sponsor white supremacists in Civil War II.

Today's radical right-winger wasn't there when we arrived, but he's there now, smiling in someone's face in front of the exit.

Emmalee spins right back around, hissing, "I'm too pregnant for this."

Switching our grocery bag to the opposite hand, I lace our fingers together. "Don't worry."

We try to exit the store peacefully, but of course we're bombarded. I'm completely unreceptive, so he singles out Emmalee, blocking her path. Her grip tightens, and I boil.

I have to pin my hand to my pocket, willing away what Brayden calls my "trauma reactive behaviors." As in this guy's KKK, neo-Nazi Alliance logo alone makes me want to punt him across the street. My brain insists I *need* to before he splashes Emmalee's blood across my shoes, and I've seen too many "non-Patriot" women killed to argue with it.

I must show it; he opens and closes his quivering mouth, threatening honest-to-god tears. Because he's "too manly" to cry in front of us, he retreats to his American flag table.

We take our chance to speedwalk down the street.

"Are you okay?" I ask.

Emmalee checks over her shoulder, huddling into me. She doesn't respond beyond a nod. It's unlike her, but I don't blame her for feeling scared. In the name of "a safer society," white supremacists killed more people than our units did, and killing was our job. But that wasn't the scariest part.

They believe in every drop of blood spilled.

And they get away with it.

When we cross the street, separating ourselves from the store by a traffic rush, Emmalee slowly exhales, dropping her head against my shoulder. "Okay. I'm okay now."

I can't relax, however. I'm tracking some men following us across the street, making eye contact to startle them. But they don't care; they stare right back. Maybe I'm having paranoia again and they're just regular dudes in baseball hats.

Emmalee and I hop into her car. She already has to dig around in the grocery bag for the anti-nausea wristbands we bought, the circles under her eyes notably darker.

"Oh, Ems… Are you still okay to go? I'd drive, but I'm still not allowed… and I kinda don't blame them."

"It's okay, I don't mind driving." She sighs, her forehead on the steering wheel. "I just have *intense* protective instincts right now. I'm freaking out inside even though we're away from him, and it's exhausting. It feels like I can't keep the baby safe enough no matter where I go… because nowhere in this world is safe."

I lean over the center console to put my arm over her shoulders. "I feel that way sometimes too. But if it's white supremacist men you're worried about, I've got you covered."

She laughs, poking my nose with hers, and I break into a smile. Emmalee plants a slow, tender kiss on my lips, filling my chest with a sedating sense of safety. I caress her smooth jawline to welcome more of her touch, and she hums into my mouth, kissing me even longer. Her icy irises glisten with my reflection, and it warms my core.

"Okay," she breathes. "Let's go."

Her jaw is still tense as she flashes her blinker, waiting for ongoing traffic before we merge onto chaotic downtown streets. I try to rub her arm to calm her, but it's not enough.

"Ems? Hang on a second."

I sound as nervous as I feel. Emmalee puts the car into park, whipping her perplexed stare at me.

"Tell me if it's still okay to touch you like this or not, but—" I put my hand on her stomach. "I'm going to do everything I can to keep you both safe, okay?"

Her forehead wrinkles, my poor best friend hanging on her steering wheel for comfort. It looks like she's about to cry. I flinch to retract my hand, but she holds it to her in desperation, squeezing her eyes shut hard. We sit in silence as she breathes repetitive, whistling exhales until her shoulders drop.

"Thank you," she whispers. "Thank you."

I haven't touched her baby belly since the first night, unsure if it was appropriate beyond that heat-of-the-moment gesture. Apparently, it's better than appropriate. This is still so new to us that we can't handle each other's flushed faces beyond a quick glance. Once Emmalee starts driving, I remove my hand to untwist myself and sit properly. She looks disappointed, ever-so-subtly sinking into herself, so I replace it with the left hand so I can hold her baby as she drives. A sneaky smile spreads across her face. It's obvious she loves it, even if she's beet-red and biting her lip in embarrassment. The only sound is her blinker and random people honking at each other for no reason.

Then she starts to giggle.

I have no idea why, but I begin to laugh too.

After we fill the silence with laughter, Emmalee says, "I can't believe any of this is happening, Niko."

I chuckle, rubbing my thumb over her warm stomach. Then an idea comes to mind.

"Hey, you know how when we were almost 17, we— Uh..."

"Had really clumsy but surprisingly amazing sex? Yes, I *absolutely* remember."

I let out a surprised laugh. "Emmalee!?"

She laughs and shrugs. "Well, what about it?"

I hide my face in my hands, despite Emmalee's complaining sigh that I let go of her. My muffled laughter into my palms raises another giggle out of her.

"What I was *going* to say is, at the time, I thought up an emergency plan."

She grins. "Oh, my God. Of course you did. For a baby-related emergency?"

I laugh. "Yes. A babymergency."

"Oh, *God*." She groans. "Did you just dad-joke me?"

My eyes go wide. "Wait. Was that my first real dad joke?"

Emmalee gasps, glancing between me and the road. "Oh, my God, did you really just say that?!"

In response to my wide smirk, her face flushes bright pink, extending to her neck.

"Nikolai!" She yells through a laugh, clutching her stomach once we stop at a light. "Oh! Please, don't make me pee my pants—"

"Oh. Wait— Are you really going to?"

This only makes her laugh harder, nodding in agonized affirmation.

I shush her as best as I can, but we only continue to laugh. I have to shut my mouth and turn away from her when her eyes bulge, nearly peeing for real.

We rush into the mall and find a bathroom as quickly as possible. I can't stop smiling. Emmalee and I always get each other into trouble, but we also always manage to have fun.

Standing guard as I wait, I turn around when I hear her soft sigh exiting the bathroom.

Her faded, dark-brown hair is neatened, gracing her cheeks, and the natural flushing on her face has calmed to a gentle rosiness. I can't help but smile.

"Better?" I ask.

She rolls her eyes and laughs. "Yep. No thanks to *you*."

Emmalee gives me a soft cheek poke before sliding her hand into mine. It still feels weird, being touchy in public like this. Like we'll get caught, or we're being watched. Except I think we really are.

Despite having driven through numerous busy intersections, Emmalee and I still have baseball hat men following us. I think they *want* me to notice them. They're hovering in my peripherals, on the storefronts' opposite side. Maybe they're preying on my "instability." Stable or not, I'm succumbing to their fear tactics.

Emmalee suddenly yanks me into a store, tucking us behind the five-foot-wide post between the entrance and front windows.

"Is being around all these people too much?" She whispers. "I can go in alone."

"It's not that, exactly…"

Emmalee knows crowds are difficult for me and can probably feel me getting jumpy. And that *is* part of it. The more people around, the less I can track everyone closely enough to ensure our safety.

She raises a skeptical eyebrow. "Will you actually tell me if you're not okay, or do I have to force you to go back home with me?"

I laugh. "Okay, okay. I'm not feeling horrible, but I'm not great. And this will probably sound weird."

"Try me."

I lean into her smirk, tempted to kiss her. But instead, I whisper into her ear. "I can't tell if I'm having a paranoid episode, or if there really are three men in baseball hats following us wherever we go."

Her grip tightens around my arms. "W-what? Where?" She peeks around the entrance, but I'm sure they hid by now. "You should trust your gut. I trust it."

"I don't have a gut instinct anymore, Ems. It's mushed together with so much paranoia that I can't tell the difference."

"Oh, I see." She stares into my chest, her eyes distant in thought. "If I had to describe the difference, instincts feel… calm. Even if they give you adrenaline to help you escape danger, instincts feel like a deep, truthful knowing when you check inside. For me, paranoia feels like pure, helpless fear. Where you don't know what to believe."

"Hmm. Or maybe my instincts are just gone."

She pats my chest. "They're still in there, love."

She's never called me "love" before. I almost melt to the floor, and Ems feels it in my stunned energy, giving her a sly smile.

Emmalee spins me around, hugs me from behind, and guides me out of the store. She wants to place her chin on my shoulder to beam up at me, but she has to wobble on her toes to do it. I just about die from cuteness overload.

She giggles. "Let's keep walking. If you see them again, we can both try to get a read on them."

Studying her bright eyes, I physically feel my spirits lift. I chuckle. "Okay."

"So." She rejoins my side to whisper in my ear. "Now that I'm not about to piss myself, what was the babymergency plan?"

I laugh, then lower my voice. "You probably won't be a fan of some of it. But I was thinking if we came up with a *new* babymergency plan, you might feel a little safer about the future."

She squeezes my hand. "O-oh. That's a good point. I'd like that."

"Yeah? Then let's come up with something together. My original idea was to get our parents' help, hiring us for safer jobs and unrecorded medical appointments. Then you could take time off once it becomes impossible to hide… But a lot of that doesn't apply anymore. These days, I think my front-liner settlement should cover us both. Wait, no—" I cup my hand over her ear. "All *three* of us."

I peek at Emmalee to find her biting back a shy, rosy smile, and I swear it gives me energy.

I continue to whisper, "If you want to keep working, I'll be able to stay home with the baby, but since my parents won't let me pay for literally anything, I have enough saved so we can both stay home for a while. But I think no matter what, one part of the plan has to stay the same: we have to tell your dad as soon as possible."

Her feet slow. "Oh, *God*."

"I know. But you need to see a doctor, Ems. We don't even know how many weeks it's been."

She chews on her lip. "What else?"

"Originally, I thought of a few ways we could get a place on our own, but that's not a problem anymore with your apartment, so—"

"Are you still moving in?" She blurts out.

My heart flips from her eager stare. I let out an elated laugh, petting her head. "Yes. Don't worry, Ems. We're in this together, like you said."

"Good. I was preparing myself to fight for it if you said no."

Her devious smile grows when I giggle. I sigh in absolute adoration of her, kissing her temple.

"So then what?" She asks.

"The rest is figuring out work and money. Like officially cutting all remaining ties with Sumner, not avoiding it by using up your vacation and sick days... Please."

Emmalee sighs. "Yeah, yeah. I'm chipping away at my notice."

"Okay, okay. So the front-liner settlement can pay for the apartment, and I can put everything into my savings that Sumner gave me for his... experiments."

Embarrassment strikes my core when Emmalee sucks in a terrified breath. She whispers, "Okay, *that* is somewhat news. We'll talk more about that later."

"I guess... But beyond that—" I cup my hand over her ear. "Maybe we could escape together."

The safehouse cabin sounds like paradise—the one my parents and a few other tenants are building in the forest for other traitors. Emmalee thinks it was cruel it was kept secret from me, but I don't think she can understand. It's too incredible of a secret to share with a wolf.

Which is why I can't mention the hideout out loud, not even in a whisper. Emmalee's eyes ignite to show me she understands.

They fade just as quickly.

She strokes the back of my hand. "Niko, I'd love to, but... I don't know about making you pay for all this. I don't have enough money saved if we're cut off from the outside and can't work. I'd have to rely on you and your parents."

I shrug. I tap, *It's unowned land,* on her palm as I whisper into her ear. "We won't have rent eating into our savings anymore, Ems. Although, it's not perfect. We'll be exiled from everyone, including your parents. And, you know, we 'just' have to fake our deaths."

Her soft chuckle ends with a sigh. "I'll have to think about that... But for now, we're here."

CHAPTER 35

Emmalee

Three minutes in, and I'm ready to break down in the changing room. We scouted a few bras one cup size up, but none of them are large enough, and this pregnancy has just begun. My whole body feels out of my control.

"Ems? You okay?" Niko calls out from the changing room entrance.

"Yeah." My shaky voice gives me away. I sigh and try again. "I'll come out in a second."

I steady myself as I put my clothes back on, reassured I still have him waiting for me. My protector.

The only thing tethering my sanity to this earth is Niko. He's been by my side through everything the past week, and I mean *everything*—vomit, constipation, and sneeze-pissing alike— without batting a disgusted eye once. The most faithful person I've ever met, Niko has redefined loyalty for me.

Niko is struggling not to pace at the entrance, rocking back and forth. He softens when he sees me, giving me a sad smile as I drop our entire findings onto an unwanted clothes cart. I take Niko's hand, leading us to the changing room's waiting area with plenty of seating.

He wraps me into his arms. "What's going on? Are you upset?"

Blubbering already, I drop my forehead into Niko's chest. "Those are already too small, and they all hurt a lot."

"Oh, Ems..." He rubs my back, taking me seriously even

though I'm crying over *fabric*. "We can keep looking, okay? There aren't any shirts you liked either?"

I wipe my nose on the inside of my shirt. "Women's clothing sucks ass. Everything is see-through or pointlessly tight. Or both."

"Then let's not shop on this side. Clothing gender labels are arbitrary anyway. You liked stealing my shirt today, right?"

"Yeah, it's super soft and thick… Sorry for snotting on it."

He just laughs, his eyes glowing with affection for me and my snot-nose. It stuns me speechless.

Niko leads me to the department store's opposite half. His shoulders are still broad from the tour, but he hasn't worked out since he got home, so they've started to shrink. I'm concerned he's losing weight too fast. Weight loss is a common symptom I've seen from Sumner's experiments, like the illness eats you from the inside out. But Niko won't mention his physical symptoms. I don't think he notices how sick he is. He's still numb.

"Look how much of your color is over here!" Niko smiles, attempting to cheer me up.

I laugh, immersed in a sea of black, gray, and navy. "You're a genius. This is much better."

He kisses my forehead. "I'm going back to look for another size while you look for some comfier shirts. Is that okay?"

"I don't know…" I scope our surroundings to ensure we're alone. "Have you seen your baseball hat guys?"

He avoids my eyesight. "They, uh— Won't bother us."

"Nikolai…"

"Okay, I'll admit, I think it's the Department keeping tabs. But I made them flinch earlier when I pretended to run at them, and I haven't seen them since."

I groan. "I don't want to be alone, then."

"You won't be. Watch." Niko backs into the opposite aisle, morphing into a tall pole amongst the short bra racks. "Turn around, then turn back."

I sigh, turning to the clothing rack at my fingertips. When I glance back over my shoulder, Niko is an inch from my nose, and I squeak.

"What the fuck? How were you so quiet, Boot Foot?"

He laughs. "A lifetime of sneaking around in clunky combat boots. I won't go anywhere I can't see or reach you within seconds, okay?"

"Okay…"

I sift through one rack, finding more than expected. I'm warming up to the idea of loose t-shirts, not being forced to wear a bra if I don't have to work anymore, and my belly growing into the stretchy fabric. It feels liveable.

No, not just liveable, but comfortable. I can't remember the last time I could choose comfort. I smile, realizing why.

"Niko?"

"Hm?"

"What size shirt do you wear now?"

"Oh, uh—Usually a Large. Why?"

"So if I buy a few of these in a Large, you can wear them too?" I turn around in time to catch his blushing smile.

"Sure, I guess I could."

"Oh, thank God. Some weirdo you live with needs everything to smell like you," I mutter beneath my breath. Niko still hears me somehow, his soft giggle fading into the next aisle.

Biting back a giddy smile, I collect quite a few black shirts, including some long sleeves and a baggy hoodie that'll come in handy soon.

Something catches my eye across the room. Whoever they are, I can feel them watching me. Just as I lift my head, they're gone.

"N-Ni—"

"I'm right here. I saw him," Niko mutters behind my head.

I reach for him, and he brings me to his chest, his handful of wireless bralettes pressed against my back. Niko's predatory stare locks onto the store's corner, and my spine shivers.

"W-who was it?" I whisper.

"Someone from the DoTD. Someone we went to school with."

I swallow hard. "Oh, no…"

"What?"

"Is it Andre?"

Perplexed, Niko studies my panicked face.

Then it clicks for him: who Andre is to me. Niko morphs from intense focus to extreme rage. After today's trigger truckload, I know he's not recovering from this one. Attempting to soothe him would be like taming a… well, a wolf.

Niko's voice deepens into a vicious hiss. "He's stalking you too, now?"

"Y-you're scaring me." I squirm from his arms.

Niko's eyes trace my face, reverting into his sad-puppy guilt. "Sorry! I'm so sor—"

Andre dives straight for Niko. I barely dodge them, catching myself on a clothes rack as two beasts of men scramble in a pile of thoughtless muscle. I think I'm witnessing a gladiator fight.

"What the hell are you doing?!" I scream.

Andre clamps Niko's throat with both hands, pinning him to the ground. But Niko's neutrality startles Andre and me alike. It doesn't look like he's bothered to fight back, let alone bothered he's getting choked out. Freaked out, Andre hesitates, leaving Niko room to mouse his way out—like he did with the neo-Nazi. Reversing their positions like child's play, Niko lands a few hits on Andre's face, fulfilling his intention to "break" it when he realized Andre broke my consent. The sound of Niko's fist pounding crackling bone makes me gag.

I'm panting now. I don't want to see anything like that bleeding Nazi again. "Please— Please, stop!"

Niko catches my stare, throwing Andre across the floor as he rises to his feet. He covers me with his whole body, pressing us against an icy, mirrored pillar at the aisle's end. I can't see Andre, but I hear him lumber to his feet with a grunt. He's shorter than Niko but much broader, packing on at least 50 extra pounds of pure muscle. But he hasn't been a front-liner, and that much is obvious: he's winded, whereas Niko's heartbeat against my ear slows to a regular standing rate.

With a quick break from the action, a store clerk peeks from behind a clothes rack, her entire body shaking. "S-sir! P-please sto—"

But she doesn't exist to Andre. "What are you doing to Richards?!"

"Protecting her." Niko steadies his voice.

"Why would I hurt her? I'm trying to save her from the fucking *Wolf.*"

"Just leave, Andre," I say. "Please, leave."

After an odd pause, Andre mutters, "Don't you have anything to say to me?"

"Excuse me?" I say. Then I think about it.

He means the baby. Just like I suspected, Andre understands the power he holds over me. I grip Niko harder, knowing once he realizes what Andre just said, there will be no off-switch on Niko's impulse control.

Luckily, Andre is still an asshole who knows how to derail any logical conversation.

"So, lemme guess, you're fucking *him* now?" Andre bellows. His anger explodes inside my chest, shaking me with fear.

Niko buries his head into my shoulder, muttering to himself in Japanese. I have no idea what he's saying, but I can feel his anger rising despite his best efforts.

"You *are* fucking him, huh? You fucking *whore*," Andre says.

Andre attempts to rip Niko off me, but nothing can move my terrifying best friend. It's like I have a hundred-thousand-year-old boulder in front of me. One that has long withstood the test of time, shielding me from an onslaught of pointless violence like that's what his body was crafted for. Niko's breath is pummeled out of his lungs with every voracious hit on his back. He only grunts when we both hear a loud crack—another one of his ribs snapping.

This is the point where I sob. I feel horrible for doing this to Niko. No matter how much we separate ourselves from the Departments, we can't live average lives. We never have, and I'm afraid we never will. Niko is struggling to become a less violent person, but he *can't* be violence-free. Not when we live in a violent world.

But I can't ask him to undo his cool, not after I forced him to back off and consequently sacrifice himself. *I* have to stop Andre.

I feed into the fire in my core. I think of what Andre has done, or as Niko put it, what he's *taken*. My physical safety and this unborn child's security. The time I needed to prepare myself for parenthood, one of my lifelong dreams. Then I picture myself as another brutish man who doesn't give a shit who he plows over. Within seconds, I become him.

"Andre!" I yell.

Niko's breath freezes beside my ear. Andre pauses in his attack, awaiting my next move.

Peeking out from Niko's shield, I catch Andre's eyes. I don't let his intimidating rage dissuade me, focusing on overwhelming him. I feel bad about it, but now I understand what Niko already does; this type of person only speaks one rageful language.

"You think stalking me and beating my best friend will make me *like* you?!" I scream. Andre blinks a few times. "What a fucking joke! Niko isn't fighting to win me over like a piece of meat. He's angry because you hurt me! Badly!"

Andre deflates.

Niko flips around, guarding me behind him. For a split second, the men's tense bodies assess whether or not they'd like to strike. But as Andre analyzes Niko, he must realize Niko is unfazed. Angry, but physically steady, whereas Andre is breaking a sweat, his rapidly-swelling cheek likely fractured. Andre sinks into a seething wrinkle of his nose. He spits on Niko's broken foot, and storms out of the store.

We've attracted a large crowd, staring like we're a zoo attraction. I don't feel bad for myself as much as I feel horrible for Niko. This all happened because of me.

So I do what I do best lately and burst into obnoxious tears.

Niko whips around, but he's hesitant, unsure if I'm still open to his touch. I lean into him, giving him permission. But his warmth is gone. He only brushes my arms while I sob.

A security woman arrives, concern overriding her expertly made-up face. "Ma'am? Are you hurt?"

I shake my head no. The terrified store clerk rushes to my opposite side, supporting my heaving torso. I choke out my words. "I-I'm fine n-now."

Niko and the store clerk sit me on the waiting area's bright orange seats. The crowd partially disperses, but stragglers gawk like we're on display. Someone points out Niko's neck, striped with bright red finger marks.

"Sir, do you need first aid?" The security guard asks.

He smiles softly. "I'm okay. I'm just worried about my best friend. Can someone get her some water? I don't want to leave her side."

The store clerk rushes to the back room, and the security officer mutters into her radio.

"I hate this," I whisper.

"I know." Niko runs his fingers through my hair.

Leaning into his touch, I allow it to soothe me. If I want to slow my sobs and stop hiccup-breathing like I'm five years old, I have to ignore the aching pain in Niko's emotions. They're tempting me to bawl again.

I made him feel so guilty for protecting me like I asked him to. Like most cis men, I'm not sure he entirely understands the gutting fear of being face-to-face with an angry man, no matter how trustworthy or loving they are. It's not their gender; it's the lack of control they've been raised with.

The store clerk returns with water and a tissue box, and I attempt to clean myself up. My hand absent-mindedly comforts my growing baby as I sip my water, pleading with the universe that they're unaffected by my stress. The clerk notices, so I hurriedly drop my hand to my side.

"Tough day?" She asks.

I laugh. "Just a little bit."

The clerk offers to ring me up while Niko dissuades the security officer from calling the cops. The cops would lead to a report clusterfuck with the Departments, which is why Andre's public assault is an even bigger insult.

Beyond that, someone is bound to realize I'm pregnant, like this store clerk. If Andre discovers his suspicions are true, the Departments might surrender my baby to him. Even worse, they'll surrender me to his "care" if I want to watch my child grow up.

I'm fucking terrified. Clara's words won't stop ringing in my head—how the Departments craved Niko since he was a fetus.

Niko isn't as paranoid as he seems. We're *both* being watched.

Once we reach the counter, the clerk leans in close. "Do you need me to call someone to get you away from him too? I can help you escape."

I look over at Niko and laugh. "Oh, no. Thank you so much for looking out for a fellow woman, but thankfully, that's my best friend in the world. He was only protecting me, even though—" I choke back tears again. "Even though he had to get hurt for my sake. I feel awful about it."

She reaches out to hug me over the counter.

It's an awkward reach since I don't want to lean on my baby, but it's still a kind gesture. Surprisingly so, considering how tense everyone is with one other from the war. It makes me cry harder.

Niko strides over, nervous about the continuous tears streaking my cheeks. He wipes them off, looking back at the store clerk. "Hey, do you mind if we sit in a changing room for a minute? I think she needs space to cool off."

The store clerk glances between us, her smile spreading. "You're not going to get me in trouble, right?"

I sniffle. "Haven't we already?"

She laughs, guiding us to a changing room in the backmost corner. "Take your time."

Niko follows me in, his gentle hands on my shoulders. As soon as we're behind a closed door, he squeezes me in a careful but sturdy hug, burying his head into my neck. We breathe in silence for a while until we settle into a whispering hum, my tears slowing into an occasional sniffle.

"I'm so sorry," he whispers.

"Niko, look at me."

He shakes his head no.

I lean back until he groans in protest, and I laugh. Cupping his cheeks, I find him closing his eyes in defiance.

"Niko!" I giggle. "Why won't you look at me?"

"Because." He suppresses a grin. "You'll tell me it wasn't my fault, etcetera, even though I behaved like a caveman." His voice wavers. "And I terrified you."

I kiss him. His eyes snap open, and he backs against the opposite wall.

"Sorry." I wipe my runny nose in my shirt collar yet again. "I didn't know what else to do if you didn't want me to use words. Plus, I kinda want to make out with you as thanks for saving my ass."

He lets out a single huffing laugh in surprise. Wandering eyes caress me, taking in what I assume is the mess of a human being I am. But he doesn't seem to see it that way. His lips soften, filling with a desire I rarely see on him.

We move at the same time, desperate to hold each other. Niko presses his forehead to mine, grasping my head, cheeks, shoulders, and waist like he doesn't know where to start. So I kiss him again, heavier this time. He hums like he wanted to say something first, but it pains me to release his full lips. Niko agrees, hugging my waist to him as our lips glide with ease. After a yearning, tongue-heavy kiss, he stops himself, breathless.

"No, actually, let's not. Not while you're this upset."

I sigh. "I'm not upset with *you*. I feel horrible for making you feel horrible."

One of his eyebrows twitches, puzzling my words together.

I laugh. "*You* didn't scare me. *Angry men* scare me. All of them. Not just you."

He mulls over my words, his eyes tracing the stained, gray carpet.

"I didn't mean for you to get hurt, only to turn off your murder mode. But I don't want you to sacrifice yourself for me either."

"Then… What else am I supposed to do?"

Niko's genuine question startles me speechless. And for a while, I don't have an answer. Not until we're five shirts, two sweaters, one hoodie, and three bralettes richer, driving back to my apartment.

"Hey." I reach over the car's center console to squeeze his hand.

He shoots me a worried glance, the guilty expression having returned to his face.

"I'm sorry for asking you to protect me without making something clear," I continue. "If you need to get angry, even if it looks scary, get angry. If you need to defend yourself, even if that means using violent force, defend yourself. But I want to protect you too. If you're putting yourself in harm's way, I'm physically incapable of protecting you. That's not what I want because I care about you and your wellbeing. Your safety matters just as much as mine."

He thinks about this for a while. "But I'm not the one carrying a baby—"

"No. Listen to my words and remember them, okay?" I interlock our fingers. "Your safety matters just as much as mine. Your safety matters."

With that, the poor boy bursts into tears.

CHAPTER 36

Emmalee

The next step in the Babymergency Plan is to reject all final calls pressuring me to continue my horrifying job before Sumner realizes I'm pregnant. Niko argued the next-next step should be seeing my dad, but I'll have to schedule *that* horrifying talk after work. For now, I hope my clipboard blocks my obvious baby from Amanda.

"I've discovered my chronic illnesses are too severe to work two shifts a day," I say. "Since I'm far past my one-month courtesy notice, I'm not showing up Monday."

Amanda's face is uncomfortably neutral. "Are you sure you can't fit in a few hours? We don't have enough staff, so I can double your pay." She eyes my uncertain expression. "How about I triple it?"

With that, I'm sent home in a huff.

As soon as I open our apartment door, I find Niko belly-down on our thrifted couch, an ice pack on his latest broken rib.

I smile, knowing what I'm about to do to him. "Wow, love. You stayed so calm when I walked in! I'm impressed!"

He buries his face into a pillow to hide his smiling blush. No matter how many times I say it, Niko still gets giddy when I call him "love."

"It's only because I knew it was you." The pillow muffles Niko's voice.

"Huh? How'd you know?"

"I can pick out the sound of your walk anywhere."

I drop my bag, stride over to him, and stop at the couch's edge. He pops up worriedly, so I have enough room to nuzzle in and prepare him for the idea of making out with me.

He draws me to him as I press into his lips. The weight of it isn't enough for me, so I dive in for more, kissing him until he's blushing so hard his freckles fade away.

"Ems," he huffs, cradling my head. "I missed you all day."

I smile. "I missed you too. But guess what? I'm finally free of all chains locking me to my shitty job."

He drops his head back, letting out a massive sigh. "Thank fucking *god*."

"You better be happy. I had to turn down three times my pay rate, and it practically killed me."

He helps me onto his lap, cuddling into my collarbone. "I'm so sorry."

"Hey, I was joking. This is what I want too. That job was so horrible on a regular day, but I puked a million times after I worked with CEO Trash Bag."

"Really?"

"Yes. It was very disturbing."

He rubs my back with a strained sigh. "I hate that."

I can't contain my giggle.

Niko pops up, his eyes wide in horror. "I know that laugh."

I bite back my smirk, giggling even more. "What? What laugh?"

"Emmalee, what did you do?"

"Well, I never liked what he was doing, so…" I shrug. "I *may* have 'accidentally' changed the dates on a few patient contracts, here and there… As in, at least a couple hundred. Just so they could end their trial early and take fewer horrible medications… And I never got caught."

He stares, speechless for a good fifteen seconds. "Oh, my god. *Emmalee Marie Richards.*"

I laugh, pushing my blazer off to my sides and holding my stomach. "Yeah, yeah, I know. Those were the days before I had something to protect."

Our focus drops to my belly. Last week, I looked like I was storing a huge food baby. Today, I look pregnant-pregnant. Niko brushes his knuckles against my baby, deep in thought. As he meets my eyes, my face grows hot.

"Ems. I can't let you wait another week. We have to check on this baby."

I chew on my lip. "Can you get my phone?"

He eyes me. "R-right now?"

"My dad might be at work, so I'll just ask him when we can come over… later this week. But you're right. I'm really worried. We've been under so much stress. What if I've been freaking out so much that I killed the baby?"

Niko raises both eyebrows. "I don't think so. This morning you ate breakfast like I hadn't fed you for days, then threw it up all over the kitchen sink because I accidentally used one extra deodorant swipe."

I hum in agreement. "Good point. I guess I need to get this over with."

Niko digs into my work bag for my phone. Just to make sure I go through with it, he opens my dad's contact for me.

I squeeze my eyes shut. "Can you press the call button for me? Please? Don't let me chicken out."

"Okay."

Then I hear it ring. I rise to my feet in a panic. "Hang it up."

"What?" Niko white-knuckles his knees with the phone in his lap.

"I can't do this, it's too terrifyi—"

"Hello?" Dad's voice sounds worried.

I clam up, my jaw sewn shut.

"Emma? Are you there? …Did you butt-dial me again, young lady?"

Niko grips his forehead, stressing out as much as I am. "Hey, Dr. Richards, this is Niko."

"Is everything okay?" Dad asks. "I thought I told you to call me Ben."

"Sorry— Um… Ben…" Niko looks at me expectantly, but I shake my head no. He sighs. "Everything is fine. Emmalee asked me to—"

"Can Niko and I come over sometime this week?" I blurt out, so nervous that I'm out of breath. "I need to talk to you."

Dad is speechless for a moment. "Emma, are you okay? You sound… not so great."

"I'm okay!" My voice cracks.

Niko covers his mouth with a clenched fist, struggling not to laugh.

We hear my dad drop his files—an epic paper slap. "Alright, I'm leaving work right now. Can you meet me at the house within 30 minutes?"

"I-I…"

"Yes, we can," Niko says.

"Do you need me to pick you up?" Dad asks.

Niko pauses, waiting for me to respond. He opens his mouth to speak, but I jump in with a quick, "No! *No*. I can drive."

"Are you sure?" Niko and Dad ask at the same time.

"Yes, I'm—"

"I'm coming to pick you up in fifteen minutes. Bye." Dad hangs up.

A smile creeps across Niko's face. "I like *Ben* more and more these days."

I groan, speed-walking to my bedroom mirror. Rolling my shoulders back, I whisper a curse symphony beneath my breath, turning to the side. It's probably hideable… if I wear my new hoodie that erases all body shape. But I don't understand something.

"Why do I look *this* pregnant?"

Niko leans his chin on my shoulder, wrapping his arms around me from behind. "Hmm. That's a good question." He runs his hands over my belly. It's still too small to hold both of Niko's calloused palms at once, which somehow makes it cuter. But usually I'm looking *down* at his hands on my belly, and not… *this*. I watch him caress me in the mirror, looking like full-blown husband material caring for his pregnant wife, and my heart almost explodes.

He meets my eyes in the mirror, traces our intimate, reflected image, and jolts upright. "S-sorry."

I turn around to smile against his lips. "It's more than okay, pretty boy."

He huffs through a nervous laugh, stepping closer to kiss

me gently. I close my eyes, breathing in his luscious scent I've craved all day.

Then I remember why I'm freaking out. Niko slips my overly baggy hoodie over my head the second I strip my blazer. I change into looser leggings—a pair where we cut the stubborn elastic at the top since I'm expanding faster than I can buy clothes. We don't have time for much else before Dad texts that he's parked out front.

I lock my door with trembling fingers, ready to barrel down the stairs to my inevitable doom, but Niko stops me.

He plants a soft kiss on my lips. "I'm here with you all the way. Whenever you feel scared or nervous, just look at me, and I'll be there. Okay?"

My shoulders loosen. "God, I *adore* you, Nikolai Blackwood."

Satisfied with the blush I've given him, I descend the stairs with a smile. Until I see Dad's car parked out front.

Niko opens my apartment complex's door for me, allowing me to lead the way and wave to my dad with an awkward smile. I hop into the front seat at both of their requests, leaving Niko to sit alone in the back. My bag in my lap has to awkwardly cover my stomach; the seatbelt isn't doing me any favors.

Dad's concerned stare softens when he sees I'm not dying. "So... What have you two been up to today?"

"I finally quit my horrible job," I mutter. "And Niko went to therapy."

"Oh, good for you, Emma. And you too, Niko."

Niko can't hold Dad's stare in the rearview mirror, checking my expression before looking out the window.

"Thanks, Dad," I say. "Sorry to make you get off work."

He glances over. "Well, should you be sorry? Or is this important?"

"It's important," Niko says before I can speak.

We turn to Niko, but he's still casually staring out the window. I sigh, sinking deeper into my seat.

Dad rubs my shoulder. "You can tell me anything, you know."

"I know..."

The walk to my childhood home's front door is even more awkward, especially when Niko stops on the sidewalk like he's not allowed past an invisible barrier. Dad's guilt isn't masked by his smile as he laughs, doubling back for the love of my life with a bro-slap on the shoulder. I wince, knowing Niko's entire back still hurts, but Niko doesn't seem to mind. The two of them smiling together is a sight I never thought I'd see.

Dad opens the door. But to my dismay, he stops in the doorway to look me in the eyes. "Should I call your mother?"

"Oh, God," I whisper. He knows. I can see it in his face. "I-I don't know."

Niko eyes us anxiously, needing yet another invitation to step through the house's threshold.

Dad leads us past the entryway, stopping at the kitchen table where my parents used to have their nightly chats. It looks unused and clean, I imagine from their busy work schedules not allowing them to even see each other. More unit members are dying in the hospital than ever before.

Dad pulls a chair out for me, and it feels way too formal. I laugh, but he only smiles. It makes my palms sweat.

"I might pee my pants in fear," I mutter.

Niko shoots me a petrified stare. "Will you?"

I sputter out a laugh, realizing he wouldn't be surprised if I really did piss myself after all the weird pregnancy shit he's witnessed. Dad glances between Niko and me, struggling to keep up as we nervous-giggle like weirdos.

Once we're seated, both men stare at me expectantly. I bury my head in my hands, groaning.

"Emma, you have to give me something to work with, here," Dad says. "I'm only getting more anxious."

I chew on my lip, revealing my true, terrified expression. Dad dissolves into a pale fear.

"Sorry," I blurt out. "It's just— This is just—"

Dad's eyes dart between us. "Do you *both* have something to say to me?"

I shake my head no, but Niko nods yes. I give Niko's arm a gentle nudge, and he gawks at me, offended.

"Don't give him the wrong idea!" I whisper, even though they can both hear me. "What do *you* have to say to *my* dad?"

"Don't worry about it. I'll tell him after you."

I know Niko wants to soothe me. Honestly, I'm aching for it. I don't think I can blame it on hormones. My body, heart, and mind are equally in love with him, and the stress of everything else makes him feel like heaven.

Niko's eyes soften with his slight smile. "Do you need me to say something to get you started?"

I bite my lip, turning back to Dad's shell-shocked stare. "Sorry, Dad. I'm okay. I'm just ridiculously nervous. And *extremely* nauseous."

Dad rises from his chair, retrieving three mugs. "How about we have some peppermint or ginger tea to calm your stomach?"

I exhale. "Sure. Thank you."

Niko steals a quick hand squeeze beneath the table, eyeing me for how I'm doing. But then Dad casually lifts his phone to his ear. I hope it's a work call.

"Monique, honey," he says to my mom. I want to die in my seat. "Can you come home? Emma has something she wants to tell us."

CHAPTER 37

Niko

It's jarring to see her this nervous. Emmalee is the most shameless person I know, loud-mouthed in the best way and forever ready to tell the world to fuck off, yet she's crumbling in her seat. I'm dying to hold her, or at least hug her, but I don't want to make her dad feel any worse. He looks ready to fall apart.

The microwave lets out a shrill beep, and I jump. Emmalee grabs my arm to soothe me, and I steadily exhale. Thankfully, Dr. Richards quickly removes the hot mugs, ending the beep. Grabbing tea bags, spoons, and a small honey jar, Dr. Richards' back is turned, so I kiss Ems' knuckles. She smiles slightly, but her jaw remains clamped shut. She looks like she did this morning at the sink.

I lean in and whisper, "Are you going to throw—"

She hurriedly shakes her head no, releasing my arm when her dad turns around.

Dr. Richards spreads the mugs and tea between us, and Emmalee's hands shake as she grabs hers. It hurts to watch her suffer like this.

I steal a glance at her father, who similarly shifts from fear to sadness.

Dr. Richards opens a jar of raw honey. "Emma, sweetheart, are you— What? What's wrong?"

"Smells so—" Emmalee's jaw clenches hard. "Sickly sweet, and I'm already—" Her skin washes gray, and my limbs feel numb. She lurches, tightening her mouth in a heavy gag.

"Ems. Bathroom. Don't hold it," I say.

Before I finish my sentence, she jumps up, sprinting upstairs.

I turn to her dad, wide-eyed.

He leans in, inspecting my face. "Did *you* do this to her?"

So this is where Emmalee gets her lion's heart. I hold eye contact, determining what to say with a hammering pulse. "This isn't for me to tell. I'm here to help her in every way I can, though."

He sits back, perplexed, and stares deep into his mug without another word.

The toilet flushes above our heads. We look to the stairs expectantly, but Emmalee doesn't come out right away.

"Do you have a bathroom downstairs?" I ask.

"Yes. Do you need it?"

"No, thank you. Just curious why she went upstairs."

He sighs. "That's Emma's bathroom. She always pukes in that one."

I give a revelatory hum as if this conversation were totally normal.

We only share another 30 seconds of painful silence before Mrs. Richards unlocks the door in a stressed rush. Her petrified eyes lock onto her husband's. Ben speeds to Monique's side, pulling her close to mutter soft reassurances.

This proves it; they have an idea of Emmalee's situation. But they don't know the worst of it. My gut churns when Monique turns to say hello, a forced smile on her face as we shake hands for the first time in years.

"I should've known Emma wouldn't be able to resist your charms the second you came home!" Monique laughs like it's a lighthearted joke, but I know it's not. It leaves a sour sting in my chest.

Thankfully, Emmalee rescues us by poking her head over the stair railing. We share a quick glance, and she puts on her best smile for me. I know she's hurting and terrified just by the slight tension in her lips. Some of the tension in my own body releases when she finally returns to my side, giving my hand a quick, grateful squeeze. I wish I could kiss her.

The four of us settle down with Mrs. Richards's help in keeping the conversation flowing.

Dr. Richards warms a fourth mug in the microwave, warning his wife, "Don't use the honey unless you're far away from Emma, *Honey*."

Emmalee groans. I laugh, tucking her hair behind her ear. Then I snap upright, realizing her dad is looking straight at me.

He smiles. "When will this stop being weird?"

"Probably never." Emmalee sighs.

All four of us laugh, but it's superficial.

We're all on edge, knowing this conversation will only get more awkward. I'm worried about her parents' reaction to *how* Emmalee became pregnant, more than anything. Emmalee sounded especially nervous about sharing the trauma aspect. Visiting them in person, I understand why: they care about her so much that Andre's abuse will hurt them too. I offered to blame her unexpected pregnancy on myself, but Ems gave me a vehement "no." She doesn't want them to paint me in a negative light ever again, but I don't see her pregnancy as 100% bad. She's falling headfirst into a different type of love, one she always wanted to feel. I'm honored that she's allowing me to witness it.

A beep chimes throughout the kitchen. I'm so deep in thought that I reflexively block the back of Emmalee's head, huddle over her to protect her vital organs, and force her to take cover beneath the table.

All she can do at first is let out a surprised squeak. "W-what the—"

"Oh, my god." I pop back up in realization.

It was only the microwave.

Her parents are half-standing, staring curiously. From their perspective, it must've looked like I randomly slammed their daughter's head into my lap.

"S-sorry!" I say.

Emmalee pokes her head up after me, gripping me by the shoulders. "What's wrong?!"

I help reposition her in her seat. "Sorry. I'm *so* sorry for grabbing you, Ems. I-I forgot where I was. That sounded just like the bombing alert on my receiver, and I didn't want you to get hurt when things started falling off the walls, s-so I—"

I'm not sure my explanation made sense, but the stress of their stares exaggerates my already heightened state. The room closes in on my lungs, depriving itself of oxygen. I flinch as Mrs. Richards approaches, but to my surprise, she hugs me.

"Shh. You're safe here." Mrs. Richards pats my back. "It's okay, sweetie."

I glance at Emmalee. She has so much admiration for us that tears form in her eyes. Emmalee extends her hands, and we take them. Between both women's nurturing kindness, I relax.

"T-thank you." I delicately pat Mrs. Richards' back. "I'm okay now."

Dr. Richards smiles at me with newfound warmth, but I don't quite understand why.

Emmalee inches her chair closer to mine, pulling my hand into her lap. We're all motionless as she clears her throat, preparing to speak.

"Do you remember me talking about Andre?"

The Richardses share a quick, knowing glance, her mom pressing fearful knuckles to her lips.

"Your ex?" Dr. Richards jaw tenses.

"Y-yes. I— He— Dammit. This is so humiliating." Emmalee brings a shaky hand to her forehead.

I run my thumb over her knuckles, and she huffs, looking into my eyes for reassurance. A quick nod from me is all she needs. She spouts her woes to her parents, keeping her eyes glued to the table.

Their expressions sink lower and lower as she explains the details, including things I didn't know. How she broke up with him multiple times, yet he kept breaking into her apartment, persuading her into sex with mutual loneliness. How deeply she blamed herself for agreeing to it. From what I've seen, she still does. We all agree this guy was more emotionally manipulative than she realized during the relationship.

It takes her a few conversation cycles to grasp our words. No matter how physically protected she is from him, Andre's abuse still has her thoughts tied. It shatters me; this is what I must've looked like to Jay.

I have to shuffle in my seat to contain my rage, wishing I beat the guy unconscious like Jay had the guts to, but then I see her father seething, and I suddenly get it. Emmalee doesn't need more anger or aggression in her life, either. She's just like me; she *needs* gentle love.

Steeling myself, I softly squeeze her hand. She squeezes back, ending with, "I need your help."

Those words send shockwaves through my system. I've never heard her say them directly before. I'm so proud of her.

Emmalee's parents take turns hugging her. Emmalee exhales with a smile, but her dad doesn't look okay at all. I'm tempted to hug him myself, but I'm not sure if that's okay.

Mrs. Richards leans into Emmalee with questions about her symptoms, but Dr. Richards excuses himself.

Without thinking, I jump up to follow him. Emmalee and her mom look relieved, giving me the same appreciative, yet somber smile.

Once Dr. Richards and I are alone in the hallway, he stops, staring at the front door. I take a risk by putting my hand on his back, expecting him to either ignore it or shoulder me off.

He swings around and bear-hugs me. I feel small in his arms, even when he quietly sobs against my shoulder. I squeeze him back even tighter, and he seems to feel a cathartic release from the pressure.

"Thank you." He steps back after a few moments with a pat on my shoulder. "Thank you for being there for her."

"I *want* to be," I say.

It's more forceful than intended, but Dr. Richards' wet eyes glisten with such sudden hope that I'm inspired to continue.

"I love her." I smile. It feels incredible to validate it out loud.

Dr. Richards continues to stare.

"I'm happy to take care of her, Ben. And I wanted to say, I'll happily help her raise the baby as my own. Or I'll be their figurative father in court so no one can strip her of her child. But it's entirely her choice. Just as long as she's safe and happy, I'll be there."

Dr. Richards traces my eyes, his lip quivering again. I'm afraid I've said something wrong, but he smiles, giving me another grateful hug.

We rejoin the women, and Emmalee weeps when she sees her father's tearful, red face. I stand back with a satisfied heart as she cuddles into her loving parents' embrace. Then I freeze in the doorway, too shocked to move when they open their arms to include me too.

CHAPTER 38

Emmalee

"Is that the heartbeat?" I whisper.

Dad sighs. "No. That's *your* heart going a hundred miles an hour. Take a deep breath, Emma."

I do as instructed, death-gripping Niko's hand. He's staring at me with an expression I've never seen. As Mom hovers over my head and Dad reapplies gel to the ultrasound wand, I try my best to figure Niko out. So far, I'm unsuccessful. It could be my rampant emotions blocking the sensation of his. Or maybe Niko is feeling something I've never felt in anyone before.

He brushes my hair behind my ear, softening into a smile. Then our attention turns to the screen. My heartbeat continues to scream through the monitor as Dad presses the wand to my stomach. Just like last time, I reflexively shove it off me.

"Sorry," I mutter. "I'm freaking out. I feel super out of control."

Niko stands from the stool beside me. "Do you want to do it yourself?"

Dad offers the wand. I shiver, unable to convince my hand to take it.

"Would you like me to do it?" Niko asks.

I groan. "I don't know. I don't know what's wrong with me."

"How about I try again and if you feel uncomfortable, control the wand yourself instead of pushing it away," Dad says.

I drop my head onto the bed's crinkly sanitary paper and accept fate. I was excited to see the baby, but now this ultrasound feels like a death sentence. Thinking of the ultrasound that way makes me feel like a horrible parent before they're even born, but I can't stop the fear growing inside me, making my heart race.

I study Niko as he examines the screen, signaling my dad is about to try again. I do my best to allow it this time, attempting to soften my tensing muscles, but then I catch a glimpse of something.

The second I see them, I forget myself. None of us move. The only movement comes from the miniature human on the screen, wiggling around beneath the wand's pressure.

I knock the wand off again.

"Is that hurting them?!" I ask.

Dad shakes his head no, unable to respond. He swallows hard. "Well, now I have proof Niko didn't do this to you."

"*Dad!*"

"Sorry, kidding. Mostly," Dad chuckles. But he doesn't smile for long. "It's just that Niko was in another state. You're further along than you thought."

"By how much?" I whisper.

"About a month, at least. I'll have to take a closer look at home. Either way, you're already in your second trimester, Emma."

I clench my teeth, reality seeping in. Not just the answer for why I'm already this big, but disgusting truths, such as how this was Andre's exact plan: surprising me when it was a month too late to illegally order a morning-after pill. I can't stop shaming my obliviousness while he fulfilled his wishes. It's mortifying.

But Niko doesn't budge. His eyes are glued to the screen, long after the image has disappeared.

Mom massages my raised shoulders. "Emma, honey, you have to hold still. It'll be over in a minute."

"I-I know, but— "

Niko absent-mindedly traces my stomach, knowing that's what soothes me best these days. And even if it's exactly what I needed to feel safer, my parents are watching. Between Niko's sweetness I don't feel like I deserve and Andre's increasing betrayal I trapped myself in, I want to dissolve into the examination table. Dad tries his best not to stare, turning back to the screen to seek out my uterus.

"Well, that's a healthy baby," Dad whispers.

The longer we watch my developing child's kickboxing practice, the more my chest burns with acidic anxiety.

"Emma?" Mom leans over me.

I choke back a sob with a ragged gasp, struggling to stabilize my breathing. Niko springs to his feet, looking at me with a sincerity I can't describe. He wraps his arms around my shoulders, cradling my head as Dad continues to work.

Instead of permanently recording ultrasound images on the Department database, Dad instructs Mom when to snap pictures with our ancient digital camera. We're storing them to analyze later, but I'm not sure privacy exists. In my heart, I know I'm trapped in the Departments for life. And because of that, my baby is too.

"I can't do this," I whisper.

"You're not doing it alone." Niko strokes my head.

He rises to his palms beside my shoulders, crinkling the paper beneath me. His tearful eyes make me cry harder, unable to hold my stomach steady.

"Sorry," I whimper.

"Well, I got what I needed, anyway." Dad's voice wavers as he delicately wipes the gel off me. "Do you want to talk?"

I sniffle, covering my face from their worried stares. "I don't know what to say."

"Do you need a minute alone?" Mom asks.

I cling to Niko's shoulder. "With Niko, please."

My parents close the door behind themselves, guarding the door in the DoH hall.

"Ems, don't hold back. Tell me everything you're thinking."

I grip Niko's shirt like it's my last thread of sanity. "He did this to me *months* ago, and I never knew."

"I'm so sorry."

"And the baby is so real, *so* real. And I—" My breathing hitches as I let out a strange cry. Niko scoops me into his arms, steadying himself a few inches above my nose. "I have a bad feeling. I don't think they'll survive, Niko."

His forehead tenses, and, shit; *Niko* is attached to the baby too. The emotion emanating from him that I couldn't put my finger on was the confusion of loving someone you've never met.

It's becoming too difficult to breathe. My eyelids flutter against my heartbeat's sudden skyrocketing, spotting out my vision. Niko holds me to his chest, urging me to copy his deep breathing. After a minute or so, I can see my surroundings again.

"Why do you think they won't survive?" He whispers, his cheek pressed against mine.

"I've done a horrible job already. I'm not myself. I can't calm myself down, pretty much ever, and I can tell my body is nearing a big health crash from the stress."

Niko cups my cheeks. "Hey, either way, we're not there yet. Let's focus on what we can do right now. You're doing what you need to, getting a checkup."

I close my eyes, shuddering through a breath. "Yeah. I'm just so sad. For the baby."

"If it helps to think about it this way, I don't think they're hurting." He smiles, and my heart shatters. "They're so damn cute, Ems, it's unbelievable. I swear to god, they have your adorable nose and—" He blinks away the threat of tears, holding a smile for me. "I don't think they're suffering, Ems. They look really active, more than I imagined. They're probably blissfully unaware while camping out in there, all cuddled in. They're safe, thanks to you. And you're doing the best you can. It'll all be oka—"

"No, it won't." I grip his shoulders, hating everything I'm about to say. "They're only here because of him. I don't know how to live with it. I don't want the kid to have to find out someday. I want them to feel wanted."

He swallows hard. Pressing our foreheads together, I can feel his thoughts mirroring mine. I don't think either of us realized how painful this would be until we got here, but I'm writhing. The cloaked abuse I tolerated sinks in for what feels like the first time, digging its nails into my skin and brandishing me with scars I can't erase.

"Are you saying you want an underground abortion?" He asks.

I chew on my lip, staring at the ceiling. "No. I'm completely in love with them, Niko. And even if I wasn't, that could kill me. I'd only consider it to protect them from the Sumners in the world."

Niko's expression sours when I say that name.

I hold Niko closer, desperate to keep him by my side. "I'm so sorry I did thi—"

He kisses me firmly. "No. It's *not* your fault."

I huff through tears, stretching to kiss him again. Softly moaning beneath the comforting pressure of his lips, I knead a few more out of him. Niko's breath turns heavy, welcoming me into his arms as I wrap my arms around his neck. When he dives back in for my lips, I sigh in relief, pulling his waist to me.

He pauses. "Emmalee, listen to me."

I catch my breath, releasing his swollen lips.

"I meant what I offered. I'll raise this baby with you as my own."

I let out a weighty sob, urging him closer. I'm *dying* to accept his help. To have a family with him. But I don't feel like I deserve it.

"I'm not just saying that, Ems. They won't have to feel like they have a shitty biological father because I'll be their real father before they ever know the difference. All you have to do is ask."

"I can't ask you to do that."

"Yes, you can. I want you to."

"Why?"

He bites back tears, wiping mine with his thumbs. His hands brush over my face, unsure how to touch me for a moment.

My tears slow on their own; something important is coming. The weight of Niko's powerful emotions pound through my heart.

"*Because*, Ems," he whispers, staring me in the eyes.

The dim lights create the deepest shade of black I've ever seen in his sparkling irises, and a soothing warmth ignites in my core.

"The second I heard your voice in my in-ear—the day you saved my life—I was reminded of what I already knew: I love you more than I can express, and you are the love of my life."

CHAPTER 39

Niko

I did it. I finally told her I love her. And now I'm getting to hold her in my arms on her parents' living room couch. I can't believe it.

The Richardses periodically check in. Ben let me borrow his old camera to stare at the baby some more. Emmalee hasn't accepted my offer, but I can't help it; I *love* her baby. Mini-Ems. It's hard to contain myself, but I'm doing it for Emmalee. Thankfully, she's smiling more and more at the photos, zooming into the ultrasound with me and giggling when I poke the baby's nose, then hers.

Otherwise, Emmalee slips between weeping, spacing out to our movie marathon, or giggling with me over nothing important, all while snuggled at my side in her oversized hoodie.

Whenever she cries, I whisper how much she means to me. At first, it makes her cry more, but then she ends up smiling until she complains her cheeks hurt.

I don't particularly like movies. Something always sets me on edge, adding to a rising pool of minor triggers, and I never know which will be the one that spills me over the brim. But today, I love how movies make Emmalee laugh, how her toes grip themselves when fictional couples argue, and how she furrows her brows when she's immersed in the action.

She falls asleep with her head in my lap. The TV has gone silent, left on the finished movie's info page. I drop my head back, listening to Emmalee's gentle, slow breath. I've never known such peace.

Her parents whisper goodnight, offering the guest room if it's too cramped in Emmalee's room. I don't know how to respond to them acting like we'll obviously sleep together, but thankfully, the Richardses accept my smile and nod as keeping quiet for Emmalee, and head upstairs for the night. My heart throbs once we're alone, relishing how incredible it is we're left alone at all. Everything is finally settling down.

But then Emmalee pants in her sleep, distressed.

"Hey, Ems," I whisper, rubbing her back.

She whimpers, and my veins throb in my neck.

"You're okay, Ems. It's just a bad dream."

She gasps awake, gripping her stomach. Her eyes dart around the room, desperately sticking to me once she spots me.

"Hey." I stroke her cheek. "You're safe. I've got you."

She lets out a massive exhale, rubbing her eyes with her sleeve. I let her this time.

She's been having as many nightmares as me lately, even if we sleep together. It's far less if we're by each other's side, but still a constant affliction.

But she hasn't told me anything that makes me think she's poisoned enough to have seen it too—an entire *alternate dimension* Sumner is patenting. With a gateway through our dreams.

Chronic Nightmare Syndrome was a coverup diagnosis to keep victims of S817 from questioning our transition to this dimension. I'm almost certain of it.

Hopefully this means that while she has been exposed, Emmalee hasn't suffered as large of a dose that I have—that she still has a chance at peace.

I hoist Emmalee into my arms, rousing a sleepy giggle from her.

She massages my scalp with her nails, wrapping her legs around my waist. "Where are you taking me, pretty boy?"

I can't help but smile, nudging her nose with mine. "Wherever you'd like me to. It seems I have parental approval to stay either upstairs or downstairs."

"Oh, *really?*" She wiggles her eyebrows.

We laugh, deciding on the guest room since we can't seem

to shut up around each other and her parents are sleeping off today's stress.

I carry her to her room for a change of clothes first. She finds two giant t-shirts she slept in throughout high school and two pairs of plaid pajama pants. Neither of us likes to sleep with pants on, but we decide to spare her parents at least a little sanity once we exit the guest room in the morning.

My focus lingers on her wall of black squares. Something about them makes my heart race.

"You finished the entire wall while I was gone," I mutter.

Emmalee doesn't respond. When I look over at her, she's chewing her pouty bottom lip again, her eyes flitting from one black square to the next.

"Ems?"

"Hmm?"

I sigh, steadying her shoulders. "What's wrong? Does this wall bother you?"

"It doesn't *bother* me, no…"

"Then?"

She groans. "Okay, okay, fine. It always meant a lot to me, but I don't want to come off like a weirdo."

"What do you mean? It's about color theory, right?"

She nods, fiddling with my shirt sleeve. When she sees my adoring smile, we both giggle.

"Then can you explain it to me again?"

Emmalee looks back at the wall with a soft hum. Then she redirects my line of sight to one of the squares. "What color do you think this is?"

I stare for a while. "I know the wall is black, but that one looks green-ish."

"Right. It looks green compared to the ones beside it, but it's still black. You could call it green-black, but the longer you look, the more you can pick out other colors, so green-black isn't the exact description for it. Kinda like there are no words to describe the color's *fullness*…"

I can't figure out what's making her so shy, but I love seeing her mental gears turn when she talks about painting, granting space for her passions again. I miss it. "So what other colors do you see? I can't see them like you can."

She blinks a few times, then laughs under her breath. "That's what used to upset me. If I'm being honest, this wall is how I see… people."

I can tell that wasn't exactly "honest," but as she meets my eyes, I tuck her hair behind her ear, giving her more space to explain.

Clear eyes beam up at me. "It's not only because I can feel people's energy. I just feel like we look at people and call them one thing, but they're made of so many little colors, and most people don't take the time to notice them. They just call them 'orange,' or maybe they'll look an extra few seconds and call them 'burnt orange.' But they're so much more than just 'burnt orange.'"

I hum, looking back at the squares in a new light. "And at the same time, endless variations of black exist, but they're still all black."

Emmalee grips my arm harder. "Yeah… yeah." She nods a few times, seemingly adding something together in her mind with small, rapid glances across the squares.

"Hey, you okay, Ems? You don't have to tell me now, but I know this means something more to you than—"

Emmalee gasps, her eyes zipping to something behind my shoulder. "What's this?" She dashes to her bedside table, holding up a folded paper that says, *Emmalee,* on the front. "It's in your handwriting."

My face grows hot. I don't remember what sixteen-year-old me wrote, but I'm positive she's holding the letter I wrote for her seventeenth birthday.

And now she's reading it. I cringe as she reads it aloud.

"Ems, happy seventeenth birthday." She gasps. "Is this— Did you finally find this letter for me?! Where was it?"

I'm speechless for a solid minute as her shaking hands cradle the creased paper. "I definitely didn't put it there, Ems. W-well, I put it in your bedside drawer four years ago, actually. I haven't seen it since."

"So you think my parents…?" Emmalee trails off, a smile growing on her lips despite her fingers pressed to them.

"Emmalee, maybe you should wait—"

She gets that mischievous look on her face, and I know it's for my own good to give up now. But Emmalee snickers, holding the letter as far away from me as possible to tease me, and I can't resist the bait. I catch her, kissing her neck until she accidentally lets out a rambunctious giggle.

Snickering and shushing each other, we settle onto her old bed as Emmalee reads the letter in silence.

"Ems, I don't trust my younger self to write something all that amazing, so—" I trail off, watching rapid emotions flicker across her expressive eyebrows.

Then her face contorts.

She meets my eyes as hers spill over. "Nikolai, my love, you've never given yourself enough credit."

I rush to hold her, and she leans into me, allowing me to read the letter along with her. As I thought, it's a generic message compared to how in love I actually was, only redeemed by my adorable baby sister's drawing: our whole friend-family— Emmalee, Jay, Lilith, Hana, and myself—stands beneath a giant rainbow, our all-black outfits spurring Emmalee into delighted giggles.

My heart races when her eyes reach the card's corner. There's a small "PS: flip to the back" in different, sloppier ink—the portion I wrote while high on Emmalee-love hormones.

Emmalee flips the letter over and buries her nose into the page. My fingers shake as I pull her curtain of faded hair back on one side, revealing the letter to me.

Emmalee, that last letter doesn't cut it for how I feel about you, and I'm sorry I've been such a wimp about it. So I'm going to be as honest with you as I can.

I'm currently looking at your ridiculously cute sleeping face, trying not to cry like a baby because I don't want to leave your side. I never do, Ems, and I hate thinking this could be the last time I see you.

I want to be a better person whenever I'm around you. And don't worry, I'm still doing it for myself, not for anyone else. But you make me like myself. I've never ~~said~~ said that in my life and it still feels weird, but you have that effect on people. The amount of care and understanding you've poured into me makes my heart full, and that's just who you are. It's beautiful, and something I can never get over about you.

I'll always have your back, from a few Departments away or hundreds of miles. I'm on team Emmalee, <u>forever</u>. You're never alone, just like you've reassured me.

Which is also why no matter what happens to me, you <u>need</u> to live the absolute best life because you deserve it. Everything heals inside me when I'm around you. And I think you do that to everyone. Your heart is powerful, Ems.

I think the world of you.

Sorry if this was too cheesy. Thanks for making me see what I was missing.

♥, N

"What were you missing?" Her stuffy nose muffles her voice. "That would've driven me fucking nuts."

I laugh, hiding my face. "I was in love with you and too scared to admit it. For my whole life, Ems. I'm sorr—"

Emmalee wriggles my hands off my face to kiss me square on the lips. When I pull back to meet her sharp stare, she points at her wall of black squares.

"Those are your eyes, Niko. All the colors I've seen in them. Well, no. In you."

Overwhelmed is an understatement. I want to witness each and every square—to imagine what she felt growing up to go to this effort level for me. But I can't right now. Not when the love of my life is in front of me, huffing through tears and passion. For *me*.

I cradle her to me, and I don't let go.

For a second, I'm afraid to accept this sincerity. But then I reverse our roles. Just like I believed for Emmalee, she believes *I* deserve this love. So, at least for tonight, I decide to accept it all.

Emmalee kisses me over and over again, swallowing hard between hiccuping tears.

I pull back, tucking her hair behind her ears. "There's something else on your mind."

"Yes, there is." Her quivering lip shakes my heartstrings as she guides my hands to her stomach. "I know you offered first, but—" She steels herself, smiling against her nervous stare. "I'd *love* to have this baby with you, Nikolai."

CHAPTER 40

Niko

Emmalee tosses off her oversized hoodie, draping it over the guest room's corner armchair. She caresses her belly in small circles, inspecting how her undershirt stretches around it as the fabric ripples beneath her palms. Her fingers are delicate with her body these days, and it fills me with tranquility. I rise to meet her just as she turns to meet me.

We've taken a while to come down from our emotional high, and we haven't said much beyond holding each other. Eventually, we've simmered down to the mushy, playful giddiness we've shared most of our lives, and that has yet to go away.

So as we embrace, it's no surprise she scrubs her forehead into my neck until I squirm away from her ticklish attack.

We climb into the small, paisley bed, barely long enough for our lanky bodies. Emmalee prowls like a lion, tackling me onto the pillows with a devilish grin.

"Be careful with yourself, baby mama."

She sits up with a gasp. "Oh, my *God!* What has you so brave today?"

I laugh. "You. You're incredible."

She turns her back, tossing off her shirt in a huff. "Pft. I don't know about that."

"Are you putting down my best friend again? What am I going to do with you?"

I stroke her ID tattoo down her spine, making her jolt in a cute little shiver. She whips around, flustered.

Instead of putting her shirt on, she slinks toward me in only her black bralette, her sly grin forming.

"Uh oh," I mutter.

Emmalee giggles, wiggling into the covers. Lacing her foot between both of mine, she wraps an arm around my torso.

"What?" She giggles. "Just saying hi."

I want to laugh with her, but the dim lamp illuminates her icy, clear eyes, and my heart and brain glitch. Emmalee grows serious alongside me, quieting her breath as I run my fingers along the length of her collarbones. I trace her shoulder, following the lines of her elegant arms, all the way down to where her hand rests on my waist. Then I travel back up again, this time skimming her soft neck and jawline.

Emmalee already breathes heavier. I can feel it too; the excitement of our bare skin touching and a room to ourselves. With an emotional closeness further than we've ever reached, we've grown into each other. Ever-adapting to each other's needs for the sake of pure love.

"I really do love you, Ems." These words are still terrifyingly raw. But I love it. I love how her breathing rhythm resets when I say it, her pupils dilating ever-so-slightly to take more of me in.

"I love you so much, Niko," she whispers.

I massage her scalp as we huddle in a lingering kiss. Her fingernails caress tingling circles across my shoulder blades, and it softens my lips. Emmalee's tender kisses lose the pained urgency they've had lately—like my confession soothed her into knowing there will always be more of my heart to share. Our tongues touch, and my lungs threaten to stop functioning beneath the drawn-out pressure of her bright pink lips. I can feel her enjoyment in her hot breath.

Her lips squirm a little, Emmalee wedging a knee between mine with slow blinks. I know what those eyes mean. She confessed she's been craving me in more ways than one, although we haven't acted on it since we were teenagers. Even with everything I've been through, I don't mind sexual attention from her. Our escalating closeness draws that side out of me. But I don't expect anything from her. I'm happy to stick with massaging her sore lower back until she sighs against my lips.

She pulls back to get a good look at me. I smile as her grin grows, gentle fingers combing my stubborn hair. First, she traces the freckles across my sun-tainted cheeks, then she outlines my lips. But eventually, she loses herself to her thoughts.

I brush through her hair, and she relaxes into my touch. But it's not enough to erase the contemplation in her eyes.

"What are you thinking, Ems?"

She glances up at me with a shy smile. "I guess I wanted to *make* a baby with you. Originally. When I dreamed of growing up and living with you. But now… We never got a chance."

My whole face flushes. "Oh."

She laughs. "Is that a surprise?"

"No, not entirely." My heart hammers as my voice softens. "But we still can, Ems. If you eventually want another, and we're ready."

Her blush brightens, flooding her swollen nose. "Oh, God. I can't even *think* about having a second baby right now."

I laugh. "Okay. That's fine."

I stroke her belly, but her mind visibly races. Readjusting our intertwined legs until my stomach can safely cradle hers, we shelter the baby between us. I've never felt so warm.

Finally, Emmalee lets out a heavy sigh. It's accompanied by a smirk, so I know what's coming is wonderfully devious.

"I don't know. Maybe this is a weird idea, but I thought— *if* you wanted to—maybe we could pretend to make *this* baby together… right now?"

My heart flips. "Emmalee…"

"What?!" She laughs, squirming in embarrassment against my side. "I told you it was weird, but I just thought, you know, maybe it'd help us feel better about everything, or that you'd also like to—"

I interrupt her with a desperate kiss. "I would. I *love* that idea."

"Oh, Jesus. You want to?"

I sit up to meet her face to face, blood pumping through my ears. "Yes, Ems. Let's rewrite their story."

She kisses me with a sudden urgency, only releasing my lips to breathe. "Please. I want this."

"I want this too," I whisper. It's embarrassingly vulnerable, but the more we say it, the more eager we get. "Let's make a baby."

"Oh, shit," she breathes, giggling as I pull her beneath me by the hips. "Please, get me pregnant."

I gape down at her, shocked.

She laughs. "What, you aren't used to me embarrassing you by now, pretty boy?"

I laugh. "That's not it. I'm not used to being so openly in love with you that I can make a baby with my best friend."

With that, Emmalee hikes up my shirt, flipping it off me once I pull it to my neck. She grins, eyeing me up and down. "Well, I'm not complaining."

"Me neither." My smile fades. I hover over her, unsure what to do next. I love her so much, it's scary.

"Hey, you okay, love?" She whispers, stroking my cheeks.

"More than okay. I just want you to be comfortable. I'm worried I might hurt you, lying over you like this."

Her sly smile returns. "Then let's sit up."

Pushing me back until I'm sitting on my heels, Emmalee climbs onto my lap. My focus shifts to the intensity of her eyes piercing into mine. In them, I see the deep trust she has in me. It means so much that my hands tremble as they slide up her back.

She kisses me like she means it, immersing her fingers into my coarse hair and grabbing fistfuls. When she gives the strands a soft pull to massage my scalp, I can't help but breathe heavier into her mouth, and she smiles through our kiss.

I comb back her hair's base to reveal soft brown roots beneath the faded black dye, burying my nose into them and kissing her neck where her roots start. She sighs into my ear, lighting a fire down my spine. While I knead her sore back with my hands, I kiss down her neck, across her collarbone, and her chest's upper ridges, making my way back up again until I kiss her soft jawline. Her breath hitches in delight. When I meet her lips again, she gives a soft whine, and I nearly die.

"Nikolai," she whispers. We stare into each other's eyes as she grinds her hips over me. "I can feel your emotions, and I—"

I must've already been verging on tears. We erupt into sobs

against each other, extending our movements beneath the weight of the lifetime we've been forcibly separated.

And it's not just that for me. Sex always came with a pressure to please that I didn't know how to escape. Not even therapy seemed to touch it, making me afraid that abuse irreversibly sewed fear into my soul. I never imagined I could *relish* in someone else's pleasure, especially not sexual pleasure, but I'm eager for hers tonight. She gave me the space to say no, but I gave myself permission to let her see me. It's a glorious, overwhelming change.

"I love you," I whisper, my shaky breath huffing against her lips.

Heavy blinks push tears down Emmalee's beautiful cheeks. "God, I love you so much."

I lean forward until she happily relaxes into my lap. "Can I touch you?"

I expect her to smile, but her playful sass is buried beneath feverish passion as she struggles to tear off her underwear. I can only get a giggle out of her once I slow her urgent hands, gingerly slipping her underwear off for her as she relaxes into the pillows.

Knowing she can feel it, I think about how much I've adored every moment with her as I tease her in delicate circles. She huffs against my lips, cradling my head. I'm thorough with my mouth and fingers, thinking about how her joy soothes my broken soul. How her loving influence helped me take back my life. And how I can only see myself living this life with her.

Emmalee grips my arm as I tease her up and down, her hips following my fingers.

"Is this okay?" I ask.

"I want more." She's not shy anymore. "You're so gentle, and— It's too good for me."

My face burns hot. "Ems, you deserve someone to be gentle with you. Nothing is too good for you. You deserve it all."

She stares in silent awe. I'm not sure if she's been properly worshiped in her life, but I'm convinced she needs to be. And I want to be the one to do it.

So I continue, "I'm going to make you feel good, but I won't rush you. I want to make sure you're better than just 'okay' with anything we do."

She leans into my touch with a yearning groan, and I shiver. "You're too sweet, Niko."

I shake my head no as we kiss, and her tongue begs me to broaden my movements. "It's only true, Ems. You deserve to feel good and safe, my love."

The more she sighs beneath my hand's pressure, the better I feel. My heart throbs throughout my body, responding to her with just as much desperation.

"I can't wait." She shifts me upright, sitting up to strip her bralette as she teases me with addictingly sweet lips. "I'm ready."

I can feel she really is, removing my wet fingers from her, so I give her space to straddle me with a pounding heart. She breaks eye contact with me to kiss my neck like I always do to her, but I gasp like I've been electrically shocked, curling into myself.

"Oh! Sorry!" She gapes in surprise. "Are you okay?"

I catch my breath, absorbing the sight of her trusting me with her whole body. I'm dying to trust her in the same way. To be free, at least with her. Why do I *still* have to be like this?

"Sorry, you don't have to answer that. I just won't do that again, don't worry." Emmalee smiles reassuringly, and I melt.

"No, I'm okay," I whisper. "With you, I'm fine with anything. I just— Well, I have to remind myself that it's you, so if we could—um—keep looking at each other?"

"Yes, love. Absolutely, we can. Stay present with me."

Emmalee slinks her shoulders toward me, her nose nudging mine like she's urging me to play. I laugh under my breath, falling for her contagious tenderness. My shoulders fall, and she eases my boxers off without dropping my eager stare. The blue flecks in her crystalline eyes stand out in the dim light, entrancing me in her comfort.

"Good job, I'm right here," Emmalee whispers. "Do you need more help feeling safe?"

I breathe through her words, struggling with the answer. Eventually, I nod.

"What can I do?" Emmalee laces her fingers through my

hair, kissing me until my eyelids grow heavy. "I want to take care of you too."

I smooth her hair back, searching her face. A soft kindness stares back, allowing my heart to roam free.

"Let's be gentle with each other," I whisper.

"Gentle. Got it." Emmalee visibly absorbs my words, gazing deep into my eyes.

Everywhere we touch, we meet skin to skin. I scoot Emmalee closer by the hips, welcoming her warmth. She rubs against me, coaxing me back until I have to prop myself up with my palm against the cold bedsheets.

She's on her knees above me, and I'm enamored by her power. It doesn't feel forceful or intimidating; it feels present. Nurturing and compassionate, like she decided to care for me just the same. I'm convinced she's the loving, valiant leader the world needs.

I caress her hips and back, giving her soft squeezes on the way up. Emmalee's tranquil blinks soothe me as much as her fingertips, scrubbing my scalp in gratitude.

Her mouth parts, welcoming my touch as I continue teasing her where I left off. She allows me to spoil her, leaning into my hand, and I eat up every second.

"Ems," I whisper, my chest rising and falling with urgency.

She doesn't say more, prodding my lips and staring deep into my eyes as she begins to stroke me with her cool hands.

We warm each other up far quicker than intended, panting within minutes.

"Do you feel okay with going further?" Emmalee whispers.

I nod, unable to form the words. She's too gorgeous— her touch's softness mixed with the incredible stability her confidence gives me. How confident she is in not just herself, but *us*.

I kiss her chest above her heart, pressing my lips into its steady beat. She wraps my whole head in a hug, reaching between her legs to adjust us both. As she eases herself above me, she meets my eyes. It's almost too intense. I'm bursting with affection for her before we've fully indulged in each other.

Her heartbeat flutters beneath my fingertips at her jawline, and I smile. Our kisses turn heavy, overcome by her fervor.

Emmalee eases her hips down over me, and we both gasp.

"Oh, shit," she whispers.

"What? Are you okay?"

Emmalee lets out a soft moan against my lips, and my whole spine lights up. "Yes," she breathes. "It's so nice, with you, that I— I didn't know it could be like this, Niko."

She pushes me deeper. Our breaths clash against each other's chests as we rub our foreheads together, immersing ourselves with one another.

I drag my hands up her thighs, kneading her hips as she snuggles into me. Emmalee gasps as we roll our movements together, our hips inching closer with every pulse of muscle.

My heart can't handle her satiated face, forcing me to deepen my breath to keep a grip on myself. She smashes our lips together, undulating with a thirsting passion. I lean back into her movements, allowing her to lead us. I admire her strength so much that it feels even better. It almost aches.

I understand why Emmalee is forcing our lips together now; her breath hitches through her nose until she can no longer suppress a heavy moan, uttering it deep into my throat. I surprise myself by returning one back, encouraging her to grip my back and swing her hips lower. Wanting to combine pleasure sensations for her, I rub my knuckles along the indents between her ribcage and her shoulder blades' edges, massaging her entire torso. Her soft, purring reaction leaves me dizzy.

Releasing my lips to desperately catch her breath, Emmalee grabs me by the cheeks. "I meant it. I haven't felt this connected to someone before, Niko."

"Me neither. The first time we did this, I realized how in love I was with you, but it's hitting me harder than ever."

She whimpers into my cheek, kissing it before returning to my mouth. "I feel it too. I'm so in love with you, it hurts. But a good hurt."

I smile. Just as I thought, she gets me.

She rotates her hips to sit on me at a different angle, and her eyebrows curl. "Oh, that's—"

I shift my free hand to steady her waist. "Does it hurt?"

Emmalee shakes her head no, and she pushes her hips into

me another time with shaking legs. A groan escapes her lips, and my eyes widen.

She doesn't have to say anything more. I thrust into her until our movements broaden. Emmalee begins to moan with every pump of our hips, unable to help herself. I tighten our lips, muffling her enjoyment so we can keep it to ourselves. This frees her to utter pleasure into my mouth, stirring an intense fervor in me to hear more.

She's encouraging a new level of sexuality within me I rarely allow myself to experience. I'm shocked by how deeply I press into her hips just to hear her voice. By how secure freedom feels under her reign. I'm convinced no one else in the world could bring this type of love out of me.

"I love you," Emmalee whispers through a gasp.

And I can feel it. No matter how much she yearns to be rough, she tames her impatience simply because I need her to.

Her love is so gentle.

"Niko? You okay, love?"

The safety I feel produces wordless sounds from my mouth I've never heard before. Emmalee gasps, moving in tandem to the automatic bucking of my hips.

"*Good job*, love," she breathes. "Let yourself go. I love it."

I gasp for her, hugging her hips and torso until our hot skin melds. Emmalee always makes a point to cuddle me back, and her tight embrace tonight doesn't disappoint. It's all-encompassing, dissolving my fears of being seen like this. I want to cradle her forever.

There's an uncontainable urge within me to lean forward, allowing myself to treat her fully. As instructed, I let myself go. When I lean her back, her center of gravity rocks against my hips, and I moan against her lips. She kisses me hard, quieting my voice. I know I'm the one being too loud now, but I can't help myself. The love of my life wants me to feel good. Her eyes are shining from my pleasure as much as mine are for hers.

All at once, it becomes too much.

"I love you," I can hardly say, burying myself into her embrace.

In a sudden burst of feeling, I'm overwhelmed by her encompassing warmth and overflow. She hugs my hips down into her, making sure I'm gratified. My body listens to her silent urging, behaving as if we're genuinely making a baby and it's desperate to fulfill her dreams. Emmalee loves it so much that I continue to love it, the honeyed, sensual ache extending with every gasp from her swollen lips.

She looks absolutely taken with me, and a momentous gratitude surges through my blood; I'm so glad I lived through hell to be here with her. I raise her hips, carrying her weight in my hands as she relaxes back into the mattress.

"Nikolai—" Emmalee grips the pillows behind her head and leans into my continued touch like she craves it.

Feeling the need to soak in every moment of her pleasure, I slow my movements into heavy, deep pressure. I watch for the subtle signs of ecstasy in her expression until I learn what she enjoys most, and I repeat it over and over. Emmalee whimpers in delight.

But then she gives my shoulder a tender bite.

I hiss through it, meeting her apologetic stare with a smile. "Is this still okay for you, or was that a revenge bite, little lion?"

She breathes out a laugh between satiated, heavy blinks, her jaw dropping. "S-sorry, I just—"

Desperate hands urge my hips deeper. As soon as I obey Emmalee's wishes, her touch on the back of my neck grows weak and she closes her eyes. Emmalee muffles her growing moans into my chest again, but this time it can't contain her enjoyment. I speed up for her, longing to hear her voice as it mimics my body's movements.

I gasp for air as she fills the room with her satisfaction's beautiful ring, burying deep into my heart. Cradling her, I ride out her waves of delight.

I can't help but weep. This is an intimacy level I've never experienced with another human being. I didn't know I could.

Emmalee gazes up at me with hot red cheeks. She's giddy with soft laughter the moment she catches her breath. We kiss softly, more of a confirmation of each other's love than a necessity anymore. Admiration replaces the desperation from moments before, languid strokes of each other's backs, sides, and faces to conclude the intense physical labor between us.

I hover over her, speechless. She can't stop smiling, lazily blinking as she sinks into the pillows. I smooth down her hair and continue to plant soft kisses over her face. We stay like this for ages, absorbing each other's love.

It hurts my heart to have to physically separate from her, but I don't say it aloud. I don't have to. Emmalee clings to me to close the gap again, in reassurance for us both. I love-drunkenly laugh at how ridiculously well we match, scooping her up and carrying her to the bathroom.

I play with her ruffled hair as she pees—she's unbothered, maybe even happy that I'm in here with her. While she washes her hands, I stand behind her to look at us together in the mirror. I'm surprised by how serene she looks after so many stressful years, but then I see I look exactly the same. Dare I say *happy*.

I hold Emmalee's beautiful little belly carrying what is now *our* baby, and it makes us cry.

We return to bed, cuddled up in mesmerization of the new life we're building. I've never doubted my feelings for her, but this solidifies a place in my heart for our love. Somewhere I can safely house it because she helped me build it: a gentle love.

CHAPTER 41

Niko

"What's your life dream, little lion?"

Emmalee giggles, sprawled over my chest and legs. "You'll never let me live that bite down, huh?"

I grin. "I'm not complaining."

"Oh, so you liked it. Good to know."

I laugh, and she props herself up with a smug grin. We couldn't convince ourselves to sleep, surprisingly hyper for how exhausted we feel.

Emmalee hums in thought. "My life dream, huh? Why do you ask?"

I tuck her hair behind her ear, kissing her exposed forehead. "Jay and I used to ask each other. To remind each other to stay alive."

Emmalee sits back, suddenly serious. "Really? Like how?"

"Hmm. We'd ask each other when things looked impossible, or not worth living through. Usually during bombings. They'd cut our communication to leave us to fend for ourselves, so we'd take turns watching out for each other. Not just physically, but mentally."

Her crystal stare flips my heart. "Niko, that's *incredible*. No wonder you held onto your heart. You taught each other compassion."

I clear my throat through the stabbing grief in my chest. "Well, if we didn't look out for each other, no one else would. But Jay was a true survivor, Ems, just like you. Even through everyone else's bullshit, he never forgot his truth. I've seen life so much differently through both of you."

Emmalee mulls over my words for a while, rubbing her fingertips across my chest in gentle circles until I shiver.

"So what was your dream you'd tell him?" She whispers.

"It's always stayed the same. I just want to marry someone I love and live a simple, quiet life with them." I avert my eyes, embarrassed. "Jay used to laugh and say it was too boring when I could dream of literally anything, but it feels like I'm asking for a lot."

I find the courage to look back up, and Emmalee beams over me in the sweetest way. "That dream sounds beautiful, love. It's not asking for a lot at all. And I also agree with Jay; you deserve even more. I'd love to see you dare to ask for your 'wants' someday."

For a moment, I don't know what to say. But Emmalee doesn't mind, supporting her belly to settle back down at my side with a grin.

"Well, pretty boy, I'll have to think about my life dream some more. For now, I'd love to give this baby a peaceful life. It's scary to think about that, though. To get too hopeful. I'm not sure a life like that exists."

"It can." I hold her belly with her. "We'll make it happen."

She strokes my cheek and kisses me slowly. I breathe into her pining lips, soaking in the sincerity between us.

Then she inhales sharply, gripping my hand. "Let's come up with a combined dream! For fun."

I smile. "That does sound fun. With the baby?"

"And the two of us. We have our whole lives together, even after they grow up."

"Hmm. You're right." I furrow my brows.

She giggles. "You're taking this very seriously, I see."

"Well, yes." I can't contain my mischievous grin, awaiting her reaction. "Now that I've gotten you pregnant, I *better* take our futures seriously."

Her eyes widen before she bursts into a contagious belly laugh—one she has to slam quiet beneath her palm. With an airy giggle, she whispers, "Okay, well, I want to live in a quiet, safe place too."

"Yeah?"

"Yeah. Somewhere that… o-our baby can actually run around outside and play."

She can't meet my eyes. I giggle, enthralled by her shy blush. "Is that hard to say still? *Our* baby?"

"Yes. I love the sound of it too much."

My chest pangs. "Me too, my love."

"Your turn."

I smile. "I'd love to see you be able to paint again. Somewhere you can relax and not feel so sick from stress, setting yourself free on the canvas."

Emmalee chews on her lip. "What about something for you?"

"I mean, I'm happy just living with you. That's more than I ever knew I could dream of until recently."

She wraps her arms around me, hiding her eyes as she snuggles into my chest. "Did you ever want to be a dad?"

"Yes."

Emmalee meets my eyes again, surprised by my rapid response, and I smile.

"My baby sister was so cute, Ems. We were alone so often when she was a newborn that… she felt like mine. It was terrifying being responsible for someone so dependent on me when I felt so young too, but I loved every second. I'd do anything to make her happy. I still picture her as my baby."

Emmalee's eyes soften. "Is she still upset with you?"

I sigh. "Yes. She won't talk to me."

"I'm so sorry, love. What are you going to do?"

"Actually, I was going to ask if you wanted to come home with me soon? To see her. Or, if you want, we could share our exciting news." I giggle when Emmalee bites back her erupting smile. "We can wait until you're ready. But I figured Hana might want to see her favorite superhero in the world rather than her asshole brother who abandoned her."

Emmalee glares, and I laugh. It makes her soften up, giving my cheeks a squish. "Don't make fun of my baby's father."

My cheeks grow hot. "Okay, little lion."

"Hey, you're just as much of a lion as me. Pinning me to the bed like that."

I cover my eyes and let out a surprised laugh. Emmalee giggles, nuzzling her way beneath my hand with her nose until she can give me a huge kiss.

"Okay, okay," I say. "We can both be lions."

"Alright, fine. But you're not an asshole, and you didn't abandon us. You didn't have a choice."

"Well, I *was* the one who screwed up. That's why we got deployed."

"What do you mean? It wasn't because of my dad's restraining order?"

Ben's fury flashes through my mind in small movie clips. Like all my flashbacks, it arrives in a Russian roulette, cycling through traumas until it lands on one that knocks me the fuck out. But Emmalee catches it early, vigorously rubbing my shoulders and hands to help me come back to the present. Once I have a clear focus on those gorgeous eyes, I slink into the pillows with a sigh.

"Sorry, my love," Emmalee whispers.

"It's not your fault... little lion." I smile, drawing a laugh back out of her. "Anyway, we *really* got deployed because I finally fought back against Sumner and it pissed him off. Before that, he only kept me home for his own gain. He'd often... experiment on me."

Emmalee falls still. "You mentioned that. What does that mean? The same experiments I saw?"

"Um, no, not exactly... His unit member experiments are different from the medical ones since we're what he uses as first trials. It all starts at the same source, S817, but then it turns into vivid nightmares... which turn into something else. He'd try to add to my trauma. For some reason, it helped the dreams work the way he wanted them to—like it would take me to where I needed to be. He was using me to figure out those dreams, basically."

She smooths my hair with furrowed brows. "I... don't quite understand. And I thought kids weren't allowed to get paid until fifteen, even in the Departments. But he's been experimenting on you since you were twelve?"

"N-no. *That* was for his own… enjoyment. A power thing. He turned those— Uh, 'private meetings' into the S817 experiment later, when I was fifteen. Which, yes, was paid. To, um, keep me quiet."

She drops her forehead against mine. "That's fucking *horrible*, Niko. All of it. I don't know how to help you recover from that, but I want to."

"You *are* helping me. You're teaching me what a healthy life can look like, just by being with me."

"That's not enough. You deserve to heal." She huffs. "Do you think he'll actually leave you alone?"

It hurts to see her staring back with such fear. When we're together, my head clears, and I can see how detrimental Sumner was to my mind. I don't feel that disgusting pressure to return to him, obeying his orders. Emmalee is my clarity.

"He won't, huh?" She whispers.

"If I let him back in, he'll grab the opportunity by the neck," I mutter. "I have to stay strong—violently strong—if I want to hold power over myself around him. I feel like I'm suffocating beneath him, even now. I don't know if that'll ever go away."

"I hear you. But look around the room with me, okay?" Emmalee draws my hands to her hips, then the baby pressed against my waist. I caress her bare legs draped over me, run my fingers along her spine until she shivers, and I see what she means.

"We're *here* right now," I whisper.

"Yes, love. You're with me. You don't have to listen to his orders anymore. We're making our own rules from now on, okay?"

I exhale. "Okay."

"Niko, I have this feeling," she whispers.

I sit up in concern. "What feeling?"

"Like… we have a connection. More than just our relationship. It sounds cheesy…"

"It's not cheesy. It's powerful. If I had to describe it, I think our souls are connected."

"Yes!" Emmalee kisses me. "Exactly. Like even if we get separated, we'll always find our way back. Like nothing can truly tear us apart because we have a secret link."

I breathe in her words, unable to contain my smile. "It's true. You've always been my guiding light."

Her eyes light up. "I feel like we can *really* do this, Niko. Like we have an unspoken promise to make it work between us, no matter what."

"Yes," I whisper, cradling her head. "Yes, I feel it too. And I love it so much."

"I love *you* so much. So whenever you feel alone, you're not really alone, okay?"

"Okay. Neither are you, Ems."

She straddles me, kissing me until we both grow lazy from blissful exhaustion. Her eyes droop against my touch, and it makes my heart ache.

"Are you sleepy?" I whisper.

"Yes. I'm sorry."

"Don't be sorry. You're busy expanding our new family."

She laughs, laying back down to huddle into my chest. "I'm cold."

I hold her steady, reaching for our untouched pajamas. As I drape a loose t-shirt over her head, she disrupts the process by pressing our lips together. She grunts in annoyance when I can't contain my laughter enough to properly kiss her back.

"Ems, I love you, and I'll kiss you more tomorrow. You don't have to squeeze any last ones in because our last kiss won't be until you're at least 100. I won't accept a year younger."

She sighs through a smile. "Fine. I won't be a cute old lady, though."

I laugh. "Yes, you absolutely will be. You'll be cute forever."

Emmalee hums, settling into the blankets. She looks so peaceful beside me that my eyes water. I rush to throw her spare shirt on and huddle beneath the covers with her, dragging them up to her chin. She burrows in, nestling against my cheek. I lightly trace her facial features, long after her breathing slows and my eyelids grow too heavy to control. Draping an arm over her, I give in to exhaustion and fall deeply asleep.

When I enter Sumner's dream dimension, I'm somewhere I rarely see.

The ground is as white as the vast emptiness above my head, everything visually meshing into an illusion of oneness. I could be falling, and I wouldn't know it beyond the sensation.

I hear a distant rumble, so I walk toward it. I want to figure out this dimension before Sumner does, but without his influence. To dismantle his lovechild, and use it against him somehow.

This place both embodies and amplifies my fears. I think Sumner wanted this dimension to traumatize me for life, but at some point, its purpose shifted within my mind; now, this black smoke dares me to conquer my fears. Facing the worst in this alternate world is slowly teaching me how to survive anything in reality. I want to use this secret, fear-busting technique to my benefit, especially if it spites Sumner.

The rumbling emanates from a spinning black smoke ball. It's weird; I've never seen one from the outside before.

Sumner won't tell me what he thinks this black substance is, but it's in every single dream. It's important to him. That's why I take every chance I can to investigate it.

But I've never tried passing through from the outside. It's always barricading me inside its cocoon—when it's not morphing into "other" me—and I'm itching to defy it.

The smoke sears my body on contact, but with how good I've felt today, I put up with it. My eyeballs burn inside my skull, my fingertips melting beneath the heat as I dig and dig. It overcomes my resolve, forcing me into a heavy panic. I back out of the smoke, rocking myself into stability on the empty ground.

My arms are as red as the ugly scars desecrating my limbs. It stings long after I free myself from the smoke's touch, but I can't give up.

There could be something important encapsulated inside the swirling smoke. Or maybe *someone*.

Hopping to my feet, I pat my utility pants for my favorite knife. I find it where I left it in last night's dream: tucked into a makeshift, secret pocket inside my right pocket. Flipping the knife over my knuckles, I analyze the smoke's movement. It's swirling to my right, so I follow it.

Suddenly, it lunges for me. I swat it off with the knife. Surprisingly, the blade bisects it with a piercing hiss.

So I dig in. I slice deeper and deeper, the knife growing so hot that my reflexes demand I drop it. But by now, I've created a gaping hole. The gap reveals another white nothingness, just large enough to squeeze into.

I close my eyes, take a deep breath, and jump through.

It doesn't hurt at all. For a moment, I experience true nothingness, bodiless and submitting to wherever my mind takes me. My very essence reassembles, materializing somewhere new.

Then I see her.

There's no question as to who she is. Even from behind, I recognize the way she breathes. How she leans into one shoulder when she sits, flipping her hair from her eyes with a quick head toss.

Her grown-out roots stretch her dark brown hair to her shoulders. She doesn't want to dye it, protecting the baby from chemical exposure—just like in real life.

"Emmalee?" I whisper.

I can't move. She doesn't seem to understand where my voice is coming from yet. Then the rest of our environment appears.

We're in a grungy hospital. She's surrounded by suffering people, *dying* people, dissolving into the stained linoleum floor in black smoke puddles.

It looks like she has given up.

When she meets my eyes, I run to her. She gasps, welcoming my embrace.

When we touch, my heart sinks. Emmalee feels real. But I don't want this to be real.

She can't be in this dimension. Not because of quantum physics, but because that would mean it's not just Chronic Nightmare Syndrome for her. Sumner medically abused her further than she realizes, dosing enough S817 to transport her soul to the Deep Sleep dimension without killing her. Just like me.

But Sumner never figured *this* out. If he realizes we can reach each other's dreams, he'd gain the ability to terrorize us from the inside out.

Not even my own mind is safe.

"Niko? What's wrong?" She whispers. "Are you sick too?"

I pull back, sobbing. "Oh, god, Ems—are you stuck here? Is this where you dream?"

She looks around us. "Sometimes. But you've never been here with me before. This is my least favorite one." She glances over the sea of suffering around us. "These are my old patients that disappeared. The ones Sumner experimented on. No matter how lucid I am, I can't stop them from dying. So now I just sit with them. I make sure they're not dying alone. I don't know what else to do."

I cradle her to my chest, watching in shaking horror as patients melt. Emmalee doesn't flinch, not even when the black smoke licks our limbs to give us a taste of its pain. It's too much for me to take in, however. I'm physically and mentally weak.

She lays my head into her lap, running her fingers through my hair as I drown in anxiety. "Niko, are you okay? You're so upset…"

I grip her blazer's base, losing myself to panic and hardly able to keep myself from waking up. "Emmalee, promise me something, okay?"

"O-okay?"

"Remember this dream. Tell me when you wake up if you can remember us talking about this, okay? You *have* to. It's really important."

"Hmm… Okay?" She studies my face with a puzzled frown. "Hey, you're okay, love. Just rest now. You look so tired."

"I am, Ems. I'm so tired, it hurts."

"I hear you. I am too. But when you're around, I can manage it."

I sigh, kissing her fingers. "Me too, Emmalee. Thank you."

"Thank *you*. Now I don't have to be alone here, either."

CHAPTER 42

Emmalee

My love for Niko has grown to an uncontainable joy I've never felt before. And it wasn't just the sex.

After feeling so afraid to love, Niko was so vulnerable with me that his loving words and actions meant even more. He left me reassured throughout the night, offloading my fears with his tender heart. It put me into such a heavy, comforting sleep that I didn't hear him get out of bed this morning.

But I'm confused why Niko doesn't feel like himself today. I'm so connected to him right now that I can sense his distress from a distance.

I seriously hope he didn't spend the night pacing. Sometimes I think Niko is still searching for Jay, unable to physically settle without his combat partner by his side and feeling guilty for surviving. As if he left Jay behind.

I wake up to a delicious breakfast smell—food that doesn't make me gag, so I figure it must be Niko.

Once my heart allows me to stand, I find Niko at the stove, softening fresh vegetables in a pan and darting around the kitchen in a nervous huff.

"Hey, love," I mumble, rubbing my eyes.

He whips around in surprise. "H-hey."

I frown as a deeper wave of his anxiety hits me in the gut. I open my arms for him. "You okay?"

Niko swallows his emotions, burying himself in my embrace with a spatula still in hand. "I'm just having a difficult morning. Sorry."

"You don't have to apologize. Was it something we did or talked about?"

"No, it's—"

"Hey, Emma, who's cooking?" Dad calls out, stomping sleepily down the stairs. Niko and I hurriedly separate, meeting Dad's eyes at the kitchen entryway. "It smells great! But, um... Am I interrupting something?"

I look up to find Niko's wide-eyed stare. He relaxes with my laugh as I scrub his hair, turning back to Dad. "Nope. I just woke up too. And was distracting our cook with a hug."

"Sorry," Niko says. "For cooking with your food. I figured you'd want us to eat, but I didn't want you to have to cook. I hope that's okay."

Dad smiles. "Hey, I'll never turn down good food. Thanks for making it."

"Thank you for letting me spend the night, Ben."

We all beam at Niko's silent victory: he finally un-militarized Dad's name to his face.

Dad strides over to pat Niko's shoulder, his grin making my heart twitch in fear of whatever dad-thing he's about to say. "Sure. You're only allowed back if you two keep quieter next time."

I gasp. "*Dad!* Oh, my God..."

Niko is motionless, his color draining away. Then he takes off for the bathroom, handing me the spatula.

"Oh. Did he not realize I was joking?" Dad asks. "I mean, we always wear earplugs because your mom and I both snore. I slept through the whole night like a rock. But you two didn't— I mean, in your childhood home? I figured you *wouldn't...*"

I chew my lip. "You can't joke about sexual things with him! He's still recovering from major trauma."

"Oh, God. So you did."

"That's not what's important, Dad!"

Mom yawns in the entryway. "Why are we already fighting at nine in the morning?"

"Just torturing Emma and traumatizing her boyfriend, apparently," Dad grumbles. "Now I have to erase that image from my mind too."

"It's your own fault!" I say.

Dad suppresses a laugh, but I'm too annoyed to laugh along with him. Maybe I'd find this funny under other circumstances. I'm already pregnant, so I don't mind if my parents know about my sex life, but Niko *really* minds.

I knock on the bathroom door and get no response. So I barge in.

Niko is sitting on the stark-white tile with his head in his hands. Without looking up, he mutters, "I just need one more minute to die and come back to life before I can face your dad again."

I kneel in front of him, stroking his hair. "It was a bad joke, love. He didn't hear anything at all."

"What?"

"Yeah. But I accidentally told him we had sex anyway."

Niko groans into his palms.

"It's okay, he's a doctor."

"He's *your dad*, love. You didn't see how angry he was with me when we were seventeen. I can't ruin this again. I can't lose you."

"Okay, let's slow down." I ease his hands off his face, kissing him on the cheek. Once his bloodshot eyes meet mine, I smile. "It's all okay. We'll go back in there and eat what you made, and everything will be great. No one's mad. We all love you."

His onyx stare makes me flush. I'm dying to lean into him and make his body feel as good as last night, but it's definitely not the time. Niko bends down, gingerly kissing my baby belly, and I almost change my mind.

"You're killing me," I whisper.

He jerks back. "Huh? Did I hurt you?"

"Oh, love, I'm sorry. I was joking." I cringe at my poor timing. He's *really* not himself today. I rub my fingers over the worry lines in his forehead, kissing frazzled his eyes. "I meant you're so wonderful that I don't know how to contain myself today. I'm dying to cuddle the shit out of you. Otherwise, I'm ridiculously fucking happy."

"Oh..." He smiles, nudging my nose with his. "Well, I'll make sure to cuddle you extra tonight."

I laugh. "Okay, good! I can't wait! Come on, let's go."

He takes my hand, following me out of the bathroom. Dad gives Niko so many "reassuring" back pats while he finishes cooking that I shrink in my seat, unable to focus on Mom's lecture about raising children.

We settle around the table with a rainbow array of tempting sliced fruit, pancakes, and cooked vegetables beneath our noses. But while everyone else is seated, Niko still stands behind his chair, gripping the backrest.

"Um, I made some eggs and sausage for you, Ben and Monique, but I hid it from Emmalee's nose in the microwave, for now."

"Oh, thank you!" Mom smiles, patting his chair. "Come sit with us, sweetheart."

He sits, presses his palms together, mutters "いただきます," and takes deep breaths with his eyes closed. I know what he's doing, but it must look new to my parents.

"Are you… religious?" Dad asks.

Niko opens his eyes and heartily laughs, then covers his mouth. "Sorry. I wasn't laughing at you; I was thanking the food, and now I'm doing the breathing technique my therapist taught me because it's hard to eat while I'm anxious."

"Oh. Well, good for you for taking care of yourself," Dad says.

I chew on the inside of my cheek, trying my best not to laugh at their painful awkwardness.

"Thanks for the food!" I load my plate. My parents watch wide-eyed as I serve myself long after everyone else is done. "Sorry, did I take too much?"

Mom rubs my shoulder. "No, Emma, I should be sorry for staring. It's just, you've struggled your whole life to eat without feeling nauseous. It's just new, that's all."

"Yes, let's leave the poor girl alone," Dad says. "She needs to gain about twenty more pounds for that baby within the next few months, anyway."

I grunt through my mouthful of food. "*Twenty?* How the hell am I going to do that? My whole life, I could hardly gain anything I lost!"

"When you weren't pregnant, sure. But dysautonomia be damned, your baby is doing great, and your body seems to be instructing you on what to do next to combat that chronic malnutrition. It's okay to eat as much as your body says you need, no matter what anyone else says."

I swallow hard. "Am I still not eating enough, though? Will the baby be okay?"

Niko grabs my hand. "Hey, it's okay."

"Yes, it's okay. You're not doing anything wrong," Dad says. "You have plenty of time to keep cooking that little bun."

"Ugh," I groan, clutching my churning stomach. "I think *I* need some breathing exercises now."

Niko chuckles, closing his eyes with a deep breath. I copy him, releasing a slow exhale. Soon, all four of us are breathing deeply at the table, Mom nudging Dad into doing it too. I let out a loud laugh at their sudden serious faces, and everyone opens their eyes, turning to me. We erupt in a giggle fit, and all is well again.

Niko lightens up as we catch up with my parents. Niko is still amused that I yelled at my boss without knowing he was a top United States official, and Dad chokes in hysterical agreement. We're all having an incredible time despite our painful circumstances, finishing our meal with laughter in the air. Until I say something intended as a joke.

"You know how when you see someone you know in a dream, and it feels all trippy the next day?"

My parents nod, but Niko freezes.

I laugh. "I have some recurring dreams, but this time, Niko was there, talking with me for what felt like *hours*. I don't know if it's from pregnancy, but my dreams are ridiculously vivid lately. It was so weird; it felt like we were talking for real, about us dreaming, even. I woke up confused if I really dreamt it or not."

Niko's fork clatters to the table.

"Niko?" Mom asks.

"What did I say? In the dream." He's staring deep into my eyes.

My brows furrow. Something feels off beyond Niko's skyrocketing anxiety. It's also coming from somewhere else.

I meet Dad's eyes, and it starts falling into place. They both know something I don't about these dreams—these nightmares.

Niko is asking because he *needs* to know, as if it's as crucial as a real-life circumstance.

But having Chronic Nightmare Syndrome from S817 and having nightmares *with real people* are two separate things. That would mean the dreams are a physical location. And *that's* impossible.

But as I look between Niko's terrified stare and my dad's, I'm unsure how to feel. All I can remember are Lilith's words, warning me the experiments could wipe my memory, and Niko's hysteria after his tour about S817 "creating a new place." How Sumner was trying to "figure out" how the dreams worked using Niko. Like the dreams were a *physical* puzzle.

"I-I... I dreamt you told me to tell you we dreamt together. I thought it would be funny? I mean, there's no way we could *actually* dream together, but while I was asleep, it felt so real that—"

Niko stands, his chest heaving. He looks my parents in the eyes. "Sorry, I— Sorry for ruining this."

"What?! What are you going to do to us?" Mom grips my arm in defense of me.

I watch her words hurt him as much as I can feel it. Niko leaves to pace in the other room. We can all hear it from the table: his limping foot clopping against the entryway hardwood. Then we hear his rapid breath, struggling for air.

"What's wrong with him?" Mom asks as I run from the table.

"Paper bags don't usually work for him, but can someone get one, in case?"

Dad understands, at least. He strides into the kitchen, searching through our drawers as I rush to soothe Niko before he hyperventilates.

But it's too late. By the time I reach Niko, he won't even let me get close. He backs against the wall, bumping his shoulder into a picture frame before sliding to the floor. He motions for me to stay back when I try again to approach. I don't want to ignore his consent, but I might have to at some point, just to ease his suffering. It's already coming close to that.

"What are you thinking? Talk to me," I say.

He stumbles to his feet. Niko backs away from me into the

living room, almost tripping over the couch. "It was *real*," he wheezes. He takes in my confused stare and continues, "The dream. I dreamt it too."

"Is he finally having a nervous breakdown?" Mom appears at my side.

I seethe. "*Excuse* me? He can hear you."

"I'm aware of that, *Emmalee*."

Dad puts a hand on Mom's tense shoulder, brushing past her with a paper lunch sack in his hands. He approaches Niko with his hands up, but it only forces Niko deeper into the living room.

"Not a good idea, Dad." My eyes water. Niko's panic sears my heart, and the guilt bursting through him pinches a deep nerve in my chest. "Don't corner him. He's afraid of hurting people, and you're getting in his space."

"*Will* he hurt me?" Dad sets the bag on the coffee table and backpedals.

"No, he won't."

Niko meets my eyes, gripping the brick fireplace mantle to remain upright. I can tell he's questioning my words' truth. How I could have so much trust in him when he has so little in himself.

"Nikolai, take the bag and place it over your mouth, like this." Dad holds his fist around his lips to demonstrate. "You can do it."

Niko shakes his head no, gripping his chest. "Dying."

"You're not going to die. I won't let you." I step past my dad. "Can I get closer to help you?"

He shakes his head no. "I can see it again."

"See what?" I ask, ignoring my dad's suspicious your-boyfriend-has-lost-his-mind stare. "He's having a flashback, Dad," I hiss.

Dad's eyebrows furrow.

"Sorry, Ben," Niko gasps. "I see Jay."

My knees shake. I grip the couch to stay upright, inching closer to Niko.

"No! Stay back, Ems. *Please*."

"Okay." I freeze in place. "It's going to be okay. Tell me what you see. Get it out of your head."

Niko breathes out an incredulous, "What?" Then his eyes flick around the room, remembering even more.

"Just try."

"Jay went to the bathroom. Someone killed him."

I choke back tears. "Sumner killed him?"

"No— He— He *ordered* someone to do it. While I was asleep," Niko says, screaming now. I'm dying to hold him, but he shakes his head no. "I should've been there!"

"Oh, my God." I swallow, holding back the acid rising in my throat. "Y-you didn't know."

"But now he has you too. In his dream dimension."

I don't want to believe it, but this sobering truth washes over me—instinct, not paranoia.

But we're not alone, and I'm positive this is classified information. Dad is still frozen behind us, but then he sees something I don't, rushing off to the kitchen. I turn around to find both parents missing.

"Niko, my love," I whisper, stepping closer to him. "Please let me help you. Please."

"No! If you're dreaming this deeply too, he'll use you because of me. He'll kill you!"

"No, he won't. We're right here, remember? We're together now, and we're safe from him, okay?"

Our heads whip down the hall the second Dad starts yelling. I've never heard him raise his voice at Mom in my life, but now he's shouting, "Give the poor kids a break! Why would you do this?!"

"Emma needs professional, medical help! She's dreaming too!" Mom struggles to yank her phone from Dad's hands. Her mind sounds set.

"I'm what?" My tears are no longer sad anymore. They're furious. "You knew about this?! I've been having nightmares for *years!*"

Niko grips my wrist, pulling me away from the kitchen. His hyperventilation has been replaced by a panting cry. "We have to get out of here, Ems."

"Why?"

"I think she called the Department of Health." He hugs me to his chest from behind, shielding me from my own parents.

I catch my mom's eyes, expecting to find her confused. When I don't, my blood boils with more than rage. Heartbreaking betrayal courses through my limbs with every pounding thump of my heart. "You did, didn't you?"

She continues to stare. "You both need immediate care. You're sick, and *he's* violent."

"Let's go. Please, let's go." Niko tugs on my shoulders to plead me out of my staredown.

"Not yet. I want to hear the truth from my mom directly."

"I did call, sweetie." Her voice shakes. "You've asked me your whole life about why we're here, and why we don't want you to be in the DoTD. Well, this is why. You were never supposed to associate yourself with someone like him. The criminals we test these drugs on."

Mom swallows hard, wincing at my obvious rage as my full body shakes. I can't bear to respond.

"They're going to lock her up like a criminal now, either way. Experiment on her," Niko snaps.

Mom doesn't spare Niko a glance, her eyes locked on mine. "I pack drugs myself, sweetheart, so that we'd never have to be the ones to take them. But now that you have, you need to detox it from your body in the hospital—by any means necessary. Especially if you're dreaming this heavily, which is a potentially fatal sign. At the very least, your baby won't survive without detoxing it." I can't breathe as she glances at Niko, leaning close to me. "I'm not sure either of you will survive anyway, with *him* around. He doesn't seem stable."

"I'm sorry," Niko whispers.

As if my mom's words didn't hurt enough, Niko's needless apology stings too much to bear when he's the only one keeping this baby and me safe. I've never been this angry with my mom in my life, but as hot, vicious sobs rip from my core, I don't feel the urge to lash out. I see it in Mom's numb, brainwashed eyes; she's as trapped as we are.

But it's no excuse for what she's done. As my mother turns her back on me, my guilt-stricken father allows Niko to take me away. He doesn't have a choice either: Mom still has no idea we're all traitors.

I know I've been betrayed, potentially sentenced to torture, by the woman who promised to protect me for life. Hurt doesn't describe it. My soul is crushed.

I'm not a parent yet, but I couldn't imagine abandoning my baby like this, and I can read emotions. No, I'd rather die protecting them.

Guarding our developing baby with my arms, I allow Niko to drag us out the door. My numb body doesn't feel like mine anymore as we stumble onto the sidewalk. But we're both such a goddamn mess that we don't make it far, armored vehicles streaming down my parents' street.

"Go," Niko yells over the mechanical hum. "I can escape, but it'll be difficult to rescue you if you're caught."

I believe him. I've never seen his eyes like this before. The person who's forever labeled a predator suddenly looks like prey.

I try my best to slip away in the shadows of my childhood home as Niko fends off at least fifteen guys at once, but it's a useless effort. These guys know who they're dealing with. They sent an excessive amount of men to flood Niko until they can dart him, his movements fading until his body falls limp.

I figure it's best to raise my arms in submission. Not for me, for our baby. Even if that means giving away our biggest secret.

"I'm pregnant. Please don't hurt me."

They don't listen. Hoisting me up like a ragdoll, they throw me into a truck beside Niko's unblinking, paralyzed body.

I'm breathless for a moment, terrified I'm staring at the love of my life, dead. But he's not; he's just unconscious, despite his eyes being stuck open.

No matter how much I plead for information, the helmeted men leave me to sob in the back. They drive us straight to Sumner Hospital.

CHAPTER 43

Niko

"Hey, Wolf," a voice whispers over me. I know this voice, but I can't open my eyes. "I can't carry *and* protect you out there at the same time—it's too fucking violent. You've gotta wake yourself up, bro. Go find Ricky and give them all hell for me, okay?"

I can't respond, stuck in a limbo between dimensions.

That couldn't have been Jay. Jay's *dead*, and this voice called me "Wolf."

But the voice has a point. I've never identified with the Wolf, a degrading nickname from people who hardly know me. But today is different.

I think it's finally time to embrace him.

The moment I open my eyes, I see someone pierced holes in my IV bags, leaving my blood to reverse a few inches through the tubes. Whoever they were, they're on my side.

So I follow their advice: I tear both IVs out. Sedation doesn't work well on me anymore, so as far as I can tell, I'm relatively clear-headed. I rip off my boot brace, leaving my achy foot to fend for itself. Then I shove any nurses and doctors blocking my path, checking every single room for her.

I need to find her quickly. There's smoke outside, pillowing against the hospital windows. With the way it's spiraling upwards—nothing like fog or clouds—I can't fight my fear that the city was recently bombed. I'm not waiting around for verification.

After three sedatives upon our arrival at Sumner Hospital, they finally knocked me out. Emmalee tried to call my mom

while we were in the truck, but Mom didn't answer. Dad didn't either. She tried them a second time, then she called Lillith, leaving hushed voicemails for all three of them. Lilith has no reception in the forest's blackout zone, but my parents always answer—unless something is *majorly* wrong. I'm worried for their safety just as much as ours.

I wasn't unconscious as Emmalee struggled; I was physically paralyzed. I had to lie there, watching her suffer. Alone, crying over me, and gripping her belly in fear.

Emmalee did everything right, complying physically but refusing to surrender any information until they gave up and let her remain silent. I trust Emmalee to fend for herself, but I don't trust Sumner to go easy on her.

The next chance I get, I'm going to kill him. I'm breaking my promise to myself to never kill another soul, committing a final wrongdoing to end the cycle once and for all.

Without Jay by my side to gut the entire system, this has become the only way to end it. Frail patients line the hallways, dead-asleep. We're all poisoned.

People turn and run screaming the second they see my eyes. I'm not sure what I look like, but the Wolf has a mind of his own. He's all my brainwashed violence packed into a neat human body, bulldozing anything that dares to underestimate my willingness to survive.

I scour the place until I'm chased by Department of Tactical Defense unit members with dart guns. It's weird; they don't care that we're surrounded by civilians, in a civilian hospital. But I think I get why. The Departments are finally siding with the white supremacists—the nation's sponsors—and no longer caring to hide it. But does that mean Civil War II has reached Santa Desierto?

They might be able to sedate your average DoTD unit member, but they don't know how long I've been running to dodge death. I'm still running in my nightmares, even if I wake up terrifyingly stationary.

Eventually, I'm sick of them following me. I leave the nearest unit member cowering on the floor, disarming him by shattering his trigger hand in my fist.

"Let me go where I want to go," I say.

And they do—after my second target crumples like a wilted rose. The DoTD falls back, instructing the hospital staff to steer clear of me. A staff member attempts to guide me, but once I pick up the pace, they yell out a room number and run.

I'm assuming everyone knows who I'm looking for. They know better than to trap me in a room; I'm the most skilled at close range, so they're gambling that by letting me find her, I'll spare them.

I attempt to soothe myself on the way there so I don't show up looking like I've come to kill her, but I can't calm myself down. Every waking meat sack is a threat, having chosen to side with greed over human beings.

According to her room number, she's in the ICU. I try not to think about what that means for her as I charge the frigid ICU halls.

Flinging open her door, I find her—motionless and isolated. The room has no windows, four white walls barely large enough to contain her bed and equipment. She doesn't notice me; she can't. She's flat on her back, unconscious with a tube down her throat and fluids pumping into her veins.

My heart breaks for too many reasons to bear. This isn't just a hazard for Emmalee, but for the baby.

I lean on her bed, attempting to wake her. I'm too devastated to quiet myself when a nurse enters to find me sobbing. Emmalee's hair has grown since I last saw her, resting below her collarbones. I've been asleep longer than I thought.

Then I lift the covers to reveal her abdomen. She's still pregnant, but she's lost weight across her entire body—weight she worked so fucking hard to gain. Her belly has hardly grown.

"She's sedated for her comfort." The nurse's voice shakes. I turn around to face him, and he flinches.

"For her comfort? How comfortable will she be when the sedative kills our baby? Has it already?"

He gapes, making strange, uncertain sounds with his throat.

"How promising. Tell me what you did to her."

"I-I'm not authorized to give out my patient's medical information to—"

I grip him by the scrubs. He goes weak in the knees.

For a moment, I see myself from the outside. I picture how Emmalee would see me if she woke up right now, lifting a helpless nurse by his shirt collar. He didn't do this. This isn't *his* fault.

But in a way, it is. He was a bystander. He might not have chosen it himself, but he certainly isn't choosing to help anyone escape in the face of horrific suffering.

"Your complacency is showing." I feel my cheeks tightening, grinning like this is some twisted joke. It has to be. This can't be real. "She didn't need a tube down her throat when I last saw her. She was finally happy. Other than our baby's safety, her main concern that day was that she wanted me to cuddle her extra. So, what did you do to her? And how long have I been asleep?"

"She got sicker over the past three weeks. We're doing everything we can!"

I release him. He crumbles to the floor, so I pick him up by the armpits and stand him upright again like an infant. He's a curious little man, suddenly lacking limb control.

"I haven't been asleep for three weeks. I wouldn't be able to walk." My voice sounds robotic, spewing out everything I'm thinking.

"N-no, you just… You have some memory loss, Sir. It's a common side effect of—"

"S817. If it doesn't kill me first. You're killing people, you know that? How does it feel? To become a killer? You can't take it back, you know. Once they die, they're dead. You'll never be able to forget their eyes when they take their last breath, not until you take yours. Good luck trying. Should've never killed people in the first place."

His teeth are chattering. I turn my back to him, knowing he's a lost cause. He takes his cue to run.

And I'm alone with Emmalee again. Her cheeks are as sunken as her eyes.

First, I want to taper off her sedatives, but they're unmarked, and I'm not sure which is which. I also don't know how to safely remove the tubes from her throat. Once she's awake, I might have to carry her for a while, but I don't have a choice. I need to get her out of here before someone important arrives for us. Beyond that, they took our personal belongings, and I don't think we can make a proper escape without clothes—half-naked with only drab hospital gowns over our underwear, trapped in the middle of downtown Santa Desierto with unit members searching to stamp out traitors. I'm sure that's exactly why they hid our belongings, but I don't want to leave her side over fucking fabric. The second I leave, they'll find another way to trap us here.

I stick my head out of the room. "Is someone willing to be a human being and help us out?"

Everyone just stares.

"Good to know."

Turning back around, I'm stunned by how nauseating it is to see Emmalee like this. They've made her vulnerable, unable to consent to anything they decide to do to her. They're likely keeping her asleep to force her to dream.

But what if she genuinely needs medical intervention? Sometimes, S817 is too much for people, no matter how low of a dose. They could be trying to counteract the damage they caused, keeping her alive by a thread. What if by kidnapping her from the hospital, I'm killing her? What if I lose *both* of them today?

"I—"

I whip around. The nurse has returned.

"I-I want to help."

He's holding our clothes. I didn't even ask for them.

He squeezes his eyes shut as I approach. I don't think he's expecting me to hug him, but I don't know what else to do. The numbness in my mind is wearing off, and my heart feels like it's rotting.

"Oh—" He gasps, patting my back as I weep. "I-it's okay. You'll be okay. You're a true survivor."

"Perpetual victim," I mutter.

He swallows hard. "I need to attend to Miss Richards before she wakes up."

I release him, standing in shaky silence as he disconnects Emmalee from dozens of wires and tubes. After disconnecting her IV, her heart rate speeds up. I lapse into a frustrated pant—she doesn't need intervention, after all. If she needed the ventilator, he wouldn't be able to suddenly take her off it. As soon as she stirs, he yells at me to stay back and stop pacing, that my presence is too overwhelming for her while she's in pain and he needs to focus. I do my best to listen.

Emmalee's eyes are wider than I've ever seen them. I bite my cheek so hard I taste blood, clutching my hair roots as I helplessly watch. He helps her cough the tube from her trachea. She grips the nurse's shoulder in fear, her fingers turning white.

"Ems, I'm so sorry," I rasp.

She just stares back.

More unit members arrive to try and stop us. The nurse makes a terrible mistake by turning around and showing his face to them, but I do what I can and protect us all. At least temporarily.

I'm confused. These guys are painfully easy to tear apart. I can break their limbs and immobilize them in seconds, and everyone seems hesitant to attack me. This is not the DoTD I know.

"Did they... kill all of you off?" I ask the guy I'm pinning down.

His eyes are bulging wide, so I stop restricting his airway. He hasn't had the same strangulation training I have. And his sheer size should've helped him kick my ass. I can tell I'm smaller than before, that S817 licked the meat from my bones. I wouldn't be able to fend them off if I hadn't been training myself non-stop for years. Particularly the past four years. On the front lines.

"Oh." I laugh, unable to stop once I start. "They killed us all on the front lines, huh?"

I let him go. He has no fight left.

The remaining DoTD members retreat. I watch them scurry away, wondering if I'm doing them a disservice by keeping them alive. The DoTD will kill or torture them worse than the quick death I could provide.

"She needs some time to adjust." The nurse wrings his hands in Emmalee's doorway.

"Okay. Don't leave yet. They'll kill you."

"Y-yeah..."

"Do you want out? I'll protect you."

Terrified tears surface, but the nurse smiles. "I can't. There aren't many nurses left. People need me."

"What are you going to do?"

"Die, probably." His voice peters out as he speaks. He doesn't look like he's accepted his fate. He doesn't want to die, either.

"I can't let you do that."

His fingers twitch, a fire boiling in him. "This is my choice."

He slips past me, darting down the hall. I respect his choice.

Emmalee is half-awake, but she doesn't look good. He left her with oxygen flowing into her nose, but her skin is still a strange yellow, her lips a soft purple. They're killing her; I can feel it. My throat tightens.

I carefully approach, lacing her fingers in mine. She rolls her head back and forth, attempting to work off the sedatives. When I kiss her fingers, her eyes snap open, yanking her hand from mine.

"S-sorry, love. I'm sorry," I say. "I shouldn't have grabbed your hand while you're so out of it. I'll ask for permission next time."

I didn't think my heart could break further, but it leaves me struggling to stay stable. Emmalee never used to pull away from me. The way she's acting… It reminds me of myself.

She's alert now that I scared her, staring up at me.

"Ems? You okay, my love?"

Emmalee continues to stare. I crouch at her bedside, attempting to look less like I'm towering over her and more like I'm here to support.

She opens her mouth, but lurches with a grimace. Emmalee grunts, grabbing her throat.

"Oh, Ems… Does it hurt to speak?"

She nods. Her eyebrows furrow, but more in confusion than pain.

The way she's staring at me makes me nervous. The familiar softness has evaporated from her icy clear eyes. They look cold.

"E-Emmalee?"

She clears her throat, wincing as she swallows.

Then she rasps, "Wh—"

"…Who?"

She nods.

I struggle in silence, trying to understand what she's saying.

"You," she croaks out a whisper. "Who— Are—" She throws her head back in frustration, flipping it back up to finish her question. "You?"

"W-who am I?"

She nods, eyeing me. She looks… terrified of me.

I don't understand it at first. Rising to my feet, I gape in disbelief. Wondering when her eyes will stop looking at me like that.

But they don't. I'm a stranger.

My world is ending.

"Um," the nurse says, suddenly behind me. It's the first time I haven't noticed someone entering a room since I was a child. I resist a primal urge to turn around and arrest him, whipping around in panic instead. He jumps, taking a few steps back. "S-sorry! She's still waking up and might not be herself for another thirty minutes."

I exhale. That, I can handle.

Emmalee continues to stare me down, so I sit in the corner. I know for a fact she will *not* be happy if I kidnap her against her will, and I don't want to traumatize her more.

"I need to get you out of here, okay? Do you not remember me?"

She shakes her head no, studying me up and down.

I push my grown-out hair from my eyes, struggling to remain calm. What if she never remembers me again?

"That's okay, you will soon," I reassure us both. "These people are making you sicker. Do you agree with me?"

She nods viciously, gripping her stomach. "My—" She coughs, reaching for me.

I rush to her side, automatically placing my hand on her belly like it belongs there. I have to choke back tears. "Does it hurt?"

She nods, beginning to cry.

"How much? A lot?"

She grips my hospital gown, whimpering and holding her throat. She can't bear to give me a yes or no, which I think is the most painful "yes" I've ever witnessed.

"Okay, love. It's going to be okay," I whisper, cradling her head to my chest.

I pull away to grab our clothes, my hands shaking. I have to pretend like I'm confident we can survive, but I'm not sure anymore. She looks so frail, and if she's losing the baby, I don't know if she can handle it on top of everything else. Not just physically, but mentally.

She gasps, slapping the bed to get my attention.

"What?! What's wrong?" I jump up with fistfuls of her black clothes.

She attempts to smile through tears. "N-Niko," she rasps, opening her arms.

"Yes!" I hoist her to her knees, wrapping my arms around her waist. "Good job, Ems! You remembered!"

We celebrate our weird victory. Emmalee is still incredibly high on sedatives, switching between an unpredictable mix of happiness, fear, and pain.

I brush her hair back, cupping her pale face in my hands. "Ready to escape, little lion?"

She plants a sloppy kiss on my lips—I'm assuming to mean "yes." Our limbs tangle, and she almost falls off the bed until I catch her.

This is going to be a challenge.

CHAPTER 44

Emmalee

It's been thirty minutes since Niko struggled to get me dressed. I'm rational enough to feel horrible for it now, even though I'm still delirious and feel like I'm carrying the weight of ten bodies as we walk. I kept trying to smother him in the hospital, half to apologize for forgetting my life partner and half because, without a filter, I'm a horny disaster.

Niko has been carrying me as he sprints, using the DoTD's required memorization of Santa Desierto's streets and back alleyways in case of martial law. I tried to tell him to save his energy and put me down, but I'm not sure he heard me. But I can't fight anyone off in my current state, so it's unfortunately up to him to protect us. Considering the way he's tossing his head around, we're being followed. Eventually, he doesn't have a choice with how he's wheezing and stumbling, and sets me on my jelly legs.

"I'm too weak to keep carrying you. I'm so fucking sorry," I think Niko whispers. But I can't fully tell. My blood pressure is so low that I can't keep my eyes open, let alone hear properly. He drags us into the streets instead of the alleyways, blending in with a sea of stress-soaked human beings so that we can move slower but remain hidden.

Niko won't admit it, but he's as sick as I am. He's discolored and exhausted, verging on throwing up. But he won't. He won't even mention he feels sick. Maybe he's unaware of it. Numb again, after all that effort to deprogram himself.

My high-vision gives me a sudden revelation. Mentally separated from myself, it's apparent how far society around us has degraded. Debris blankets the street, I've seen numerous people bleeding, and everyone's pissed off and rushing. I don't understand why. A stranger knocks me into Niko, angry with how much I'm bumping into people by mistake; my feet are slurring as much as my words. They must have known, seen we were struggling, but they didn't care. Shoving a sick, pregnant woman to the floor is the new normal. Niko wants to hit them, I can tell, but he prioritizes stabilizing me on my feet, keeping us moving.

I stop us for a moment, shuddering beneath the pain in my gut. It's forcing me to bend over and grip Niko's arms with a pathetic whimper.

It took me the longest time to remember I'm pregnant. Up until five minutes ago, I had no idea. I think I know why, but I don't want to admit it.

I feel empty. Emptier than I've ever felt in my life.

"Hurts," I mutter.

"Fuck," Niko whispers.

I think he knows, but he's trying to stay hopeful. I groan, realizing *Niko* is more optimistic than I am, and he's not in his right mind. Neither of us is. Something happened to us, but I don't know what. I can't remember.

"You're going to be okay, my love," Niko coos over me, begging me to move. "Breathe through it and keep walking, okay? I'll take care of you for as long as you need as soon as we're safe."

We keep walking through the sea of dead eyes. The world as we knew it is gone, but everyone's carrying on with their individual realities, fending for themselves and themselves alone. If you keep your eyes up, you'll see federal soldiers in the street, keeping everyone on track. Cops beating people on every street corner. Department unit members chasing anyone who tries to escape. But I'm not sure anyone else wants to see it.

We *can't stop* seeing it—un-knowing doesn't exist. And according to the rageful men chasing us, we know too much. But I don't feel like I have an upper hand. My memory is so hazy that I can't remember what day it is, where I live, or where we're going.

All I know is that I don't like the men chasing us, gaining on us. Walking death sentences.

Planes hum, flying low. Everyone starts running, ignoring the soldiers' orders to remain calm. People trample one other in front of us, but I don't know how to move anymore—in genuine traumatic shock.

But Niko is truly the Wolf in human skin. Hoisting me over his shoulder with shaking arms, we ditch the sidewalks for the alleyways again. It's too loud to decipher the sounds enough to comprehend what's happening to us, but Niko understands. And if Niko's energy blazes with fear, I know it's the right time to be petrified.

He manages to evade the source of smoke, billowing across the street—a lung-strangling dust coating the air and making our eyes water. Niko covers my mouth and nose with his sleeve, but all I can think about is his bleeding ears.

He runs for what feels like ages. By the time we step back onto the sidewalk, a pathetic fraction of our hearing returns. But we don't need our hearing to see that the shop windows no longer exist, and there are far fewer people to hide amongst— well, *living* people.

"—can't fly—cursed forest," is all I can read from Niko's lips, but I can put the pieces together: planes can't fly over the forest's electromagnetic radiation.

Niko bursts into a sprint. I cling to him harder, feeling utterly useless. My legs tremble with every heave of my abdomen, and I understand exactly what's happening no matter how much I want to deny it. If we even live through this, we'll be childless. Not because my body failed, but because no one cared enough to end our suffering. Worse, some intentionally injured us.

At the same time, I feel like a failure. I thought I could finally be someone's hero.

The mess of bodies confuses me. It's like someone sloppily hit the trigger, bulldozing civilians, police, and the "National Guard," or today's disguise for the Department of Tactical Defense, indiscriminately. For the sake of pure death. It's no wonder they didn't catch up to us until now—they're all out of living worshippers to fight on their side.

Niko's body finally gives out. The "National Guard" doesn't give up on us; we still know too much.

This is it. As the men approach us, ready to dart Niko to sleep again, I understand our fate. I'm not just losing my baby, I'm losing my life partner.

Before they can strip me away from Niko, I huddle against my lover's chest, my sole remaining comfort.

"I love you," I say, but I can't hear myself. I hope he can read my lips. I hold his wet cheeks in my palms and say it to him again. "I love you. Please don't blame yourself."

But he does. I don't need him to voice it to understand the searing guilt in his energy. This alone might kill him. He tries to fight back—we both do. But once again, in a never-ending cycle, we're separated.

It's too much. Allowing myself to go limp where I lay in the back of a Department utility vehicle, I simply breathe. Numb all thought. With a new dose of sedatives pumped into me, I squeeze my eyes shut, and my mind travels somewhere else. Just like Niko said, interdimensional travel. To the place where we all dream.

CHAPTER 45

Emmalee

Jostled in the back of the DoTD transport van, this is one time I prefer this nightmare dimension.

Before the dream dimension opens, there's an all-consuming emptiness. The black waiting room. Where emotions heighten until the dream realm feels more alive than waking reality, and everything you've bottled down comes spurting out.

It's the only place I can remember everything, so memories flood my head.

I was only transferred to the ICU yesterday. For weeks before that, I was crammed into a room of other patients. Other *dreamers*. Each time I'd get a new roommate, I'd outlast them. They'd flatline out of nowhere sometimes, but usually, they'd simply never wake up. Braindead.

Dr. Sumner loves me; he made sure to let me know. He'd tell me how interesting I was, just like his "vital patient," Niko. How we outlive anyone and anything that happens to us.

Every day was the same. I'd beg Sumner to give me "the antidote," to which he'd laugh in my face. I'm pretty sure it doesn't exist. He would've been interested in "harvesting" our baby, he once said, "if it was actually Blackwood's." So he left me to become disturbingly intimate with our unborn child's slow death. "Trauma is useful, Miss Richards," he always says. "It teaches us everything we need to know about ourselves."

Sumner only cared about one thing: how we managed to link our minds in our dreams. Until we teach him, he won't let us go. In the meantime, he studied our bodies' reaction to S817 all hours of the day, minutes stretching into torturous lengths.

At least, that's how it started.

When we arrive back at Sumner Hospital, they leave me for three days to miscarry alone with a nurse I've never met. It's the worst thing I've ever done.

The minute I'm coherent enough to sit upright, they bind my mouth and wheel me to a new room. It's the first time I see Niko again, but his mouth is bound too. Even though it kills to admit, I'm dying to tell him the worst news about our child. But I can't even do that. They decode our childish tapping language—even though I only used rapid flicks of my eyes—and threaten to hurt Niko if I continue communicating with him. But Niko's eyes tell me he understood. All we can do is stare at each other, grieving in hideous silence.

Niko escapes his restraints over and over again—until they sauter him into a metal restraint chair in front of me and *actually* torture him. The longer I gaze into his empty eyes, the more the future horrifies me.

My deepest fear comes true, having to feel every inch of Niko's pain through my empathic senses without being able to help. But Niko isn't scared of the pain; I can't stop screaming, even though his greatest fear is me seeing him like that.

Until the tenth day. Seemingly out of nowhere, Niko's face falls blank, staring back at me as they work. It changes his entire face, erasing the Niko I knew.

"Interesting. Thank you," Sumner says when I shit myself in fear in front of everyone, even though no one laid a hand on me.

But Sumner's words give me the answers I fear.

They're never going to stop. Not even if we tell them how we connect in the Deep Sleep. This data is worth just as much; he wants to know how to destroy someone's health without touching them, leaving no evidence, and it's working on me. Especially because my memory is broken, proving my abuse testimony "unreliable."

We're perfect subjects to destroy each other with, all because we fit together. It's the first time I've regretted loving Niko, but I can't stop aching for him even though it's killing him. The guilt from loving him is killing me too, stripping the weight from my bones until I'm a wheezing skeleton.

One day, Niko doesn't recognize me, his eyes furrowing in confusion when I croak his name. I knew it was coming—Niko's forgetfulness has been his trauma response for his whole life—but that doesn't stop it from hurting. I'm not sure he'll ever see me again. This realization makes my whole body shake, burning my limbs and stomach until I feel nothing at all. It's too much to feel.

I finally understand why Niko forgets. As long as I love Niko, they're going to hurt him. I'm afraid I have no choice but to forget too.

When I sleep, it's nothing but black.

CHAPTER 46

Fourteen

I only dream in vivid nightmares. It took me a while to remember this nightmare land—the Deep Sleep—is its own dimension.

The tenth dimension. We created an opening to it, attempting to rationalize our earthly suffering. Here, we can see every possibility imaginable, and work through it without losing our lives. The power of human minds is limitless. Especially in survival mode.

But the physical place I'm trapped in is far from amazing.

In a newly constructed hospital wing, they drug us to sleep, holding us in this dimension for longer. They feed us through intravenous nutrition or nasogastric tubes shoved down our noses and throats to keep us alive while we sleep for days.

And we dream.

We dream until our skin is infected from pissing and shitting ourselves in our sleep. We dream until some of us can't any longer, mentally flatlining in screams, word salads, or eternal silence. Physically disintegrating to a skeleton-like version of "living." They intend for us to dream until we die.

35 of us have survived from our experiment cell's original 100. The cell is a large cement box with one window. Two walls are cement, the one with a door is shatter-resistant glass—that I've tried to destroy, multiple times—and the fourth is a *giant* one-way mirror.

We can't escape the shells of ourselves, facing our twisted

reality in the massive mirror wall. I can't recognize myself. My hair is long, I'm lean and lanky, and my skin has bleached beneath the fluorescent lights. The only grooming they do to us is to shave our faces and limbs, making it even colder.

Still, my favorite times are once I'm finally awake.

I feel like a horrible person for staring at one woman in particular, stationed across the room. My guiding light. We're almost always awake at different times, but on the rare days we're on the same bed-cleaning schedule, her smile warms my heart.

They call her "Fifty-Five" to match her ID number. None of us are allowed to talk to each other, so I don't know her real name. I vaguely recognize the ID down her spine, but I think that's because she has the same starting number as Jay's: 26. She doesn't have the additional "1" tattooed at the start of her ID to signal she's part of the Department of Tactical Defense, so we couldn't know each other.

But I want to know her. Her long hair is a gentle brown, darker at the wavy ends. The dark circles beneath her eyes suit her badass attitude, giving our nurses and doctors absolute hell the second they step into the Cement Box. It makes me laugh every time, which spurs her on in an improvised, beautiful rant. Other times, Fifty-Five won't say anything at all. She won't even sit up. She raises her leg in the air, holding people back with her bare foot smashed in their faces.

Her lionhearted comfort brings cheer to our whole group, but she's a complete nuisance to our captors. No one wants to work with us because of her. She's making the experiment impossible, just like I am.

Sometimes I'll open my eyes to find her staring at me first. Every time, she smiles back. I don't know if either of us has a reason why we stare or smile, besides the pure comfort that we're at least not alone. We witness each other.

I've physically broken at least 50 guards threatening to harm other patients, to the point where only 3 willing guards remain. Now, they're forced to take unmanageably long shifts all week.

But I'm too tired to get up and talk to Fifty-Five because of it, struggling to conserve my limited energy. I need it to fight for those who can't, including her. I hope she understands. If I had energy left to go sit with her, I would.

I hope her smile doesn't fade any day soon. That she keeps up hope.

I try my best to connect with my cellmates in the Deep Sleep Dimension, slicing into their black smoke cocoons. Once I'm inside their dreams, I beg them to settle on a simple escape plan. If we all rush the door together, they can't handle our collective force, no matter how disabled we are.

But everyone's too terrified to follow through. Many of these people are chronically ill civilians, made even sicker by S817. Their remaining hope in society has long since shattered.

The next time I wake up, my back is warm. It's unusual for our metal beds to be warm beneath the constant air conditioning, so…

Someone else is on my bed.

Something within me knows they're safe to be around, nuzzled into my back with their limp arm around my waist. I don't move them, fighting to remain still as I shed tears—instantaneous from being cuddled for the first time in years.

Studying their pale hand flopped in front of my chest, I can't shake the feeling that I know these fingers. But they're a deep reddish-purple between the frigid air, non-stop IVs, and poor blood circulation—unrecognizable, even if I tried.

I look up to check on the woman across the room. Her bed is empty.

I sit up in a panic, terrified we've lost her. Our resident fighter. My favorite fellow experimentee.

With a quick headcount, I spot 33 heads in the beds around me. I'm number 34. So the 35th person behind my back is…

Fifty-Five's expression contorts, distraught I've broken our body heat bundle.

I lay back down as fast as I can, tucking her limp arm around my waist like it was a moment ago. She's spooning me once more, her frustrated breath slowing against my exposed back. This gives me an excuse to warm her cold hand, cupping it in mine as I gape at the silent room around us.

We've never spoken, but she understood my dilemma. How

I was aching to sit beside her. To meet her. She *chose* to lay at *my* side. To provide me with an overwhelming, rare sense of comforting touch beyond the quick hugs I've received for kicking guard ass.

This is absolutely not allowed, which makes it even better.

I can't get over how she smells. We're all sweaty and share a disgusting single-person bathroom that we hardly have the energy to shower in, but she smells good to me in the most nostalgic way. I can't put my finger on it. She smells like home. Warmth. And she feels like it too. Her cold hand somehow warms me. I weep, the metal beneath my cheek clouding with my breath's heat.

It feels safe to sleep with her by my side.

In the Deep Sleep, a swirling black cloud encases another dreamer for the first time in months. I try my best not to raise my hopes, diving into the undulating smoke even as my nails rot off.

Throwing myself headfirst into the whited-out nothingness, I'm shaking with impatient excitement as I wait for my soul to reincorporate. To enter someone else's mind.

Then I see her brown hair. I'm so elated that I stand agape for a moment, watching her mull around in the white nothingness as I choke back tears.

Fifty-Five whips around at the sound of my joyous sobs. My laugh echoes as she cheers, bounding her way over with both arms flung high in the air.

She throws herself at me. I struggle to catch her in my embrace, too weak from laughter and the sudden, confusing pain in my heart.

Taking my cheeks in her gentle hands, Fifty-Five smiles with her delicate, gray eyes. We gaze at each other in awed silence. I'm so happy, I could kiss her. Actually, I almost do, catching myself just before I bend to meet her lips.

I don't know if she saw through my mistake, but her giggle proves she's up to something.

"Hi!" She breathes.

I laugh. "Hey."

We separate and sit on the floor. Neither of us can stop grinning, even if I stare at the white space between our crossed legs.

Fifty-Five chews on her lip. "I heard from someone else you have a plan?"

"Oh!" I perk up, startling her into a jump. We both laugh. "Sorry. I do have a plan. It's a simple one: messing with each other's sedation feeds until we're all timed to wake up on the same day, then charging the door together when the nurse rotates our feeds. It's not foolproof, but I'll protect everyone as they escape."

Her eyebrows furrow. "What does that mean, 'protect' them?"

She's the first person to ask. I pick at my fingernails, unsure what to say. "Well, I mean, I'll defend everyone from any guards trying to stop us."

"Right…"

"And I'll make sure I'm the last one out. Just in case I need to hold them off. To keep them occupied and make sure everyone else escapes."

Fifty-Five crosses her arms. "You're not doing that."

"Oh. Why not?"

"Because! I'm not leaving you behind, Fourteen!"

I smile. "You sound like an old friend of mine."

"Yeah, well, good. They sound like a good friend."

I laugh. "He really was."

Her expression softens. She leans closer, grabbing my hand to stop me from fidgeting. We stare into each other's eyes.

Fifty-Five says, "If you're set on that, then I'll be the last one out with you. The last two."

My heart clenches. "Okay, wait. You don't have to sacrifice yourself for—"

She raises her eyebrows, giving me the most contagious, mischievous smile I've ever seen. "Okay, *Mr. Sacrifice*. Give me a real reason why I shouldn't be your escape buddy, and I'll consider listening."

I laugh. "I'm your escape buddy?"

"Well, I have a heart condition and need someone to carry me. I can only run in short bursts without passing out. So, will you be?"

"Yes." My cheeks flush. "Of course I will. But why me?"

"Because I know your secret."

I freeze like I've been caught, even though I have zero clue what she's talking about.

Fifty-Five sighs. "You could've *easily* escaped already, Fourteen. On your own."

I bite my lips, unable to hold eye contact with her anymore. "Please don't point that out to anyone else."

"What the hell is keeping you here, though?" She scoffs. "It better not be some fucked-up version of punishing yourself."

I shake my head no, but that's not enough for her. She crosses her arms, and I know I'm in trouble. "Okay, fine. I don't think I'm the greatest person, but that's not why I'm here. I just couldn't imagine leaving. I'd feel horrible leaving everyone here to— Well…"

"Leaving us here to die, you mean?"

I nod, wary of Fifty-Five's response. If I shared the full truth, I'd tell her I especially don't want to leave *her*, but that sounds totally creepy. This is the first time we've spoken, yet I'm feeling things for her that I shouldn't. Powerful, gut-twisting emotions. I've had them for a long time.

Even though she's irritated, she breaks into a smile the second we lock eyes. "The truth is, I like you, Fourteen. That's why I want to be your escape buddy. I don't *know*-know you, but I like your smile. And I like the way you think of other people." She squeezes my hand before letting it go. "But I *don't* like how you sacrifice yourself for all of us. It's not fair to you. So I'll be the one to make sure you get out alive."

I can't smile anymore. "What about you? What if I drag you down?"

"You won't. We're both survivors by nature."

My heart swells in the face of her confidence. It inspires

a strength, down to my soul, that I haven't cultivated for a long time.

It may be violent and messy, but the escape is a fight I can get behind—intended to save lives rather than end them. It feels like me.

"Okay," I say. "Let's do it."

She grins until her upturned nose scrunches at the top, and we laugh together. We laugh as we plan the escape details to my parents' safe cabin in the forest, giddy with excitement. We laugh as we recall previous examples of the remaining guards' weaknesses, according to our obnoxious antics. We laugh just to finally laugh.

My face hurts in the best way. So when she abruptly awakens without me, ripping her from this dimension, it kills me.

Enough to startle me awake.

My sedatives are still pumping full-course, leaving my vision in a bleary haze, but it's easy to see what's wrong. Fifty-Five clings to my bed's edge with panicked screams. A guard yanks her off the bed, yelling and reaching for his taser as she protests.

I don't think I've punched someone so hard in my life. 5 of us awake dreamers watch the guard go limp where he stands, far before he hits the ground with a resounding thud.

"Is he… dead?" Twelve, my bed-neighbor, asks.

"I… I don't know." Fifty-Five rubs the bright red handprints on her arms.

Twenty-Three, a retired nurse, slips her fingers to the guard's neck. "He's alive. For now."

I slouch to the floor. "Sorry. I didn't mean to hit so hard."

Everyone mumbles reassurances, checking the glass door over their shoulders.

Then excitement hits me; the guard didn't have time to call for backup. We're alone until his shift ends. *Unmonitored.*

We have a little under seven hours to wake everyone up. To escape.

Fifty-Five meets my eyes, the same deviance flashing through her wide stare. "Hey, Fourteen, do you know how to tie a good knot?"

After stopping our sedatives, we tear pieces off our hospital gowns until we can fashion a sturdy enough rope. While Twenty-Three inserts her next round of IV sedatives into the guard's arm, I allow Fifty-Five the honors of flipping off the security camera, seconds before I disassemble it, popping apart the lens and internal microphone wiring without making a sound. Now that no one can hear us on playback, Fifty-Five fills in the awake dreamers on the plan—the modified plan, happening *now*—and I tie the sedated guard to my bed, bind his mouth with some leftover cloth, and strip his weapons.

It feels weird to hold a gun after all these years—weird enough to place it as far away as possible within arm's reach. The guard doesn't have a tactical knife, souring my mood.

"I can't *sprint*. Where will I even go, out there?" Sixty-One, the oldest man among us, hisses behind my back.

"Follow me into the forest," I say. "I'll protect you from behind and go at your speed."

"The fucking *cursed forest?* Hell no."

I shrug. "I understand your concerns, Sixty-One. It's not a baseless rumor or a superstition; it *is* 'cursed,' in a way—with electromagnetic radiation. But I know of a safehouse there. The people there have technology that'll block out the EMR 'curse,' so to speak. These guys don't have it, so they won't chase us."

"I don't see you holding this miraculous, otherwise undiscovered tech. Don't people die within fucking minutes? Where the hell are you going to find something like that?"

"I don't know. I just have to hope my family's still alive, and that we can somehow alert them to give us blockers on the outskirts."

Sixty-One eyes his fellow awake dreamers, waiting for someone to take his side. When no one does, some muttering how dying in a cursed forest still beats dying here, he scoffs, stomping back to his bed in the corner. Fifty-Five meets my eyes with a suppressed smile, and we both struggle not to laugh out loud.

Fifty-Five stands, addressing the entire group. "You're welcome to follow us, but Fourteen and I can't help you if you split off on your own. The choice is completely up to you. We'll guide you out of the Cement Box either way. Right, Fourteen?"

"Right, Fifty-Five." I hide my blushing smile, turning my back to unhook another dreamer from their sedatives.

It takes four hours for everyone to wake up and another two to get everyone coherent enough to move their bodies. Exhaustion creeps in. But I'm afraid if any of us take a nap, we won't be able to wake up from how accustomed we are to sleeping for days at a time.

An hour remains to escape the cell. Once we exit the Cement Box, people will come after us, guaranteed, so we're only racing the clock for the next guard's shift.

But I'm counting on our guardless head start. I need it to station everyone safely behind me... before I become the Wolf.

"How long do you think we've been held here?" I whisper to Fifty-Five.

"Hmm." She furrows her brows, huddling up to my side. The sudden closeness between us makes my heart throb. "It's impossible to know, really. I'm guessing a couple years, judging by your hair length."

"Yeah, me too," I say. Fifty-Five stares at me expectantly, so I continue, "I asked because I'm not sure what it'll look like out there anymore. It might look worse than in here."

She laughs. But then she realizes I'm serious. "*Worse?* Like how?"

"Like, there might be a lot of... decay."

"Of people?" When I nod, she gasps, her eyes darting around the room. Fifty-Five inches closer to lower our voices further. "What makes you say that?"

"I recognized the superweapons that started about a month or two ago. They make that weird metallic *ping*. They... don't leave much behind."

She studies my eyes for the truth. "Did you help make them?"

"No. I've been a test subject, long before this. I was the only one who outran those."

I turn away, not looking forward to her reaction to my weird life. Cool hands slip around my waist, squeezing me into a melting warmth as her body heat spreads across my bare back.

"I'm so sorry," she whispers. "I'm sorry you've seen worse than this."

I can't believe she believes me. It tempts me to cry.

After a moment of enjoying her comfort, I grasp her hand, turning to face her again. "Maybe it was so I could help you all escape without fear. So I could be the unbothered one."

"But you're *not* unbothered." She gives our interlaced hands a knowing, scolding squeeze, and I laugh.

"No, I'm not. But I'll have to seriously injure anyone who tries to stop us, and pretend I'm unbothered by my actions. I do care, and I'll try not to hurt anyone too badly, but this is life and death. I won't blame you if you never want to see me again after this, okay?"

She opens her mouth with a rebuttal, but something stops her. "Okay."

Fifty-Five gives me a wary smile. With a heavy sigh, I gather the courage to tuck the guard's handgun into its holster, hooking his utility belt around my waist. Unfortunately, it's about five sizes too big for my emaciated body. It clatters to the floor the second I drop the belt, so I resort to strapping it over my left shoulder. Then I use a leftover hospital gown scrap to tie the top half of my long hair.

Fifty-Five and I make sure everyone has an escape buddy. We pair our strongest runners with five dreamers who can't walk, allowing them to ride out the escape on wheeled metal beds. But by "strong runners," I mean those of us who don't stumble around enough to passably jog. I'm trying not to show it, but if the DoTD is still outside, we're screwed.

"So, the plan is to conserve, conserve, conserve," Fifty-Five says. "If we don't have to run, don't. Save that energy for when it's absolutely necessary. Once Fourteen and I call out to run, don't look back and *go*. Go as far as you can and find shelter. As for the trackers in your arms…"

"I'll find a knife and antiseptics on our way out of the Cement Box," I say. "Line up in front of me, and I'll slice it out of your arm."

"Will you be able to numb us first?" Eight asks.

Fifty-Five bites back a laugh. "No, Eight. No, we will not. I don't think they know numbing cream exists in this shithole."

"It doesn't really hurt, anyway," I say.

Everyone, including Fifty-Five, shoots me a skeptical glance. They must view my opinion on pain as weightless. Blatantly ignoring me as I laugh at myself, they carry on, rehashing the plan.

But by the time we're all ready to go, I have a horrible feeling.

"What?" Fifty-Five asks. "What's wrong?"

"We have to leave. *Now*," I say.

The entire room falls silent.

A few people question me, telling me we still have another thirty minutes or so until the guard's shift ends, but Fifty-Five stops them. "I believe him. Something feels off."

I open the door with the guard's keycard, peeking down the hall. It's silent. We funnel into the narrow hallway, anxiety urging everyone toward the door.

"Back up," Fifty-Five yell-whispers.

No one over 40 listens to her in an unspoken display of sexism, and I hate it. I squat, offering to lift her onto my back. She giggles, hopping onto me. At our combined height, she towers over the entire group. Everyone falls silent, captivated by her regal aura.

"Listen to me closely from now on. We *have* to work together," Fifty-Five says.

Once they actually take a moment to listen to her, no one questions her. She has a savior's voice.

Fifty-Five continues, "Do *not* trample each other. Everyone will make it out. We'll *all* work to make sure of it."

The dreamers nod, and I can't erase my smile. I feel better already.

After allowing the metal bed buddies to squeeze themselves ahead of the pack, I open the hallway door. Again, we're the only sign of life.

We pass through the sterile halls, doing our best to remain perfectly silent minus the nerve-wrackingly squeaky bed wheels. Apparently, our Cement Box is one cubby of an even larger Cement Box, and the neighboring boxes are empty.

I part from the group to snatch a scalpel, a gauze pad tub, and plenty of antiseptic swabs from a supply room. The doorknob doesn't have a lock, so it takes mere seconds.

As everyone waits their turn to have their arm sliced in pure silence, I'm starting to get antsy, sensing everyone else pushing the group from behind. Fifty-Five, at the pack's head, raises her hands to tell everyone to give each other space.

I weave my way back to her side, and it settles my nerves a little. As I flick the tracker out from her left arm, I wince along with her.

"Hey, that wasn't too bad," she whispers.

I smile, swapping the guard key between my teeth with the scalpel handle. "Don't say that too soon."

My timing is painful. Once we open the exit with the guard key, an alarm starts.

"Whoops," Fifty-Five laughs it off.

But I can't laugh; I see what she hasn't yet.

We can't run as planned. We're not on the ground floor—we're at an equivalent height to Sumner Hospital's top floor, separated by a thin bridge.

Above the city.

The only way out is through the hospital.

CHAPTER 47

Fifty-Five

"Alright, so maybe this is a *little* bad." I chase after Fourteen like a floppy seal.

He motions to follow him with a sharp wave. I'm sure his urgency is because of that fucking alarm, but part of me wonders if it's because we're hovering over a literal 100-foot death drop, speed-walking across a narrow metal bridge with nothing beneath us except asphalt. It's a panic attack waiting to happen amongst severely ill individuals.

I make the mistake of looking down, and my head spins. Luckily, I have my escape buddy. He cinches me tight to his side with a firm arm, keeping me on my feet.

Turning over my shoulder, I'm hit with a wave of the dreamers' pure fear. Straightening my back, I steady my shaking voice. "Look straight ahead at the dreamer in front of you, and nothing else. Move as quickly as you're physically able to."

But we run into a serious problem.

"Stop!" A man in all black and a tinted helmet screams. He's holding a "rifle" of some sort, but it doesn't look normal.

Fourteen steps in front of me before I can react. With his hospital gown fluttering to his sides, Niko marches deadpan toward the loaded barrel. Just his agitated back sends a chill down my spine, and I'm not alone. The armed man shrieks, cowering on the ground from Fourteen's mere *approach*.

The second Fourteen disarms the attacker, slicing his wrist tendons with the scalpel, it sinks in: Fourteen is not a normal human being. His warning about what I might see him do was a serious one. I don't know how to feel about it.

But then I feel his concern for us. He swings the confiscated weapon over his shoulder, shooting us a mother bear's apprehensive glance. "Stay in a line behind me. Don't even give them a *limb* to target. These aren't regular weapons, and I have a feeling they'll gladly blow us apart. Let me be your shield."

"Hey, no," I hiss, gripping his arm. "I'm not letting you sacrifice yourself, remember?"

His dark eyes soften for me. But when we open the door at the bridge's end, we're met with clunky footsteps charging up the stairs.

Fourteen unhooks a cased weapon off the wailing, limp-handed man at his feet. Grinning as he whips out a scary knife, Fourteen flips the blade over his knuckles faster than I can track. And he laughs, really *laughs*. It sounds… wolven.

But wolven is what we need him to be. Masked men lunge at us, one after another, as we enter the hospital. It's hard to look away from the violence unfolding, but I have to redirect my focus. To urge the last dreamers over the bridge while Fourteen uses the knife to physically disable anyone who approaches us.

He's slashing bodies in graceful, *horrific* motions, all while muttering ridiculous things to himself like, "How do you like my gown, honey? You picked it out for me."

This is the scariest moment of my life, but I find myself laughing with him. He's been silent for years, but now that he's finally opening his mouth, he sounds as damaged as… well, me.

"What now, Fifty-Five?" Fourteen's pupils are dilated and jumpy. It looks like his body unleashed a hormonal version of speed.

Everyone who approached us has sprinted in the opposite direction, well-aware they're no match. We're at a crossroads. Fourteen nods me toward the stairs versus the elevator.

Our initial plan was for me to act as a Guide while he does the grunt work. But this is a terrifying decision to make alone. If we choose the stairs, I don't know how the metal bed dreamers will make it down. And if we choose the elevator, we won't all fit. We'd have to take separate elevators with no way to protect everyone. But we're supposed to be in this together, so there's only one shitty option.

I turn around, met with a horde of petrified eyes. "Who's capable of carrying some weight? At least two people per metal bed, and help whoever you can down the stairs."

We're a fumbling disaster, but we make it down one floor. Then the next.

I didn't realize Fourteen had blood on him, but now he furiously scrubs at his skin, verging on panic. I grab his elbow just in time, making sure he doesn't miss the last step onto the seventh floor. For whatever reason, the way he looks at me in surprise makes me smile. Maybe it's to reassure him, or maybe it's because that's all we've been doing for years. Silently giving each other a reason to trudge on.

He shoots me a shy glance, startling me as he pulls me into his chest on the final step. But the surprise cuddle is only because someone charged up behind me.

They don't last long.

I'm trying not to theorize why Fourteen seems to hit my assailants harder. A flash of desperation in his energy ripples through me as he protects me. Like it terrifies him to see me nearly hurt. But maybe he does that with everyone. We *do* have a silent connection, but I'm not sure how he feels about it. I've hardly heard him speak in his luxuriously gentle voice before today, and I don't want to get needlessly attached. With him, it's too strong of a connection to survive if I'm let down. His smile is the only thing I've had to look forward to for years.

Fourteen has confiscated more weapons than he can hold, so now I have a few strapped onto my back. The people we've encountered won't bother us again, even if Fourteen let them live. If they're not wounded enough as it is, they'd have to work through severe primal fear before returning. Or to be even more afraid of someone else.

On the fourth floor, we find "someone else." Someone our attackers are both terrified of and taking orders from.

A Commanding Officer bursts through the stairway door, yelling demands to his cowering unit as they retreat without permission. I don't understand his words, but I don't need to. He has the energy of a bull.

Fourteen wastes no time. It's the first time I've seen him struggle in a fight since we were placed in the Cement Box. The Commander seems feral.

A memory worms its way through my head as Fourteen struggles beneath him on the floor. Something that feels important.

But this isn't the time for reminiscing. I can't stomach standing back and watching another second. Striding up to the Commander, I tear off his helmet and start beating him with it. He *definitely* doesn't appreciate that.

Fourteen's eyes bulge as the Commander grasps for my hair, but I'm yanked backward into a man's chest—one weapon short.

"Stand back, Fifty-Five," Sixty-One hisses, aiming the gun at the Commander's head.

I'm not a gun expert, but I don't think "gun" is the right word. It's jet-black, but it has a liquid tank compartment to replace the ammunition. The ammunition tank walls look comically thick, but I can still feel heat emanating from it. The energy I sense from the liquid is *putrid*.

When Sixty-One pulls the trigger, I'm temporarily blinded by the light bursting from it. Fourteen scrambles out of the way, tackling me into a bunch of dreamers. Before we can berate him for bowling us into a heap, we're stunned silent at the sight before us. My ears are still ringing from the screeching metal *ping*, but I'm too distracted to care.

There's no top half to the Commander. I don't think I can mentally assemble his torso back together, smeared across the walls like strawberry jelly. And I don't have time to.

"Don't look! Keep running!" Fourteen yells, snatching the weapon from Sixty-One's hands. "Don't think about it, Sixty-One."

Sixty-One hobbles between Fourteen and me, hardly able to fumble down the stairs. "I just— K-ki-*killed*—"

"I know. Trust me, I *understand*." Fourteen's eyes have dimmed, mirroring the dull ache I feel in his core. "Don't think about it, not right now."

Sixty-One can't shake himself off. "What just— I'm a gun owner, and I— What *is* that thing?"

I give Sixty-One a side hug, urging him forward. "Sixty-One, what do you want to do once you're free?"

He stares like I've lost my mind, but Fourteen illuminates in realization of my intentions.

"Everyone, tell us your life dream. One by one," Fourteen says. "Starting with Sixty-One."

It takes Sixty-One a while, but eventually, he whispers, "I want a new dog."

"What kind of dog?" I ask. "What will you do together?"

Sixty-One wants to adopt a hunting dog from a shelter, one calm enough to lay at his feet while he fishes. Someone recommends a few different breeds of setters, retrievers, and pointers.

Eight wants to write a fucked-up memoir about all this and retire 20 years early. Plenty of us second him.

Twenty-Three wants to take sewing classes and start a small throw pillow business. We'd get a trauma-family discount, of course, but none of us are willing to take it.

We each focus on something to strive for as we barrel down the stairs, slipping, panting, and trying not to pass out from how horrific we feel. *This* type of dreaming gives us a purpose for running ahead. And we need it; the whole cavalry is set on stopping us.

Somehow, we reach the first floor. Fourteen stops at the hospital's glass entrance to check for more ambushers on the streets. When he finds nothing, he urges us forward. We try our best to drag everyone out the doors, but with the end in sight, everyone is so desperate that they're making careless errors.

As my peers scramble out the hospital doors like severed worms, my gut churns with dread. Something bad is coming.

The hospital PA system chimes, revealing a familiar voice.

"No survivors," Sumner says. I can hear his smile. "Fire at will."

A marching horde startles us from behind, metal-pinging weapons raised. With a death trap coming straight for us, a stampede is inevitable. Before I can lose sight of my escape buddy, he scoops me off my feet with a powerful hug beneath my ribcage, dangling my legs in the air.

We try to yell at everyone to stay calm, but we only manage a few screaming orders before Twenty-Three is obliterated in front of us all.

I can't hear myself scream, but I can feel it with my whole body. The screeching weapons must be damaging our ears, leaving me in sudden silence. And we have to *move* if we want to avoid these "bullets." If it weren't for Fourteen's infallible focus, I'd be carpet jelly.

I feel like I'm watching a silent, unnecessarily convincing horror film. The sight of drugged, armed men racing after skeletal adults sends a flashback through my system of a warzone I witnessed once. I can tell it's the same memory attempting to surface from earlier, but I'm confused; I've never been on a battlefield. Regardless, I see a vision of someone sprinting from white-hot orbs, their terrified breath panting in my ears.

The flashback ends, and I still can't hear, but the sensation of someone's exhausted breath doesn't stop. I realize it's Fourteen wheezing against my bare back, and the actual battlefield is happening *now*.

Fourteen yells something, but I can't understand him. I can only read his lips as he sets me on my feet. "Run," he mouths, wide eyes pleading with me as he puts his entire body into the single-syllable word. "*Run.*"

So we do. The hot asphalt sends painful shockwaves through my creaky limbs, but that's hardly a problem compared to being blasted to mincemeat. Fourteen yanks on my arms to redirect me, keeping me out of firing range. It's almost to a fault, forcing him to miss a wide-sailing shot that even *I* could see in time. When I yank him out of the way of fire, he looks at me like I'm a god granting his second life. Somehow, I'm still able to smile. He has no idea how much of a hero he is. That he's the *only* reason I'm here.

When my hearing returns, I feel even less human. None of this seems real. Where buildings lined the street, only a quarter remains amongst towering slabs of scorched rubble. Another dreamer ceases to exist with every minute that passes. Tanks hum a few blocks away as our bare feet hammer the asphalt, sprinting as far as our legs allow. Megaphone orders strategize how to gain a better angle on us.

They're exterminating bugs.

I grip Fourteen's arm, choking out my words. "Don't you have a gun?"

"Unfortunately." He frowns, plucking it from the holster strapped across his chest, and fires off a few rounds.

I hadn't realized how much returning fire would slow us down, but Fourteen must've, so I hope my inexperienced suggestion was worth it. I do a double-take when I look back to find half the men after us writhing around on the floor, mostly with hand or leg injuries.

"Fuck," he mutters, stretching his firing hand. "This isn't my specialty. I almost hit an artery on that last one." Then he continues returning fire. Fourteen notices my shocked stare and laughs. "Told you I'm a monster."

"*Please* keep being a monster," I grunt, struggling to stay on my feet. My heart is pounding so hard that my vision warps in waves, like throbbing liquid on a thumping speaker.

Fourteen heaves me onto his shoulders in a fireman's carry, but I can tell it slows us down. Between both my decisions in a matter of seconds, we've lost the distance we gained. The guilt crushes me, panic crawling up my throat.

Just like in private school, I'm the one holding everyone back.

With a six-and-a-half-foot view of our surroundings, I can see the true monsters clearer. The Tactical Defense unit members don't look bothered by eviscerating us. Worse than this situation seeming normal to them, they think their actions are *justified*. My entire existence can't convince them otherwise. It shakes me to my core, making me cry out in fear above Fourteen's head. The sound of my own scream makes it real, echoing in my head over and over again to remind me how long this trauma will last.

Fourteen grasps me tighter, his rasping lungs begging for air. "I've got you! You're alive."

He's convincing us both. Especially when we round a corner and he lets out an exasperated groan.

This. This metal-pinging *cannon.* This is what I saw producing deadly white-hot orbs in my flashback, not those *baby* "rifles." Our fate hits hard, the cannon's molten core charging up before our eyes. I know what that's about to look like—what *we're* about to look like—and taking cover is impossible unless we cross the street to the next building. The blast will be too wide to clear otherwise.

Fourteen's panic mortifies my body, his feet digging even harder into the eroded asphalt as the metallic ping pierces the air. I tighten my muscles, attempting to lessen my weight for him. I can't do much else. He throws us across the last stretch of crosswalk, my side crashing to the ground in just the right way to knock the air out of me and freeze my diaphragm. That's not enough to overcome my cannon fear, clinging to Fourteen as we squeeze past the nearest building's edge. Our backs are blasted with hot air, terrifying me into finally sucking in a breath.

For a moment, I wonder if I'm on fire; Fourteen rolls over me on the ground with heaving gasps. He's patting me down like he's putting a fire out, but then I realize the fire is his anxiety. He's checking to make sure all of my body is still here, horrified with the prospect of my potential loss when *he's* the one who was behind *me*—the last to safety. Staring up into his bulging, black eyes, I don't think I've ever felt so loved.

"We're okay!" I croak, rising to my feet. "We're okay!" It's my turn to pull on his arms, dragging his heavy feet down the sidewalk.

I can finally see the forest peeking through the city alleyways. This gives us a silent push forward, magnetizing us toward our life-saving goal.

Fourteen looks behind us, sucking in short, horrified breaths.

"What are you doing?! Run!" I yell.

He snaps out of it, a little more wide-eyed than before. "*The dreamers.*"

My hope evacuates my heart; he's right. *Everyone* fucking *died*.

We're the sole survivors. And I think I need Fourteen to live in order to mentally, emotionally survive *that*.

"Don't look back!" I scream, tugging him forward. "Survive! Please, survive!"

He takes my pleading to heart, lacing our fingers and flying down the street. Tears gush down his hollow cheeks.

I had a foolish hope they'd give up once we gained enough distance—dodged them enough times to simmer down their vengeance. My vindictive side is taking over now, their poison seeping through me as they, in fact, continue to bombard us.

I'm not sure how either of our bodies is still functioning, but mine hardly is. By the time they're following us in a massive SUV, participating in a ridiculously unfair shootout with Fourteen and somehow still losing against him epically as he sneaks us through back alleyways, I'm about to pass the fuck out. Fourteen hoists me onto his back, darting down the closest narrow alleyway he can find to evade anymore cars.

But Fourteen *stops running*. It feels instinctually incorrect, tempting me to panic again.

A disgusting energy accosts our immediate surroundings. I squirm out of Fourteen's arms to look, but he tucks me behind him, his shoulders tensing toward his ears.

At the end of the alleyway, a black SUV barricades our exit. Dr. Sumner hops out of the passenger's seat, dusting his clothes like it's just another day at work.

That malicious craving for revenge spikes back up in my blood. I can tell Dr. Sumner is about to open his mouth, and neither of us will like what he has to say. The men around him charge up their weapons, preparing to aim at us. But there isn't the same deadly intention behind their movements—a hesitation they haven't shown until now. Something is different.

"Fourteen," I hiss.

He isn't listening, unblinking as he tracks Sumner's every move. We know Sumner well by now, so I understand Fourteen's silent, curdling fear, as well as his fingers twitching toward his weapon stash.

The men flinch at Fourteen's rising hand, so I grip his fingers, securing him against my side. I'm not sure why, but Fourteen's panic increases my taste for blood. I'm not just "seeing red," I'm envisioning a strawberry jelly smear of a doctor at our feet.

I refuse to let Sumner speak another poisonous word.

When I step in front of Fourteen, his energy bombards me

into halting in place—frigid, catastrophic dread piercing my thoughts. Fourteen forces me behind him again, and I don't even know if he's thinking about it. His eyes are primal.

But I catch something he doesn't; they lowered their weapons when I was the one in front.

"How do you fire these weapons?" I whisper.

Fourteen's head slowly turns, his eyes igniting in a different type of fear.

Sumner sucks in a breath to laugh, his smile crumpling his cheeks. Until I step back in front of Fourteen.

Just like last time, the men lower their weapons. They're not going to shoot me.

I have to act fast, rebelling against both Sumner and my unstoppable escape buddy. It throws Fourteen off when I hoist one of the metal-pinging weapons from my back—probably because I almost pointed it at him like a reckless freak and he had to dodge the barrel—but I can't let my mistake faze me. I have to look confident. Purposeful. I sink as deep as I can into my need to murder.

The look on my face alone is enough to silence Sumner. His smile drops as I raise the weapon, aiming for his head. Everyone seems to move at once as I fumble around, clicking off the safety far easier than I think should be legal. And to my own surprise, I willingly pull the trigger.

As soon as the heat releases, knocking me backward into Fourteen's panicked chest, I'm struck with intense, confusing feelings about what I've done. I've never come close to killing a person in my lifetime, and I didn't think I'd start today. Yet I've now attempted it. I have no clue if I've succeeded; my detonation's flashing light forces me to squeeze my eyes shut.

Fourteen disarms me and drags me down the alley before I open my eyes. We're back on the main streets by the time the SUV explodes in a ground-shaking boom.

Fourteen breaks through his fight-or-flight silence, throwing his head back in rabid laughter. He keeps us running, dragging my stunned face forward. "You blew up their fucking shootout car!" He shouts, rejoicing toward the sky.

"S-Sumner— Did I?!" I croak, unable to form a full thought.

"No, but he won't fuck with *you* again!" Fourteen continues to cackle.

I breathe out my relief, hardly able to laugh. I almost killed a man, and it was *completely* intentional. Even now, I only regret missing. This is a thought I vow to keep to myself, running for the growing trees on the horizon.

CHAPTER 48

Fifty-Five

Darting through the park, it's somehow more terrifying than running barefoot through martial law streets. It's far too open. Hiding is unfathomable as they shoot from a distance, hell-bent on killing us.

We're nearing the treeline with every step, betting on the forest's ability to shelter us. So far, I have a good feeling about our plan. Their distance from us is widening—they're lagging as they reassemble their units with awkward, cumbersome equipment—but this only means they fire off more rounds in an attempt to reach us. They want us downright *obliterated*, not just dead.

And we're traveling on sloppy feet. Fourteen has to pick me up for the umpteenth time, and I groan in frustration. "I hate how I'm like this."

"Well, I'll probably pass out too if we have to keep this up, so you're not alone." And it's true; he's struggling to breathe as much as I am.

I can feel him quivering beneath me, and it makes me cling to him tighter, wishing I could magic away our pain. It feels like weeks have passed since I decided to cuddle his frail body this morning, hating the sight of him shivering alone across the room.

They gain on us, of course, and this time, they're far from letting up. Watching our backs slows Fourteen more than his exhaustion, so I cling to Fourteen like a koala, counting the energies barraging us; I've decided to Guide Fourteen to safety.

He understands what I'm doing without explanation, submitting to my warnings about which direction to go. The shots fire toward his back, but he no longer turns around to spot them. It startles me how much he trusts me. My throat tightens in doubt of myself, at least until Fourteen sharply readjusts me in his arms and the jolting movement shocks my soul back into my body.

I clear my mind to retain my nerves, but it's not enough. I can't warn Fourteen of every man swarming us, flooding the park with trucks, cars, SUVs, and in the distance, slow-rolling tanks.

Fourteen shrieks.

It's a sound I never expected to hear from him, so I wonder if he was somehow shot. But as I turn to see what his eyes are locked onto, I spot two human beings. They're sprinting toward us so fast they look animalistic. They've identified themselves by removing their helmets, and I recognize them both.

Coming to our aid are two old friends; Lilith, my ex-girlfriend, and Jay, my *dead* friend.

Except Jay is clearly *not* dead. Sweeping to our side with a familiar smirk, Jay hunts our hunters like this is a normal day. He disarms the men in the distance by shooting their firing arms, just like Fourteen. When Lilith charges in from behind Jay to take over, Jay sprints toward us. I watch in petrified awe as Lilith slaughters hordes in seconds, forcing them back with her expertise alone.

"Don't you fucking cry, Wolf!" Jay cackles, his voice booming behind my back. I expect Fourteen to set me down, but I'm even higher in the air, moving *faster*.

I look down to find Jay holding Fourteen, who is still holding me. Fourteen and I look at each other and warily laugh, joy still foreign to us.

"What the fuck, Jay?! Are you superhuman?!" I scrub his rich, brown curls.

He snickers, charging on ahead. "Pretty much! I *really* know how to run now! Right, Wolf?"

Wolf must be Fourteen's nickname, unless that's his name-name. It suits him: fierce, but in the name of loving loyalty.

Fourteen lets out a breathless laugh, more like a whimper.

It's clear to Jay and me that he's unable to speak, marveling at Jay's existence.

"Here come the guys!" Jay beams.

Traitors spill from the trees. I would never have noticed them if Jay hadn't pointed them out, slithering from the tree roots in complete silence until they start firing.

I peek over my shoulder to find no one chasing us anymore. They don't want to; Lilith is leading the traitor army.

Before the traitors can get close enough to cause genuine damage, our attackers scramble away, giving Lilith the widest radius. She struts across the forest's outer rim, flinging her rifle in proud circles. I shiver. She's not just a terrifying force—some part of her enjoys this. She's playing.

"Oh, my God," I whisper. "They're retreating at the *sight* of her."

Fourteen huffs a short laugh, croaking out a shaky, "Yep, that's my sister."

"Wait, what?!" My heart stops, fumbling over itself. I grip Fourteen's shoulder, and he jumps in surprise. "I dated her once."

Fourteen juts his chin back in shock. "You dated *my* sister?"

"Uh, guys?" Jay's feet dance through the knotted tree roots, the forest thickening by the millisecond. "What in the actual fuck are you saying?"

"W-what? What do you mean?" Fourteen asks.

Jay looks at us with the most contorted, confused face I can imagine. "Oh, my fucking *god*. You're both *serious?* Okay, nevermind. I think you're more fucked up than you realize."

Fourteen and I gape at each other, reflecting pure perplexity.

"Don't worry, we'll get you sorted! ...I think." Jay takes a heavy, burdened breath as we slow to a steady fast-walk, and I know it's not because he's tired.

"Jay, what—" I start, but Fourteen stares at me so curiously that I lose all thought.

"You know Jay too?" His focus is unwavering. "My *best friend?*"

Now it's sinking in: something is amiss. I couldn't be tied to Fourteen's intimate circle without knowing him. Not in the Departments.

Before I can speak, Lilith approaches us from behind.

"You two okay?" She calls out.

"They're fucking *alive!* Can you believe it?!" Jay beams, setting us down. "But, uh— Something's going on here, Lils."

Lilith strides up and punches Jay in the arm. "Stop making my name sound cute. It's weird."

"There are more— Uh— Pressing problems right now, *Blackwood.* With these two."

Jay eyes us up and down, and I realize I'm clinging to Fourteen's hospital gown like a nervous duckling. As I step away, Fourteen continues to stare at the ground, his brain overstimulated with information. But he can't let go of my hand, almost like he's afraid to. Until Jay steps into his personal space, sorting out Fourteen's frazzled, long hair.

"Look at you: a true Lionheart!" Jay chuckles.

Fourteen doesn't seem to hear him. He lifts his shaky hands toward Jay's face, hesitating to touch him like Jay might evaporate into forest mist.

Clearing his throat, Jay drops his eyes. "Bro, I— I'm so fucking sorry. I really thought you'd make it out of the hospital on your own, otherwise I would've come back for y—"

"Jay!" Fourteen crumbles against Jay's chest. He lets out an agonizing sob that echoes through the forest, shaking my heart's depths. True grief, vocalized. "You died!"

"*That's* what's wrong? I didn't die, bro." Jay chuckles softly, cradling Fourteen's vibrating, limp body. It's a shocking contrast to the athletic resiliency I just witnessed in Fourteen. "You told me to run, so I ran."

"Part of me died with you." Fourteen's quiet words sink into us all, dissolving our energy into sympathetic pain.

Jay nuzzles into him, soothing Fourteen's violent tears with soft strokes of his long hair. By the severe shattering in Jay's emotional energy, I'm surprised by how well he's keeping himself from crying. It's enough to make *me* weep.

"It's okay, bro. I've got you now. Our unit of two is back together. It's all going to be okay."

"Will it?" Fourteen whispers.

He means it. I bite my lips, huddling into Lilith for comfort. I'm terrified of the answer to Fourteen's question just the same.

"Yes, I promise you." Jay embraces him tighter. "Your baby sister is alive and safe in the cabin." With these words, Fourteen cries out in relief. Jay smiles. "You've got parents waiting for you, and a whole crew ready to defend your life. It's time to be loved, bro."

My tears fall with Fourteen's. He meets my eyes with an elation amongst so much grief, and I'm convinced we'll be alright.

Jay and Fourteen stand in a cuddle ball for a while, not wanting to budge. I don't know what to do with myself, but thankfully, Lilith holds me close, giving me a grounding squeeze.

With Fourteen glued to his side, Jay seems to shine brighter. "Don't you worry, Ricky. You'll be the safest woman in the forest between us three."

I give Jay a grateful smile, but something in his words unsettles me. I can't remember if Jay knows my parents or not, but I hope they're okay. Alive, at least.

Our escape's gravity sinks in. No matter how much I want to, I can't forget that the dreamers all died. Everyone but us.

We start down the forest path, distancing ourselves from the armed men behind us. But Fourteen is quickly winded, squatting into the dirt. It shatters my heart.

I dash to his side. "I'm so sorry! I made you run while carrying me for *so long!* I owe you my fucking life."

Fourteen shakes his head, grabbing fistfuls of leaves. "How did this happen? Any of this?"

"We heard firing and came running to help," Lilith says, nonchalant. "We rescue people all the time."

"Yup!" Jay grins. I've *so* missed his gloating. "The safehouse cabin is fucking huge, man! We wanna fill the place up with survivors eventually, so Lilith and I make daily runs. All that brainwashing finally paid off for something good, dude."

Lilith gives a rare smile. "Although, we didn't know we'd be rescuing our best friends today."

"Best… friends?" Fourteen whispers, at his sanity's edge.

He looks up at me with fresh unfamiliarity, and I'm just as

stunned. I can't place if Lilith meant that we're each separately close, or if *all four of us* were once best friends. It can't be the latter, right?

"Um, Lilith?" Jay's concern overrides his confidence. "I think I need to talk to you. Privately. Now."

After hooking radiation blockers onto our hospital gowns, Lilith steps over Fourteen's hunched back. "We need to keep moving as soon as you can, but this forest is too confusing for newcomers to navigate. Stay close."

She's satisfied with my nod, trudging ahead with Jay as they whisper to each other. Fourteen and I know they're talking about us, but neither of us mentions it. This mystery is too exhausting to solve. I'm still trying to process my gutted, wavering happiness that we're alive.

But I don't know how to help this crumpled shell of a man next to me. We're vibrating with more than just anxiety and adrenaline—we're trapped in the mindset of prey. I'm terrified we'll never stop feeling victimized. Unwillingly vulnerable. I'm even afraid of my crushing fear. That it might dissolve the rest of me, leaving me only with my primal core. Or it might glue us to the forest floor, just long enough for someone to come find us and devour us alive.

I can feel Fourteen feeling the absolute same, and although I hate that for him, it's oddly comforting. At least one person gets it. Gets me.

Maybe it's a message from the universe, or maybe it's my survival-mode talking, but a voice in my head tells me to *just get through today*. And if today is too much, then just the next minute. The next second. That sounds much more manageable.

I sit beside Fourteen, resting a hand on his heaving back. "Do *I* need to carry *you* now?"

It starts off small, but eventually, he huffs out a genuine laugh. Rising to his feet, Fourteen gives me a weary smile. I weave beneath his arm, draping a bit of his weight over my shoulders to support him down the path.

The cursed forest is brambly and overgrown, reaching titan levels of gigantic. Its striking hush leaves us to our thoughts. Almost simultaneously, our emotions morph into post-traumatic survivor's guilt. I can acknowledge it in myself, but that doesn't lessen it an ounce. Its foul taste permeates every part of me.

"Do you think *anyone* survived?" I shiver, my mouth watering from instant nausea.

Fourteen's eyes remain glued to our blackened feet. His silent pat on my shoulder says enough.

We dive deeper into the forest's reign, gladly dipping our toes into its reality. As we pass into the thick of it, I glance at Fourteen. Despite the horrors we've witnessed today, he looks stable enough to survive. Staring at our unstoppable friends' backs as they guide us to Fourteen's family cabin, I know exactly why.

We're headed toward safety. It wasn't without loss, but we did this *ourselves*. We took everything we were handed and scrambled it into unidentifiable bits, rearranging our destinies to create new paths. We're not just survivors; we're creators of ourselves, despite ourselves. Fate defiers.

"We're alive," Fourteen whispers.

His earnest relief burns my eyes.

In his relief, I still hear neglect. Someone who's been abandoned by more than the ones he loves—by humanity itself. But he's right; we *are* alive. We're alive, even if almost no one else wants us to be. But *we* want each other to be. Right now, that's all that matters.

So I stop him, pulling him close. Fourteen accepts my embrace as if he craved it, cradling me to his chest. I listen to his frantic heart, realizing I cherish its every beat. These heavy feelings still don't make sense to me.

I don't know how long we've stood here, but it must've been a good minute. Lilith and Jay are stopped ahead of us, patiently waiting as they whisper to each other.

When I pull back, Fourteen is looking into the distance, lost in thought. He isn't eager to let me go until I drop my arms, snapping him back to this reality with darkened cheeks.

His shy humanity strikes me. No matter what he said, he's not the monster he believes. He risked his life for the dreamers for *years*. When he could've lost all hope during our bloodbath escape, he risked his life for *me*.

And I gladly risked my life for him. Something is there between us. Something powerful. Maybe that's all I need to know.

I hold his thin hand, redirecting us down the path.

"What do you think that's all about up there?" I nod him toward Lilith and Jay's back, desperate to hear more of Fourteen's gentle voice. It's soothing. Maybe I'm feeling this way because he's my official hero.

Up ahead, Lilith shows a rare instance of shock, glancing between us and Jay.

Fourteen sighs. "I don't know what they're saying *exactly*, but… I think we have some memory loss."

"Y-yeah… Do you think the cabin is safe?"

He smiles, his adoring gaze latching onto our friends' backs. "Yes, Fifty-Five. That, I can say with confidence."

I suck in green-scented oxygen, relaxing into the idea of somehow-safety in the murder forest.

Then I have a striking thought. "Hey, Fourteen?"

His midnight eyes meet mine, and I almost forget my question. "Hm?"

"You don't have to answer if you don't want to, but… Do you remember your name, at least?"

I'm met with a precious smile that could kill, and my heart melts. Fourteen laughs softly. "Yes. Thankfully, I can remember my own name."

"Then…?"

He tilts his head in wordless confusion.

I giggle, poking his side. "I'm trying to ask what your name is, Fourteen!"

Fourteen stops in his tracks. He doubles over, bursting into a breezy cackle that urges me to laugh along with him.

"Oh, my god, *Fifty-Five!*" He wheezes, sucking in a desperate breath with tears in his eyes. "We just risked our fucking lives for each other without knowing each other's *names?*"

It's my turn to giggle my ass off now. "Apparently so!"

We lean into each other, soaking up each other's laughter. But then he releases me, holding out his hand to shake like he's greeting me for the first time.

I laugh, grasping his right hand in mine. "Emmalee—that's my name. Emmalee Richards."

He smiles. "Niko. Nikolai Blackwood."

"Nice to meet you, Niko!" I shake with authority until his smile bursts with a giggle to match mine. "I'm sure we'll be fast friends."

Fourteen— No, *Niko* laughs, draping his arm around my shoulder. "I'm sure we will. Nice to meet you too."

I swear I can feel the confidence of our successful partnership in our steps. Each footprint we press into the leaves brings us closer to a new reality—thankfully one that doesn't revolve around interdimensional nightmare travel.

It's stunning to believe it, but I think I'm no longer alone. I've spent years wrangling my independence, trying to survive the loneliness in a cold, cement box of a world. But right now, Niko's warmth doesn't feel all that bad. No matter how safe the cabin truly is, if Niko is there, it's somewhere I can create safety. I have absolute faith in our strength.

"Hey… Emmalee?" Niko's energy jumps as he says it.

I'm not sure what he's thinking, but his emotions rumble into a power that stuns me silent. There's so much love, but he only said my name. My breath shakes as I search his eyes, and he flushes.

"*Emmalee,*" he whispers. His emotions jump again.

For some reason, it makes me cry. I hold his cheeks in my palms, staring into his eyes. He's crying too.

"Nikolai," I whisper. I didn't expect it to overwhelm me so much, but my voice quivers through all three syllables.

A grin bursts through his tears. "*Emmalee Richards.*"

My heart restarts itself. I've never heard someone say my name like that. Like *I'm* his hero.

I've never been a hero before, but the way he beams down at me makes me want to believe it. My eyes blur with tears. For once in my life, maybe I *am* a hero. Even though it was just one person I helped escape, I was able to save *him*. To be my hero's hero.

"*Nikolai Blackwood.*" It comes out as a choppy, pathetic gasp, but I hope he feels the love when I say his name.

His emotions don't just erupt, they flutter to new, uncontainable places. Niko makes a helpless sound, his smile mixing with upset.

We grapple to embrace each other at the same time, our sobs interrupted by the force of our chests colliding. It makes us laugh, but as we grip each other's backs, nothing can make us feel close enough. After squeezing every inch of his torso, I wrap my arms as far as I can around his waist and stay there, shifting my head to lay on his shoulder. Gazing up at him.

His panicked breath softens when our eyes meet, his nose only an inch from mine. With shaking fingers, Niko delicately brushes my hair behind my ear. He wipes my tears that rush out from his touch, then immerses his fingers into the roots of my hair. Holding my head to him like he wants me there.

Then we stay there. Holding each other. Staring into each other's eyes.

I've never felt someone's energy interact with mine like this. His presence fills me with so much peace that for the first time in years, my heart slows into perfect balance.

"It's going to be okay," I whisper.

Niko nods through a sigh, his gentle breath warming my cheeks. "We'll be okay."

My heart leaps; he said *we*.

In case I'm reading him wrong, I brush the gentlest kiss onto his cheek, just beside his lips.

At first, a rush of Niko's flustered, erupting excitement pushes a giggle out of me. But within milliseconds of my invitation, Niko dives in, kisses me straight on the lips.

I'm flooded with elation, followed by the most unfamiliar, comforting sensation; blissful, quiet safety. Grasping at Niko's hospital gown, I huff through short, desperate breaths against his cheek. I swear my soul is reigniting. And it's like he knows; Niko cuddles me closer, wrapping one arm tighter as his other hand massages the back of my head. He deepens our next kiss, easing my eager grip into a tender, grateful hug.

Within seconds, I've melted in Niko's arms. I stroke his bare back as I hold him close, breathing in every second of his

intimate presence. My instincts scream, "*stay with him.*" I have a feeling it means forever.

After kissing me dizzy, Niko pulls back with the cutest puppy-dog expression I've ever seen, his eyes scanning the fluttering leaves surrounding us.

"Sorry, I forgot where we were," he whispers.

My cackle echoes across the trees, and Niko's resulting giggle only amplifies it.

He holds his hand out for me. "Let's go home."

With weepy smiles, our hands interlock—a silent vow to never let go.

TO BE CONTINUED IN BOOK 2

As Emmalee and Niko find sanctuary in the forest, they seek key answers: what happened to them in the Cement Box that they can't remember? Are they truly safe now in the Blackwood cabins? Most perplexing of all, who are they to each other, really?

Despite their faded memories, the pair dives into a love they never had a chance to explore on Department land.

But as they purge the past from their minds, the experiments they endured left a lasting consequence that threatens to overpower them and everyone they know; S817 submerges its victims into Dimension 10 whenever they fall asleep, and it appears to have something to say.

ACKNOWLEDGMENTS

Most people don't expect a psychological thriller to save their lives, but this one saved mine.

Ten years ago, I was a bedridden teenager, clinging to every weekly manga chapter release of *Tokyo Ghoul* by the awe-inspiring Ishida Sui—who happens to be the first person to whom I owe my thanks. Ishida-sensei's story drove me to follow my dreams, showing me I could do what seemed impossible: to help at least one person out there to feel less alone, even if they're isolated in bed and within the last inches of their life.

Soul Survivors didn't begin as a novel. My first webcomic, *Chronic Nightmare Syndrome*, was not only the first makings of *Soul Survivors'* dystopian universe, but also my life-saving project.

Lyme spirochetes had taken over my system. Many of you might view the medical system a bit like this: when patients are sick, they can go to the doctor, get diagnosed, trust that their doctors are guaranteed to care for patient lives over pride and power, and treatments given in response (treatments that exist in the first place) help patients feel better upon receiving them.

Unfortunately, many disabled and chronically ill folks, like myself, live through the opposite of every single one of those points. Reckless medical experimentation; life-threatening mistakes that were never accounted for; treatments that nearly killed me on my way to "health" because, well, that's just how they worked; giving up on me as a potential liability; governmental dismissal and erasure of real diagnoses; and a general disdain for disabled people despite it being their job title to care. These are some of the many horrors I experienced within the medical system—as a child—and they are not original.

I still don't know how I survived. I've always had the impression that Lyme enjoys watching its host suffer; even as it dies off, it releases a dangerous load of toxins into your system. If killed too quickly, and without adequate detoxing methods, those toxins can potentially be fatal. I didn't want to live a life where I'd have to violently kill anything, but Lyme continued to eat away at me, forcing me to play its game of "damned if you do, damned if you don't" combined with "fuck around and find out." There were many points where I wanted to scream at it, "Don't you realize you're about to kill yourself alongside me?"

I'm certain it came very close to taking us both out—only saved by sheer fucking willpower. Each day, I experienced the war waged inside my body, unable to escape it. So when the cathartic, tragic account of Kaneki Ken's medical experimentation within *Tokyo Ghoul* spoke to my soul, opening my eyes to the life-saving power of fiction, I started writing.

Now, Reader, what I'm about to say is a lot of pressure to put on an audience, so I've never thanked you in this way. However, I want to use this experience to emphasize that you matter to the world around you: I don't think I could've pulled through as easily if it weren't for my very first handful of *Chronic Nightmare Syndrome* readers. I knew some readers would come and go (and please, feel free to despite me telling you this). I was also very aware that the comic might never be discovered at all. All of that was okay with me. But the thought of you enjoying this story pushed me when nothing else worked; if I didn't wake up another day, future readers would never know how the story ended.

Amazingly, you did show up, and you doubled my determination to live through hell. Thank you for being there the whole way through, even when you had no idea how vital your presence was to me.

Although I discontinued the original *Chronic Nightmare Syndrome* comic, this story has remained something I've returned to—revising, rewriting, and growing with it—until finally, *Soul Survivors* was born. Within these ten years, I can't believe how many incredible people have supported me in becoming a better storyteller.

I'm so honored to thank the following family, friends, and more loving supporters who helped me bring *Soul Survivors* to life:

To Soul Survivors' editor, Kayla Vokolek, thank you for creating a safe place from the very beginning for me to share this story, allowing me to grow exponentially as a writer and editor. Despite how headachingly complex this storyline can be, Kayla patiently and enthusiastically edited this book with me twice: once in 2021, when we achieved a near-possible task of reducing word count by thousands, and once more in 2024 after a year of listening to me describe a vague, OCD-riddled obsession that "something was off." Thank you for helping me navigate this beast both times, guiding me to craft it into a story I love.

Mom, I know you don't usually like thrillers, but you've shown up countless times for me as the best audience ever for this freaky story. Thank you for reading *Soul Survivors* with me in all its forms, including so generously sitting down and reading the entire, massive thing aloud with me to help me hear how it sounded—a memory I will always cherish. Your kindness allowed me to greatly improve my storytelling skills, teaching me how to better imagine readers' experiences of my writing.

Whenever I look at my first version of this story, *Chronic Nightmare Syndrome*, I think about how my dad encouraged me to grow through my art rather than hide evidence of my growth from the public. Thank you, Dad, for breaking me out of harsh internal rules despite times of intense self-criticism. Thank you, also, for letting me recount the entire plot in great detail, listening and asking questions for literal hours as we drove from California to Oregon for our huge family move. I'll always remember how much that meant to me.

My best friend of a sibling, Blake, has always been someone who gets me. Thank you for encouraging me through literally anything I make, allowing me to tell you all about it—no matter what chaos I come up with—and continually showing up to be my biggest supporter.

Uncle Andrew, thank you for so generously reading this story's first novel version. Your feedback was so encouraging and insightful, so much so that your advice still resurfaces in my head as I write today. Thank you for so compassionately guiding me to become a better writer.

A special thanks to some of my dearest friends who have been there from the first story outline:

Jamee, not only were you Arielle's (and Emmalee's) very first fan, but you've also been the best friend I could imagine to create art alongside. Thank you for giving me a reason to push myself to come back to life, just so we could make more silly inside jokes.

Thank you, Jun, for spending so many days with me at the very start of my creative journey. I'm not sure you ever knew how much our old art streams gave me so much to look forward to in my darkest days, but our live streams helped me re-discover my voice when, in person, illness had physically silenced me.

Layla, thank you for always supporting my weirdest endeavors over the past ten years, and especially for allowing your beautifully weird heart to shine alongside mine. Your best friendship has continually allowed me space to learn how to be a freer, more authentic version of myself.

Lukas Kazmirski not only beta-read *Soul Survivors*, but did so three whole times! I can't tell you how thrilled I was to implement your initial feedback and see how much it improved Emmalee and Niko's story, let alone have the privilege to witness your excitement over the second-to-last draft of the story. You've been so generous with your time and energy to support my dreams.

To my sensitivity readers, thank you for taking the time and care to boost this story into a more authentic version of itself. Thank you, Quill Chiaki Hogan, for your incredibly thoughtful comments, helping me add so much depth to not only Niko, but also to every character's internal journey. Anonymous, your incredible generosity in reading and commenting on Niko's side of the story despite outside stressors is something I can't thank you enough for. Thank you, Michelle Soto, for jumping in with Spanish help at the last minute, including putting up with my long-winded explanation— all over a single word! I'm so grateful to have you as a dear artist friend I know I can always count on.

My dear friends Lindsay, Elizabeth, Malama, Dahlia, Julia, Aileen, Alyce Sarich, Erin Dean, and so many more have kept me inspired and excited to keep following my storytelling dreams—for an entire decade(?!?). Thank you to Dahlia, Julia, Elizabeth, and Alyce Sarich for reading excerpts of this story in various stages, giving me more fuel and feedback to improve my craft. I'm so grateful to have such generous friends in my life.

Alongside me in my creative journey, my Patrons on Patreon have been some of my most dedicated, kindhearted supporters. Thank you so much to everyone who has supported me the past ten years: Lukas Kazmirski, Katy, Anonymous, Phokoro, Stacie, Aileen,

E the cat caterer, Mitchie, ZeroShift, Cass, Ollie, LC, Mel, Jennifer B., Courtney, Drask, Jade, Reece, Sara, Leyth, AlexLBJD, Shinya Sahaku, Erin Dean, Zen, Alisha, Kim Warren, Annie, Jodie, Croc, Just a Jinx, Philip, Bella, Katelyn, Katelyn R., Rob, Silivrens, Aaa Bbb, Jessica R., Naomi, Nicole, PrKitty, Wren, Julia K., Laura E., Lukas G., J, Sarah, Strawberry Sticks, Robin, GenderBender LLC, MiaBeecraft, Pinkalien_99, Jason, Mix, Jessica P., Sparky2154, Jessica M., Megan W., Saer_Riley, Tiger Lilee, Tvgold, Kylynn, Sawyer, Chiral_Leaf, Emily P., J.F., Sky, Valerie, Noah, and Zeela.

Thank you so much to every reader who has read and supported the first version of this story on Tapas, including my first internet friends—B, Scythe, Tay, and Landon—who accepted me at every awkward stage of my coming-out journey, as well as every Tapas tipper who has generously donated to each story I've written.

Inkitt, Wattpad, and new Tapas readers, your support has been so heartwarming to see as it carries over to each new story. Thank you for continually showing up for me.

And finally, I'd love to thank you, dear Reader, for reading Emmalee and Niko's first book. I can't tell you how important it is to have you here, rooting for two disabled protagonists, especially for someone like me. Thank you for helping me to do what I love, and continually re-invigorating my original goal: to help others feel less alone in their struggles, just like I was helped. I hope you know how much you matter to those around you, even if you have no idea of the depth of your importance to them (which I can guarantee is immeasurable). Take care, and see you soon for another wild ride in Book 2!

You matter to me. If you or someone you know is struggling, please flip to the following page for mental health resources.

RESOURCES

You deserve support and free access to knowledge. Please utilize the resources below whenever you need them. The world needs you here.

International Society for the Study of Trauma and Dissociation
https://isst-d.org

RAINN (Anti-Sexual Violence Nonprofit)
https://www.rainn.org

Psychology Today - Find a Therapist (International)
https://psychologytoday.com/intl/counsellors

Trans Lifeline
https://translifeline.org

The Trevor Project
https://thetrevorproject.org

International Association for Suicide Prevention
https://www.iasp.info

International OCD Foundation
https://iocdf.org

MORE BY RIVER KAI

BOOKS

My Shy Alpha
Book 1 of the Steamy Shifter Romance Series

Freeing My Alpha
Book 1 of the Steamy Shifter Romance Series

Book 3 of the My Shy Alpha Series (2025)

Unraveling with You
A Steamy Contemporary Romance

COMICS & GRAPHIC NOVELS

Resonance
Space Gays Vol.1

What-Sexual??
Vol.1

What-Sexual??
Vol.2 (Winter 2024)

ABOUT THE AUTHOR

As a bisexual and transgender creator, River Kai specializes in LGBTQ+ Romance, Sci-Fi, and Fantasy with mental health and disability representation, creating stories for readers like him to see they're not alone. While he writes in multiple Romance sub-genres, his stories share three recurring themes: empowering character arcs about healing from trauma, authentic representation of transgender or bisexual main characters with depression, anxiety, PTSD, and OCD, and a sweet-but-spicy emphasis on consent.

For current updates, follow River Kai on social media
@riv_kaii   *@riv_kai*   *River Kai*   *River Kai Art*
or sign up for the River Kai Art newsletter at
riverkaiart.com/newsletter